I Want You to Want Me
The Survivors: Book XII

Shana Galen

I WANT YOU TO WANT ME
Copyright © 2022 by Shana Galen

Cover Design by The Killion Group, Inc.

All rights reserved. Except for use in any review, the reproduction or utilization of this work in whole or in part in any form by any electronic, mechanical or other means, now known or hereafter invented, including xerography, photocopying and recording, or in any information storage or retrieval system, is forbidden without the written permission of the author.

All characters in this book have no existence outside the imagination of the author and have no relation whatsoever to anyone bearing the same name or names. They are not even distantly inspired by any individual known or unknown to the author, and all incidents are pure invention.

Also by Shana Galen

REGENCY SPIES
While You Were Spying
When Dashing Met Danger
Pride and Petticoats

MISADVENTURES IN MATRIMONY
No Man's Bride
Good Groom Hunting
Blackthorne's Bride
The Pirate Takes a Bride

SONS OF THE REVOLUTION
The Making of a Duchess
The Making of a Gentleman
The Rogue Pirate's Bride

JEWELS OF THE TON
If You Give a Duke a Diamond
If You Give a Rake a Ruby
Sapphires are an Earl's Best Friend

LORD AND LADY SPY
Lord and Lady Spy
The Spy Wore Blue (novella)
True Spies
Love and Let Spy
All I Want for Christmas is Blue (novella)
The Spy Beneath the Mistletoe (novella)

COVENT GARDEN CUBS
Viscount of Vice (novella)
Earls Just Want to Have Fun
The Rogue You Know
I Kissed a Rogue

THE SURVIVORS
Third Son's a Charm
No Earls Allowed
An Affair with a Spare
Unmask Me if You Can
The Claiming of the Shrew
A Duke a Dozen
How the Lady Was Won
Kisses and Scandal (three novellas)
The Highlander's Excellent Adventure
Sweet Rogue of Mine
Her Royal Payne
From Rags to Kisses
I Want You to Want Me

THE SCARLET CHRONICLES
To Ruin a Gentleman
Traitor in Her Arms
Taken by the Rake
To Tempt a Rebel

THE ROYAL SABOTEURS
Beauty and the Thief (coming August 2022)

STANDALONES AND ANTHOLOGIES
Snowbound with the Viscount (novella)
Stealing the Duke's Heart (duet)
The Summer of Wine and Scandal (novella)
A Royal Christmas (duet)
A Grosvenor Square Christmas (anthology)

Dedication and Acknowledgments

It's been such a pleasure to write the books for each of the men in the Survivors. This last book is dedicated to all the readers who loved the series as much as I.

I'd like to acknowledge Sophie Jordan for giving me the idea for the series as well as all the people who have worked behind-the-scenes to make the books available, including Gayle Cochrane, Abby Saul, Kim Killion, Maddee James, and Sarah Rosenbarker.

One

"My lord."

Nicholas looked up in surprise. The footman must have stepped into the drawing room and moved across it so unobtrusively that Nicholas hadn't even realized he'd entered until the servant stopped beside the couch to lean down and murmur near his ear. Not that Nicholas minded. His mother and the marquess had been lecturing him for over an hour.

He turned his head slightly. "What is it, James?"

"There is a woman crying in the stable."

Nicholas raised a brow

"Thirty is a very good age to marry," his brother the marquess was saying. "I married at nine and twenty, only a few days shy of thirty."

"Who is she?" Nicholas asked the footman.

"I am not certain, my lord. The groom came to tell us."

"Did the groom say what was the matter?"

"No, my lord."

"Why doesn't the groom ask her to leave?"

"Nicholas," the dowager said loudly, her voice echoing off the walls of the drawing room. "Are you attending? Your brother makes a very good point."

"I am listening, Mama," Nicholas said, smiling at her. He'd been listening for almost an hour now, but he didn't mention that. He'd known what this afternoon was about as soon as his sister and the marchioness went off together for a walk, leaving him alone with his brother and mother for a friendly chat.

But this chat was more reminiscent of his time in the army and a general giving him his marching orders. He had been listening, even as the footman relayed his message, even as the pain in his leg grew from uncomfortable to unbearable. Both of his legs had been crushed when his horse fell on him during the war. The right leg had healed for the most part, though it still hurt and was terribly stiff in the morning or when the weather was damp. His left leg was mostly unusable. He could put a little weight on it and had some range of motion, enough that he could walk if he leaned heavily on a cane. His left knee, in particular, had suffered the worst of the damage and it pained him any time he had to bend it for very long. He'd now been sitting with it bent for almost an hour and he'd been in agony for approximately forty-five minutes of that hour. He desperately wanted to prop it up on the couch and stretch it out, but if he did so in front of his mother, she would look at him with that awful pity in her blue eyes, and his brother Henry would look away as though embarrassed.

"Henry, do go on. You were saying thirty is a good age to wed." Nicholas inclined his head toward the footman. "Does she refuse to leave?"

"No one can get close enough to her, my lord. She has a pig guarding her."

Nicholas almost laughed at this, but the footman's expression was deadly serious. "I see," Nicholas said, forcing his expression to remain somber. "Assure the groom I will be there as soon as I can to deal with the situation."

"Yes, my lord." The footman bowed and made his exit.

"As I was saying," his mother continued, "I think a house party is just the thing. We will invite a half dozen or so of the most eligible young ladies to come to Battle's Peak for a week of games and riding and the lovely summer weather. At the end of the week, you will choose one to marry." She produced a sheet of vellum. "I have made a list of the ladies I think we should invite. Your dear sister-in-law was kind enough to add her own suggestions." She held the vellum out to him. "Would you like to peruse it?"

Nicholas liked anything that would allow him to move from his present position. He stood awkwardly, grasped his walking stick, and made his way across the room to his mother. Though it was only a few steps, it seemed to take hours. His mother looked away as he moved toward her, pretending to take in the newly remodeled drawing room. His sister Florentia had done it in the Greek style, with columns in white and white plaster and moldings on the walls and ceilings. Groupings of chairs and couches, all upholstered in pale cream and gold, were placed throughout the long, rectangular room.

Nicholas took the paper and stood in front of his mother, forcing her to look at him.

"Are all of the ladies from London?" the marquess asked. "None are local?"

Undoubtedly, he was thinking of the daughters of Mr. Kentworth, whose land bordered Battle's Peak on the south.

"Your dear Mary made inquiries there, but the eldest girl is only eight," his mother said. "There is the Blackstock family," she said. "Mr. Blackstock was a gentleman, but he passed away a few months ago, and I'm afraid Miss Blackstock has been allowed quite shocking freedoms since then."

Nicholas could only wish he'd be allowed the freedom of escaping from this room. He finally looked down at the list. He recognized the family names but none of the ladies. Even without knowing them, he knew they would be gently bred girls who were accomplished in all of the feminine arts—drawing, singing, playing pianoforte, and embroidery. They would speak French and wear the latest fashions and they would pretend they didn't mind that he was a cripple, but inside they would be completely disgusted. No lady of Society would consider marrying him unless her parents were desperate for a good match or in need of money. Without thinking, Nicholas crumpled the list into a ball and tossed it in the hearth. His mother gasped and his brother sputtered, "What's this now?"

"I'm not marrying," Nicholas said.

"But we just discussed—" his brother began.

"You talked, and I listened," Nicholas interrupted. "I *did* listen," he added before they could protest. "Not once did either of you mention the most important consideration. I am a cripple."

"Nicholas, do not speak that way," his mother chided him.

"Why?" He leaned heavily on his stick to make a point and also because he needed to take some of the pressure off his left leg. "Because if we pretend I do not have an injury it will go away? I have unfortunate news, Mother. I will not be miraculously healed, and you know as well as I that every lady on that list will pity me and pray to God her parents don't force her to marry me."

His mother opened her mouth but didn't seem to know what to say. Henry stepped in. "They're young and foolish. Mary and I didn't wed for love. That's something that comes in time."

"Mary also didn't feel pity and disgust for you."

"What are you saying, Nicholas?" the dowager demanded. "You have been back from the war for over three years. I have been patient. I have been understanding. You wanted to come here and recover, we allowed it. You did not want to travel to London for the Season, we allowed it. But if you will not come to London, then I must bring the eligible ladies here."

"No," he said.

She waved a hand. "You cannot possibly mean that you will never marry."

"Plenty of men don't marry—"

"But you are the son of a marquess. You *must* marry."

"Third son and, as Henry pointed out, I am thirty years old. I don't *have* to do anything."

Now would have been the time for a dramatic exit. And if he could have walked faster than a snail, he would have made one. As it was, he hobbled across the floor and was able to hear all of his mother's muttered insults, including how he was spoiled, willful, and stubborn.

He was stubborn. Nicholas could admit to that. But so was his mother.

He'd told her a dozen times, probably more, that he wanted to be left alone. What had she done? Sent his sister Florentia. Nicholas liked her well enough, and she stayed out of his way, but now his mother had come with the marquess in tow, seemingly for the sole purpose of prodding him into marriage.

Nicholas made his way toward the door that opened to the back of the house. He was closer to the stables that way. He nodded at the footmen he passed. Years ago, he would have strode quickly past them and not even noticed. Now he had plenty of time to take in their appearances and note whether they looked happy or irritable, weary or well-rested. At this moment the servants looked strained, as though they too were feeling the stress of his mother's visit.

He finally reached the exit and stepped into the warm afternoon. The sunlight poked out from a blue sky filled with puffy clouds. It was a perfect day for riding, except he didn't ride any longer. If he had, he would have saddled a horse and escaped his family that way. He would have come back in a much better temper as riding always restored his good mood. Now his escape options were far more limited. He wondered if it was time to seriously consider the ultimate escape—Canada. He had been contemplating booking passage on a ship and starting over where no one cared if he was Lord Nicholas St. Clare. He could just be Nicholas St. Clare, a cripple. And no one would pity his mother or his family or whisper behind their fans about what a shame it was because he had been such a handsome, athletic young man.

He'd reached the stable and a groom ran to meet him. The lad doffed his cap. He was sixteen at most and looked relieved to see him. "My lord, I don't know what to do. The lady refuses to leave."

"Why has she taken refuge in my stable?"

"I don't know. I can't get close enough because of the pig. I tried to talk to her, but I had to shout, and she was crying so hard I don't know if she heard me."

Nicholas looked about. "Where is John Coachman and the other grooms?"

"Lady Florentia and Lady Mary asked the coachman to drive them about."

Nicholas nodded. "I see. Well, leave her to me then."

"Yes, my lord." The groom doffed his cap again. "Be careful, my lord."

Nicholas smiled and hobbled toward the open door of the stable. During the war he'd been known as a horse whisperer—all of his life, really. He'd always had a way with horses. He seemed to understand their fears and their needs and how best to respond. The ability to connect to his horse made him a good rider, and it also served him and his troop well during the war when he was frequently called upon to steal horses. He never had a problem convincing a horse to go with him. It just took some soft words and a bit of coaxing—maybe a little treat—and he won the horse over easily.

Pigs were another matter, he thought as he stepped into the stable and was met with a large white pig covered with bristly white hair and several large, black spots. The pig had round, floppy ears that pricked up at his arrival, and she or he pawed at the ground and snuffled. There was no sign of a lady, but with one glance down the row of the stable, he saw several horses snorting with their heads high—a clear sign they were uncomfortable or detected danger.

The pig snorted as well, but Nicholas was not well-versed in pig vocalizations and wasn't sure if the pig was friend or foe. He stopped just inside the stable, deciding not to test his luck with the pig. "Hullo!" he called. "Is anyone here?"

No answer except more snorting and head tossing from his horses. He moved inside, another slow step, and the pig watched him warily. "Hullo? Miss?"

Still no answer, but he thought he heard a telltale sniffle.

"If you are inside, might you call off your pig? I'd like to talk to you," he said, beginning to feel rather like an idiot. "Nice pig," he told the animal, who was grunting loudly now. "Is this a Hampshire pig?"

"A Gloucestershire Old Spots. Now go away," said a feminine voice.

Nicholas took the words as a good sign. He was making progress. They'd come from the right rear of the stable. There were a couple of empty stalls there and she was probably hiding in one.

"I can't go away," Nicholas said, edging closer. "I live here. I'm Nicholas St. Clare. Who are you?"

"I can't go away either," she said, her voice muffled with congestion. "I can't go home."

"Why is—" This was ridiculous. He did not want to yell down the length of the stable while a pig directed a menacing stare at him. "Miss, would you mind very much calling off your Gloucestershire Old Spots so we might speak face to face?"

For a long moment there was no answer, and then he thought he caught sight of a head peeking out from a stall. A moment later, there was a shrill whistle. The pig's ears twitched, and the creature turned its head. "Sweetie, come!" the woman called.

With a last look at Nicholas, the pig lumbered back toward the stall. Nicholas followed, lumbering himself as he made his way past the stalls of horses. He spent most of his days in the stable. He didn't ride any longer. He would never ride again, but he enjoyed the company of the horses, and grooming and caring for them took his mind off his shattered legs. Finally, he came to the stall and peered down at a woman sitting on a small stool and dabbing at her eyes with a handkerchief. She was pretty, even with red-rimmed eyes and splotches of pink all over her face. She had hair the color of amber—not brown but not quite blond—and large brown eyes with long lashes. Her eyes reminded him of a fawn's eyes. They were wary but curious. She was dressed simply in an earth-colored under dress and brown over dress. Her hair fell in wild waves about her shoulders and was sprinkled liberally with hay. At one point it might have been pinned up, but Nicholas rather doubted it.

"You are Lord Nicholas," she said.

He gave a slight bow and waited for her gaze to slide over his damaged legs and his walking stick and for the pity or horror to creep into her eyes. "I am," he said. "I don't think we've met."

"We haven't." Her gaze didn't waver from his face. "I don't go out into Society. Until recently." And with that, she started weeping again. She covered her face with her handkerchief and sobbed quietly, her shoulders shaking. Nicholas would have knelt beside her, but of course he couldn't manage to do more than lean on his stick.

The pig, who had gone to the far end of the stall, glared at Nicholas, and he would have sworn it wore a look of reproach. Nicholas gave the animal a pleading look, and perhaps it worked because the animal nudged the woman with its snout. The woman sniffed and rubbed the pig's head. Finally, she sniffed again, and straightening her shoulders, dabbed at her nose and eyes. When she had composed herself, she took a breath. "I'm sorry to have disturbed you. I shouldn't have come here. I was out walking, and I began crying and—well, you see the state I am in."

Strange. Certainly, she must have noticed his walking stick or the way he stood awkwardly with all of his weight on it. Her gaze had dipped down, but she hadn't seemed repulsed.

"Has something happened?" Nicholas asked. "Are you ill or is anyone in your family—"

"No but thank you for asking. My problem is not that sort."

She was definitely educated. She spoke well and if she knew who he was, she must be local. "I've been told I am a good listener. If you want to talk," he added.

She shook her head. "No. Not about this."

"Then would you like to come inside? I could have the cook prepare some tea. We have several comfortable chairs where you could cry."

She gave him a watery smile. "Thank you. But I have almost wrung myself dry. I should probably go home."

He found that he didn't want her to leave quite yet. He hadn't had a conversation with anyone but a family member in some time. Not only that, but for once the conversation didn't involve his injury or marriage. This woman—whoever she was—hadn't seemed to care that he was a cripple. She couldn't have failed to note the stick and the way he favored his left leg, but she didn't immediately offer him a seat or behave as though he was an invalid.

"I would escort you home," he said, "but—" And he gestured to his leg.

She glanced at his leg impassively. "I don't live very far, but thank you. You have a lovely stable. I will recommend it to anyone else who needs a good cry."

"Please don't," he said. "The horses and grooms rather prefer tearful humans to go to the house. I believe I mentioned we have several comfortable chairs. Perfect for long or even short bouts of weeping."

"I shall keep that in mind." She rose and he noted she was of medium height, slender, with a hint of curves below the waist and more than a hint at her neckline. He might never plan to marry, but he was still a man, and he couldn't stop himself from looking. "And I am sorry to have troubled you."

"It was no trouble," he assured her. She gave him a dubious look and then whistled as loudly and shrilly as any man might do. "Come, Sweetie!"

The pig trotted to her side. She gave a quick bob. "Good day, my lord." Lifting the hem of her skirt, she started away, the pig at her side as though it were a dog. Nicholas noted the lady's rear view was as pleasing as the front. If he was not mistaken, she had a nicely rounded bottom.

Right before she reached the door, Nicholas pulled his gaze from her backside. "Wait," he called. "I didn't ask your name."

She glanced over her shoulder, all that amber hair whipping around. "Amelia Blackstock," she said. "No doubt you've been warned about me." And then she disappeared through the door, taking her Gloucestershire Old Spots with her.

Two

Amelia had walked for about ten minutes before she realized she was heading in the wrong direction. Actually, Sweetie realized it and nudged her legs then stopped walking, plopped down, and gave a stubborn grunt. Amelia glanced back in bewilderment then looked around and realized she had gone south when she should have gone north. Leave it to Sweetie, whose first priority was always her stomach, to alert Amelia to her mistake. Sweetie didn't like to stray too far from her feeding trough this close to mealtime.

"Oh, no," Amelia said, feeling silly. "I wasn't even paying attention."

As always, Sweetie listened with interest and then rose to her feet as soon as Amelia changed directions for home. Now Sweetie trotted in front of her, leading the way. She was surprisingly fast for such a large animal. Amelia kept her gaze on Sweetie and tried to keep her thoughts from wandering again. That was rather difficult when she was still flustered by her meeting with Lord Nicholas. She hadn't expected him to be so handsome. He had golden hair that fell in a perfect wave over his forehead. His eyes were a pale blue that reminded her of the summer sky. She looked up. Yes, exactly the color of a sun-washed summer sky. He'd been tall and dressed in clothes that certainly accentuated his broad shoulders and slim hips.

She'd heard he had been injured in the war and not paid much attention as she'd been consumed by her own worries at that time. Now she realized he must have injured his legs somehow as he used a cane to walk. Why hadn't anyone ever mentioned how beautiful he was?

And why was she thinking so much about his looks? Wasn't she in trouble right now for admiring another man overly much?

She had to walk quickly to keep up with Sweetie, and it was less than a quarter hour before she'd reached her family's small estate, which bordered Battle's Peak for about a half mile on the northern edge. Catmint Cottage, the name her great-grandfather had given to the house he'd had built on the land he'd inherited, had been named for the profusion of purple-blue flowers that bordered the area around the gray stone house. The estate had been larger a century ago, but her father had had to sell a portion to pay for his mother's long illness and then an even larger portion to pay the taxes when, a few years later, he was injured. Now they had only two tenets and enough money for Rose and a cook two days a week. Most of the rooms at Catmint Cottage were closed and the furnishings covered. Amelia and her mother were the only family members who lived here now. No need for all the extra bed chambers and sitting rooms.

Sweetie gave a little squeal of delight and began to run. Amelia looked up and spotted Rose, the maid, hanging clothes to dry on a line. "Now what do you want?" Rose asked sternly when the pig stopped before her and looked up hopefully. "So sure I have something for you?"

The pig made a snuffling sound and sniffed the ground then looked back up hopefully.

"Very well," Rose said, reaching her red, work-roughened hands into her apron and pulling out a dried apple. "Here you are then."

Sweetie took it and crunched loudly as Rose wiped her hand on her apron.

"You spoil her," Amelia said as she came closer.

The lines around Rose's mouth deepened as she smiled. "And you are one to talk, Miss Blackstock."

Amelia managed a smile that she didn't really feel. "Guilty as charged."

Rose reached for a shift and pinned it up, her white hair glinting in the sun. "It's good to see you out and about. You were locked up in that house for too many years. I've always said a long walk does wonders for a body."

She had said that often, and it was one of the reasons Amelia had gone for the walk that had ended at Battle's Peak. But though she felt more energetic than she had before, her worries still lay heavy on her shoulders.

"Next time see if you can convince your mother to go with you."

That was a Herculean task if ever she had heard one, but Amelia nodded. Sweetie nosed about her boots, sniffing hopefully for scraps to eat. Amelia went to the bucket with scraps that hung near the house, Sweetie right on her heels, and dumped the food in the trough. She checked the pig had fresh water and walked back to Rose. She would have helped hang the clothes, but her hands were dirty from her walk.

"How is she today?" Amelia asked. "Is she awake yet?"

"She is," Rose said. "I made her some tea and toast."

Amelia didn't ask if her mother had eaten it. She would see that for herself in a few moments. "How did she seem?" Amelia asked.

"About the same," Rose said, not looking at Amelia. That meant she was still not doing well. She had gotten out of bed today, which was something. Amelia tried to take solace in that small victory.

"I'll go check on her."

Rose nodded and continued pinning a petticoat to the line. Amelia went in the back door of the house, leaving the door open so Sweetie could come inside if she wished and Rose did not have to fumble with the latch and the heavy laundry basket. She passed through the small kitchen, pausing to check the herbs she had hung last week, and then made her way into the house proper. Built in the last century, the house was drafty and damp in the winters but actually quite comfortable in the spring and summer. The carpet was worn and there were empty rectangles on the walls where paintings had once hung before being sold. The doors to the rooms on the ground floor were all closed, making the vestibule dark. Amelia glanced at the closed door of the dining room then decided to try the drawing room instead.

She entered the dark room and found her mother immediately. Marianne Blackstock sat in a chair, her black-clad body looking small against the high back. On the table beside her sat a tray with untouched tea and toast. Amelia wanted to turn right around and walk back out, but she forced herself to be cheerful. "Good day, Mother," she said, her voice bright. She crossed the room to the curtains.

"Oh, don't—" her mother began, but Amelia was merciless and pulled them wide to allow the sun in. Her mother held up a hand to shield her face. Her skin looked even paler in the warm glow of the afternoon light.

"You haven't touched your tea or toast," Amelia said, coming to stand beside her mother. Her mother made no response, just pressed her hand to her temple. Her hair, a slightly lighter shade than Amelia's, was streaked with white. It lay heavy on her shoulders as she hadn't bothered to pin it up. She also hadn't taken the time to dress and still wore her nightgown and a robe over it.

Amelia sat in the chair opposite her mother. "You must eat and keep up your strength," she said.

Marianne Blackstock lowered her hand and looked at the tray as though just seeing it. "I will," she said.

"Why don't you allow me to help you dress?" Amelia asked. "I'll brush your hair and pin it up then make you a fresh cup of tea."

"No, thank you, my love," her mother said, her voice faint. "I have a megrim today. I'm not feeling at all well. If you could help me back to bed, I would be grateful."

Amelia tried to hide her sigh, but she rose and helped her mother back to her bed chamber. The task seemed to take hours as her mother walked slowly, and the bed chambers were on the first floor. Once Amelia had her tucked into the dark room, she went to fetch a fresh cup of tea. Sweetie had found the abandoned toast and was chewing the last crust in the drawing room. Amelia didn't even scold her. No point in wasting it. Instead, she took the empty plate and cup to the kitchen and heated a fresh kettle of water.

A few moments later, Rose entered with the laundry basket on her hip. "Oh, Miss Blackstock, I can do that."

Amelia waved a hand. "It's no trouble. Mrs. Blackstock has a megrim and went back to bed. She can take tea in her room."

Rose looked as though she wanted to say something then closed her mouth again.

"What is it?" Amelia asked. "Go ahead."

"I don't want to speak out of turn, Miss, but…"

Amelia raised her brows and nodded.

"I wonder if we should call that doctor back. Your mother does not seem to be improving."

A cold finger of fear pressed against her back and tried to push its way in, but Amelia had years of practice pushing back. "It's only been a few months since my father died," Amelia said, trying not to sound as defensive as she felt. "She needs more time. And I'll never call that doctor back. He wanted to bleed her, as though putting leeches on her would cure her of grief."

"We could consult another doctor."

"I'll think about it," Amelia said to mollify her. The truth was she didn't have the money for fancy doctors and treatments. She knew what troubled her mother. For eight long years, from the time Amelia had been five until she was thirteen, her mother had nursed Amelia's paternal grandmother. The woman had been like a mother to Marianne Blackstock, who had grown up without a mother of her own. They'd spent thousands of pounds on treatments and remedies. They'd consulted a dozen doctors. None had been able to heal Georgiana Blackstock or stop her slow, agonizing decline.

The death of her grandmother had been followed by three years of relative happiness. Her father and mother had begun to talk of the future, Amelia's future. They had discussed balls at assembly rooms and even a shopping trip to London. Amelia had been poised to make her come out shortly after turning sixteen and then her father had been injured in a hunting accident. The poachers had been on their land illegally and hunting out of season. They had mistaken her father for an animal and shot him. And then the cowards had fled, leaving her father lying on the ground in a pool of his own blood.

By some miracle, her father had not died. The pistol ball had gone right through him. Unfortunately, it had torn through his spinal cord on its way out, leaving him paralyzed from the chest down. For the next ten years Amelia and her mother had spent every hour of every day caring for her father. He was prone to respiratory troubles and the doctors had advised them to make sure he was not prone for too long. They also had to keep his leg muscles from atrophy and that involved a regimen of moving the legs and exercising them. He had to be bathed and fed and his waste dealt with. Some months, he was in good spirits and health for weeks. Other months, he was dejected and begged for his wife to put him out of his misery.

He had never expressed such sentiments to Amelia and he never spoke them when she was nearby, but she had overheard them on more than one occasion. Luke Blackstock did not want to be a burden to his wife and child. Sometimes Amelia wished her mother would agree to her father's wishes and free all three of them from this prison. But mostly she was glad her mother was strong and refused. Amelia had loved her father, and his death six months ago, though expected, was painful.

Her mother had immediately gone into mourning. She'd taken to her bed for days at a time. Amelia had as well. They were both so tired from years of caretaking that it seemed they could not rest enough. But eventually Amelia had recovered her strength and her energy. Her mother had not. And her mother's inattention had allowed Amelia freedoms she would not normally have had. Though she was a spinster at six and twenty, she had been all but locked away for a decade. She craved freedom and people and excitement.

At first, she had felt a niggling in the back of her mind that she had forgotten something—that she needed to be home to care for her father. When she realized he was gone, grief washed over her. But she found that if she went into the village and spoke with shopkeepers and the girls she had grown up with but lost touch with, those feelings faded. And, of course, there were handsome men to flirt with, and when she was with them, she forgot all her heartache.

Except one of those flirtations had gone too far, and now her monthly courses were late and she had a new worry. This time she had no one but herself to blame. What would she do if she was with child? What would her mother do? Her poor mother could not even manage to eat without being cajoled. She couldn't offer Amelia any solace or advice.

Amelia finished steeping the tea and placed the teapot, a cup, and a few biscuits on a tray, which she carried to her mother's room. Sweetie, ever hopeful at the prospect of more food, followed her up the stairs, but Amelia closed her mother's door before the pig could go inside. Her mother did not mind the pig, but there were limits to her tolerance and her bed chamber was one of them.

"Mama," Amelia murmured. "I brought you tea and biscuits."

"Thank you, my love," her mother said, her voice faint and muffled by her bed covers.

"Would you like me to help you sit?"

"No, love. I just want to rest. I'll take the tea soon."

Knowing her mother would probably do no such thing, Amelia placed the tray on the bedside table and sat in the rocker by her mother's bed. "Is there anything I can do to help? A cold compress?"

"Amelia, dear, you have spent enough time at sickbeds. I just need a nap, and I'll be fine. You go have fun."

Amelia had listened to her mother one too many times and now she was dealing with the consequences of her *fun*. Amelia rocked slowly in the chair. "I'd rather stay close to home today, Mama."

Her mother reached out and patted Amelia's hand. Her mother's hand was pale and bony, and Amelia wished she could force her mother to eat and walk in the sun and do anything but waste away like this. "You always were a good girl," her mother said.

Amelia felt her cheeks heat. She was not a good girl. She was a ruined woman who would soon be shunned by everyone of good society. She'd bring shame on her mother, who was already buried in grief. A pregnancy would be the last nail in Marianne Blackstock's coffin.

"I try," Amelia whispered.

"You know your father always wanted a girl," her mother said, her voice growing weaker as she began to drift into sleep.

"I didn't know that," Amelia said, a bit surprised at this revelation. Her father had never behaved as though he was disappointed he did not have a son, even though the lack of one meant his property would all go to his cousin one day. Fortunately, that cousin had been in India for the last decade. The lawyers had written when her father passed away, but thus far there had been no reply. Amelia hoped that when he returned, he would allow Amelia and her mother to stay at Catmint Cottage, but there was no guarantee.

A few days ago, that had been Amelia's greatest worry. Now, she had an even bigger one.

"He was so pleased when the midwife told him he had a daughter. He couldn't wait to hold you and show you to all of the tenants."

Amelia smiled at the description. It was lovely to think of her father happy and joyful and not the shriveled man who had begged for death.

Amelia took a breath. "How did you tell him?" she asked. "How did you tell him you were expecting a child?" She made her voice light and curious, but she had a serious reason for wanting to know. Although she did not know how to reach Jonathon Wickersham, she knew who did. And she wondered if she should let Wickersham know he was to be a father. Was it too soon? Would he care? Or would he rush back to beg her to marry him?

Somehow, she doubted the latter would occur. Wickersham was a soldier, and he seemed to enjoy traveling about the country. He probably had a pretty girl in every town he visited. Would he even remember Amelia? He wasn't in love with her any more than she was in love with him. It had been a mistake to lie with him. It had been an enjoyable evening, and she hadn't regretted it…until now.

"Oh, I didn't need to tell him," her mother said. Amelia had almost forgotten that she'd spoken. "He figured it out all on his own. He probably knew before I did." She squeezed Amelia's hand lightly. "And he was so happy. So happy."

Amelia did not move until her mother was asleep. She left the cooling tea on the table and moved quietly out of the bed chamber. Sweetie was no longer outside the door, but Amelia found her on the floor of her own room sleeping on an old mattress that she'd given to Sweetie when the pig had taken up only a quarter of the bed. Now when Sweetie stretched out, she was larger than the mattress. Amelia went to her dressing table, opened a drawer, and pulled out a sheet of foolscap. She didn't spend much time brushing and primping and the drawers of the table were full of books and pamphlets and clippings from magazines or papers. She rummaged around more and found a quill and ink and then stared at the paper before her. Finally, she dipped the edge of the quill in the ink and wrote, *Dear Corporal Wickersham.*

The tip of the quill broke and the M smudged and Amelia sighed. She'd have to start again. Except she'd begun this letter three times already and had never gotten further than the salutation. What was she supposed to say? *I'm carrying your child? I think.*

Perhaps she should wait until she was certain.

Except she had never been late before. Never.

Amelia did not know much about pregnancy, but she'd never been excluded from conversations or restricted from reading what she liked. She knew a missed cycle was one of the first indicators of pregnancy. Every morning she woke and checked hopefully for signs of blood on her nightshirt or bedclothes. And every morning there was nothing. This morning she'd been so distraught, she'd left early with Sweetie to go for a walk. That hadn't ended well. Lord Nicholas had to kick her out of his stable. He'd done it nicely, of course. She should be thankful he was a kind man.

She didn't deserve kindness, not when she would bring shame and scandal upon her family nine months from now. Hadn't her mother been through enough? She was so close to breaking, and Amelia had no doubt that she would be that final straw. It was enough to make her weep again. Amelia buried her face in her arms and sobbed.

***

Nicholas had never had the gift of strategy or negotiation that his friends in the war had possessed. He'd been asked to join Lieutenant-Colonel Draven's troop of doomed soldiers because he had distinguished himself in the cavalry and he had a way with animals. He could coax oxen into going another mile with their heavy burden of weapons or supplies. He knew what poultice to use when a general's horse was hobbling. But what had really captured Draven's interest was when Nicholas had managed to sneak into the enemy camp under cover of darkness and lure three dozen of their horses to the British camp. Not surprisingly, the British victory at dawn the next day had been quick and decisive.

Less than a fortnight later, Nicholas had stood before Colonel Draven who explained that his troop would be far from supplies and would need to be self-sufficient. Not only was Nicholas a decorated cavalry officer Draven wanted to fight with his chosen troop, he wanted Nicholas to ensure the troop always had horses at their disposal.

Nicholas had agreed right away, but Draven had raised a hand to stay his answer. "Let me ask you this first, my lord," the colonel had said, his bright blue eyes fixed on Nicholas. "Are you afraid to die?"

Nicholas had thought the man a bit strange and the question rather odd. But then some of these older soldiers had been fighting for so long they had become somewhat eccentric. "Of course, I'm afraid to die," Nicholas had answered.

The colonel had smiled. "You're the first man I've recruited who's told me the truth, and so I'll tell you a truth, my lord." Draven leaned close. "There are worse things than death."

At the time, Nicholas had assumed the colonel meant the demise of the British empire and rule under Napoleon. Now he understood better. How many times had he wished he'd died rather than come home a cripple? There were days, early on, when the pain had been so bad that he'd prayed for death. Now the pain was tolerable and most days he did not want to die. Except today. Today he wished someone would put him out of his misery.

When Nicholas had returned from dealing with the woman in the stable, his mother and brother had started in right away about the matchmaking house party. Florentia had returned shortly thereafter and helped Nicholas escape, but she would not be able to save him during dinner tonight. Even as his valet finished brushing his coat and moved to help Nicholas don it, Nicholas was dreading the hours' long ordeal.

He had to think more like Stratford. He needed a strategy for escape. But how could he escape his own home? Impossible.

"Is that all, my lord?" his valet asked.

"Yes, Mr. Glick."

The valet gave Nicholas his walking stick and moved away and into his dressing room. Now Nicholas would have to make his way down the stairs and to the dining room. His leg ached just thinking about it. Perhaps if he thought hard about how to deal with his mother and avoid an onslaught of silly, young women in his home, he would be able to forget the pain. He made his way toward the stairs, passing the portraits of his ancestors in the gallery. Finally, he started gingerly down the stairs, his stick tucked under his arm and his hand gripped about the railing as though his life depended on it—which it did.

What he really needed was Stratford to swoop in, assess the situation, and draw up a battle plan. But he was on his own, and thus far he could see no escape.

Three

She couldn't find Sweetie. It was her own fault. Even though she'd vowed to stay home and stop flirting with men, she couldn't say no when the girls from the village came and begged her to go to the assembly rooms with them for the dance. Amelia had agreed and then everything had been a flurry of hair and dresses and gloves, and she'd forgotten to feed the pig.

She'd remembered just after eleven and had left the dance early to feed poor Sweetie. She felt awful that she'd forgotten, so awful that she hadn't even minded that she would have to miss her dance with Charles Woolf, who was the most handsome man in the village. It was probably for the best that she did not dance with him. She'd gotten into enough trouble with handsome men.

But when she arrived home, she couldn't find Sweetie. The house was dark, and her mother and Rose were abed. Amelia had taken her lantern into the yard and searched there and the barn. Then she'd gone to all of Sweetie's favorite spots, but she hadn't found the pig. What she had found was ground that had been uprooted. Like any pig, Sweetie loved to root in the earth and had a strong snout for just that purpose. The pig had obviously been looking for food, and Amelia followed the upturned earth. There were stretches where the ground was undisturbed, and Amelia feared she'd lost the trail, but then she'd find another area of destruction and continue on. After about a quarter of an hour, she knew exactly where Sweetie had gone—Battle's Peak.

She should have thought of that before. Sweetie had eaten all of the horse feed she could find when Amelia had stopped in the stable a couple of days ago. Sweetie was ruled by her belly and would remember the food there and return. Of course, the stable would be closed for the night. It was nearly midnight, after all, so she just hoped Sweetie would be rooting around there still. Lifting her skirts, Amelia hurried toward the Marquess of Averstow's property. She despaired of the state of her shoes after trekking through all the mud, but it was too late to salvage them now. She couldn't even feel too bad about ruining them. It had been years since she'd run about in the dark, and she'd forgotten how much fun it could be. She'd forgotten how the sky was full of stars on a night like this, so full that she felt she could almost pluck one from the sky. And she loved the sounds of insects chirping and owls hooting and the stillness of the world blanketed in darkness but for the beam of her lantern.

Finally, she reached the stable and stopped. The door was open. Amelia didn't know how Sweetie had done it, but she managed to open the door and was probably inside eating Lord Nicholas out of horse feed. Amelia swore. She did not want to enter the stable at night. This property was a breeding farm, and the horses were extremely valuable. What if she was shot under suspicion of being a horse thief? She'd just have to be quick and quiet.

She lowered the lantern's shutter and picked her way across the yard until she reached the open stable door. She stepped inside, allowed her eyes to adjust to the darkness, and was about to whistle for the pig when she heard a man's voice speaking low. Amelia couldn't make out the words, so she moved silently closer.

"You're not so scary, are you?" the man was saying. "You're simply protective. Like a guard pig."

She moved closer again and peered inside an empty stall to find Lord Nicholas half-sitting on a tall stool, one leg stretched out before him. He was scratching Sweetie on the head, while Sweetie happily slurped up whatever was in the trough. Of course, as soon as Amelia peered around the corner, Sweetie must have heard or smelled her. She lifted her head, made a loud whining sound, and came to snuffle at Amelia's skirts. "You are a very naughty girl," Amelia said. She looked over at Lord Nicholas to see him push to his feet. She wanted to tell him not to go to so much effort for her, but she knew it was probably a point of pride for him. "My lord, I am so very, very sorry Sweetie has disturbed you."

"No apology necessary," he said. She caught the wince of pain he gave as he put weight on his left leg. "She's a clever girl." He glanced at her as she dipped her head back in the trough, grunting happily. "She opened the stable door all on her own. Of course, if I hadn't been here, it would have been locked."

"I wouldn't put it past her skills to unlock it. She's too clever for her own good." Amelia tilted her head in curiosity. "If you don't mind me asking, why are you here this late? Is one of your mares in labor?"

He shook his head. "Nothing like that. My mother and brother are visiting and have invited the Kentworths for dinner. This was the only place I could think to escape and catch a moment of peace and quiet. And what about you?"

"Me? Oh, you mean why am I here in the middle of the night?" She'd been staring at him, admiring his male beauty, and was taken off guard at his question. "I was looking for

Sweetie, of course. It's completely my fault she went wandering. I forgot to feed her before the ball this evening."

"Ball?" His gaze slid over her, making her whole body flush with warmth. "Ah, that explains the dress. At the assembly hall?" His brows rose.

"Yes. I left early—as soon as I remembered." She gestured to the pig who was sniffing at the now empty trough, hoping to find some overlooked morsel. If she kept her gaze on the pig, perhaps he wouldn't notice her pink cheeks and the difficulty she was having catching her breath. He was having quite the effect on her. "Apparently, it was not soon enough. I am sorry to have disturbed your peace and quiet."

"I don't mind. I'm pleased to see you are no longer in tears."

Amelia felt her cheeks burn hotter. Little chance the light was dim enough that he didn't notice. "I was hoping you had forgotten about that."

"A man doesn't forget a pretty woman weeping in his stable."

Her cheeks were flaming now. She was tempted to put her hands against them to cool them. A few months ago, she would have mumbled some response and ran away, but now she had some practice in the art of flirtation. And though she had never flirted with anyone as esteemed as the son of a marquess—and a war hero at that—she was not intimidated. Well, not very intimidated.

"No more than I have forgotten the brave man who came to my rescue."

"Brave?" He leaned against the stall opening, the gesture casual. She could almost believe he did it out of habit, but she could see it also took weight off his bad leg without him having to use his cane.

"You were the only one brave enough to take on the ferocious Sweetie."

He glanced down at the pig, who was now snuffling about the hay on the ground, moving it here and there. "She is quite fearsome."

"You should see her when she's hungry."

"I'm afraid, Miss Blackstock, even my bravery has limits."

She smiled at his quip and realized in the past few moments with him she had smiled more than she had in weeks. Not only was he handsome, he was charming. A dangerous combination, especially for her. She'd been snared by his charms, and now every smile he gave her caused her belly to flutter.

Sweetie had discovered some edible item just beneath the trough and frantically pushed at the wooden box in order to reach it. The trough jolted sideways, right toward Amelia. She heard the screech of the wooden legs just in time to jump out of the way. The only place to jump was toward Lord Nicholas, who caught her just as she careened into him. But her momentum was too great, and she put them both off balance and they tumbled to the ground. Fortunately, her landing was soft, as he held onto her so his body cushioned her fall.

"I'm so sorry!" she said as soon as they landed. "Are you hurt?"

"I'm fine," he said. "The hay softened my fall. And you have nothing to apologize for. It's my damn leg that gave out."

"Rubbish. I crashed into you like a pair of oxen." She was still lying half on top of him, her skirts tangled under his legs, making it impossible for her to move away. He would have to shift his weight, and she worried it might be painful. Fortunately, she had landed on his right leg, which seemed the stronger of the two. "I should try and stand but you're on my skirts…"

"Ah, sorry." He seemed to blink and come out of a trance. "Give me a moment to catch my breath."

He was in pain. He didn't want her to know it, but she could see it in his eyes. They creased at the corners as though he was trying to avoid flinching.

"Take all the time you need. I'm perfectly content to sit and admire your eyes. They really are the loveliest shade of blue."

Lord Nicholas went perfectly still, his gaze darting to hers and holding. Amelia realized too late that she shouldn't have spoken her thoughts out loud. Women were not supposed to compliment men. It was considered forward. Not to mention, she should not be complimenting a man she just met. He would think her some sort of wanton.

Which wasn't far from the truth.

"I shouldn't have said that," she whispered. "You will think I have no manners." She looked away from that piercing gaze, lowering her chin.

"Actually," he said, his voice soft. "I rather like your lack of pretensions. It's a refreshing change."

She glanced up at him. "It is?"

"Not to mention, it's nice to have someone mention my eyes. No one looks at anything but my legs these days." His voice was low and like velvet over her skin. Her thoughts were all muddled now at the feel of his body against hers and the warmth of him. The scent of him.

"Don't be ridiculous."

"It's true."

"It's not. Why, when I was here the other day, I couldn't stop staring at your eyes and your face and that hair." She really should stop talking. "Why should I care about your legs?"

He shook his head, seeming not to believe her.

"Do you know I even started home the wrong direction because I was so busy thinking about how your eyes matched the color of the sky?" She gestured to Sweetie, who had eaten whatever it was that had drawn her attention and was now back to snuffling about. "Sweetie had to correct me and remind me of the right path."

Lord Nicholas stared at her as though she were a unicorn. She couldn't help it. Her gaze lowered to his lips. *This is how you end up in trouble*, she reminded herself. This wasn't exactly how it had started with Wickersham, but she now knew that a kiss led to a touch led to…well, a baby. And that led to ruin.

But the way he looked at her. The way his gaze slid over her lips made her forget she was ruined and her life was in shambles. What was one more sin? How could she possibly resist when he was looking at her like she was a tropical island, and he was a man who'd been swimming in the middle of the ocean for weeks.

"Would you think me terribly forward if I kissed you?" she murmured, her voice low and seductive without her even meaning to make it so. A kiss would take very little effort. They were so close that she only need lean forward slightly.

"Yes, but I think I should mention that I'm coming to realize I like forward women."

Amelia smiled and tilted her head, leaning close until their mouths were just a breath apart. Although she had intended to kiss him, he was the one who finally bridged the gap and pressed his lips gently against hers. A frisson of pleasure coursed through her at the barest brush of his mouth. Her hand closed on one of the buttons of his coat. She needed something to keep her grounded.

He nibbled lightly at her lips, and Amelia's chest grew so tight she feared she couldn't breathe. And then she feared she would never breathe again if he didn't kiss her more— kiss her fully. She yanked at the button she held, pulling Lord Nicholas closer. His hand, which had been resting on the small of her back, slid up to cup the back of her head as he deepened the kiss. His mouth slanted over hers, his tongue flicking out to taste her lips. Amelia couldn't stop a small moan from escaping. She craved physical touch, craved the sensation of being held, pressed close. Her breath quickened, and she met Lord Nicholas's tongue with a touch of her own. He started in surprise then yanked her closer and kissed her more deeply.

And then Sweetie gave a loud squeal and scrambled to one side of the stall, jolting Amelia and causing her to fall completely onto Lord Nicholas. He gave a grunt of pain as her weight pressed on one of his legs and then the bright light of several lanterns temporarily blinded Amelia.

She shaded her eyes with her hand and looked up into the faces of three angry people.

***

He didn't know why he'd done it. Once upon a time, flirting with an attractive woman, bantering with her, and even kissing her would have been an everyday activity for Nicholas. But even before the war and his injury, Nicholas had not been an idiot. He would never have risked spending time with the unmarried daughter of a gentleman in a stable alone where they might be discovered and she compromised. Nicholas could only attribute the mistake now to the fact that it had been so long since he had touched a woman that he'd quite lost his head.

And now they would both pay for it.

"What is the meaning of this?" the dowager marchioness demanded, staring down at Nicholas and Miss Blackstock with fire in her eyes. It was probably just the reflection of the lantern one of the footmen held, but she truly appeared to have flames blazing from her eyes. "Who is this person and what are you doing?"

Henry cleared his throat. "I think it should be obvious what they are doing, Mama."

She gave the marquess a quelling look, and he stepped back. Just behind him, Nicholas spotted Mr. and Mrs. Kentworth, Florentia, two more footmen, and a groom and the coachman. Nicholas would be damned if he wasn't well and truly caught.

Miss Blackstock seemed to come to her senses first. She jumped to her feet, placing herself between her enormous pig and the onlookers. "I'm terribly sorry to disturb you, my lady." She bobbed a quick curtsy. "My lord. Mr. and Mrs. Kentworth—and er, my lady. And you, my lady."

Nicholas wanted to put a hand to his face. The whole house had come to the stable.

"I just came to collect my pig. I'll be on my way now." And she actually tried to scoot around his mother and brother. The dowager held up a hand, and that was all it took to stall Miss Blackstock's progress.

"Not so fast, Miss—?"

"Blackstock," Mrs. Kentworth supplied.

The dowager's fiery gaze narrowed then focused on Nicholas, who was trying to set his walking stick upright so he could grasp it and haul himself up. It would have been an awkward and painful process if his brother hadn't stepped forward, offered his hand, and hauled Nicholas up, saving him the embarrassing struggle.

"Explain yourself," his mother demanded.

Nicholas thought the explanation was rather obvious for anyone to see. They'd all seen him kissing Miss Blackstock. If he had been thinking about anything besides her lovely hair and her large eyes and her…other assets, this would never have happened. He would have known the party would come for him.

He had indeed been hiding in the stable. Mr. and Mrs. Kentworth had been so careful in their speech to him, apologizing once when they only mentioned the word *war* in reference to their children. He'd withstood the pity in their eyes as long as he could, and then he'd fled to the one place in the world he felt he was not judged—among his horses.

When the pig had snuffled in, interrupting his solitude, Nicholas had known it was growing late and the Kentworths would want their carriage soon. The grooms and coachman knew better than to disturb him, so he would have to come out soon so the horses and carriage could be readied. But just as he was about to do so, Miss Blackstock had come in.

And then Nicholas had forgotten about everything but her. She'd been windswept from her brisk walk, her cheeks pink from the night air. Her hair was down about her shoulders in delicious waves of amber that gleamed in the lamplight. He couldn't stop staring at that hair. He wondered how it would feel in his hands, and he could imagine it was as slick as silk.

If it was just her hair or her eyes that had entranced him, he might have been able to think clearly. But once again, he was drawn into conversation with her. It had been three years at least since he had flirted with a woman, and he would have sworn he had forgotten how. But with Miss Blackstock, it came so easily. She didn't look at him with the pity that had weighed him down in the dining room. She looked at him as though he was a man—a man she desired.

Of course, she had mentioned his leg, but when she did so it was in a matter-of-fact manner. She didn't feel sorry for him or treat him like an invalid. She treated him like he was whole and undamaged.

And then she'd tottered against him and they'd both lost their balance, and suddenly he was on the ground with a beautiful woman in his arms. She was soft and smelled of crisp green apples and enticing woman. And when he met her gaze and she teased him with the promise of forward behavior, he couldn't resist. He knew he should resist. In the back of his mind a clock was ticking away the minutes and seconds until the Kentworth coach would be needed, but it had been so long since he'd had a woman in his arms that that incessant ticking was difficult to remember.

Most likely the grooms had started to come in and then noted he was not alone and slipped back out again. When the requested carriage did not appear at the house to take the Kentworths home, his mother, who was impatient and bad-tempered when her wishes were not quickly fulfilled, had led the whole party to the stable to see the task done herself.

Nicholas didn't need to have been there to know exactly how it happened. And now he had ruined Miss Blackstock.

He would have to marry her.

"Mama," Henry said, the head of the household as always. "The Kentworths must be tired and ready for their beds. Perhaps we could speak of this later." What he really meant was privately. No need to discuss this personal matter in front of neighbors and staff.

"Of course, Averstow," she said, using his brother's title. "Lord Nicholas and you, come inside." She pointed at

Miss Blackstock who looked like she wanted nothing more than to escape along with the Kentworths.

Miss Blackstock followed behind the dowager, the marquess and marchioness, and Nicholas. His sister, Florentia, fell into step beside her. Nicholas heard her whisper. "Don't look so worried. Everything will be fine."

"Somehow I doubt that," Miss Blackstock muttered. Then more loudly, she said, "Come, Sweetie!" The grooms all made way, as did the Kentworths, as the pig and Miss Blackstock left the stable. Outside, the family bid farewell to the Kentworths, who were assured their coach would be ready momentarily. But as the rest of the party started back for the house, Miss Blackstock slowed. "I should take my leave. It's late and—"

"Come inside," the dowager said, and her tone made even Nicholas hesitant to disobey.

Obviously, Miss Blackstock did not realize the danger she was in because she shook her head. "Thank you, but my pig—"

"Can wait in the kitchen," the dowager said, her tone brooking no argument. "Come inside or I will have you carried bodily."

Miss Blackstock's expression was mutinous, but she gave a stiff nod. "I suppose I could stop in for a moment."

Florentia patted her shoulder, and the family went inside, the dowager leading the way to the drawing room. When they were inside, she moved in front of the footman, shooed him out, and looked back at the party. "Lady Averstow and Florentia, you may go to bed."

"But Mama!" Florentia said, her tone pleading. She was two years Nicholas's senior, but she had never married and was a woman, so their mother still treated her as though she were a child of ten.

"Good night, Florentia," the dowager said, her face stony. Florentia gave Nicholas an apologetic look and left, Lady Averstow right behind her. Mary might have argued her right to stay more successfully, being that she was the marchioness, but no doubt she had little inclination to listen to the lecture her husband and mother-in-law were preparing.

As soon as the ladies were gone, the dowager closed the door with a final thud. Then she turned and glared at Nicholas. "What were you thinking!" she hissed. It wasn't a question but an accusation.

"Clearly, he was not thinking, Mama," Henry said.

Nicholas shot him a look of disdain for his lack of loyalty.

"Was this pre-arranged?" his mother asked. "Had you planned this rendezvous?" She looked from Nicholas to Miss

Blackstock and back again. Nicholas opened his mouth, but Miss Blackstock spoke first.

"Of course not. I was at the assembly rooms this evening and when I arrived home, I couldn't find Sweetie."

"Sweetie is the pig," Nicholas supplied. "A Gloucestershire Old Spots."

"That's right. I looked all about our house and the yard for her, but all I could find was evidence of her rooting about. I followed it and it ended at your stable. I found the door open and Lord Nicholas sitting with her. We spoke for a moment, and I was just about to return home when you came in."

"You did more than speak, girl," the dowager said.

Miss Blackstock's cheeks colored, but she kept her head up and her shoulders straight, her back not touching the chair where she'd been directed to sit.

"We were knocked off balance by Sweetie, and that is why we were on the ground. We both found the entire situation amusing and shared a kiss. That is all."

"That is everything!" his mother all but shouted. "Because not only did you share a kiss, you were alone and discovered. If you had been seen by only the family, we might have kept this a secret. But the Kentworths saw you as well as numerous members of our staff. You, girl, are well and truly compromised."

Miss Blackstock's face froze in a stunned expression. She went quite pale, and Nicholas could almost see her trying to grasp the implications of everything his mother had said. Then his mother turned her angry gaze on him, and Nicholas felt the blood drain from his face.

"What do you have to say for yourself?" she demanded. But she didn't wait for an answer before she shook her head in disgust. "I never thought I would have to worry about this from you."

Nicholas would not have wondered why, even if his mother hadn't gestured to his legs. The dowager couldn't believe that anyone would want a cripple like him. She'd thought she would have to entice women with a house party at Battle's Peak and Nicholas's family name in order to generate interest in him. She really did pity him and think him pathetic. He glanced at Miss Blackstock again. She was watching him, her brow slightly furrowed in confusion. How could she not understand his mother's implication? How did she manage to look past his injury when no one else could?

"I am a gentleman," Nicholas said. His mother gave a disbelieving huff. "I will marry her."

"Yes, you will," his mother said. "And what a waste of all my plans." She directed her steely gaze to the marquess.

"You will go with him to Doctors Commons for the special license. I want this done quickly and without fanfare."

"Of course, Mama," Henry said. The discussion over, his mother and Henry started for the drawing room door.

"Wait a moment." Miss Blackstock stood. Nicholas realized they had forgotten about her family. Her mother would need to be informed of the plans.

"I will send word to your mother first thing in the morning," the dowager said, not looking at her.

"There's no need," Miss Blackstock said. "I will not be marrying your son."

Nicholas raised a brow, too surprised to be insulted. He'd only offered to marry her to save her from ruin. Once word was spread that she had been found alone in his presence, practically on top of him, lips locked in a kiss, she would be cast out of all good society. Her entre family would suffer from the scandal. Not only would she not be invited to any more assembly balls, local merchants might refuse to sell them bread or bolts of cloth or seeds for their farmers.

"I don't see how you have any choice," his mother said, echoing his own thoughts. "Unless you plan to flee to the Continent, but even that will not spare your mother the shame of your actions."

"But I didn't do anything," Miss Blackstock said. "It was a little kiss. Can we not simply explain—" No one cut her off. She seemed to realize the ridiculousness of what she said mid-sentence. "No, of course not." She sighed, the sound one of utter defeat. She looked at Nicholas then. It was the first time she had done so since they'd been discovered. Her large brown eyes were filled with regret.

She really would refuse to marry him. Even though it meant ruin for her and her family. There could be only one reason for that—she couldn't stand to marry a cripple.

Four

Lord Nicholas's expression changed. He'd been looking at her with a mixture of resolve and concern, but now his face hardened. She couldn't tell what he was thinking when he did that, which was probably exactly the point. She could hardly blame him for being angry with her. No man wanted his marriage proposal refused—even if that proposal had only been made out of duty and obligation. "My lord," she said, trying to keep her voice from wavering. "Might we speak privately?"

"I think you have spent quite enough time alone!" the dowager marchioness said. The marquess leaned down and spoke quietly in her ear. Her eyes narrowed, but whatever he said must have swayed her. "Fine," she said. "You have five minutes." And she turned her back and swept out of the room. The marquess followed, closing the door as he left and leaving them in the silence of the large room.

Amelia had never been inside Battle's Peak before. She knew the outer façade of the house almost as well as she knew Catmint Cottage. But the family did not live or often host entertainments here. They used it strictly as a stopping point when traveling from one home to another or when looking in on their stables. In fact, it wasn't until Lord Nicholas and his sister had come to Hungerford a couple of years ago that the house had been staffed and inhabited fulltime. Not that it had mattered to Amelia, initially. Her life with her ailing father went on much the same as it always had. And by the time he died, the excitement over Lord Nicholas's arrival had waned. Lord Nicholas did not seem at all interested in hosting balls or dinners or anything worth gossiping about.

She looked about the drawing room now and tried to commit the gold and white furnishings to memory. The style reminded her very much of descriptions she'd read of Greek temples. She would have to describe it to her mother—if her mother was still talking to her after tonight.

Lord Nicholas stood stiffly in the same spot he'd had occupied since entering the room. He was dressed in evening clothes except he wore trousers instead of breeches. The starkness of his black coat and trousers made him look taller and more imposing, especially in the flickering candlelight. It was hard to believe she had kissed him just a short time ago. Now she was half afraid of him.

"My lord, if you will allow me to explain myself," she began.

"There is no explanation necessary," he said. "You do not want to marry me. I won't force you, though I do fear for your future. But one can hardly blame you for refusing."

Amelia blinked in surprise. This was not at all what she had expected him to say. "You think I am refusing you because we hardly know each other?"

He let out a derisive snort. "I think we both know the real reason."

Amelia didn't see how he could possibly know the reason as no one but she knew it.

"I don't think you do know my reason, and I feel I owe it to you to explain." Even the thought of telling him about her transgression and the trouble she might be in made her feel hot and uncomfortable. Would he call her names? Would he think the worst of her? She certainly had not behaved as she had been taught. When Corporal Wickersham had pulled her into that empty room late at night, she had known she should not do as he asked. But she'd been so tired of rules and denying herself, she'd pushed down that voice and done it anyway.

Tonight, with Lord Nicholas, she hadn't kissed him to thumb her nose at rules and restrictions. She'd done it because she'd wanted him. In the moment, kissing him had seemed right and natural. How could she possibly resist?

Obviously, she should have resisted because if she had, she wouldn't be in this lovely room with an angry man staring at her.

"Spare me the explanation of what I know all too well," he said. "I don't need to be told I am a cripple."

Amelia opened her mouth to ask what he was talking about then closed it. She felt as though she were a fish washed up on shore and flopping about in an attempt to return to the world she knew. "You think this is because of your injured legs?"

"What else?"

The arrogance of this man—to believe everything in the world was about him and his limp. "Have you considered that my refusal might be about *me*?"

"Rubbish. There's nothing wrong with you."

"There's nothing wrong with you, either."

"Are you mocking me?"

Amelia closed her eyes and tried to focus on the task ahead of her. "No, my lord. I'm trying to tell you that my refusal to marry you has nothing to do with you. In fact, I'm trying to save you."

"You're not making sense. I knew as soon as we were discovered that I would have to marry you or you and your family would be ruined by scandal. I don't need to be saved. If we don't marry, the worst that would happen to me are some whispered remarks I won't even hear as I have no intention of going out in Society unless absolutely necessary."

"And while I do appreciate your sacrifice, my lord, I can't allow you to make it. Not when I am carrying another man's child."

Whatever Lord Nicholas had been about to say next—some refutation of her argument, no doubt—her announcement shut him up. His gaze lowered to her abdomen, which would tell him nothing as it was far too early, and then back up to her face. "I see," he said. "You are in love with another man."

"No." She shook her head. "You don't see at all." She threw herself on a couch and covered her face. "This is mortifying. I haven't even told my mother or my friends, and now I must confess my transgression to a man I don't even know."

She felt the couch dip as he took a seat beside her. "You don't know me very well, that's true. Let me assure you I am not one to judge. I have made my own transgressions in the past."

"Yes, but you're a man." She parted her fingers and peeked out at him.

He shrugged. "I didn't transgress by myself. Does this man know about your—er, condition?"

She closed her fingers again. "No. He's a soldier and his regimen has moved on."

"I see. Have you written to him?"

She shook her head. "No. I thought about it, but…" She trailed off. She could not tell him the real reason she hadn't written. The *real* reason she had not begun that letter.

"But?" His voice was quiet and did seem kind.

She lowered her hands and squeezed her eyes shut. "I don't want to marry him. Honestly, it was just a bit of fun. I know how that makes me sound, but why should I ruin his life just because mine is ruined? At least that was my thinking." The words had spilled out in a torrent. Now she opened her eyes and stared into his lovely blue ones. "What an idiot I am. I have now put you in the same position. I seem to have a knack for ruining men's lives. I will write to him tonight and there will be no need for you to marry me." She jumped up. "I will fetch your mother."

But just as she started away, he grasped her wrist and tugged her back. She turned back to him, puzzled.

"Wait a moment," he said. "Let's think this through."

"I have thought it through."

He gave her a dubious look, and he did not release her wrist. Amelia looked down at his hand holding on to her and wished she didn't feel flutters in her belly at his touch. "If I understand correctly, you do not want to marry this soldier."

"Not particularly. He made me laugh and he could dance until I couldn't breathe, but I don't think he'd make a very good husband. Or father," she added.

"And no one knows you are carrying his child?"

"You know."

"Besides me." He furrowed his brow. "Are you even certain you *are* carrying his child? When was your rendezvous?"

Amelia's jaw dropped open and she pulled her arm away from him. "I don't have to answer that!"

He gave a sigh that indicated he was struggling to tether his patience. "Is it possible you are not breeding?" he asked, his gaze again falling to her flat abdomen.

"I suppose," she finally conceded.

"And are you opposed to marrying me?"

Amelia took a step back. "I beg your pardon."

Lord Nicholas stood, a bit slowly and stiffly but with a hint of the grace he must have had before the injury. "It seems to me your choices are limited. You must marry, if not because we were seen together this evening than because in a few months your other predicament will be made clear. There is only one way to save yourself and your family from shame and social exile. You must marry." He paused, seeming to give her time to digest what he had said. Amelia knew he spoke the truth. She'd been contemplating her family's ruin for about a week now. And it seemed she'd made a bad situation impossibly worse.

"The best solution might be to marry me."

Amelia stared at him. Was he really suggesting they marry? The silence went on for a long moment before he shifted uncomfortably.

"I understand my injury is off-putting. I assure you, I expect nothing from you. I am willing to accept a marriage in name only."

Amelia's head was spinning. She could not seem to make any sense of what he had just said. Why did he think she cared about his injury? And what did it mean that he expected nothing from her? *A marriage in name only.*

"You mean we would not have marital relations?" she asked, feeling her cheeks heat.

"Correct."

Was that supposed to convince her to agree? The kiss they'd shared in the stable had been the best kiss she'd ever experienced. Granted, she'd only been kissed a handful of times, but never before had her toes curled and heat infused her from her belly down to…well, she'd been quite warm. If there was any benefit to marrying him—besides his family's fortune and this large house and his lineage—it was sharing his bed. But then he might not want her now that he knew about her condition.

"You would marry me, even though I carry another man's child?"

"Yes."

"You would claim his child as yours?" she asked. Her mother would have fainted dead away if she had heard the way Amelia was speaking, but Lord Nicholas already knew her darkest secret. Why not shove everything into the open now?

"I would. The child would be mine under the eyes of the law, and I would treat him or her as my own."

"Why?" she demanded. She hadn't meant the question to come out like a challenge, but she wouldn't take it back. She wanted to know his motivations. She deserved to know.

"I have my reasons for wanting to marry, just as you do."

"Such as?"

He gave her a tight smile. "My mother will be back in a moment, and I'd rather we sort this before she returns. Do you agree or no?"

Amelia stared at him. His blue eyes were calm and his expression patient. If she said no, he would probably nod and wish her the best. If she said, yes...that was the real question. If she said yes, her entire life would change.

It wasn't the change she'd wanted. Of course, neither was bearing a child out of wedlock. On the other hand, she'd been dreaming of a change for ten years—longer than that if she thought back to all the years her grandmother had been sick. She'd wanted to go somewhere new, do something different, not have to worry about medicines and money and whether Rose needed help with the chamber pot or making dinner. She'd asked for change, and now the chance at an entirely new life—a new world—had been tossed in her lap. All she need do was grasp it.

"I agree," she said. "I'll marry you."

He hadn't exactly asked her, but she wouldn't let a small thing like a proposal ruin this moment. On impulse, she stepped forward, rose on tiptoe, and kissed his cheek. Of course, his mother picked that moment to open the door and return.

***

Nicholas had been too stunned to say anything when Miss Blackstock kissed his cheek. He'd wanted to pull her close and see if he could catch the scent of apples again, but his mother's horrified gasp put a damper on that idea. Before she could sputter something about decency and propriety, Nicholas announced, "Miss Blackstock and I are agreed. We will marry posthaste."

That announcement took the wind out of her sails. The dowager seemed to deflate at the words. Finally, she gave a tight nod. "I cannot say I am happy about this turn of events, but I am reassured that you are both willing to be reasonable." She directed her gaze at Miss Blackstock as she spoke. Little did his mother know that Miss Blackstock was actually quite reasonable. Not only that, but she was honorable. She didn't have to tell him about her pregnancy. She could have hidden it from him until after they were married. The fact that she was honest and open with him made him like her all the more.

"Henry," his mother said, turning her head slightly to indicate Nicholas's brother, still standing in the doorway. "You will go with Nicholas to secure the special license tomorrow."

"Of course, Mama."

The dowager looked at Miss Blackstock again. "You will marry the day after tomorrow. Eight in the morning in the family chapel. Do you understand?"

"Yes, my lady."

"Good. Now I suppose we should see if John Coachman can take you home."

But Miss Blackstock shook her head. "I'd rather walk, my lady. It's quite difficult to persuade Sweetie to climb in a carriage, and we can be home by the time your grooms have the horses hitched at any rate."

"Miss Blackstock," the dowager began. "It is after midnight. You cannot think to wander about the countryside alone. It is not safe."

"Thank you for your concern, my lady, but I'll have my pig with me. She is quite adept at protecting me."

"A pig! Nicholas, tell her no."

Nicholas wasn't about to step in the middle of this. The best thing to do would have been to offer to accompany her home, but he couldn't possibly walk that far, especially in the dark when he couldn't see the uneven spots in the ground that might put him off balance. "Can we at least send a footman to accompany you?" he asked.

"Please don't," she said, and before anyone could argue further, she said farewell and was gone.

"Nicholas," his mother's voice was sharp. "Go after her. She cannot walk home alone."

He stared at his mother, wondering if she could possibly be serious. Had she really forgotten his injury?

"Nicholas!" she said, staring at him with annoyance.

"Mama," the marquess said quietly. "He cannot go after her. His legs…" The sentence trailed off, leaving Nicholas to wonder what he might have said had he continued. No one ever mentioned his injury in his hearing. He rather doubted they mentioned it among themselves. What would Henry have said? *His legs are crippled? He is useless?*

His mother showed no embarrassment or acknowledgement of her mistake. Instead, she quickly changed course. "Ask a footman to accompany her, Henry. Thank you."

Henry went out on perfectly healthy, normal legs, leaving Nicholas alone with the dowager. She gave him a narrow look. "Well, what do you have to say for yourself?"

Nicholas shrugged. "You wanted me to marry."

"But did you have to go and ruin a girl to do it?"

He sighed. "I kissed her. That is hardly ruining her. Despite what it might have looked like, it really was just a kiss. Ridiculous that now I should have to marry her over it, but I understand that in your world the way something looks is much more important than the way it really is."

His mother sat heavily in a cream chair, her white head resting on the curve of the back like a snowy bird. "Why must it be *that* woman? Was there no one else you wanted to kiss?"

Nicholas wouldn't answer that question. Not only was there no one else he wanted to kiss, he hadn't even realized he'd wanted to kiss Miss Blackstock until he was kissing her. Instead of pursuing that line of thought, he said, "What is the matter with Miss Blackstock? Her father was a gentleman, and his land borders ours. I should think it a decent match."

His mother lifted her head, slowly. "As I mentioned the other day, that lady has become quite wild of late. Her father died some half a year ago, and since then she has been left to her own devices."

"What does that mean, precisely?" Nicholas asked. "She lives alone?"

The marquess came back into the room, half out of breath. "I sent a footman, Mama, but he could do no more than follow at a distance. Miss Blackstock's pig did not take kindly to his presence."

Nicholas coughed to hide the hint of a smile.

"Henry, Nicholas was just asking about Miss Blackstock. Tell him why I am so despondent at this betrothal."

Henry looked at his mother and then at Nicholas. At twelve years Nicholas's senior, Henry had never felt much like a brother to Nicholas. Their father had died when Nicholas was only nine, and for almost as long as he could remember, Henry had been the head of the family. He always seemed like more of an authority figure than a sibling. Henry was closest in age to Richard, who was eight years older than Nicholas, and the two of them had always been on good terms. For a few years during his childhood, Nicholas and Florentia had been playmates, she being only two years older than he, but when their youngest sibling, Anne, had been born, Florentia had been more interested in playing at being her nursemaid or mother and dressing Anne up like a doll than playing rough and tumble games with Nicholas.

It was because he was alone so much that Nicholas had developed a love of horses. He spent a great deal of time in the stables with the grooms and stablemaster, and he had learned everything from how to properly muck out a stall to how to saddle his own mount. When he'd gotten older, he'd learned all there was to know about breeding horses as well. He took a keen interest in pairing the right stallion with the right mare and for years he had not missed the birth of a single foal.

And then the war had come.

Henry was still looking at him, and Nicholas raised a brow in question. Although his earlier conversation had given him a good idea at what exactly his family might object to about Miss Blackstock, he wanted to hear their impressions for himself.

"I haven't any experience with her personally," Henry said. "But I have heard she is frequently at assembly balls without a chaperone."

Nicholas waited for him to say more, but it seemed no more was forthcoming. "She seems of an age," Nicholas said after a moment of silence. "She must be five and twenty."

"But she is unmarried and thus should have a chaperone," his mother said.

Nicholas wanted to roll his eyes at the absurd dictate, but he said nothing.

"And I have seen her in the tavern in the village," Henry said. Nicholas was surprised at this statement. Henry was not the sort of man to frequent a village tavern. He was not a very social man, and he was very particular in his tastes. He bought his coats from Weston, his boots from Hoby, and his watch fob from Rundell and Bridge. When it had come time for him to marry, he'd had one condition: she must be the daughter of a duke. Henry was not the sort to rub elbows with farmers and laborers.

"*You* were in the village tavern?" Nicholas asked.

"Briefly," his brother said, his lip curling to show his distaste. "And while I was there I observed Miss Blackstock and some of her friends laughing and chatting with some of the young men from the village."

"Is that all?" Nicholas said. He knew from the lady's own lips that was not all she had done, but if she was to become his wife, he would start protecting her name and reputation immediately.

"That is not all," the dowager said. "As I told you, she has quite the wild reputation, and the proof of that is in her behavior tonight. Not only was she in our stable in the middle of the night, found in flagrante delicto—"

"A kiss is hardly in flagrante delicto."

"—she insisted on walking home again alone. The woman is quite wild. I do worry for you, Nicholas. If only the Kentworths had not been present to see you with her, I would have found a way out of this!"

"I thank you for your concern, Mama," Nicholas said, "but you needn't worry for me. I'm sure I can manage one woman who has spent her entire life in Hungerford. And now that I will be married in a few days, you can go back to husband-hunting for Florentia."

His mother blanched, which was exactly the response he'd wanted. Anything to take the attention away from him. "Florentia," his mother all but wailed. "What am I to do about her? Two and thirty and not married. I despair of ever marrying her, and now that you will be wed, where will she go?"

Nicholas tried to add that she could stay right where she was. Battle's Peak could comfortably house a troop and would not be crowded with the three of them, but his mother rose and continued bemoaning her spinster daughter until finally Henry offered to escort her to her chamber. He left with her on his arm, shooting Nicholas a dark look.

Finally, left alone, Nicholas heard the tall clock chime two. He rubbed a hand over his face, knowing he should go to sleep. It would be a long day tomorrow. They'd have to travel all the way to London and back, and that meant leaving at sunrise and returning late into the night. It also meant having to sit all day, which would be torture for his leg. He hadn't liked sitting in a carriage for hours on end before the injury, but now he had no choice. He couldn't ride.

The pain tomorrow would save him pain later, he told himself. He wouldn't have to host a house party of debutantes. He wouldn't have to endure the pity in their eyes. He wouldn't have to argue with his mother, who seemed incapable of hearing him when he said he did not want to marry.

Now she would have her way, but so would he. Yes, he would marry, but it was on his terms. He would spare Miss Blackstock the disgust of seeing his injury, and he would spare himself from having to watch her grin and bear his attentions. The irony was on him, of course, because Miss Blackstock was the first woman in a long time that had actually drawn his interest. Yes, that was in part because she hadn't looked at him with pity. But there was no denying he was also attracted to her. If he hadn't been, he wouldn't have kissed her.

Now he just had to find a way to forget that kiss because he'd all but ensured it wouldn't happen again.

Five

Amelia hadn't thought she would sleep at all. When she'd finally climbed into bed—well after three in the morning—her mind had been spinning with thoughts of how she would tell her mother she would marry in two days. She didn't want to think past telling her mother to the actual wedding ceremony and marriage. But she did need to sort out how she would broach the topic. And that was her last thought before a soft voice roused her awake.

"Miss Blackstock, are you ill?"

Amelia opened her eyes, surprised to find her room bathed in pale sunlight that filtered through the drawn curtains. She sat up. "I must have overslept."

Rose nodded. "You tired yourself out with dancing last night. Would you like me to bring you a tea tray?"

Amelia shook her head. "No. I know you have plenty to do. I'll get my own." She paused in the act of throwing the covers back. "How is my mother today?"

Rose smiled. "She seems a little better this morning. She is having tea and toast in the dining room.

A rare good day, and just when Amelia needed it. "I'll join her."

"Very good, miss."

Amelia dressed quickly, pulling her hair into a long tail at the back of her neck and rushing down the stairs. Her mother was seated in the dining room, and she looked up when Amelia entered. Amelia tried not to show her concern, but sometimes when she saw her mother in the sunlight, it was difficult not to notice the changes in her. Once she had been a beautiful woman with hair the color of ripe wheat, eyes a lively green, and a smile almost too big for her face. Now that hair had faded and was streaked with gray. Her eyes were surrounded by lines of worry, and she hadn't smiled in years. Amelia might have thought she'd imagined the woman she'd once known as her mother if there hadn't been a portrait of her as a young woman in the drawing room.

"Good morning," her mother said. "You slept so late I asked Rose to make sure you were well."

"Too much dancing last night," Amelia said. "But how are you? You look better today."

"My megrim is gone." She sipped from her tea.

"You should rest today to make sure it does not come back." *Until I tell you about my impending nuptials,* Amelia thought.

"I would," her mother said, "but I worry I put too much burden on you and Rose. I cannot place the management of the estate completely on your shoulders."

"You managed it for years, Mama, and you showed me how to do everything. I don't mind at all."

"But I do. You are a young woman. You should go to dances and dinner parties. Enough of your life has been wasted in this place." She gestured to the room, but Amelia knew she meant the cottage as a whole.

"I would never consider a single day spent with Papa or Grandmama a waste. I wouldn't trade a single moment with them for even the grandest ball."

Her mother's eyes filled with tears and Amelia rushed to her. "Don't cry. Please. I didn't mean to make you weep."

"It's just that you are such a good girl."

Amelia wanted to cry out that she was *not* a good girl. She had become pregnant out of wedlock and all but ruined herself by kissing a man in a stable the night before. Good girls did not do such things.

"I wish things had been different for you."

"And I wish they had been different for you, Mama. But all we can do is hope things are better in the future."

"Yes." She patted Amelia's hand. "How did you become so wise?"

She wasn't wise at all. She was an idiot, and she'd made terrible mistakes. Amelia eased into the chair to sit beside her mother. "There's something I need to tell you, Mama."

Her mother sipped tea again, and Amelia wondered if she'd even heard.

"Mrs. Blackstock!" Rose appeared in the doorway with a letter in hand. "This just came for you and Miss Blackstock."

Her mother shook her head. "A bill from the doctor, no doubt." She rubbed her temple. "I will look at it later."

"No, madam. It came from Battle's Peak."

Amelia watched as her mother's hand fell away from her temple and an expression Amelia had not seen for years crossed her features. She looked…curious. The expression made her look younger and seemed to ease some of the lines at her eyes. Amelia stared at her mother as she reached for the letter.

And then Amelia blinked, realizing what the contents of the letter probably held.

"Wait!" she said before her mother could break the seal. Her voice was so shrill that even Rose glanced at her sharply.

"What is it?" her mother asked.

"I think I had better speak to you before you open that letter."

"Why? Do you know what it is about?" Her mother's voice sounded younger, so youthful. "It has been years since we received any correspondence from the Averstow family. How curious that something should come today."

Not so curious if one had been in the stable at the Averstow estate the night before. "Rose, would you leave us for a moment?" Amelia asked, wanting privacy to tell her mother what she must. Rose would find out at any rate, but her mother should be the first to know.

"Of course, miss," Rose said. Amelia didn't miss the look of injury on her face. Not only had she been sent away just when an exciting letter had arrived, she was also being excluded from the confidence of the two women she had worked beside for more than twenty years. Amelia promised herself she would make it up to Rose. Somehow.

Rose closed the door as she departed, and Amelia turned back to her mother. She blanched when she saw her mother had not waited for her and opened the letter already. "How curious," Mrs. Blackstock said, looking from Amelia to the paper and back again. "We have been invited to dinner this evening at Battle's Peak."

"Have we?" Amelia squeaked.

"Yes. It will be the dowager, Lady Averstow, and Lady Florentia. It says an informal repast with ladies." Her mother lowered the letter to her lap. "Whatever shall I wear?"

"It didn't mention anything else?" Amelia asked.

"Such as?" her mother asked, her tone all innocence.

"Might I see it?" She held out her hand, and her mother placed the heavy cream paper in it. Amelia scanned the letter and saw that it was, indeed, just an invitation to dinner. The men would likely still be en route from London, and the ladies probably wanted to do something to welcome the Blackstock family, considering Amelia would soon be one of them.

"That's very kind of them," Amelia said.

"I didn't realize the dowager was in residence." Mrs. Blackstock lifted her teacup again. "I wonder where Lord Nicholas is. Or perhaps he does not care for company."

"He doesn't," Amelia said. And then, realizing what she had said, she continued in a hurry, "I hear he is somewhat reclusive."

"That's too bad. He never used to be, but the war changes people." She glanced at the wall where a portrait of

Amelia's father hung. He looked down at them, his dark eyes smiling, even if his expression was serious. Amelia understood her mother's thoughts then. They had been through their own war, first with the illness and death of Amelia's grandmother and then her father's injury a few years later.

"I don't suppose I need to think overly much about what to wear," her mother said. "I only have one black dress fit for a dinner. But what shall you wear? You are too young to wear mourning."

At six and twenty, Amelia was not too young, but she had taken advantage of her mother's indulgence and worn bright colors or white in company these past few months. Right now what she would wear back to Battle's Peak was the last thing on her mind. "Mama, I believe I know why we have been invited to dine."

"There is a reason?" her mother asked.

Amelia nodded. She knew she should simply tell her mother everything right then, but the words stuck in her throat. Her mother had always thought her such a good girl, and it was not easy to disabuse her mother of that idea in one fell swoop.

In the long pause, her mother lifted her hand to her temple again, and Amelia knew she would be the cause of the next megrim.

"It has to do with Lord Nicholas, Mama," Amelia said carefully. "And myself."

Her mother said nothing. She simply waited for Amelia to go on. It was the way she always accepted bad news. She stood stoic and silent before doctor after doctor, absorbing the dire predictions for her husband's fate, never asking or soliciting. It was not her way.

"Something happened last night," Amelia said. "And I am betrothed to Lord Nicholas."

Anyone else would have gasped in shock, but Mrs. Blackstock had suffered worse shocks than this. Her expression did not change, and she did not speak. Amelia explained how she had arrived home from the assembly rooms and found Sweetie missing and how she went to find Sweetie and found her in the stable at Battle's Peak. She did not mention she had been there before.

"Lord Nicholas was inside. As I said, he prefers solitude, and his mother had invited the Kentworths for dinner. I believe he slipped out for a few moments and encountered Sweetie. We were talking and…well, one thing led to another, and he kissed me. Or I kissed him. I'm not sure which. It was only a kiss, but, well, we had fallen to the ground, and it looked like much more and that was when Mr. and Mrs. Kentworth came for their carriage followed by the dowager countess and Lord and Lady Averstow and Lady Florentia."

Mrs. Blackstock closed her eyes as though pained. Amelia pressed on anyway because what else could she do?

"The dowager said I was ruined, and Lord Nicholas offered to marry me, and I accepted because I don't want a scandal. I don't want to hurt you, though I'm aware I am probably hurting you now—" She was aware she was babbling, but she couldn't seem to stop. She always talked too much when her mother became silent. It was as though someone or something needed to fill the hush surrounding them, and she always stepped into the void.

"Lord Nicholas and his brother went to London to get the special license. We're to marry tomorrow."

Her mother took a deep breath then reached over and pressed her hand to Amelia's. Amelia stared at her, hoping she would say something. The press of her hand was a good sign, but Amelia needed absolution. Instead, her mother rose and walked with her back straight and stiff to the door. "I think I shall lie down for a little while. I'm not feeling well."

Amelia stood. "I understand. Can I bring you anything?"

Mrs. Blackstock opened the door. "No, not just now."

"Mama," Amelia called. Her mother paused but did not look back. "Will you attend the dinner this evening?"

Without an answer, her mother walked away.

***

Obtaining the special license had been a simple matter. It had taken no more than a half hour and then Nicholas and his brother were standing outside in the gloom that passed for sunshine in London. Somehow the summer heat seemed more oppressive in Town.

"That was quick," Henry said. "While we are here, I should look in at Averstow House and pay my solicitor a call."

Nicholas was in no hurry to fold himself back into the coach and relished some time to stretch his legs. And now that he was here, he supposed he should look in at the Draven Club and see his friends. He didn't generally like to do anything that would churn up memories of his time in the war, but how could he not go when he was so close? "I'll be at the Draven Club," he told his brother.

The marquess raised his brows with interest. "Very good. "I'll collect you there in say"—he pulled out his pocket watch and checked the time—"three hours?"

Nicholas nodded.

"You take the carriage," the marquess offered. "I feel like a walk today."

Nicholas doubted it, but he couldn't walk all the way to St. James's Square. If he didn't take the coach, he would have to hail a cab. The brothers parted and Nicholas climbed gingerly into the coach and gave the coachman the direction. The streets of London hadn't changed much from the last time he'd been here, and the snarl of horses and carts and coaches made the journey take far longer than it ought. But he finally arrived and made his way awkwardly up the steps to the club.

Porter, the Master of the House, opened the door immediately. "Lord Nicholas," he said as though his appearance there was commonplace. "How good to see you. Come in."

Nicholas couldn't help but look down at the wooden peg Porter used in place of the leg he'd had amputated. Colonel Draven had told them Porter lost his leg in war, but Nicholas had never asked for more details. Now he wondered.

Porter took his hat and gloves, while Nicholas attempted not to look at the large shield opposite the door. The shield was cut in half by a medieval sword and around the shield were eighteen fleur-de-lis that symbolized the men who had not come home from the war.

"Is anyone else here?" Nicholas asked.

Porter opened his mouth and then closed it again, seeming to consider. "Mr. Payne is here."

"Rowden?" Nicholas hadn't seen the former pugilist since he'd come to Hungerford for a boxing match and ended up married.

"He is in the dining room."

"Alone?"

Porter paused again. Odd that. Porter seemed almost flustered. Nicholas might not be a regular at the club, but he knew Porter enough to recognize that something was the matter.

"I cannot say, my lord."

"You cannot say whether or not he is alone?"

"Correct."

"Shall I go up and see for myself?"

Porter gave a sigh of relief. "That might be best, my lord."

"Very well." Nicholas eyed the winding staircase carpeted in royal blue. Stairs were the bane of his existence. It hurt like the devil to walk up them as most men did, but he'd have to suffer the pain unless he wanted Porter to witness the usual humiliating way he managed stairs.

Porter went ahead of him, seeming to manage them with ease. Nicholas gritted his teeth and started up, leaning heavily on the banister and trying not to bend his left knee. That meant the bulk of his weight was supported by his right leg, which was the stronger leg but still pained him when strained. He had reached halfway when he glanced up and saw Porter waiting for him, eyes fixed on a spot just above Nicholas's head. Like any well-trained servant, Porter would never allow Nicholas to know he was being observed.

Nicholas didn't know why he spoke then. Possibly because he was out of breath and wanted a reason to pause for a few moments longer. "I don't suppose you have any suggestions for making this climb easier."

Porter's gaze did not move from the distance. "I do, my lord. If you take the walking stick you have crooked on your elbow and place it on the stair ahead of your left leg then it will take some of the weight off your right leg and provide balance."

Nicholas looked down at his ebony stick and unhooked it. He did as Porter said and though the effect was not substantial, he did see the benefit. At this point, he could use any small improvement. "Thank you, Porter," he said when he finally reached the top.

"No thanks is necessary, my lord, I assure you." He started toward the dining room. "This way, my lord." His voice was unusually loud, almost as though he was warning Rowden someone was coming. He paused at the dining room doors a bit longer than was customary and then opened them wide, showing Rowden sitting alone at a round table covered with a white linen cloth. He had his hands folded in front of him as though he had been sitting alone and twiddling his thumbs.

"Lord Nicholas," he said. "I didn't know you were in Town."

Nicholas looked about the room. It appeared empty other than Rowden. "May I join you?" he asked.

"Ah…of course."

Nicholas crossed to the table and took a seat.

"Do you still prefer port, my lord?" Porter asked.

Nicholas did, but he'd noted that there was already a bottle of wine on the table and two glasses. "I'll have a glass of wine. It appears there is already one here for me."

Porter looked at Rowden then back to Nicholas. "I will fetch you a clean one, my lord."

When that was done, he hurried out of the room, and Nicholas gave Rowden a long look. "Am I interrupting something? Some sort of clandestine meeting? Should I go?"

"No, you might as well stay," came a voice from under the table.

Nicholas looked down then back at Rowden, who covered his mouth to hide what was an obvious smile. Slowly, Nicholas lifted the material from the tablecloth and peered under the table. Rafe Beaumont sat cross-legged, smiling up at him.

"What the devil are you doing under there?" Nicholas asked.

"I panicked," Rafe said. "I needed somewhere to hide."

"I think he means why are you under a table at the Draven Club when you are supposed to be in the Americas?" Rowden said.

"Oh, that." Rafe waved a hand. "I came back for a visit."

"A visit? Aren't you wanted for treason?" Nicholas asked

"I suppose. Can you hand me that glass of wine?" Rafe pointed to the table above him where a glass sat.

"Come sit in a chair, Beaumont," Rowden said. "No one is coming here to look for you. Porter wouldn't allow them entrance."

Rafe reluctantly crawled out from under the table and took a seat just as Porter returned with Nicholas's port and a plate of steaming food. Nicholas's stomach rumbled. He was hungry after a day of travel. As soon as Porter left them, Rafe leaned over the table and looked from one side to the next as though making sure they were not observed. Which was ridiculous as no one else was in the room.

"I came back to see my parents. My stepmother wrote that my father was not well. Indeed, I believe he was quite ill over the winter and is only now recovering. But his recovery was not at all assured, and as it takes weeks to cross the ocean, I didn't want to wait."

"I hadn't heard Lord Haddington was ill. I'm glad he is improving," Nicholas said. "But that doesn't explain why you are here, hiding under the table."

Rafe gave him a look that said the answer to that question should be obvious. "Draven said I might come back in a few years when the entire collaborating-with-a-spy-nonsense blew over."

"But the woman was a spy and you married her," Rowden said. "I'm not sure that qualifies as nonsense."

Rafe waved a hand. "She was only spying to protect her father. She never passed any information along, and now they're both in Bos…in an undisclosed location in the Americas, and I thought I might test the waters here, so to speak. But I'd only been at the earl's town house for a few days when Draven came to call and told me the Foreign

Office was aware I was here and preparing to take me in for questioning."

"It sounds like the spy nonsense hasn't blown over."

"Apparently, not. Thank God I didn't bring Collette or the baby."

Nicholas choked on his port. "You have a baby?"

Rafe's chest puffed up. "I do. A boy who is almost one now, and sink me if he isn't the most handsome young lad you've ever seen. I'll bring him next time."

"Next time?" Rowden sputtered. "Do you think there should be a next time?"

"Hell's teeth, there has to be. Boston—er, the undisclosed location—isn't completely devoid of fashion and Society, but I'll not stay there forever. London is home. Just not yet."

Nicholas managed to eat a few bites of mashed turnips. "What will you do now? Hide here until you can book passage on a return voyage?"

"That was the plan when Draven sent me here, but he said it might be weeks before I can chance appearing at the docks. They'll be looking for me. I'm to stay here until he says it's safe."

"Then you'd better listen to him," Rowden said.

"And what if they trace me here? Then not only will I be taken into custody, Draven's loyalty will be questioned. He could lose his position."

Rowden made a show of looking under the tablecloth.

"What are you doing?" Nicholas asked, conscious of his crippled legs underneath.

"Looking for the real Rafe. He never thought about anyone but himself."

Rafe eyed Rowden, unamused. "That's not true, and you know it. I always think of the lady and make sure she climaxes first."

Nicholas was glad he was not drinking when Rafe said that. He probably would have spit the liquid out.

"Of course, there is only one woman now, and I assure you, Collette—"

"Rafe." Rowden raised a quelling hand. "Your time might be better spent thinking of a plan rather than boasting of conquests."

"I have a plan."

Rowden and Nicholas exchanged a look. Nicholas started, "You just said—"

"I said I didn't want Draven to be in danger, which means I need to leave the club. I'll go with you." He pointed to Nicholas. Nicholas was all but ready to glance over his shoulder.

"Me?"

"Yes. You never write, but Phin does, and he says you're almost as much a recluse as Nash. I had thought to go to Wentmore, but Nash is too far away. You're hiding away at Battle's Peak, and that's only a few hours."

"I don't think that's a good idea."

"Why? Are you not returning to Hungerford?"

"I am. My brother will be here in a few hours with the coach."

"Which brother?" Rowden asked. "Henry or Richard?"

"Henry."

"Ah, he's a good chap then," Rafe said. "We can trust him."

"Yes, but my mother is at Battle's Peak and my sister and well…there's another snag."

Rafe shrugged. "Nothing we can't handle, I'm sure."

Nicholas rather thought it was something he couldn't handle. "I'm marrying in the morning."

Six

Amelia stared at herself in the mirror over her dressing table. It only showed half of her body at a time, but she had never thought she wanted a full-length mirror before now. She'd chosen a white muslin dress with sprigs of green in a pretty pattern throughout and an apple green ribbon at the waist. She'd tied the ribbon at least three times, but she couldn't see her back and still wasn't sure if it was straight. Her hair looked presentable. She'd been doing her own hair for years, and had pulled most of it up, leaving a few tendrils to fall over one shoulder. That seemed to be the style lately. Thus far she had not heard a sound from her mother's room down the hallway. She supposed that meant she would be dining at Battle's Peak alone.

Not that she blamed her mother. It couldn't be easy to learn that your daughter was not the person you'd believed for all these years, especially when she was the only family you had left.

But Amelia wouldn't think of that now. If she did, she'd start weeping, and then her nose would be red.

She took a deep breath, pulled on her white gloves, and opened the door to her room. Lifting her skirts, she descended the stairs, keeping her head high. The dowager had said she would send a carriage, so there was no cause to worry about soiling her slippers on the walk over. She had taken the added precaution of feeding Sweetie a little extra this afternoon and then closing her in the library so she could not get out to forage for more or harass the coachman when he arrived.

Amelia went to the window and parted the curtains, looking for any sign of a carriage when she heard a step behind her. She turned and gasped.

Her mother stepped into the front parlor wearing a deep purple dress that brought color to her cheeks. She looked ten years younger.

"Mama!" Amelia finally managed. "You look…" But she didn't have the words to describe how lovely her mother looked. Yes, the dress was out of fashion and subdued as befit a widow. The garment was probably ten or more years old, but it fit her well and highlighted her lovely white neck and collarbone. Mrs. Blackstock had pulled her hair into a fashionable twist and the gray that streaked through it actually looked very distinguished. At her ears were a pair of glittering lilac gems.

She caught Amelia looking and touched them gingerly. "They are just paste, but I like how they glitter."

"*You* glitter," Amelia said. "You're beautiful!"

"I don't feel beautiful. I feel old, but I hope I make a good show. I don't want to embarrass you."

Amelia went to her mother, taking her hands. "Embarrass me? Mama, after what I have done, if anyone is to be embarrassed, it's you."

"Don't think I have nothing to say to you on that account, Amelia," her mother said, her voice scolding, which was a tone Amelia rarely heard from her. "But now isn't the time." She gestured to the window where the coach could be seen approaching.

"Oh, dear. I don't think I can do this!" Amelia squeezed her mother's hands tightly.

"You are a Blackstock, Amelia. We don't run from trouble. *It* runs from us."

It was something her father had been fond of saying, and Amelia smiled at the way her mother imitated her father's way of saying it. But she couldn't help think that her father had never had to contend with the Dowager Marchioness of Averstow.

The carriage ride to Battle's Peak was far too quick, and in a matter of minutes they were climbing out of the conveyance and being guided inside the large manor house.

Amelia had not really looked at the grand entry when she'd been led inside the night before. She'd been too distraught. Now she noted the width and height of the foyer and the expanse of polished wood flooring, laid in an intricate pattern. The dark wood gleamed under the light of the candles sparkling in the crystal chandelier. A grand staircase in marble curved gracefully up to the first floor and Amelia spotted at least two paintings by Renaissance masters on the walls. A large vase of daffodils was set in the middle of a round mahogany table in the center of the floor. The scent was lovely, and Amelia inhaled deeply then caught her breath as Lady Florentia appeared. They had not been formally introduced, but Amelia had seen her in Hungerford a few times these past few months and knew who she was.

Lady Florentia was a few years older than Amelia and considered a spinster. Regardless, she did not look like a spinster. She had dark hair and dark eyes and offset them with a dress of cream with gold embellishments. She looked like she might have just arrived from ancient Greece, which Amelia supposed was the effect she wanted. The Grecian style of the drawing room made perfect sense now.

"Mrs. Blackstock. Miss Blackstock!" Lady Florentia gave them both a stunning smile and a curtsy. Amelia and her mother followed.

"Thank you for the dinner invitation," her mother said. "We are delighted to attend."

Amelia couldn't help staring at her mother. She hadn't heard her speak like that in years.

"It is long overdue," Lady Florentia said, coming forward to take Amelia's hands. "And of course, we have such good news to celebrate. I am overjoyed that we shall soon be sisters."

"Thank you," Amelia said, her voice catching in her throat. She hadn't expected such a warm welcome.

"Please come to the dining room. Lady Averstow and the Dowager Marchioness are waiting."

Amelia exchanged a nervous look with her mother and then she returned to the drawing room where her fate had been sealed the night before. A liveried footman opened the door, and they entered, finding the marchioness and the dowager seated on a pale couch whose upholstery gleamed in the lamplight. Amelia and her mother both curtsied and the marchioness smiled in welcome. The dowager made no attempt to make them feel welcome. Amelia felt her eyes sweep over her in a dismissive manner.

A footman brought small glasses of Madeira for Amelia and her mother, and once everyone had been seated, the marchioness asked after their health and made a few comments on the weather. They were the sort of comments intended to put one at ease, but Amelia could hardly feel easy when the dowager stared at her so intently.

"I was so sorry to hear of Mr. Blackstock's passing," Lady Florentia said after they had discussed the recent rains in as much detail as possible.

"Thank you," Amelia's mother said, looking down. Amelia clenched her fists, hoping that her mother did not tear up or suddenly fall ill with a megrim before they had even gone to dinner.

"I did not know him well," Lady Florentia continued, "but the few times I encountered him, he was always smiling and seemed to have a very amiable disposition."

"He was always in good spirits," Amelia said, sparing her mother from having to reply. "He always had a kind word or a wry observation. Indeed, he always made us smile."

"He will certainly be missed," Nicholas's sister said.

She was kind, and she was trying her best to show Amelia that she would welcome her with sisterly affection.

"When did your father pass away?" the dowager said, her voice harsh after Lady Florentia's quiet tones. It was the first word the dowager had spoken.

"Almost seven months ago, my lady," Amelia said.

The dowager's gaze swept over Amelia again, and she forced herself to sit still in her chair and not to fidget.

"And you have already set aside your mourning clothes," the dowager observed.

"That is my doing," Amelia's mother said, much to Amelia's surprise. She hadn't thought her mother strong enough to speak when the conversation had turned to her late husband. "Amelia is young and has spent most of her life caring for the sick or infirm. I did not think she should spend a moment longer than necessary in mourning."

"She is not so young," the dowager observed. "How old are you, Miss Blackstock?"

Amelia did not particularly like the question, but she did not see how she could avoid it when it had been asked so directly. "Six and twenty, my lady."

The dowager looked back at Mrs. Blackstock. "Not so young. Practically on the shelf."

"Mama," Lady Florentia chided. "Miss Blackstock barely looks a day over twenty."

"And from all accounts, she behaves as though she were closer to sixteen. Have you encouraged her reckless behavior as well?" the dowager asked her mother.

Amelia watched her mother stiffen and her spine straighten. How dare the woman say such things to her dear Mama? Before she could offer a rejoinder, though, her mother held up a staying hand. She cleared her throat. "My lady, I am fully prepared to take responsibility for all of my daughter's actions."

Amelia didn't think her mother quite knew the extent of those actions or she might not have claimed them all.

"I am aware that some in the area like to whisper about trivial matters over tea."

"Trivial matters?" the dowager said, her brows rising.

"Yes, such as whether a lady of six and twenty needs a chaperone or dances with the same man too many times or laughs too loudly at a public inn. These matters do not concern me."

"I see."

"At the end of the day, what really matters is whether or not my daughter or I or any of us has a rich, fulfilling life. I have learned that life can be short and in a single moment, everything can change. One must live life to the fullest because we never know what day the Lord has set as our last."

Lady Florentia was nodding her head, but the dowager looked angry. Her cheeks had dark splotches of color on them. "It would seem you actively encourage Miss Blackstock's wild ways."

"I would never do so, but I also know my daughter and she is not wild. She is a good girl and always has been."

Amelia felt hot tears prick the backs of her eyes, and she bit the inside of her cheek to keep from crying. How could her mother defend her? She knew Amelia had been ruined. She was not a good girl.

"I would hardly call her behavior in the stable last night that of a good girl. She was practically on top of my son. We caught them in flagrante delicto."

"Mama," Lady Florentia interrupted. "It was only a kiss."

"Hmpf. That is all we *saw*."

Marianne Blackstock rose then, her shoulders straight and pushed back, her chin high. "I have been a widow now for seven months, and I know something about what happens between men and women. No woman ruins herself. The man must also participate. In fact, the man is usually the instigator and we women are unfairly blamed for his misconduct."

Now the dowager rose to her feet. "My son would never seduce this woman." She pointed to Amelia. Amelia sat stiffly in her chair, uncertain whether she should stay seated or rise and defend herself. What was happening? They hadn't even gone to dinner yet.

"Clearly, he played some part," Amelia's mother said.

"He was a victim of her schemes to marry him," the dowager spat. Even Lady Averstow, who had been silent up until now, gasped at that accusation.

"My daughter does not scheme. If she was indeed engaged in a kiss with Lord Nicholas, it was mutual."

"It couldn't be mutual," the dowager said. "My son is a cripple."

Amelia's hands flew to her mouth. How could a mother speak so about her son? Her tone was full of disgust. She jumped to her feet. "He is *not* a cripple. He is a war hero."

The dowager turned her head to stare at Amelia. "Sit down, girl."

"I will not allow you to speak about Lord Nicholas as though he is an invalid. He has an injury to his legs but I assure you, he is still very much alive and perfectly healthy."

"Sit down."

"And the last time I checked, a man does not need his legs to kiss a woman."

"Sit down! I will not tolerate this insubordination."

"And we will not tolerate this lack of regard," Mrs. Blackstock said. "I am afraid I am feeling unwell and will be unable to stay for dinner. Amelia, come. Let's go home."

Amelia followed her mother as she swept out of the drawing room. Her head was spinning. Never before had she done anything so bold. She couldn't remember her mother ever doing such a thing either, but then perhaps all of the times she debated and argued with doctors over the years had given her a spine of steel. At that moment, Amelia thought her mother the most amazing woman in the world. She caught up to her and they walked across the marble floor side by side.

"I cannot believe we just did that," Amelia said under her breath.

"Neither can I." Then she stopped and Amelia had to lurch to a stop under the chandelier.

"Have you changed your mind?"

"No. She's a horrible woman," her mother said. She looked down at her hand. "I just realized I am still carrying my wine glass." She downed the wine, then walked forward and passed the glass to the footman. The butler appeared, breathing heavily, and Amelia realized he must have raced up from the kitchen to meet them in the foyer. He took their wraps from the footman and offered them very formally.

"Miss Blackstock! Mrs. Blackstock!"

Amelia looked up and saw Lady Florentia racing toward them, hand fisted in the long train of her gown.

"Please wait!"

Amelia glanced at her mother, who had paused in donning her shawl.

"I am so sorry for my mother's behavior," she said in a loud whisper. "She is overwrought and not herself."

Amelia rather thought the woman was probably behaving exactly as herself, but she said nothing.

"I am afraid I really am unwell," her mother said. "I cannot stay for dinner."

"I must see my mother home," Amelia said.

Lady Florentia glanced at the footmen who were pretending not to listen in. "Have the coach brought around," she said.

"That's not necessary," Amelia said. "We can walk." But of course, she should have considered her mother's condition. Perhaps they should accept the coach.

"Let me do this small thing for you, Miss Blackstock," Lady Florentia said.

"Thank you," her mother answered. Lady Florentia glanced at the footmen again and they moved away slightly. She took Amelia's gloved hands in her own. "I am sorry about my mother, but I assure you, after the wedding, she will return to London or our estate in the country. You shan't have to see her again."

"Ever?" Amelia asked.

Lady Florentia smiled. "I cannot promise that, but it will be rarely. Please don't cry off."

Amelia glanced at her mother. "I can't cry off. I'm ruined."

Lady Florentia shook her head. "Somehow I don't think that really matters to you." She squeezed Amelia's hands. "My brother is a good man, and you're the first woman—the first person—he has taken any interest in since he returned from the war. I think you two can make a go of it."

Obviously, Lord Nicholas had not told his sister about his plans for a platonic marriage. But the rest of what she said was true. Lord Nicholas was a good man, and at this point, Amelia did not have any other options. "I will be in the chapel at eight in the morning," she said.

Lady Florentia gave a little hop. "I will see you then. Tomorrow at this time, we will really be sisters!"

"My lady, the coach is outside," the butler said.

"Thank you, Tiggs." Lady Florentia released Amelia. "Off you go then. Mrs. Blackstock, I do hope you feel better tomorrow. And again, I am sorry."

In the coach again, Amelia's mother laid her head back on the squabs and sighed.

"That did not go as planned," Amelia said.

"The dowager marchioness is just as haughty as ever," her mother said, but her voice lacked the vim it had held before. "I remember now why I never liked her."

"Lady Florentia seems kind."

"She does, yes. She will be a useful ally, but—" She lifted her head and looked straight at Amelia. "You do not have to go through with this wedding."

"But the scandal!"

"After all we have been through these past few years, I can weather a little scandal. I'd rather that than have you in an unhappy marriage."

Amelia wished she could tell her mother about the pregnancy then. When she gave birth to a bastard out of wedlock, it would be no *little* scandal. And Lady Florentia had made a good point in that Amelia would not be marrying the dowager marchioness. She would be marrying Lord Nicholas, and thus far he had been nothing but kind and understanding toward her. Not to mention he was devilishly handsome and kissed well enough that her toes tingled. Being married to him would not be a hardship—unless he really did insist on treating her like a sister rather than a wife. Perhaps she could change his mind over time?

"It won't be an unhappy marriage," Amelia said after a long silence during which she was aware of her mother watching her closely. "Lord Nicholas is a good man."

"And handsome, I warrant, if the look on your face just now is any indication."

Amelia felt her cheeks heat. "Very handsome."

"If this is what you want, then I will stand with you in the church tomorrow."

Amelia reached across the coach and took her mother's hands. "Thank you, Mama. You have always been there for me."

But Amelia did wonder who would be there for her mother when Amelia moved to Battle's Peak, and her mother was alone with her memories in Catmint Cottage.

***

It was after midnight by the time Henry, Nicholas, and Rafe arrived at Battle's Peak. Nicholas and Rowden had convinced Rafe they needed former soldier Colin FitzRoy to come to the club and devise a disguise for Rafe. Colin had been known as the Pretender during the war as he'd always been in disguise, infiltrating enemy lines. He hadn't lost his talent. Rafe was now masquerading as a vicar who had gone to Eton with Nicholas and who had been in London visiting family for a few weeks before taking his new post at a parish in the west. Colin had dressed him in plain black with a white collar and an ugly hat. He'd told Rafe to keep his eyes downcast and brush his hair over his brow as much as possible. The disguise was believable in the dark and from a distance, but if one looked Rafe in the face, he was far too handsome to go unnoticed. And anyone who had known Rafe before would know him immediately if he flashed those violet eyes or that rakish smile.

"Osgood," Rafe was muttering as the coach pulled into the drive. "Alfred Osgood." He looked at Nicholas. "Should I try it with a Yorkshire accent?"

"Can you manage a Yorkshire accent?"

"Just keep your mouth shut or you'll have us all arrested," Henry said. He had been less than pleased to have Rafe accompany them back. They'd tested the disguise on Henry when he'd arrived at the Draven Club to fetch Nicholas, and it had taken Henry about two minutes to realize Alfred Osgood was Rafe Beaumont. Of course, he'd been friends with one of Rafe's older brothers for years and knew Rafe better than the average gentleman. At least that was what the men told each other as they pushed Rafe into the coach and out of London. Rowden would write when it was safe for Rafe to return. "A fortnight at most," he assured them. Henry had glowered at Nicholas and then Rafe, who didn't seem bothered by the evil looks in the least. Rafe was far more interested in hearing about Nicholas's bride. He'd asked about a dozen questions before Henry had enough and told him Nicholas had ruined the chit and was forced to marry her.

Rafe, of course, had not looked shocked at all. Instead, he patted Nicholas's arm and said, "I didn't know you had it in you."

"If you are done congratulating your protégé," Henry said sarcastically, "how do you intend to be sure my mother and wife do not see you? Neither can be trusted with a secret, and they will both know you on sight."

"That's easy," Rafe had said.

"Go on," Henry said when Rafe didn't elaborate.

"You obviously have no head for strategy," Rafe told Henry, which made Nicholas laugh as the only strategy he had ever known Rafe to possess was the best way to woo a woman. "Laugh if you will, but you're not the one who waltzed right back into London under the Foreign Office's nose."

"I'm not so sure that wasn't stupidity," Henry said. "But do tell us your strategy."

"I'll hide," Rafe said succinctly.

Nicholas waited to hear more and when no more was forthcoming, Henry said, "That's all then?"

"It's perfect. What more need I say?" Rafe sat back and looked pleased with himself.

"A bit more, I think," Nicholas suggested before Henry jumped across the coach and strangled Rafe.

"It's the middle of the night, so presumably the house will be abed," Rafe said. "We'll pretend I'm ill for the benefit of the servants and you can stash me away in the dreary, seldom used north wing."

"We don't have a north wing," Henry said.

Rafe didn't acknowledge the interruption. "I'll stay hidden away until after the wedding guests depart. Then it will be just you and me, Nickers."

Nicholas hadn't heard that sobriquet in years. The men of Draven's troop had given it to him because he sometimes imitated the sounds horses made when interacting with them.

"And his bride," Henry said.

Rafe pointed to the marquess. "Is he always like this?"

Nicholas nodded.

"Will your bride know me, do you think?"

"I doubt it. She's been caring for her sick father in Hungerford for several years. She might know of you, but she won't know your face."

"Then she'll simply assume I am the Vicar Osgood."

"That's what we're going with?" Henry said as the coach slowed to a stop. "No one will believe it."

"I'll add my Yorkshire accent," Rafe said just as the footman opened the door.

Rafe kept his head down and stood in the shadows, waiting for Nicholas to climb out of the coach. It was an arduous process because Nicholas wouldn't accept any help, and his legs were stiff and hurt more than usual. Finally, he was on solid ground again and able to walk slowly and painfully toward the house, where another footman held the door open. "Right," Nicholas said to Rafe, his voice low. "Henry will show you to a room, and I'll have one of the maids leave a tray outside in the morning. If you stay inside and keep hidden away, no one will be the wiser."

"If you send summat to eat then I'll keep missen busy," Rafe said in what Nicholas supposed was his Yorkshire accent but sounded more like a Frenchman with a Spanish accent attempting English.

Nicholas closed his eyes. "That was truly horrible. It would be better if you said nothing."

"I won't say nowt."

Nicholas laughed and then blew out a breath as much to ease the pain of walking as to calm himself. Now that he was home the realization washed over him that he would be marrying in just a few hours. He had the license in his coat, and it seemed to be burning a hole through the superfine as the night wore on. Would he really marry a woman he barely knew in the morning? Was there even any way to avoid it at this point? What if Miss Blackstock jilted him? Everyone would pity the poor cripple and he'd rather be known as a scoundrel who ruined women than the cripple no woman wanted.

And of course, this was exactly the position he'd hoped to avoid putting himself in by agreeing to marry her and thus thwarting his mother's plans to put him on display in the marriage market. At the door, Nicholas took another deep breath. He just needed to make it a few more hours. Then he would be married and all of these worries would be a thing of the past.

"There you are," Florentia said, coming out of the parlor just off the foyer.

"What are you still doing up?" he asked as Rafe hastily ducked his head and pulled his hat low on his brow.

"Don't fret. Mother is asleep, as is your wife," she said to Henry. "It's just me, and I wanted to talk to you." She glanced at Rafe. "But I see you have arrived with a guest."

"Yes," Henry said. "This is the Vicar Osgood. He is an old friend of Nicholas's from school. Vicar, this is our sister, Lady Florentia."

Florentia gave a quick curtsy and Rafe muttered, "How do?" in his pathetic attempt at a Yorkshire accent.

"Will you be performing the ceremony tomorrow?" Florentia asked.

"No," Nicholas and Henry said at the same time.

Florentia stepped back. "Very well then. I was only asking."

"The vicar is not feeling well," Henry said, putting an arm about Rafe's shoulders, which was rather awkward as Rafe was taller than he. "You and Nicholas have a chat while I show him to his room."

"Good idea. Might we speak in the parlor?" Lady Florentia asked Nicholas.

Nicholas wanted nothing more than to go to bed. Climbing the stairs was an arduous task on the best days, and it would be even more so tonight. But Florentia would not have waited up if it was not important, and he had a sinking feeling it was something to do with Miss Blackstock. "Of course," he said.

"Good night, Henry. Good night, vicar," Florentia said.

"Good night," Rafe said, forgetting his accent. Florentia's brows wrinkled as she led Nicholas to the parlor. She had the fire banked, but the room was warm, and she poured Nicholas a glass of port. He sat on a couch, stretching his left leg out. He didn't need to pretend he wasn't in pain with Florentia. She sat in a chair across from him.

"That vicar looks oddly familiar," she said. "Did he ever come home with you from school?"

"Probably," Nicholas said. "But he is quite ill, so I suggest we all keep our distance. It might be catching." He sipped the port. "What happened here while I was away?"

"Mama invited your betrothed and Mrs. Blackstock to dinner."

Nicholas took another sip of port. A longer one. "Why?"

"Ostensibly as a gesture of goodwill to your future bride and her family."

"What did she do instead?" he asked, setting the port on the table at his elbow.

"She insulted them both and accused Miss Blackstock of seducing you."

Nicholas put a hand to the bridge of his nose where a headache was blooming. "Should I go first thing in the morning and apologize?"

Florentia shook her head, sipping her wine. "It's bad luck to see the bride before the wedding."

"If I don't apologize, there may *be* no wedding."

Florentia leaned forward. "I don't think she'll jilt you."

Nicholas knew Miss Blackstock was desperate, but there might be a limit to what even a woman in her position was willing to tolerate. "Why not?"

"She stood up for you. She told Mama you were a war hero."

Nicholas might have been pleased if he hadn't known the only reason the mention of war would come up was with regard to his injury. It did not take him more than a few seconds to work out how the conversation had gone. "Mama did not think I was capable of seducing her."

"More or less," Florentia agreed. "But Miss Blackstock said the last time she checked, a man did not need his legs to kiss a woman."

Nicholas smiled despite the pit of dread forming in his belly.

"And did Mama throw her soup bowl at her?"

"Oh, this was before dinner."

Nicholas's eyes widened.

"We never made it to dinner as Mrs. Blackstock said she would not allow her daughter to be treated like that and that she was ill and could not stay." Florentia sipped more wine. "I did not think the lady had so much mettle in her. She looked pale and frail, but she is like a sapling."

"She bends but doesn't break," Nicholas said.

"Exactly. I went after them, of course. Well, I told Mother she had behaved horribly and then I went after them. I apologized and Miss Blackstock said she would be here at eight in the morning."

"I'm sure she only said it to avoid more confrontation."

Florentia shook her head. "She meant it. I think she fancies you."

Women, Nicholas thought, were always imagining some romance where there was none. He kept that sentiment to himself, though. "She doesn't even know me. That kiss in the stable the other night really was all there was."

Florentia shrugged her shoulder. "People marry every day who know each other far less well. My friend Lady Louisa was betrothed to her husband without ever meeting him. In a letter she received at school, her father told her who she was to marry, and she only met her betrothed a few days before the wedding."

"And how has that gone for Lady Louisa?"

Florentia made a face. "She writes that he is tolerable. They have five children now, so I suppose they get on or at least stomach each other. My point is, at least you know the woman you are marrying, and I assume you like her, considering the way we found you."

Nicholas wouldn't allow any further speculation about a love match. "As a gentleman, I'm honor bound to protect her reputation." He struggled to his feet. "This is more of a business arrangement than a marriage."

"We'll see," Florentia said. "Now, I had better get to bed else I will look a fright in the morning. Good night, Nicholas." She kissed his cheek.

"Good night."

She left the door open when she went and Nicholas peered out, observing the rest of the household had gone to bed. Good. No servants to see him crawl his way up the stairs. He lifted his glass to finish his port before making the trek but started when Rafe stepped into the room.

"Was that Florentia?" Rafe asked, looking over his shoulder. "I haven't seen her in ages."

"What are you doing? You are supposed to be hiding in your chambers. If Florentia sees you, she'll know you right away. She already commented that the vicar looked familiar."

Rafe's brows rose. "Really? I should think so. I was the first lad to kiss her."

Nicholas started again. "You kissed my sister?"

Rafe waved a hand. "Years ago. She was not even fifteen, and it was a very innocent kiss."

"If she was fifteen, how old were you?"

"I don't know. Twelve?" He shrugged. "All in the past now. I haven't even looked at another woman since I met Collette. Well, I suppose I have looked but not *looked*—"

"Rafe, if you want to get home to your wife and child, you should stay in hiding."

"I would, but I'm famished. I can't sleep on an empty stomach. I thought I would put you to bed then have a look about the kitchen."

"Put me to bed?"

Rafe's eyes, usually so animated and mischievous, went wide. "Did I say that? I wasn't supposed to say that."

"Why would I need help getting to bed?"

"No reason."

Nicholas stared at him.

"Fine. Rowden mentioned you have a bit of trouble with the stairs. I thought I could lend a hand—or shoulder."

"I don't need help."

"Fine," Rafe said. "Point me in the direction of the kitchens then, if you don't mind."

Nicholas told him the fastest way to the kitchens then waited for him to leave before approaching the stairs. The problem with the stairs at Battle's Peak was that they were wide and the marble slippery. The curving banister often meant he had to reach to obtain a good grip and his walking stick had slipped more than once on the stone. The only way he really felt safe ascending them was to sit on his backside and move up them that way.

With Rafe gone, Nicholas sat and began levering himself up one step and then the next. He moved quickly, but it was still far slower than he would have liked. He was about three-fourths of the way to the top when Rafe appeared, carrying a plate of bread and cheese.

He arched a brow at Nicholas and walked up the stairs then stopped beside him. Nicholas felt like kicking Rafe's legs out from under him. He made it look so easy. It *was* easy for him. Nicholas remembered traversing these stairs and others hundreds of times and never thinking about it. Now, he dreaded them.

Rafe held out the plate. "Piece of cheese?"

"I'm busy," Nicholas said.

"Sure you don't want help? I could have you to the top in a—"

"I can do it myself," Nicholas said, jaw clenched.

"Very well." Rafe started up again. "I know now why you were always so good with recalcitrant horses we always seemed to be stuck with during a mission."

"Why is that?"

"Because you're even more stubborn than they."

Seven

Amelia sat shaking in the coach outside the church. She didn't know if she was excited about the future or terrified she was making the biggest mistake of her life. She would walk into the chapel Amelia Blackstock and walk out Lady Nicholas. After today, her life would never be the same again. The idea was equally scintillating and petrifying.

Her mother's hand was warm and comforting on her arm, and when she squeezed, Amelia looked up into her mother's green eyes. "You're sure?"

Amelia nodded. "You should go in. I'll be right after you."

"I wouldn't blame you if you stole the Averstow carriage and ran away," her mother said with a smile. "Wouldn't that be an adventure?"

"It would." But she had nowhere to run, and even if she did run from Lord Nicholas, she couldn't run from the real problem, which was inside her body. "But you know what Papa always said—Blackstocks don't run from trouble."

"It runs from us." Her mother kissed both her cheeks, looked at her long and lovingly, then opened the carriage door. A footman handed her down and Amelia watched as she went into the small Averstow family chapel. The door closed behind her, and it was just Amelia and the footmen, who were looking rather bored of standing around waiting for her.

Trouble runs from us. Ha. Trouble had never once run from the Blackstock family. In fact, it seemed a constant shadow. And like a shadow, this current trouble couldn't be wished away. She'd embrace it and make the best of it. She took a deep breath then pushed the coach door open. At the door to the Averstow chapel, the butler nodded at her and put his hand on the latch. "Are you ready, Miss Blackstock?"

Amelia looked down at the simple dress of white she'd worn. In her hand she held a small bunch of yellow daffodils and catmint from near the house. The yellow and purple looked cheery against her white glove. She looked up at the butler again. "Is my bonnet straight?" she asked. She would have reached up to be certain, but it was difficult with the flowers.

"Yes, miss. All looks in order."

She blew out a breath and nodded. And then blew out another breath.

"Shall I open the door now, Miss Blackstock?"

"I suppose you must."

"Very good." He pulled the door open, and Amelia saw movement in the pews. Everyone turned to look at her. Fortunately, *everyone* was only about a dozen people. Even if they had wanted to invite more, the church was small and probably couldn't accommodate more than twenty. It was a lovely church, though. The walls were white and the pews a smooth, honeyed wood. Behind the altar was a small stained-glass window of the sun breaking through clouds.

"Go ahead, Miss Blackstock," the butler whispered.

Amelia realized she should start walking. Was there supposed to be music? Perhaps someone was playing. She couldn't hear anything but the thrumming of blood in her ears. Her gaze lowered from the window to the Anglican priest and then to her betrothed. Lord Nicholas gave her a reassuring smile, and Amelia could have hugged him for it. As soon as she saw him, the tightness dissipated from her chest, and she could breathe again. Was she really marrying him? She'd definitely noticed how handsome he was before, but somehow he looked even more so this morning. His golden hair was the color of the sun in that stained-glass window, and his eyes the color of the sky behind the clouds. He was clean shaven, his face turned slightly toward the side so she could admire the lines of his cheekbones and the straight slope of his nose.

Marriage to this man did not seem a hardship. She wouldn't mind waking up next to him every morning. She smiled back at him as she reached the front of the church and took her place beside him. It seemed natural for her to be there.

She continued to stare at him as the priest began to speak. At one point Lord Nicholas took the flowers from her and passed them to someone behind her, then he took her hands in his and spoke. She wanted to listen to what he said, but the blood in her head was rushing for another reason now. She was imagining going to bed with him tonight. Kissing him. Running her fingers through that golden hair.

Except…he'd said they would have separate bed chambers. He wasn't marrying her for love or even infatuation. This was duty. It was probably a duty he detested. What man would want a woman carrying another man's child?

Lord Nicholas squeezed her hands, and she wondered if he could see the concern in her features. And then she realized she was supposed to speak, and everyone was looking at her.

"I'm sorry, what was I supposed to say?" she asked, feeling completely ridiculous.

The priest repeated the vows, and she said them, keeping her eyes downcast. She didn't deserve to marry this man. More and more it seemed an enormous mistake, and yet, here she was, sealing her fate with the words on her lips.

And then she was done speaking and Lord Nicholas put a finger under her chin, lifted her face to his, and kissed her very gently and very briefly on the lips. It was so gentle and brief, Amelia almost wondered if she'd imagined it. Until he turned her to face the guests and there was polite applause and then she was being shepherded to Battle's Peak and somehow the entire ordeal was over.

***

The wedding breakfast was a blur. Amelia couldn't stop thinking about the kiss Lord Nicholas had given her. It had been so soft and sweet. It made her feel as though he cared about her. That he wasn't just marrying her out of duty. But she had to remember that this was duty for him and necessity for her. She'd married him because she needed a father for her child.

She'd tried to eat something, mostly at the urging of her mother. Finally, the breakfast had ended, and the dowager and Lord and Lady Averstow had announced they were returning to their country home. Lady Florentia took Amelia and her mother upstairs and opened the door to a large, airy bed chamber. "This is your bed chamber, Amelia—may I call you Amelia?" she asked.

"Of course." Amelia stared at the large room with its four-poster bed and whitewashed furnishings. The pale green walls reminded her of the surrounding fields in late summer, before everything turned golden yellow from the heat of the sun.

"I hope you will think of me like your sister and come to me if you need anything," Florentia said. "My sister Anne married a few years ago, and I've missed her."

"That is very kind of you," Amelia's mother said. "Do you know if Amelia's trunks have arrived yet?" Amelia and her mother had stayed up late, packing two trunks with everything Amelia held dear. Even though Catmint Cottage was close by, Amelia's mother said it was best to take everything she would need in one fell swoop.

"They arrived during the breakfast, and I've asked O'Malley to unpack them."

Amelia raised her brows.

"The lady's maid," Florentia clarified. "If you don't mind, we will share one."

"That's very generous."

Florentia shrugged. "She can manage us both as we don't entertain much. I'll leave you to settle in," she said and left Amelia and her mother alone, closing the door as she departed.

"This looks nice enough," her mother said, opening all the drawers and cupboards and making certain everything was as it should be. Amelia went to the windows and looked out at the manicured lawns of the great house. She had a view of the back, which was bordered by a grove of trees and trim shrubbery. The grove also boasted a fountain. A couple of birds were splashing about in the fountain and shaking their feathers. She moved about, looking at the furnishings, and stopped before a closed door. She tried it, wondering if it was a dressing room, but it was locked.

"That is the door to Lord Nicholas's room," her mother said.

Amelia felt her cheeks heat, and she dropped her hand immediately.

"Oh," she said, feeling ridiculous. For a moment, she had forgotten she was not a guest here, but the mistress. She was a wife now.

"I have been putting this conversation off," her mother said, "but I suppose we had better have it before I go."

Amelia turned to look at her. "You're leaving already?"

"I'm very tired, my love, and I am sure you are as well. Besides, your husband probably wants you all to himself."

Did he? Lord Nicholas had barely spoken to her throughout breakfast. He hadn't really even looked at her. She wondered if he was in his room now or if he'd gone to the stable. She really should go there too and make sure Sweetie was settling in. She'd wanted to bring the pig inside, but her mother said the dowager would probably frown upon that.

"I worry about you," Amelia said, allowing her mother to draw her away from the connecting door and to the bed. "Alone at Catmint Cottage."

"I have Rose and plenty of ledgers to keep me busy. After a few days' rest, I will be ready to look at the accounts and perhaps visit all the tenants."

Amelia had heard all of this before. Her mother often made plans she promised to start once she was rested, but days would pass and then weeks and nothing would be accomplished.

"I will come visit you tomorrow," Amelia promised. "We can have tea."

Her mother laid a hand over Amelia's. "That would be lovely, but it might be best for you to stay close for a few days. Your husband will want you near."

Amelia couldn't think why. "Catmint Cottage isn't far."

"Yes, but you are married now, and when a man and woman marry, their lives change. You see, sometime today, probably this evening, but possibly this afternoon, your husband will want to visit you in your chamber. When he does, he will probably want to kiss you and get into bed with you."

Amelia suddenly realized what her mother was trying to explain to her. Of course, she already knew all about what happened between a man and a woman under cover of darkness, but she couldn't tell her mother that.

"And then he will…"

"I think I know what you are telling me, Mama," Amelia broke in. She did not want the mortification of her mother explaining sexual relations.

"How would you know?"

Amelia hadn't thought far enough ahead to anticipate that question. "I, er, I have seen animals. All those foals and piglets and lambs that are born every spring result from all the, er, activities in the few months before."

Her mother nodded. "It's a bit different with men and women. In nature, the male mounts the female from behind, but humans—"

"Mother!" Amelia cried, resisting the urge to put her hands over her ears. "Lord Nicholas and I will figure it out, I am sure. There's no need to explain in detail." Amelia prayed her mother would agree and stop talking.

"Very well," Mrs. Blackstock said, looking relieved as well. "If you do have questions, you can always come to me."

"Thank you, Mama. I will." Amelia hugged her mother, and her mother hugged her back, embracing her with surprising strength.

"Oh, darling girl, this is not how I imagined your wedding, but I can't claim I am unhappy. You are a lady now—married to the son of a marquess. I always wanted you to marry above your station. Your father simply wanted you to be happy. Now you will have both, yes?"

Amelia had no idea if she would be happy or not, but it was too late to change her mind. "I will be, Mama. I am happy."

"Good." Marianne Blackstock kissed her daughter's cheek and rose.

"I'll see you out, Mama."

She held up a hand. "I know the way. You stay here and rest. You may not sleep much tonight."

Amelia smiled weakly, and as soon as her mother was gone, she flopped back on the bed and blew out a breath. As embarrassing as the conversation with her mother had been, Amelia was saddened by it. She was not a nervous bride waiting for her bridegroom to come to her bed. Lord Nicholas wouldn't be coming to her bed. He'd said they would not have marital relations. How could she blame him? She was ruined, even before he'd met her. Of course, he wouldn't want her. That door between their chambers was closed and locked and would remain that way.

***

Nicholas stood in Dominion's stall, brushing the stallion. Dominion was temperamental and wouldn't allow anyone but Nicholas and Bowen the stablemaster to tend to him. He seemed to know he was a magnificent beast and deserved the best.

"There you are," said a voice, and Rafe peered around the wall of the stall.

Nicholas quickly looked about the stable, hoping none of the grooms were about. Rafe clapped him on the shoulder. "I already checked. They're in bed. No one will see Reverend Osgood."

"You're a vicar, not a reverend."

Rafe cocked his head. "I thought I was a reverend. No, we're both wrong. I'm a rector."

"You're a vicar, and you had better remember it because we've told everyone the Vicar Osgood is not to be disturbed."

Rafe sat on a wooden barrel. Somehow he looked elegant and sophisticated, even surrounded by hay and burlap feed bags. "What is the difference between a rector and a vicar? I've always wondered that."

"Didn't your father want you to go into the church?"

Rafe smiled as though thinking fondly of some long-lost memory. "He did until he caught me...well, that's not relevant. What are you doing here? Why aren't you in bed with your bride?"

"I hardly think that's any of your concern." Though Nicholas had been thinking along those same lines too. He rather wished he was in bed with Miss Blackstock, now Lady Nicholas, but every time he considered the possibility, his leg gave a painful twinge, reminding him he was a cripple, and no woman would want him. He hadn't married for a bed partner. He'd married so he could avoid his mother's marital machinations.

"Too true. But if my wife were there"—Rafe pointed toward Battle's Peak—"instead of an ocean away, I would be in bed with her. I can assure you of that."

"If you ever want to see your wife again, you need to learn to stay in your bed chamber."

Rafe leaned forward. "If you want me to stay in my bed chamber, you have to remember to feed me."

Nicholas closed his eyes. "Right. In all the chaos today, the servants must not have remembered to leave you a tray. I'll fetch you something from the kitchens now." Nicholas gave Dominion a last pat and put the grooming tools back in their place.

"I'll go with you," Rafe said. Nicholas might have argued, but it would be hard enough to go upstairs without having to manage a tray of food for Rafe as well.

The two men entered through a back door, Rafe going ahead to check that their path was clear. He peered around corners and slinked through shadows as though he had been trained as a spy. Which he hadn't. During the war, Rafe had been known as the Seducer. It had been his job to gather information by seducing the wives of officers for the French. He'd saved the troop from more than one ambush, but despite the fact that he always asked for dangerous missions, he'd never been given any.

And then after the war their commander, Lieutenant Colonel Draven, had pulled Rafe aside and given him the dangerous mission he'd always wanted. From what Nicholas had heard, Rafe had been tasked with gathering information about a woman suspected of being a French spy. She was the daughter of a notorious French assassin and living in England under a false name.

But instead of turning the woman in, Rafe had fallen in love with her. She was indeed the assassin's daughter and she'd been in England spying for the French—apparently under duress—and Rafe had fled with her to America. The official story was that the two of them had disappeared, but Nicholas and the other men of Draven's troop—the twelve Survivors—knew the truth.

Rafe had taken a great risk returning—not that Nicholas blamed him. Lord Haddington was a kind man and a loving father. Of course, Rafe had wanted to see him in his hour of need. But if Rafe was caught, he'd be hanged, and his wife would be a widow and his son an orphan. The stakes were life and death.

Which was why Rafe probably shouldn't be the one leading the reconnaissance. "Get behind me," Nicholas hissed. "If I'm seen, no one will comment."

Rafe sulked, but he did as he was told. After Nicholas checked the kitchen was empty, he motioned for Rafe to enter. Rafe proceeded to begin filling a plate with whatever he could find.

"Cover that back up," Nicholas instructed. If Rafe left the kitchen in a shambles, Cook would not be pleased. Rafe was sampling cheeses and pastries as he went, and Nicholas was just about to tell him to take the plate upstairs when the door opened, and his bride stepped inside.

Both Rafe and Nicholas froze, Rafe in the middle of biting into an apple.

"I'm terribly sorry to interrupt," Lady Nicholas said, her gaze going from Nicholas to Rafe and back again. She was dressed for bed, her hair plaited in a long river of amber over her shoulder. She wore a white robe cinched at the waist and her feet were in slippers.

Rafe looked at Nicholas, the apple still clenched between his teeth. "My lady." Nicholas gave a stiff bow. "I don't think you have been introduced to my friend Vicar Osgood."

Rafe chewed through the apple and lowered it from his mouth. "How do?" he said.

Not the Yorkshire accent again. Nicholas wanted to hit him. Lady Nicholas greeted him, but before Rafe could answer, Nicholas said, "The vicar is originally from Yorkshire, but he lost most of his accent as he's lived in London for some time now."

Rafe shook his head, but Nicholas ignored him. "Did you need something, my lady? You can always ring for your lady's maid."

"Every time you say that, I look around for someone else."

Nicholas raised a brow.

"When you say, *my lady*," she qualified. "I've always been a *miss* before."

"That is the beauty of the sacrament of marriage," Rafe said in a preachy tone. "It makes two, one."

Lady Nicholas blushed, and Nicholas tried again. "Is there something you need?"

"Not for me," she said. "But Sweetie is hungry."

Rafe shot a confused look at Nicholas, who realized he hadn't seen the pig in the stable. "The grooms fed all of the animals," he assured her.

"She wasn't in the stable," Lady Nicholas said. "I brought her to my chamber. She's not used to sleeping outside."

"Who is Sweetie?" Rafe asked.

"Lady Nicholas's pig," Nicholas answered. "A Gloucestershire Old Spots."

"Oh, of course." He put his plate down and appeared intent on staying and listening to the rest of the conversation.

"Have you just arrived, sir?" Lady Nicholas asked Rafe. "I don't remember meeting you at the wedding breakfast."

"The vicar arrived last night and has not been feeling well," Nicholas said. "He needs rest."

"And food," Rafe said. "I'm famished."

Nicholas gave him a hard look. Rafe looked back then seemed to understand. "But I am indeed very tired. I will take my plate to my chamber."

"You needn't leave on my account," Lady Nicholas said. "I will just gather a few scraps and go."

Rafe made a show of yawning. "No, no. Too tired to stay. Good night, my lady. Good night, Nickers."

When he was gone, Lady Nicholas turned to him. "Nickers?"

"I don't suppose you can pretend you never heard that?"

"Probably not. Will the cook mind if I take a few scraps?" She lifted a small pail near the door and gave Nicholas a questioning glance.

"Not at all. She puts vegetable scraps just there." He pointed to a corner.

"Oh, that's perfect." She crossed to the rubbish bin and emptied it into her pail. Nicholas couldn't quite keep himself from staring at her bottom as she bent. Then he forced himself to look away. No point in coveting what he could not have.

She turned back to him, seeming unsure what to do next. "It was a lovely wedding," she said.

Nicholas detested awkward conversation, but he could hardly avoid speaking to his own wife. "It was. You looked beautiful."

"So did you." Her cheeks colored again. "I mean—"

"Thank you," he said. "Are you settling in? Is there anything you need? Other than food for Sweetie, that is."

"No, I have everything. My bedchamber is exquisite. Green is my favorite color."

He gave her a questioning look.

"The walls are green," she said.

"Of course. I haven't been in there for some time."

The mention of him in her bed chamber caused her cheeks to turn an even deeper shade of red. Suddenly, she shook her head and blew out a breath. "I don't know why we should be so awkward around each other," she said abruptly. "We never were before."

He smiled, glad she had broken through the formality between them. "I suppose neither of us is used to being married."

"I am certainly not used to being referred to as Lady Nicholas."

"Would you allow me to call you Amelia?" he asked.

"I'd like that, yes. Shall I call you Nickers?" Her brown eyes glinted with amusement.

"Nicholas will do."

She looked around. "The house seems quieter now that everyone is gone."

"Now that my mother is gone, you mean."

She gave a small smile. "I suppose I am not used to living in a house this big with so many servants. I expected it to be…busier."

Nicholas shook his head. "It's quiet here. That's why Florentia and I like it. Neither of us care much for balls and dinner parties. I hope you don't find it too tedious." He was very aware that she had been shut up for years, caring for an invalid. He didn't blame her for wanting a bit of fun after all those years of drudgery.

"Not at all," she said.

Nicholas wanted to offer to walk her to her chamber, but there were the stairs to contend with. "You should go back to your room before you catch a chill," he said.

"Or Sweetie comes looking for me. Good night, Nicholas," she said.

"Good night."

She left, carrying her pail, and Nicholas leaned against the worktable. The idea of a platonic marriage had seemed like the perfect solution to both of their problems two nights ago, but now that he was married, now that the woman would be sleeping in the room adjoining his, he was not at all certain he hadn't just made things worse.

The problem was that he was attracted to Amelia.

Eight

Amelia breakfasted in bed the next morning, which was a mistake. Sweetie bothered her incessantly and she ended up giving half of her meal to the pig. O'Malley would not enter her room while Sweetie was present, so Amelia dressed herself and pinned her hair up as she did at home. Then she took Sweetie into the yard where there was a pen for a goat, several chickens, and a cow and calf. She gave her pig more food and left her to go back inside. Now that she was Lady Nicholas, she wanted to look the part, and a rumpled dress and lopsided coiffure would not do.

But when she stepped inside, she met Lady Florentia, who greeted her warmly. "Good morning, Amelia," she said with a smile and a pretty curtsy.

"Good morning." Amelia gave her a curtsy as well.

"I am so glad to see you. I thought you might like me to show you around, now that you are the lady of the house."

"Yes, I'd like that." Amelia glanced about, wondering if perhaps Lord Nicholas might join them. Florentia linked her arm with Amelia's.

"Shall we begin with the ground floor, or would you prefer to see the kitchens and servants' quarters downstairs?"

"Now might be a good time to visit with the housekeeper and the cook. If we wait too long, they will be busy with dinner preparations."

"Perfect." As they walked toward the stairs to the kitchen, Florentia told her the servant's names and how long they had been with the family and any other personal information she could remember. The housekeeper, for example, had a sister in Norwich and the cook had trained in one of the best houses in London. Amelia tried to listen, but she couldn't quite stop herself from looking for Nicholas. It didn't help that once they reached the kitchen, memories of seeing him the night before flooded back. He'd looked so handsome, with his cravat loose and falling in white waves over his chest and his hair tousled and peppered with stray pieces of straw.

She should never have agreed to marry him and definitely never agreed to separate beds. Amelia might not be the worldliest of women, having rarely left Hungerford, but she had read quite widely. She'd often had little else to do on long, tedious days when sitting by the bedside of her grandmother or father. And reading had been an escape as well. She could travel in books to places she would never visit in real life.

She'd read so many books where the fallen woman was punished and the virtuous one rewarded, but Amelia had never felt that was quite fair. The man who had debauched the fallen woman was every bit as culpable as she, and why should he win the virtuous woman? Not to mention, Amelia did not think he'd be happy with a woman who blushed when he just looked at her—not when he'd had nights of passion with the loose woman.

Amelia would far prefer to be the fallen woman and live life to the fullest. She didn't regret her night of passion with Jonathon Wickersham. She'd wanted the experience of being held by a man and made love to. She'd enjoyed it and only wished that she could have been the man and not had to bear the consequences. On the other hand, now she would be a mother. She'd rather despaired of ever marrying or having children after her twenty-fourth birthday. Now she would have both, and it was not a punishment at all.

But of course, Lord Nicholas would not want to share a bed with her. He hadn't given her reasons, only alluded to his injury. Did his injury prevent him from enjoying the marital bed or was it just an excuse because he did not want to bed a woman carrying another man's child?

"You won't see him," Florentia said as she opened the library.

"Who?" Amelia asked, but she knew she had been caught. She'd been looking for Nicholas in every room. Lady Florentia gave her an indulgent smile.

"Your husband. He keeps to himself most days. I can sometimes find him in the stables with the horses, but more often than not, I don't know where he goes."

"Has he always been so solitary?" Amelia asked, going to the shelves and running a hand over the old leather-bound volumes.

Florentia took a breath and seemed to consider her answer. "Yes and no."

Amelia looked at her, waiting for an explanation.

"He was never the sort to have dozens of friends and frequent balls and pubs every night. He's always loved his horses, always preferred horses to people, and his favorite activity was always riding. He rode every day without fail, sometimes he would be gone for hours. So yes, Nicholas has always enjoyed his solitude, but he was never solitary. He enjoyed dancing and dinner parties and had many friends at school and in Town. After the war, he wanted no one near him but me." She looked at Amelia and smiled. "And now you."

Amelia did not point out that he had not wanted her. He'd been stuck with her.

"The war changed him," Amelia said.

"Not so much the war as his injury," Florentia said, sitting in one of the chairs near the cold hearth. "His legs were crushed by a horse during the battle, and he will never be the same again. He can't ride, and I think that was the biggest blow of all. It's as though he is lost without that part of his life."

"Then perhaps we should find a way for him to ride, even with his injury."

Florentia shook her head. "A rider controls the horse with his legs. Nicholas cannot do that. He would rather not ride than ride poorly or have a groom lead him about as though he were a child again."

"I understand." And she did. Her father had his pride as well after his injury. He liked his hair kept neat and his jaw shaved. Although her mother could have done both of those tasks, Amelia and her mother paid for a manservant to come twice a week to shave her father and trim his hair every month. He needed those small things to feel attractive and human.

"Does he dine with you?" Amelia asked. If she wasn't to see Nicholas during the day, perhaps they could dine together and read or play cards after dinner.

"Not always," Florentia said. "Often I eat by myself."

Amelia went to sit beside her. "Are you not lonely?"

"Sometimes," Florentia admitted, "but I am here by choice. I can always go to London or the country estate. When I feel like I want a bit of company, I go away for a few weeks. The problem is that the last couple of years I have always felt so badly about leaving Nicholas. Now that I know you are here, I will not worry so much."

The rest of the day seemed to pass quickly. Amelia met all of the servants and felt she had a rather good understanding of how the household ran. O'Malley dressed her and styled her hair for dinner, and when Amelia went down, she hoped Lord Nicholas's eyes would light up when he saw how well she looked. But he did not make an appearance, and she and Florentia ate alone.

Amelia didn't mind spending time with Florentia. Over the next day or so, the two spent a great deal of time together. Amelia learned about Nicholas's brother Richard and his younger sister Anne, neither of whom had been able to come to the wedding on such short notice. Both were married and had children. Only Florentia was now unmarried, and she seemed content to remain so. She made a comment one afternoon that Amelia found quite revealing. She mentioned friends that had married and how unhappy they all seemed. Florentia wanted to marry for love or not at all.

Amelia wished she'd had that choice, but she was apparently married to a specter because she never so much as caught a glimpse of her husband. Once she thought she heard him in the adjoining bed chamber late at night, but when she woke the next morning, she was not certain if she had really heard him moving about or only dreamed it.

On the third night, she decided enough was enough. She dismissed O'Malley then sat in bed reading until well after midnight. About half past one she heard the unmistakable sound of the door beside hers opening and light footfalls in the chamber next to hers. Lord Nicholas was in his room, preparing for bed. Amelia pushed back the covers, pulled on a wrapper, and padded to the adjoining door. She pressed her ear to the door, listening. She thought she might have heard the sound of water being poured from a pitcher and the clink as it was set back on a wash basin.

Amelia lifted her hand and knocked.

Her heart was pounding, which might have been the reason she heard absolutely nothing. Had she imagined hearing Lord Nicholas in the room and moving about? She tapped on the door again then tried the latch. To her surprise, the door swung open, and she peered into the adjoining room.

She didn't see Lord Nicholas at first. The room was lit by several candles and a hearth, and it had a warm, cozy feel. The wood-paneled walls were burnished golden in the candlelight and the rugs on the floor were rust and gold in color. The chamber was bigger than hers, and it took her a moment to take it all in—the tall boy, the desk, the sitting area near the fire, and the large bed with the ornately carved wooden frame.

And then finally she found Lord Nicholas.

He was standing, seemingly frozen, near a painted screen. He held a towel in one hand, and the front of his white shirt was wet. She had indeed interrupted him as he was washing. The washstand must be just behind the screen.

His coat had been dropped on the floor as had his neckcloth and waistcoat, and his shirt was open at the neck. He wasn't indecent, but this was still a very intimate glimpse of him.

"Miss Blackstock," he said. "Did you need something?"

Her throat was quite dry now that she had caught sight of him. The wet shirt molded to his chest, and she could see the outline of muscles under the fitted shirt. "I'm Lady Nicholas now," she said, her voice sounding very far away.

"Of course. Are you well?"

Oh, she was quite well now that she saw him. In the space of three days, she had forgotten how handsome he was with that golden hair and those beautiful blue eyes.

"Perfectly well," she said, stepping into the room and closing the door behind her. She leaned against it, needing the support. "How are you?"

He used the towel suspended in his hands to pat his face dry. Even from across the room, she saw a trickle of water snake down his throat. Oh, my. She had to remind herself this was a marriage of duty, not of passion.

"I am well." He looked at her, seeming to expect her to say something more, but she couldn't quite think with that drip of water snaking over his skin. "Well, if there is nothing else…" he began.

Amelia snapped out of her trance. He was dismissing her, and she had better say something or she would have to leave. "I've missed you," she said quickly.

His brows came together in confusion.

"I haven't seen you since the wedding, and I've missed you."

He seemed taken aback and unsure of what to say.

Amelia moved closer, leaving the security of the door. "What have you been busy with the past few days?"

"This and that," he said. "I thought Florentia had shown you about the house and made sure you were comfortable."

"She did. I am quite comfortable, and Sweetie seems to enjoy all the extra space. I couldn't even persuade her to come in from her paddock this evening. I think she's made friends with the other pigs." Amelia was closer to him now. He hadn't taken a step back, but he was eyeing her warily. "I am thankful for Florentia, and I know we will be great friends. But I haven't seen you."

"Yes, well, I would have thought she told you that I am not often about. I keep busy in the stables."

"She did tell me that, but I didn't think *I* wouldn't see you. And I've looked for you in the stables. You never seem to be about when I am there."

"I apologize. I did not know you wanted to see me." His eyes lowered just for an instant to the bare skin visible beneath her wrap above the U of her nightgown. Then he met her gaze again.

Just for an instant, though, Amelia had felt that same frisson of excitement she'd had the night they kissed in the stable. And she knew that he was avoiding her intentionally. Why? Because he felt an attraction to her? Perhaps he did and he did not *want* to desire her. She stepped back again.

"Of course, I want to see you. You are my husband."

"My lady—"

"I thought you would call me Amelia and I would call you Nickers."

"No. I never agreed to Nickers," he said.

She smiled. "Nicholas then. Can we at least use Christian names when we are alone?"

"Of course. Er—what was I saying?"

"You were about to tell me why I shouldn't see my husband."

He shook his head. "That was not what I planned to say. I wanted to point out that our marriage was not really that sort of marriage."

"The sort where people see each other?" She knew she was making this difficult for him, but he did not seem inclined to give her answers unless she pushed and prodded.

"I thought when we agreed to wed, you understood the conditions," he said.

"I understand you don't want to share a bed," she said, knowing that was quite forward and willing her cheeks not to color. She felt them heat anyway. "I'm not asking you to come to bed with me." Unless he wanted to. "I just want to be friends. I'll settle for acquaintances at this point."

He turned away from her then, his movements somewhat stiff as usual, but she thought some of the stiffness must certainly be due to his discomfort with the conversation.

"Why does the notion of a friendship between us make you uncomfortable?" she asked.

"It doesn't," he said, still not looking at her. Unfortunately, that meant she had little choice but to admire his backside. His shirt was not wet in the back, but without a coat, she had a lovely view of his bottom. It was nicely rounded and probably quite firm under those dark trousers. He glanced at her, and she pretended to be staring at the painted screen. A large bird with outstretched wings spread over the panels. And the bird seemed to be on fire. A Phoenix?

"Amelia, I'm not sure it's wise for us to become friends."

"Why not?"

"I think you know why not," he said, and this time he allowed his gaze to travel to the swell of her breasts. Her nipples hardened just at his look, and she had to take a shaky breath before he looked away.

"We are both adults," she said, her voice low and somewhat breathy. "I am certain we can behave as such."

Though why they should need to if he wanted her and she wanted him and they were married was a mystery to her. Except, of course, if he wanted her against his better judgement. She was, after all, most likely pregnant with another man's child.

"Nicholas," she said before he could begin giving her reasons they should not spend time together. "I have spent most of my life caring for others. I don't regret one day I spent with my grandmother or my father. I would not trade them for anything."

"That's very noble of you."

She shook her head. "It wasn't noble. It was duty and my pleasure. My mother needed my help. When my grandmother was ill, I was young and did not know what I was missing. But with my father, I knew once I reached a certain age, I would never have a Season, never be a debutante, never go to Vauxhall Gardens or Covent Garden. I wouldn't trade the time I spent with him."

"You can still do all of those things."

"Of course, but I can't reclaim my youth. I sacrificed it for the people I loved, but even love doesn't remove the drudgery of wiping brows and making broth and emptying chamber pots. Six months ago, I lost my father. I would have mourned him for months or even years, but he told me he didn't want that. He wanted me to live the life I hadn't been able to with all the responsibilities of caring for him. I finally had permission to spend all day walking with Sweetie if I wanted or dance all night or sleep until noon." She looked down at her slippered feet. "Admittedly, I let the freedom go a bit far. And that's why you and I are here."

"One can hardly blame you, I think."

She looked up at him and smiled. "I hoped you would think that way because I don't want to lose any more of my life, not when there's no reason to do so." She spread her hands. "I want to live every day to the fullest. I want to experience all that there is in the world. And if we are not to be lovers, I respect that, but why can't we be friends? Why can't we experience the world together?"

"Because I can't," he said, the sharpness in his tone making her jump. "You may be free of your burdens now, but I will never be free."

"I don't understand."

He blew out an angry breath. "I can't go on long walks. I can't dance with you at Vauxhall Gardens. I can't even go to Town without my leg feeling like it's on fire and causing me excruciating pain for days. My world is right here." He gestured to the chamber. "I have no freedom any longer."

Amelia felt a sudden pang of concern. He had just gone to London to obtain the special license. Was he still in pain from that journey? "Are you hurting now?" she asked, moving toward him. "I didn't realize how much a journey to London would hurt you."

"Don't." He held up his hands, keeping her back. "I don't want your pity."

"This isn't pity. This is the same concern I would have for anyone in pain."

He eyed her warily, as though he didn't quite believe her. "It's better now. Tolerable."

"Good. Then I needn't feel bad for scolding you." Her hands went to her hips. "What a pile of utter rubbish you just spewed."

His brows rose. "Pardon me?"

"No, I won't. You act as though your life is over, and why? Because your legs have been injured? My father couldn't move the lower two-thirds of his body, and he never gave up. You can do anything you want, anything you set your mind to do—yes, even dance. It may not be the dancing you used to do, but you could dance in your own fashion."

"You don't know what you are talking about."

"You just want others to feel sorry for you."

"No. Not at all. That's exactly what I don't want."

"Then stop feeling sorry for yourself. I don't pity you or feel sorry for you. You have your life. Thousands of men never came home from that war."

His blue eyes turned icy. "I am the last person who needs to be reminded of that, my lady."

"Good. Then stop behaving as though your life is over and join me in the garden tomorrow morning." She turned on her heel to the door between their rooms. "Ten o'clock sharp. And if you are late, I will come and find you." She marched back through the door and turned back to close it, but Nicholas slammed it shut before she could manage it. She heard the lock turn and his muttered curses on the other side. For some reason, that made her smile.

***

The woman was mad. That much was clear. He should have listened to his mother when she told him marrying Amelia Blackstock was a mistake. The chit was wild, she'd said. He would regret it, she'd said.

Nicholas, being the son of the Marquess of Averstow, could have found a reason to cry off—duty or no duty. He hadn't wanted to cry off. Obviously, he'd allowed a pretty face and a lovely figure to cloud his better judgement.

Actually, what had mostly clouded his judgement was that kiss they'd shared in the stable. He hadn't felt that way after kissing a woman since—he didn't think he'd ever felt that way after kissing a woman.

So he'd let lust get the better of him, and now he was leg-shackled to a harridan. A Xantippe. A shrew who demanded he join her in the garden the next morning. What did she have planned? A hike through the countryside? Would he have to fall on his face to prove to her he couldn't do it?

Perhaps he would, but one thing Nicholas St. Clare never did was back down from a challenge, so he was in the garden at quarter to ten the next morning. Devil take him if Amelia wasn't already waiting for him with that enormous pig of hers. The pig was nosing about the flowers surrounding the fountain, while Amelia was making tut-tut sounds and sitting on the bench with her parasol shading her from the summer sun.

She looked up as he approached. He hated for people to watch him walk. His gait was uneven and unsteady, but in this case, he wanted her to see. But she didn't look at his legs or even at his body. As soon as she saw him, she looked into his face and smiled.

It was the most beatific smile he had ever seen. Nicholas actually looked over his shoulder to see what could have made her so ridiculously happy. But no one was behind him.

"You came," she said, standing and still beaming at him.

"You doubted I would?" he said, his tone gravelly and sharp.

"I thought you would. I always heard you were a man of bravery."

"No braver than most." He stopped in front of the bench. "I'm here. What now?"

"I thought we could take a stroll around the fountain—Sweetie, no!"

The pig made a sound that even Nicholas understood was displeasure when Amelia caught her nosing about the flowers.

She stood and took his arm. "Shall we?"

"I don't stroll, Amelia."

"You do today." And she gifted him with yet another huge smile. Why on earth was the woman so happy? Her face was almost as bright as the sunlight. She took a small step forward, still holding on to his arm, and he stepped forward as well. He might not walk gracefully, but he could manage a turn about the fountain. The weather was warm and breezy and the sun not yet too hot or bright in the sky. Seeming curious as to what they were about, Sweetie followed them in their slow-moving circle.

"Lovely weather we are having, isn't it?" she said.

The woman might not have ever had a Season, but she certainly knew the role of the debutante. She looked up at him and smiled and said something about the blue of the sky.

"Why are you so happy?" he asked.

Her eyes widened in surprise. "Why shouldn't I be happy?"

"You seem happier than usual," he said. "Why?"

"Oh, I've just had good news this morning."

"A letter this early?" he asked.

"Not that kind of news. I'll tell you at another time." And she looked away. Was she blushing? The color in her cheeks couldn't be because of their exertions. He was moving slower than a snail.

"I saw the rector this morning," she said, obviously changing the subject.

Nicholas halted. "The vicar, you mean? Vicar Osgood?"

Her brow knitted. "I could have sworn he said he was a rector. He has such an odd way of speaking, though." She tilted her head as he began walking again. "He says he is from Yorkshire, but old Mr. Pliney who ran the mill was from Yorkshire, and he didn't sound anything like Mr. Pliney."

"He's not from Yorkshire. What was he doing?"

"Just standing over there." She pointed toward a neat hedgerow, trimmed within an inch of its life. From above, all the hedgerows made the shape of an A for Averstow encircled by another set of hedgerows. Those hedgerows kept the gardeners busier than the flowers most years. "He had his hat off and was looking off into the distance. His eyes are quite the loveliest shade of blue. Almost violet." She glanced up at Nicholas. "Of course, I prefer your shade of blue. Although the two of you make me feel quite ordinary."

"There is nothing ordinary about you," Nicholas said before thinking.

"Oh, really?" She released his arm and moved to stand in front of him. She was smiling that beatific smile again. "Whatever do you mean, my lord?"

Nicholas felt completely at sea in that moment. Not only was he not entirely steady on his feet, he felt as though his world was jolted. What woman didn't prefer Rafe and his legendary good looks to him? Nicholas had never had his eye on the same woman as Rafe, but it seemed when Rafe was nearby, every woman forgot every other man in the room. That had been true in the ballrooms in London before the war and in the villages they passed through in France. But now this woman was not asking him about Rafe. She was smiling at Nicholas and flirting with him.

He hardly knew how to play these games anymore.

"You know you are an attractive woman, Amelia," he said.

"I know some think so. Do you?"

"Of course." He started to walk again, but of course, she just took his arm and moved with him. He wouldn't be able to outpace her.

"You act as though that's a foregone conclusion. But we really had no courtship to speak of. I have no idea what you think of me."

"I kissed you," he said, glancing down at her. "Of course, I find you attractive."

"Oh, I don't know. That might have been an impulse of the moment."

"An impulse driven by your deep brown eyes." He allowed his gaze to dip to the swell of her bosom under the pale blue morning dress she wore. "Among other things."

She looked up at him, her cheeks pink but her eyes sparkling. "What other things, my lord?"

"Probably best to avoid enumerating all of your alluring qualities if we plan to maintain separate bed chambers."

"That might be your plan," she said. "It's not mine."

Nicholas was certain he had not heard her correctly. "Pardon?"

Instead of responding, she pointed toward the house. "Oh, look! There is your sister."

Florentia waved to them. She had just stepped out of the house, a golden shawl wrapped about her creamy white gown. "Am I interrupting?" she called.

"Yes," Nicholas muttered.

Amelia elbowed him in the ribs. "Not at all. Come and join us."

Florentia did just that, linking her arm with Amelia's other, so that his wife was between the two siblings. Nicholas didn't know why he should be surprised. Of course, Amelia had won his sister over. She seemed to have such a sunny temperament. It was difficult to imagine her locked in Catmint Cottage for years caring for her ailing father. She seemed to belong in the sun and under the blue skies.

"I'm so glad you took my advice to take a turn in the garden in the morning," Florentia said. "And you managed to convince my brother as well. I have been trying for years." She winked at Nicholas, who returned her smile with a scowl.

"The fresh air is good for all of us," Amelia said. It was a sentiment Florentia readily agreed with. As Nicholas listened to the ladies chat, he realized that the two were already becoming friends. He hadn't considered Florentia when he'd married Amelia, but now he realized his taking a wife would benefit his sister immensely. Florentia was a spinster at the age of two and thirty, and her friends had all married and settled into family life. She saw them on occasion, but Florentia often complained she had little in common with these wives and mothers who bore almost no resemblance to the girls she'd known. Even their sister Anne had married and now had two very young children. Her husband's land was in Northumberland, and they only came this far south perhaps once a year. Florentia almost certainly missed female companionship—*any* companionship, as he knew he was a poor companion most days.

"And have you seen him?" Florentia was asking.

"I did. Just this morning, as I was telling Lord Nicholas," Amelia replied. Drat. She was speaking of Rafe, and Nicholas had not been paying close enough attention to turn the topic before they'd settled on it. The last thing he needed was Florentia becoming curious about the Vicar Osgood and discovering the good vicar was actually a man she had known all of her life. A man wanted for treason.

"What does he look like?" Florentia asked. "The servants say he has been in his chamber day and night. The only reason they know he is still inside is that he eats the food they leave."

"Oh, he is very much alive and seemed quite well to me."

"What is his ailment, Nicholas?" Florentia asked.

"Some sort of stomach complaint," Nicholas said, as it was the first thing he could think of and an ailment not observable.

"Really?" Florentia said. "Cook reports he eats so heartily."

Both ladies looked at him questioningly. Nicholas was not a good liar. He was better with horses than people. "Then it appears his time here is helping," he said.

The women seemed to accept this. "He looked quite well to me this morning. He was in the garden, hat off and he turned to greet me. His hair was dark and wavy, quite thick really, and his eyes were fringed with dark lashes. The color was truly remarkable—"

Nicholas made himself stumble. He felt like an absolute idiot, but Rafe's eye color was rather unique and Florentia might be suspicious if Amelia mentioned it. His sudden jolt forward caught Amelia off guard, and she also lurched forward before righting herself and lending him a steady arm to regain his balance. Even though the action had been purposeful, he did need that steadying arm to find his feet again.

"Are you alright?" she asked, putting one arm about his waist and the other on his elbow.

"Quite. I just missed a step."

"You should go inside and rest," Florentia said. "You will tire yourself."

Nicholas was about to snap that he knew his own limits, but Amelia said, "Oh, one stumble is nothing. I trip over my skirts a half dozen times a day. I really should ask O'Malley to hem them for me."

"She would be happy to do it, and she's very quick with a needle and thread. Should we ask her now?"

"Would you? I'll be along in a moment."

"Of course. Good day, brother." And Florentia started back inside.

Nicholas gave Amelia a sidelong look. "I've never seen you trip over your skirts."

"And I haven't seen you stumble like that. Is there some reason you don't want me to discuss the vicar? I can keep a secret, you know."

"I assure you, it was merely a loose pebble that moved unexpectedly underfoot."

"Well, then, watch your step." She reached up and kissed his cheek, then lifted her skirts and started back for the house. The kiss had been friendly, not at all romantic, but he still felt the pressure of her lips on his skin long after she was gone.

His bride seemed full of surprises. Not only was she perceptive and clever, she seemed innately protective. Not in a coddling way, as his sister and other family members could sometimes be, but in a way that protected his independence.

He liked her more for that. He liked her very much.

Nine

Amelia endured the fussing of O'Malley as she pinned several of Amelia's dresses perhaps an eighth of an inch. Her skirts were not too long, of course. She'd said the first thing that had come to mind when Florentia had suggested Nicholas go inside to rest. No man wanted to be treated like a child, especially not a man with as much pride as Lord Nicholas. She knew his sort. Her father had been the same. She and her mother had spent years caring for him without being too obvious about that care.

Perhaps what Lady Florentia did not realize was that her brother did not need her to look after him. If he had needed a nursemaid, Amelia would have fought their marriage harder. She did not want a husband she had to care for like a child. She wanted a partner who would care for her just as she cared for him.

And she wanted a husband who felt something more than duty toward her. She had resigned herself to the possibility that was all Lord Nicholas would feel for her—at least until after Wickersham's child was born—but all of that had changed this morning.

She'd come slowly awake before the sun was even up, her lower abdomen cramping enough that she turned this way and that to try and get comfortable and go back to sleep.

And then she'd come wide awake because she knew exactly what she was feeling. It was the same twinge of discomfort she felt every month during her courses. She lit a lamp and rushed to the chamber pot and let out a little whoop of joy when she'd seen the small drips of blood on the linen she used to dry herself. Her monthly courses might be late, but they were here.

She was not with child.

And that changed everything—in her mind, at least.

Now that she was not carrying another man's child, there was no reason she and Lord Nicholas could not be married in truth. Unless, he really had no interest in her as a bed partner. The walk this morning had put that notion aside. The way he'd looked at her, spoken to her—there was an attraction there. And it was wholly reciprocated.

But how to act on it? As a wife, she was supposed to wait for him to come to her. But why would he come to her if he thought she was breeding? Or if he thought she didn't want him? She needed to tell him she'd been mistaken and hint that she desired him. But how to broach that subject with a man? Her experience in this area was limited, and she'd never had to initiate. Wickersham had taken the lead.

She pondered her approach the rest of the day and hoped for some opportunity to speak with him that night, but he did not knock on her door, and she fell asleep before she heard him come to bed.

The next morning, she went to the garden again, hoping to see her husband, but instead she found the vicar again.

He turned to her as soon as she approached, almost as though he'd been waiting for her. Amelia stopped in her tracks. Goodness but a direct look from him was enough to stop her heart. She'd never seen such a beautiful man. He probably had every lady in his parish fawning at his feet.

"Good morning, my lady," the vicar said, giving her a smile she imagined made hearts flutter far and wide. From the way he watched Amelia's reaction, he knew the power of his smile. "I have been waiting for you."

"Have you?" she asked. "Was there something you needed?"

"There is actually." He reached in his coat and pulled out a stack of envelopes. "I wanted to ask if you would be so good as to send this correspondence for me."

Amelia took the envelopes. There must have been almost a dozen. "Of course. I would be happy to do so. How are you feeling today, sir?"

"Perfectly—er, that is to say, better than I have been. My ailment comes and goes, you see. I never know when it might strike." It seemed to always strike at mealtimes as she had invited him to dine with them several times, and he had always declined.

"I'm sorry to hear that. Is there anything I might do to make your stay more comfortable?"

"No. I'm perfectly comfortable. Thank you."

She wanted to ask how long he might be staying, but she couldn't think of a way to inquire without sounding rude. Instead, she gestured to a stone bench. She sat, and he joined her on the opposite side. With his looks, the man might very well be a rake, but he didn't seem intent on seducing her. Of course, he'd probably never had to seduce a woman in his life.

"Perhaps if you feel well enough, you might join us for dinner this evening," Amelia said, thinking that a personal invitation might be more persuasive.

"You are very kind to offer, but I have so much prayer and meditation to do this afternoon."

Amelia raised her brows. "Is there a certain amount one must accomplish each day?"

"There is, and my illness means I am woefully behind."

Amelia found this very strange, but then what did she know about the church other than the sermons she heard on Sunday mornings? Because of her father's illness, she had often not been able to attend church, so she probably knew less than most. But one thing she did know was that the clergymen who had called at Catmint Cottage over the years had often consoled and counseled her mother.

"You have known Lord Nicholas for a long time," she said.

"We went to school together?" the vicar said, almost as though he were asking her to confirm it.

"Yes. Do you mind if I ask what he was like before his injury? Was he always so aloof?"

"Nickers?" The vicar smiled again, his gaze fastening on a far-off point as though he were seeing the past. "He was never the sort to seek out a crowd. In fact, he's always seemed happiest in the company of his horses. He probably talked to them more than any of the troo—the other students."

"He talks to almost no one now," Amelia said. She didn't add, *not even his sister. Not even me.*

"He has become quite the recluse since his injury. Part of it, I imagine, is that he's mourning what he's lost."

Amelia frowned. "And what is that?"

"He can't ride anymore, my lady. And for Nickers, riding was everything."

"I wish you would speak to him about it. Why shouldn't he ride? It's only his pride—"

The vicar shook his head. "A man needs some pride. He's not a child, and I can't blame him for not wanting to be led about like a toddler on a pony."

Amelia nodded. "Yes, I see what you mean. But why should he shun people as well?"

"Is that what he is doing?" the vicar asked, violet eyes narrowing. "Has he been avoiding you?"

She didn't want to be disloyal, so she said, "It feels like it. I feel as though I hardly see him."

The vicar considered. "May I give you some advice, Lady Nicholas?"

"Of course." Now was the time when he would start quoting Bible verses. Something about women submitting to men or Adam and Eve, she expected.

"Men are idiots," the vicar said.

Amelia blinked. "Pardon?"

"Men are idiots. I'm sorry to say Lord Nicholas is not exempt. He has no idea what you require from him or what you want. He has probably not even considered it. If you want him to know, you will have to tell him."

Amelia stared at him in silence for a long moment. "Isn't that rather forward?"

He shrugged. "Men don't mind forward behavior from a wife. And, knowing Nickers as I do, I think that you will have to, er—think of it like chess."

"I don't play chess."

"I don't either, but someone has to move their piece first, yes? The game won't begin if both players sit and stare at the board."

"That is a good point."

"It rather is, isn't it?" He looked inordinately pleased with himself.

Amelia rose. "I will go post these now." She tapped the letters in her hand. "I must say, I expected you to offer me more scripture references."

"Oh, I did. I offered you loads. I just couched them in everyday conversation. It's a new method employed by the Church. Makes us rectors more relatable."

Amelia bid him good day and went inside. As she made her way inside, she couldn't help but glance down at the letters she carried. Her brows knit at the names of those addressed.

Lieutenant-Colonel Draven
Mr. Neil Wraxall
His Grace The Duke of Mayne
Mr. Murray

That last one was addressed to a man in Scotland. Amelia puzzled over the odd assortment of men. None looked to be in any way affiliated with the Church. And wasn't Colonel Draven the man Nicholas had served under during the war?

She gave the letters to a footman to send with the other correspondence and went to fetch the scraps from the kitchen for Sweetie. She found her pet in the barn with the other animals, seemingly enjoying lying in the summer sun. But Sweetie jumped up upon spotting Amelia and ran over to greet her. Amelia spent some time scratching Sweetie behind the ears and making sure she'd eaten her fill before calling the pig to walk to the stable with her. But Sweetie was more interested in taking another nap, and Amelia went alone.

She greeted the grooms, who were taking the horses out for exercise. Each horse paraded past her seemed more beautiful than the last. It was no wonder Battle's Peak was known for its breeding stock. These creatures were magnificent.

"Good morning, my lady," the stablemaster said as he approached her. "Did you wish to ride? I have a gentle mare who would suit you."

"No, thank you." Amelia did not ride and did not intend to start now. She enjoyed looking at horses and perhaps feeding one an apple or two on occasion, but she did not want to sit on one's back. "I was looking for Lord Nicholas. Have you seen him?"

"Yes, my lady. He is at the end of the stable with Lady Flame."

"Lady Flame is a horse, I take it."

The stablemaster nodded. "A good old girl. She's not been feeling well lately."

"Thank you." Amelia lifted her skirts and entered the stable. She could understand why Nicholas liked it here. It was cool and not dark but comfortably dim. The smell of manure was present, of course, but mostly the scent of clean hay and oats and oiled leather reached her nose. She found Nicholas in a middle stall with a reddish-brown horse. He was brushing her mane and talking to her softly. As soon as she approached, he paused.

"Good morning," she said, feeling awkward at having interrupted him.

"Were we supposed to meet this morning?" he asked. His blue eyes swept over her face, and her belly fluttered. Vicar Osgood might be a beautiful man, but Nicholas was also easy on the eyes. And when Nicholas looked at her, Amelia felt all warm and prickly inside. The prickly might have been slight annoyance. After all, she'd hoped he would want to make a morning walk with her part of his routine, but he had obviously taken it as a one-time event.

"I understand you are tending Lady Flame. She hasn't been feeling well?"

"A bit of arthritis, I think," he said, seeming to relax and beginning to brush her again. "She's getting on in years and she's been walking a bit stiffly. I just finished rubbing some ointment on her legs."

That was the scent she'd noticed when she'd come closer. The ointment smelled fresh, like mint or pine. Amelia ran a hand along the horse's neck. "She's a beautiful horse."

Nicholas looked at her over the mare's back. "Do you know anything about horseflesh?"

"Nothing at all."

He smiled. "She is a beauty, quite prized for her coloring." He set the brush he'd been using aside and gathered the silky strands of the horse's mane in his hands. As Amelia watched, he quickly plaited the horse's mane into an elaborate braid.

"There are many ladies who would pay handsomely for those hair dressing skills," she said.

He gave her a look of bemusement. She hadn't seen him smile very much, and that casual happiness made her heart beat faster. She wanted to make him smile every day.

"I'm only good with horse hair," he said. "Besides, ladies like all of those curls at their temple. I'd have no idea how to manage those."

"Nor would I," she said. "A few years ago I begged my mother to let me cut my hair so I could have fashionable fringe, and she said I'd regret it. I did, and promptly allowed it to grow out again."

His eyes roved over her again. "You made the right decision," he said.

Amelia tried to suppress the shiver of desire that speared into her when he looked at her like that. She couldn't think what to say, so even though she might have liked to turn the conversation from hairstyles, she said, "Your sister has that style, though, and it suits her."

He nodded, either not wanting to disagree with her or feeling non-committal. The silence dragged on just long enough for her to feel awkward. The vicar had told her to ask for what she wanted because men were idiots. She wasn't sure how to begin, but if she didn't say something now, Nicholas would move on to another stall or horse and she'd have to chase him to get a word.

"Do you remember the other night when we spoke in your bedchamber?"

His gaze lifted to hers, the blue of his eyes icy. Clearly, he was remembering some of the less pleasant things she had said.

"I told you I wanted us to be friends."

"Among other things."

"Yes, well." She moved carefully around the horse so she was on the same side as Nicholas. Now that she was close enough, she dropped her voice. "I thought we might work more on our friendship. I want more time with you."

His brows lowered. "I told you—"

"Time like this," she said before he could tell her why he couldn't give her what she wanted. "I just want to be part of your life. We could talk while you groom horses or over breakfast or, I don't know. But that is what I want—time with you every day."

"I see," he said slowly.

"It's important to me," she added, moving closer to him so she could make her point.

"Fine."

"Fine?" Amelia couldn't believe how easy that had been. The vicar was a genius. "I mean, yes, fine, good." She was so happy she threw her arms about his waist and hugged him. He was stiff and immobile for a moment, but then he put his arms around her and hugged her back. Oh, my. His chest was quite solid where she pressed against him, and he felt warm and smelled like mint. She couldn't resist turning her head to look up at him, which put their mouths much closer than she had anticipated. Her heart pounded in her chest as she remembered that kiss they'd shared in the stable before their wedding. She wanted another kiss like that. She wanted him to pull her closer, hard against him, and kiss her like he wanted her as much as she wanted him in that moment.

He looked down at her, and his gaze went to her lips. Amelia felt as though her legs were made of jelly. She wanted him to kiss her so badly. She tilted her head up, offering her lips.

"Amelia!"

She started and Nicholas stepped away from her.

"Amelia!"

Seemingly completely unfazed, Nicholas called, "We're here, Florentia."

Amelia had enough of her wits about her to turn her head as Lady Florentia approached. One look at her face and all of the heat from the embrace a moment before evaporated. "What is it?" Amelia asked. Florentia's lips were pursed and her cheeks bright red. She was breathing hard as though she had either run or walked very quickly.

"Your servant from Catmint Cottage is here. She says your mother needs you right away."

Amelia reached out and grasped Florentia's arm. "Is she well? Has something happened?"

"I don't know. But your servant said right away."

Amelia didn't know what to do. She was frozen, a million thoughts racing through her mind. Rose would not have come for her if something were not very, very wrong. "I'll go now," she said, lifting her skirts.

"Wait." Nicholas caught her arm, and Amelia had the urge to shake him off and run. But he turned her and took both of her arms in his until she looked up at him. "It will be faster if you take the gig."

"Too long to saddle," she said.

"My men are fast, and it's only one horse. Plus, if you need a conveyance when you arrive, you will have one."

"I can run there faster."

"Not much faster, and you'll be tired."

"I—"

"Stop arguing with me and let me give the orders."

Amelia closed her mouth and nodded. He walked stiffly off to speak with the stablemaster, who was nearby, having seen Lady Florentia running to the stable. Florentia put her arms about Amelia's shoulders and Amelia turned to her and buried her head against her shoulder. "I should have called on her before now. I have been so selfish."

"Shh." Florentia stroked her back. "You'll go now, and it will all be well. You'll see."

But Amelia knew things had not been well since her father died. She should never have left her mother alone at Catmint Cottage. If anything had happened to her, Amelia would never forgive herself.

***

Nicholas finished telling Bowen to have the gig readied and returned to find Amelia all but sobbing in his sister's arms. Florentia gave him an anguished look over his wife's shoulder, and Nicholas clenched his fists, wishing there was something he could do to make the grooms hurry. But they were good men and moving as fast as they could while still ensuring all was done properly and safely.

He felt completely useless, standing there beside his weeping wife and unable to do anything to help her. But that seemed to be his lot in life—he was useless these days. She hadn't been wrong that she could have run to Catmint Cottage quicker, but if they needed to fetch a doctor or additional assistance, it would help to have the gig there. Not to mention, if they took the gig, Nicholas could drive her. Perhaps that was selfish of him—to suggest the gig so he might be able to go along. But somehow in the last few days his wife had roused something inside him, a sort of protective instinct. He wanted to keep her safe and shelter her from unhappiness.

He tried not to think how ridiculous it was to believe a cripple like him could keep anyone safe.

Finally, the gig was ready, and the coachman helped him into the box. A groom helped his wife, a task Nicholas would have performed before his injury. Then he would assist a lady into a coach, letting his hands linger on her waist for just a moment too long before rounding the vehicle and leaping up himself. Now he was the one requiring assistance.

The carriage horse, Molly, was a good girl, and Nicholas had to do very little to direct her. He had been a better horseman than driver, but he supposed his driving skills were more important now. He guided the horse onto the road, and when she found her stride, he urged her faster.

Once they were on their way, he chanced a look at Amelia. Her face was red and blotchy, but she was not crying. Poor girl. The strain evident on her features tore at his heart. He would have reached over to take her hand, but he hadn't driven in some time and wanted both on the reins. Still, he felt he should say something. He wasn't any good in these types of situations, though. What should he say?

"I'm sure all will be well," he said finally. It sounded as hollow as he'd feared, and he winced a bit.

"I shouldn't have left her," Amelia said, her words like a torrent she'd been damming up. "I knew she was not strong, and I knew she was struggling. I should have gone to see her. I shouldn't have listened to her. Why did I listen to her?"

"What did she say?"

She glanced at him. "To stay at Battle's Peak and dedicate time to being a new bride. I didn't need to do that, now did I?"

Nicholas felt the barb strike him just as intended. He turned his head to stare straight forward as the horse ate up the final length of road to Catmint Cottage. As soon as the gig pulled before the door, before Nicholas could even engage the brake, Amelia had jumped down and run into the house. That left Nicholas to find a way out of the conveyance on his own. This was why he didn't drive any longer, and there was no one to help him. He moved awkwardly onto the step with his good leg then pulled his bad leg into position. Holding tightly to the box, he then lowered his good leg. Of course, it buckled, and he went down, his face in the gravel of the drive and his left leg pulsing with pain.

"Damn it," he said, pushing his face off the ground. There was no easy way to stand from a position on the ground, and he took a moment to roll over and look up at the sky and assess the status of his legs. The left was settling down now. It hadn't liked the quick bend at the knee or the jolt of hitting the ground. But he didn't think he'd injured anything other than his pride. His gaze shifted to the carriage box, and he spotted his cane looking down at him smugly. Fat lot of good it did up there. He'd have to slide over to the coach, grasp the wooden frame and haul himself up. He could imagine the state of his coat after that—not that he would normally care, but this was the first time in his wife's home, and now he would have to go in dusty and dirty.

"My lord!" The voice came from the house, and it wasn't Amelia's so he could only assume it was the servant who had come to fetch her. "My lord, are you hurt?" The older woman came running around the gig, her hands going to her mouth in horror when she saw him.

"Perfectly fine," he said. "Just took a tumble." Of course, he was not perfectly fine. If he was perfectly fine, he wouldn't be lying on the ground.

"May I help you, my lord?" the servant asked, coming to stand near him.

"That would be much appreciated."

"What should I—"

He managed to push himself up using his elbows and nodded at the box. "If you could hand me my walking stick."

She looked at the box, saw the stick, and pulled it out right away. It was so easy for her, and how Nicholas envied the ease at which she accomplished the task. Of course, it was an easy task for everyone but him.

She handed him the stick, and he set it on the ground and began to pull himself up. Without being asked, the servant went to his other side and helped lift him that way. A moment later, he was upright again with a fine sheen of perspiration along his forehead.

"Thank you," he told the servant, though he would have rather pushed her away and told her he was fine on his own, thank you very much. But that would have been uncharitable and untrue, and what was one more instance of swallowing his pride? His belly was full of it these past few years. "How is Mrs. Blackstock?" he asked, brushing off the sleeves of his coat.

"I couldn't rouse her this morning, my lord. She has been rising later and later since Mr. Blackstock's death, but never this late. I went to her chamber, and she didn't wake, not even when I shook her."

Nicholas raked a hand through his hair to try and tame it. He looked about and spotted his hat on the ground. Bloody hell. "Have you called for the doctor?"

"I sent our odd job boy for him, but he hasn't returned yet." She bent and retrieved his hat, brushed it off efficiently, and handed it to him.

"Thank you. Again. Would you mind showing me to Mrs. Blackstock's chamber?"

"Of course, my lord. Lady Nicholas has already gone inside."

Nicholas followed the servant into Catmint Cottage. The house was bright and cozy. Everything was clean and neat and uncluttered. The walls were papered or painted cheery colors with portraits or landscapes on the walls. The morning sun streamed into the windows lighting the vestibule as the chambers whose doors were open to invite him to look, but he felt the sadness within. Almost as soon as he had the thought, he dismissed it as ridiculous. Houses did not have feelings or emotions. And they didn't absorb those emotions from their inhabitants.

"This way, my lord," the servant said as she started up the stairs.

Of course, the bedchamber was upstairs. Nicholas considered saying he would wait below, but Amelia was up there, and she needed him. So climb he must. He tested the banister to make sure it was solid and sturdy, then put his cane on one step and held tight to the banister with the other and pulled himself up. He would have preferred to go up as he did at home, but he wouldn't do that in front of a servant. In any case, these stairs were narrower and wooden, as opposed to the wide, curving marble steps at Battle's Peak.

The servant turned away, pretending not to notice his difficulty and smart enough not to offer assistance. She moved slowly ahead of him and pretended to busy herself at the top of the stairs until he made it. By then Nicholas was breathing heavily and cursing himself for thinking he could be any use whatsoever to Amelia. It would have been better to send Florentia and stay back at Battle's Peak.

"This way, my lord," the servant said when she'd given him a discreet moment to catch his breath. He followed her to a room at the end of the corridor with the door flung open.

The servant stood aside so he could enter, and as soon as he did, he spotted Amelia on the bed beside her mother, who was propped on pillows and looking at Amelia as her daughter spoke softly to her and bathed her brow with a damp cloth.

Amelia glanced over her shoulder as he entered, her expression slightly annoyed. She probably wondered what had taken him so long. Then she spotted the servant. "Rose," she said, "would you fetch some broth and a cup of tea, I think."

"Of course, my lady." The servant bustled away, and Nicholas took his hat off.

"How is she?" he asked Amelia, who had glanced at him again, the annoyance gone from her expression now.

"She's given us quite a scare," she said, obviously aware her mother was also listening. "She hasn't been eating, but we'll get some food into her and build her strength up."

"I haven't...been...hungry," the widow said.

Nicholas knew that feeling. For months after his injury, he hadn't felt hungry. Nothing seemed to give him any pleasure—not food, not wine, not friends, not cards, not even his horses. Nicholas moved into the room. "You must eat to keep up your strength," he said. The words echoed in his mind as people had said them to him many times.

"He's right, Mama. You must eat." She glanced at Nicholas. "Is the doctor on his way?"

"I should think so. Do you want me to ride out to fetch him?"

"No. Stay with me." Amelia looked at her mother again. "I want you to sip some tea and broth. No arguing."

Mrs. Blackstock nodded, seeming too tired to argue. Nicholas couldn't keep his gaze from Amelia, though. She'd asked him to stay with her. She'd wanted him nearby. He'd forgotten what it was like to be needed by someone. Since he'd come home from the war, he'd had to rely on others. It was a dramatic shift for him. Hard to believe now, standing in this room supported by a cane and still breathing heavily from his trek up the stairs, that at one point he had been an integral part of an elite group of soldiers.

Draven's troop had its own mission and orders—to do everything possible to sabotage the French war effort, to gather information for the British generals, and if possible, to assassinate Bonaparte himself.

Since the group was largely on its own, away from supply lines and the bulk of the British army, they had to find their own food and transportation. Aidan Sterling was the thief of the troop and could steal anything from a loaf of bread to a wagon. He had little experience with horses, though, so it took Nicholas's skill with animals to steal cart horses or war horses. He'd been in the cavalry before being asked to join Draven's troop, and he'd brought his own horse, Charlemagne, with him. In addition to playing horse thief, he was an accomplished equestrian who was a crack shot even at a gallop. He often rode in front of the others to scout ahead and assess the possibility of an ambush. And when there was a skirmish, he and Charlemagne charged into the middle of the fray without hesitation.

He'd been a warrior.

Now he could barely make it up a set of stairs.

The servant returned with a tray, which she set on a bedside table. Amelia immediately began to feed her mother with a practiced hand. She'd obviously done this many times, most likely for her father. She had managed to get a little broth and a sip or two of tea in the woman when the doctor arrived. Nicholas took himself out of the chamber then to give his mother-in-law privacy.

A few minutes later the doctor emerged. "May I speak with you, my lord?"

"Of course," Nicholas said. "Should I ask Lady Nicholas to step out as well?"

The doctor looked over his shoulder at the bed chamber door, considering. He was an older man, perhaps sixty. He'd been the doctor in Hungerford for as long as Nicholas could remember and one of the reasons his mother had objected to him staying at Battle's Peak. Doctor Evans was competent but certainly not educated in the latest medical techniques. His training had taken place forty or more years ago, before the French Revolution. Perhaps before the American Revolution. Much had changed, and the dowager had worried a country doctor would not be able to treat Nicholas effectively.

Nicholas had argued that he didn't need further treatment. The specialists in London had done all they could, and what he needed was peace and quiet and to be left alone. Indeed, the only time he'd sent for Evans was when one of the servants or Florentia felt unwell. Nicholas had no need of the man.

"I think it best we speak man to man," the doctor said.

Nicholas should have expected this answer. Of course, the doctor would not want to involve a woman in a matter he didn't expect she would understand. But with her experience, Nicholas knew Amelia understood far more than he. Still, he would not force the issue and take her from her mother's side.

"Go on," Nicholas said.

"May I speak frankly, my lord?"

"I'd rather you did so we don't waste time."

The doctor nodded his white head, seeming to approve of this answer. "Mrs. Blackstock has been in a steady decline since the death of her husband. She seems to have fallen into a malaise. I have been here regularly the last four months, and in that time, she has lost weight and color and grown more and more listless. If I were a fanciful man, I would say she is sick from a broken heart. I am not a fanciful man," the doctor said, unnecessarily. "And yet, something must be done or Mrs. Blackstock will follow her husband to the grave."

"Lady Nicholas feels guilty that she has not come to call since our wedding. I do believe she intends to call more often."

"That would help, but though a new bride might have time to visit her mother, there are other concerns. Have you considered the estate? If something is not done soon, it will fall into disrepair."

Nicholas glanced at the bed chamber door again. "The estate is not mine to oversee. I believe it is entailed."

"To Mr. Blackstock's nephew, yes. But the man has been in India for years. Has he been notified that he now has property?"

Nicholas had no idea. He hadn't known anything about the entail, he'd only briefly glanced at the marriage contract the lawyers had drawn up. Amelia had come with a small dowry and no land. He remembered seeing that the estate was entailed and had thought no more of it.

Perhaps he'd even been a little relieved that he would not have to trouble himself with the land and tenets.

Clearly, he'd been too quick to judge.

"I'll have to look into that, sir. In the meantime, what do you suggest for Mrs. Blackstock?"

"I think she needs rest. For a decade she has been taxed with managing everything, and I believe that, in tandem with the understandable grief as a result of the loss of her husband, those responsibilities have overwhelmed her. The more that can be done to relieve her burdens, the better."

"I see. Thank you for your opinion, Doctor."

He nodded and started away. Then he paused and turned back. "May I say one thing more, my lord?"

Nicholas raised a brow. "Speak your mind, sir."

"I have known Miss Blackstock since she was an infant. Lately there has been some less than congenial whispering about her and about the hastiness of your marriage."

Nicholas had been in the army long enough to have perfected the art of keeping his feelings from showing on his face. He'd been coolly composed even when given the most asinine of orders. Now, his blood began to boil at the idea of gossip about his wife, but he didn't blink at the mention of it.

"I don't hold with any of it. Miss Blackstock—pardon me, Lady Nicholas, was always a good girl. She cared for her grandmother and then her father with a devotion I have rarely seen. Never once did I hear her complain. Never once could I fault the care she gave to either of her relatives. She was conscientious and kind and patient. If she wasn't the daughter of a gentleman, I would have tried to convince her to work for me as a nurse."

"That's good to know, Doctor."

"I thought you should know. I thought you should also know that if, after all those years of tending to others, she wanted to have bit of fun herself—to dance or meet friends at a pub—I hardly think she should be faulted for it."

"I agree, and I hope you don't think I do fault her."

"Many men would."

Nicholas didn't say the obvious—that he was not like *many men*. He simply met the doctor's eyes with his own steady gaze.

"I'll leave Mrs. Blackstock to your care then," Evans said. "And take my leave."

"Good day, sir."

He walked away, his movements agile and easy even for his age. When he had gone down the stairs and left Nicholas alone outside the bed chamber, Nicholas drew in a breath. He knew what must be done, little as he wanted to do it.

Ten

Amelia didn't hear the door open or Lord Nicholas return to the bedchamber, but she knew the precise moment he entered. He was remarkably graceful in his movements for a man who walked with a limp and a cane, so it wasn't clumsiness that alerted her but a shivering sense of awareness she was coming to realize was present whenever he was near. Her spine tingled and the hairs on the back of her neck prickled in a sort of ticklish way. But instead of turning to acknowledge him, she kept her focus on her mother, who had eaten a little and now had her eyes closed and was resting. Amelia watched the slow rise and fall of her chest and knew she could not leave her. Amelia might be a new bride, but she was also a daughter. Her mother needed her.

Nicholas had made it quite clear he did not.

The timing was bad, she told herself as she stroked her mother's brow. She had just begun to make some headway with Nicholas and if she spent time away now, she would certainly lose ground.

But it couldn't be helped. She had to do what was right, even if it meant a blow to her fledgling marriage and losing the potential of happiness. It was harder to do this time—to give up her own happiness and the chance of a future with a husband—but that didn't make it any less right.

Lord Nicholas moved behind her and put his hand on her shoulder. The gesture surprised her. She wanted to lean her cheek against his hand, but she resisted.

"Is she asleep?" he asked quietly.

"For the moment, yes."

"We should speak privately."

Amelia did turn her head to look at him then. She hadn't expected him to suggest they speak. She'd thought he would say they should return to Battle's Peak—or at least, he would say he wanted to return. Perhaps he would say it now.

She rose and followed him, closing the door softly behind her. Once outside, she gestured to the nearby chamber, which happened to be her own. She hadn't been inside since the morning of her wedding. It had only been a few days, but it seemed so much longer. The room, which had once been as familiar as her mother's face, now seemed like it had belonged to someone else. The pale blue walls and white curtains looked so childish and unsophisticated. On the window ledge lay a doll she had played with as a child and tacked on the wall was a drawing of Sweetie she had made. She was no great artist, but she'd been proud of it.

"We should go somewhere else," she said, trying to turn back, but Nicholas did not move away from the door.

"This is adequate." He looked about. "Was this your chamber?"

"It was."

She hated to see his eyes skim over the room, no doubt taking in the doll and the awful drawing. He must think her so silly and green. "It's charming," he said. "Is that a horse?" He nodded to the picture of Sweetie.

She glanced at the drawing again. It was bad but not that bad.

"It's a pig," she said. "Can you not see that?"

"Of course. My eyes aren't what they were."

But there was nothing the matter with his eyes. She had made the legs too long and the snout a bit narrow. She wanted to rip it down, but instead, she folded her hands in front of her. "What is it you wanted to speak about?"

"Your mother," he said without preamble. "The doctor told me she requires more care than she has been receiving."

Amelia took a deep breath. "I was thinking the same. I need to spend more time with her."

He nodded. "I agree. It would also be helpful to take some of the burden of the estate off her shoulders."

"Yes. She's in no state to deal with tenant requests or oversee the harvest in a couple of months."

"Then we are in agreement."

"I should stay here," she said.

"What?" He looked completely taken aback. "No."

"But you just said—"

"You cannot stay here. I mean, you could. I'd rather…" He trailed off and she raised a brow. "I think it would be best if you returned to Battle's Peak. Florentia will miss you if you are not there."

"Florentia." Not exactly what she wanted to hear.

"Your mother should remove to Battle's Peak as well. She will have the best care, and you will be close by."

Amelia was genuinely stunned. She had not expected him to suggest her mother move into Battle's Peak. Not that the house didn't have room. She hadn't even seen the whole of it yet, but she thought it boasted at least eight bed chambers, possibly more. "You don't mind?" she asked.

"Of course not. I would have suggested it sooner had I known. As to the estate, I would send for one of the assistant land managers from one of my brother's larger estates. The manager can review the situation at Catmint Cottage and put affairs in order as well as oversee things as long as necessary."

Amelia hadn't considered this idea, hadn't considered there was any way to manage the estate without taking it upon herself. "Why would you do that?" she asked.

He gave her a confused look. "Why wouldn't I?"

"The estate is entailed. You won't make any profit. Your family will not profit."

He shrugged. "Not everything is about profit. You need help. Your mother needs help. If I can provide that, why wouldn't I?"

She didn't have an answer to that question. She just knew that many men would not have even considered making such an offer, much less actually seeing it through. Amelia supposed she should have some pride and refuse the offer, but she couldn't see how pride would serve anything but itself in this instance. "Your offer is generous," she said, "and I accept."

"Good. Then I will return to Battle's Peak and make the arrangements. You pack what your mother needs. I'll send the coach back in a few hours."

Amelia felt an overwhelming rush of gratitude. She doubted Nicholas would quite know what to make of her if she started crying and blubbering her thanks. Instead, she flung her arms around him. He caught her, wrapping his arms about her. His body was stiff with surprise.

"Thank you!" she said, kissing him on the cheek. "Thank you."

"Of course," he said, stepping back. He seemed awkward, which made her feel awkward as well.

She brushed her hands on her skirts. "Should I see you out?"

"No, I can manage. Should I send Florentia or O'Malley to help you pack?"

"Rose will help." She didn't look at him. Things hadn't been awkward between them before, but she should have comprehended he wouldn't know what to make of her profuse thanks. It was just so rare that anyone ever offered to help. Years ago, when her grandmother had fallen ill, her mother said that neighbors had come and given their help and support. But after a few years, their generosity had waned. Since Amelia could remember, the family had no one to rely upon. She hadn't realized what a weight that was. Now it was as though Nicholas had lifted it from her shoulders and she was so much lighter she could almost fly away.

"Then we will have her settled by this evening," he said.

"Yes."

"Excuse me then." He bowed slightly and then opened the door and went out. Amelia had the urge to watch him leave, but she knew he would not appreciate an audience as he maneuvered the stairs. Instead, she returned to her mother's chamber and sat on the bed for a long moment. She couldn't tell if things were going poorly or well. Did he want her at Battle's Peak, or did he just feel it was his duty to help? He'd said she'd be settled by evening, but he didn't mention dining with her or seeing her then. It seemed impossible to know what he thought or felt. It was even more impossible for her to know how to react.

She hadn't realized marriage would be so complicated. She supposed she hadn't thought she'd care quite so much. But of course, she did. How could one not care for a man like Nicholas St. Clare?

A few moments later Rose entered, carrying a valise. "Lord Nicholas said you would need help preparing Mrs. Blackstock to remove to Battle's Peak."

Amelia stood. "She'll be staying with me for a time, Rose. Will you be lonely here without us?"

She set the valise on a chair. "Oh, a bit, I suppose, but there's always plenty to be done."

The two packed quietly, Amelia telling Rose about the land manager who would be coming and assuring her that she would be welcome at Battle's Peak. "Mama will be happy to see you."

"Oh, don't you worry about me," Rose said when the carriage had finally arrived, and they had helped Amelia's mother inside. "You've made the right decision," Rose said, patting Amelia's arm before helping her inside and stepping back so the footman could close the door. As the coach started away, Amelia waved to Rose and then turned in her seat to watch Catmint Cottage. Rose had said she'd made the right decision. Was that the decision to move her mother or did she mean a larger decision? Perhaps the one to marry Lord Nicholas?

***

The next few days were a blur. Amelia's mother was more ill than Amelia had anticipated. The doctor called often and when Amelia was not busy implementing his instructions, she met with the land manager to go over the books with him. Finally, the third day after her mother's arrival, she'd improved enough that Amelia felt she could sit in a chair and close her eyes for a few hours. She'd barely taken the seat beside her mother's bed when the door opened, and Lady Florentia entered. She gave Amelia a look of disappointment. "You look exhausted," she said.

"I'm fine," Amelia lied. She was exhausted. But she had felt like this before, and a few hours' rest would refresh her.

"You need to go to bed," Florentia said. "And that's just what you shall do. Now." She grasped Amelia's hands and pulled her up from the chair. "I will sit here, and you go to your chamber and sleep."

"There's no need to do that—"

"There's every need. Do not argue with me. I am older and wiser."

"You're not very much older."

Florentia elbowed past Amelia and took her chair. "I am the big sister you always wanted."

"Actually, I always wanted a little sister."

"That's what I thought until Anne was born. Trust me, it's better to be the little sister. Now off with you! If your mother needs you, I'll have O'Malley wake you."

Amelia didn't see how she could argue further and finally went to her chamber. She wouldn't be able to sleep. She was tired, but her mind was too full of what ifs. What if her mother did not recover? What if the land manager discovered the situation at Catmint Cottage was worse than she suspected? What if Lord Nicholas had just brought her mother to Battle's Peak to serve as a barrier to keep Amelia at bay? Every time their relationship moved forward, he seemed to take a step back.

In her chamber, O'Malley waited and cajoled her until she stripped down to her chemise and let her hair down. Amelia insisted she did not need to climb under the covers, so O'Malley compromised by covering her with a light blanket. Once she was alone, Amelia stared at the window and tried to remember the last time she had seen Nicholas. It was at Catmint Cottage several days ago. She hadn't so much as glimpsed him since her mother arrived. And she hadn't had time to tell him that she was not breeding, as she'd thought.

Would it even matter to him? He hadn't married her solely for that reason. Her eyelids felt heavy, and she closed them for just a moment. Another quarter hour, and she would go back to her mother's chamber. A moment later, she tumbled into a dreamless sleep.

***

Nicholas tapped quietly on the door adjoining his room with Amelia's. When there was no answer, he tried the latch and found the door unlocked. He pushed the door open and took a moment to allow his eyes to adjust to the darkness. No fire was lit in the hearth and the curtains on the windows were still open. Moonlight filtered through the glass panes. The small form on the bed was motionless.

"Amelia," he said. The form did not move. He rapped on the door and repeated her name. No response. Nicholas entered the room and crossed to the bed. He stood to the side to allow the moonlight to illuminate her. She was in a deep slumber. One hand lay open on the pillow beside her cheek. Her hair flowed like rich amber over the white pillow, and her lashes made a shadow on her cheek. Her mouth was parted slightly and her breathing deep and even.

He tried to stop his gaze from moving lower, but he couldn't quite muster that much self-control. The shift she wore had fallen off one shoulder and slid so low it revealed the rounded fullness of her left breast. If he'd nudged the material just a fraction, her nipple would be visible. His tongue wet his dry lips as he drank in the sight of that pale, round flesh. How long had it been since he'd seen a woman's body? How long since he'd touched a woman?

His gaze slid lower where the blanket tangled at her waist. One leg was covered, but the other leg was free, and her foot and calf were naked for him to see. She had long, narrow feet and slim legs. He wanted to run a hand up that leg, cup the calf, and then slide a finger to the soft skin of her inner thigh.

With some effort, Nicholas dragged his gaze away and took a deep breath. He'd forgotten what a beautiful woman she was. It was easy to forget when he was not with her, harder to forget how she made him smile and how her kindness made him feel. But he didn't think the image of that all-but-bare breast would be quite so easy to block from his mind. The feeling of desire would linger as well.

Nicholas reached for the blanket, untangled it, and drew it up and over his wife until it reached her neck. Once she was covered, he shook her shoulder lightly. "Amelia."

Her eyes opened and she stared at him as though she had no idea where she was. Then she blinked and sat straight as an arrow. "My mother. Did something happen?"

"No." Damn it all to hell. The blanket had slipped down when she sat and so had her shift. One rosy nipple was very clearly visible now as was a firm, rounded breast. "Your mother is fine."

"Oh, good." She lay back and pulled the blanket back up. "I had a moment of panic there."

"Of course. My sister took her dinner with Mrs. Blackstock and reports she ate a bit of soup. Afterward, Florentia read to her for a little while."

"Dinner?" Amelia sat again. Thank God that this time she held the blanket in place. "What time is it?"

"Almost midnight."

"What?" She started to climb out of bed, but Nicholas blocked her.

"There's no need to rise. Florentia asked me to check on you since you did not eat. I have a tray in my chamber."

"I should check on my mother."

"We have a servant watching over her. Your mother is sleeping, and there's no call to go in and disturb her. I wouldn't have disturbed you, but my sister said you haven't eaten but a few bites the past few days, and I'd rather you didn't fall ill."

"I'm not hungry." She slid off the bed, and since he did not step back, they were incredibly close. Finally, he turned to the side.

"You must eat. Think of the baby."

Her reaction was completely unexpected. She jerked and grasped the blanket then looked at him with an expression that seemed uncharacteristically guilty.

"What is it?" he asked. There was no denying something was the matter.

"I have been wanting to tell you." She swallowed and her hand at her throat tightened. "There won't be a baby."

Nicholas stared at her for a long moment before his gaze lowered to her abdomen. Without thinking, he reached out and pulled her into his arms. He'd wanted to comfort her, but when she went willingly, he found himself surprised to be holding her. "I'm so sorry. Should we call a doctor? Are you in pain?"

"No." He felt her shake her head. "I didn't lose the baby."

He pulled back to look down at her.

She avoided his gaze, her cheeks pink. "I was mistaken. I was not breeding. My monthly—er, courses, were simply late."

And then he understood. She was not carrying another man's child. She would not be having a baby.

"I feel so awful. I did not mean to mislead you. I'd never been late before, and I assumed it was because—"

He pulled her close again. "There's no need to apologize. Are you upset?"

"No," she murmured, pressing her face into his shoulder. "I'm actually relieved. I know you said you would treat another man's child as your own, but I did wonder. And now we can start over. Perhaps we can have a real marriage."

Nicholas stiffened and pulled back. "I see I've given you the wrong impression."

She looked up at him, her wide brown eyes full of puzzlement.

"This changes nothing for me. Our marriage is still one in name only." He saw the pain slice through her features at his words, and though he should have seen all of the signs, he was surprised. Something had happened in the last week since they'd wed. She'd changed her mind. She wanted more from him. Was it because she had lost the baby, or did she have feelings for him?

No matter. Even if she wanted a real marriage, he couldn't give that to her. He was only half a man, and she had simply forgotten that for the moment.

"There's a tray in my chamber," he said. "Come and eat something."

He turned and walked stiffly to the door between their rooms. He was painfully aware she watched him as he walked away, and though he hated people to see his infirmity, perhaps it was for the best this time. It would remind her that he was damaged.

"Why?" she said. Her voice rang out in the silent room. He stopped and glanced over his shoulder.

"To keep up your strength. You won't be much good to your mother if you fall ill."

She shook her head, her amber waves falling about her shoulders. "No. Why is our marriage in name only?"

Nicholas crossed his arms over his chest. "That was the agreement."

"And I needed to agree with you at that time because I was desperate and ruined. I would have agreed to almost anything, but I made a mistake agreeing to be a wife in name only. I want more."

"It's too late for that now," he said, his voice icy. "The agreement has been made."

"Then let's change it."

"No."

Her hands went to her hips and the blanket drooped, revealing the low neckline of her shift again. "Why? Why did you want a platonic marriage? You never told me."

"It doesn't matter." He started for the door again, but she had two perfectly good legs—two lovely legs, if memory served—and she raced in front of him and stood in the doorway, blocking his way. Her arms were stretched wide, and the fire from the hearth in his room was at her back. The effect was predictable. He could see the outline of her body under the thin, linen shift perfectly.

"It matters to me," she was saying, even as he tried to look away from those delectable curves. "I know you want me."

His gaze jerked to her face. Had she seen him looking at her?

"You kissed me in the stable just the other day," she said, obviously not noticing his roving eyes. "That has to mean something."

"It means I wasn't thinking."

"You weren't trying to remind yourself that you don't want me, you mean? Why not? What is wrong with me?"

Oh, dear God. She thought something was wrong with her? She was perfect. "Don't be daft," he said sharply. "There's nothing wrong with you." His words were so curt, she dropped her arms. Unfortunately, that meant the bodice of her shift dropped too, all but revealing her breast. Nicholas's gaze dropped, and so did Amelia's. She lifted her hand, perhaps to pull the neckline back up, but then she hesitated. She looked at Nicholas, and their gazes met.

Oh, no. He would not be lured in by her body. He was stronger than that. The pleasure would be short-lived. Once she saw his legs, her desire would turn to disgust. But he couldn't stand here with her half-dressed. He'd tug that neckline up himself. He reached for the linen, took hold of it, and stopped. His hand brushed the silky, plump skin of her breast. She inhaled sharply, and their gazes met again. He should pull the linen up now, wrap her in the blanket, and push her to the tray of food.

He should hurry and cover her. He should not look down at the skin his hand touched.

But he did look down, and then he moved his hand slightly so the back of it brushed over the top of her rounded breast. Her skin was warm and so impossibly soft. He couldn't seem to stop his hand from drawing the material down to reveal her entire breast.

His hand brushed over her distended nipple, the point teasing his skin as it pebbled beneath his touch. He turned his hand, closing his palm over her breast and testing the weight of it. Amelia moaned, and when he looked at her again, her eyes were closed and her teeth biting the edge of her lip. She liked his touch. It made him want to touch her more, touch her everywhere.

Instead, he bent and brushed his lips over hers.

"Yes," she murmured and kissed him back.

He continued to fondle her breast as she opened her mouth and his tongue tangled lazily with hers. There was nothing rushed about the kiss. It was slow and sensual and when the kiss deepened, he tugged lightly on her nipple, making her gasp and press closer.

He moved forward then, intent on pressing her back and pushing his hard cock against her soft belly. But his leg was stiff, and he couldn't unlock the knee for a moment. He almost stumbled and released her, swearing.

"What's wrong?" she asked, her eyes large and hazy with desire.

"Nothing." Everything was wrong. Everything. He was a fool. He grasped the material of her shift, and this time he pulled it up and covered her. Then he took the blanket and dropped it over her shoulders. "That was a mistake."

"Why?"

"I told you."

"But I liked it. I liked you touching me."

Nicholas clenched his hands to keep from dragging the blanket back down and touching her all over again.

"It was a mistake. It won't happen again."

"But—"

"Amelia, just eat now, yes? I'll see you in the morning."

And because he didn't know what else to do, he limped into his room and then right through the outer door.

He closed it behind him, ignoring the sound of her voice as she called after him. Instead of waiting for her to come out and look for him, he shuffled along the corridor and ducked into the alcove where the door to another bedchamber was situated.

He stood there quietly for some time before he heard the door behind him open. He hadn't thought of where he was going, so he assumed he'd see Florentia behind him. But it was Rafe.

"Well, hullo. I thought the house would be asleep," he said, indicating Nicholas's full dress.

Nicholas frowned at him. "Don't tell me you planned to wander about."

He shrugged. "A man can only spend so much time reading or staring out the window. At least I waited until everyone was asleep." He narrowed his eyes. "Why aren't you asleep? Or at the very least in bed? You have a bride to keep you entertained, do you not?"

Nicholas let out a frustrated sigh, and Rafe's brows lifted. "You'd better come in."

Nicholas would have refused, but where else was he to go? He couldn't go back to his chamber. Not with Amelia there and only half dressed. "Just for a moment," he said.

"Have a glass of wine, will you?"

Nicholas moved inside and closed the door behind him. Rafe's chamber was in complete disarray. Clothes were strewn about, the bed was not made, and half a dozen books lay about on chairs or the floor. Three trays of half uneaten food were piled near the door. Seemingly unaware of Nicholas's shock at the state of the room, Rafe crossed to a decanter of wine and poured two glasses. Nicholas doubted there had been wine in the room when Rafe arrived, and he wondered where it had come from.

Rafe handed him a glass, and Nicholas sipped it then pulled back and looked down. "This is very good. Where did you get it?"

"I have my sources." Rafe smiled his charming smile, and even Nicholas found it difficult to be cross with him. "I'm sure you thought I would be gone by now," Rafe said.

Nicholas shrugged. "It takes more than a week for interest in capturing a traitor to die down."

Rafe winced. "I wish everyone would stop calling me a traitor. I didn't betray my country."

"Those who wanted to take the spy and daughter of the notorious French assassin Fortier into custody disagree."

Rafe waved a hand. "Collette was only spying to keep her father alive. She never gave the French any information. This is all just a misunderstanding, and as much as I hate sea voyages, Boston is not half bad. It's not London, but it's not bad." He pushed several garments onto the floor and sat in a chair. "Now, tell me how you have been. How is your wife?

She's very pretty and charming, except for her fondness for that pig."

Nicholas felt a rush of blood go to his face. "What do you mean, pretty and charming?"

"Exactly what I said. And unclench your fists. I don't have any designs on her. I'm a married man. Collette would murder me in my bed if I so much as looked twice at another woman."

"Twice?"

Rafe nodded. "One can't help but look once. I'm not dead, old boy."

"Well, don't look at Amelia. Or Florentia."

"No plans to, but I will say that your wife seems to be alone more than I would expect a new bride to be."

"I told you the circumstances of our marriage. It's not a love match."

"That doesn't mean you can't make the most of the circumstances. Or"—Rafe set his glass on a small unused space of a table—"are you not attracted to her?"

"I'm attracted to her," Nicholas said, thinking of her lying on the bed just a short time ago. And then he was thinking about how he'd lowered her shift and touched her breast. He was *definitely* attracted to her.

"Is she not attracted to you then?"

Nicholas scowled. "How could she be?"

Rafe looked him up and down then raised a brow. "I'm no expert, but you seem attractive enough. You could do with smiling a bit more, and you might have your valet style your hair like this—" He rose and reached toward Nicholas's head. Nicholas batted his hands away.

"It's not my hair, you dolt."

"Then what is it?"

Nicholas stared at him, his anger growing. Finally, Rafe said, "Oh. Your legs."

"Yes, my legs. Would that I could forget the infirmity as easily as you." He downed the rest of his glass and turned to go.

"It's easy to forget. It doesn't seem like much of an impediment for you."

Nicholas looked back at him. "I assure you it *is* an impediment. I can't ride. I can't climb stairs. I can't even sit for long periods of time."

"What has any of this to do with your bride? Has she rejected you?"

Nicholas did not want to discuss this. On the other hand, it had built up inside him to the point where he felt he must say something to someone or burst. He slumped against the wall. "No, she hasn't rejected me. But she will."

"How do you know?"

"What do you mean? I know she will. Once she sees my injury, she'll be disgusted and recoil."

"It's that bad?"

Nicholas nodded.

"You're sure she hasn't already seen? Even with the candles blown out—"

Nicholas shook his head. "She hasn't seen. I haven't... bedded her." Nicholas stared at a point on the ceiling to avoid looking at Rafe's face, but he heard him sputtering in disbelief.

"You haven't taken your *wife* to bed? Because of your injury? Did the injury prevent you from, er—performing?"

Nicholas leveled a look at him. "No. My leg was shattered. My cock works just fine."

Rafe seemed to consider this. "So your concern is she'll see the scars and reject you."

Nicholas didn't answer. That was it, but he didn't like having it spoken so boldly.

"Let me see."

"What?" Nicholas started in surprise. "No."

"Go on. Take off your trousers and let me see. I'll tell you how bad it is. I'll be honest."

"I'm not taking my trousers off so you can gawk at me."

"I can think of a thousand other things I'd rather gawk at, but I'm offering you my services as a friend. I've been in war and seen my share of wounds. I also think I have some notion of what women find attractive. If your leg is likely to send your bride screaming into the night, I'll tell you straight."

Nicholas still didn't move.

"Who else can you trust?" Rafe asked. "I have no reason to lie. Go on."

"Fine." Nicholas loosed the fall of his trousers and pushed them down, letting gravity take them to his ankles. His shirt hung down to his upper thighs, but it didn't hide the devastation that had been wrought when Charlemagne fell on him. He knew without looking what Rafe would see. His right leg bore some scarring along the calf and the shin, but it hadn't received the worst of it. His left leg was pale, thin and misshapen. The flesh bore several bright red scars from surgeons' attempts to repair the devastation. His knee was particularly damaged. It hardly bent any longer and one side protruded unnaturally.

Rafe made no comment, just lifted the lamp and studied his legs. Then he moved behind him and looked from that angle. Nicholas had thought he'd feel odd or awkward, but Rafe made it seem like nothing out of the ordinary. Finally, he returned to his chair and said, "Pull your trousers back up, and I'll give you the verdict."

Nicholas appreciated not having to hear the bad news bare-arsed. When he'd fastened his trousers again, he looked at Rafe. "Go on then."

"It's not pretty," Rafe said. "Some women might be repulsed by it, I won't disagree."

"I told you—"

"I've not finished." Rafe held up a hand and Nicholas waited. "I don't think your lady is one of those women."

"And how would you know? Have you shown her other deformities and gauged her reaction?"

"No, but she doesn't strike me as the sort of woman to put much stock in physical perfection. You know the sort I'm talking about."

"Do I?"

"All the pampered ladies in London who half-faint if the smell of horse manure touches their nose. Lady Nicholas is a country girl with a pet pig. She's been caring for her ill mother, and other ill family members, if what I hear is correct. I'm sure she's seen worse."

Nicholas let out a bitter breath. "That doesn't mean she wants to go to bed with a cripple."

"You won't know unless you try. Do you really think she'll reject you?"

Nicholas thought of the way she'd pressed against him, the way she'd moaned when he caressed her breast. "No."

"Then nothing is stopping you. Well, except me. Tonight is as good as any to consummate the wedding." Rafe shooed him out of the chamber and closed the door behind him.

For a long moment, Nicholas stood in the corridor and considered going back and taking up where he and Amelia had left off. But Rafe hadn't seemed to realize that pride was stopping him. Pride and fear. Because rejection might not be the worst outcome. What would he do if she accepted?

Eleven

The next morning was overcast and drizzly, and Amelia frowned at it through her mother's window. "I was hoping we could go for a walk today." She tried to keep her voice cheerful.

"I don't feel up to a walk," her mother said.

Amelia had known she would say that. She didn't seem to want to do anything except lie in bed and sleep. She had no appetite and no interest in anything. Amelia had tried to tempt her with all of her favorite foods, but her mother nibbled or took only one or two bites unless Amelia cajoled her. As for entertainment, Amelia had brought books, magazines, even chess into her mother's room. All sat untouched on the bedside table. Amelia had hoped for sun today. A bit of time outdoors in the warm sunlight always made her feel better, but the weather had not cooperated.

"The first sunny day, we are taking a stroll," Amelia said. "No arguments."

Her mother didn't argue. She didn't agree either. She seemed indifferent, which was somehow worse. "Let's look at this magazine," she said, pulling a copy of *La Belle Assemblée* from 1814 off the table. The fashions were outdated, but as they'd never paid much attention to fashion, many of the styles would be new. She set the magazine on her mother's lap and turned pages at regular intervals. Amelia made comments about the hats or dresses. Her mother made sounds, but Amelia could sense she wasn't really listening.

Amelia's heart wasn't in it today either. Since the kiss with Nicholas last night, her attention had been only half engaged on any given task. It seemed she would remember the feel of his hand on her breast or the slide of his tongue into her mouth at the most inappropriate moments.

She wanted him to touch her again. Now that her monthly courses had ended, she wanted him to do more than touch her. She wanted him to strip her naked and lie her down and press his body against hers. She'd felt shame when she'd wanted that from Wickersham. But Nicholas was her husband. There was nothing sinful about their lying together.

The problem, of course, was Nicholas didn't want her. He'd left her out of breath and wanting more and hadn't come back to his room until she'd finally given up and gone back to her own chamber. Even then she'd listened for him but had fallen asleep before she heard him return. Perhaps he hadn't returned. Any sensible woman would infer from his behavior that he didn't want her. But she couldn't quite forget about that kiss. The way he'd touched her and kissed her had definitely shown desire. So why wouldn't he act on it?

She'd told him there was no baby, and he'd said nothing had changed. So the impediment had nothing to do with her. What was keeping him from doing what he seemed to want? What she *definitely* wanted? And if she kept turning these thoughts in her head, she would probably go mad enough to be sent to Bedlam.

A tap on the door roused her from her thoughts. "Come in."

Florentia peered in and smiled when she saw Mrs. Blackstock awake. "Good morning," she said.

"The weather is a bit dreary to call it a good morning," Amelia said, feeling irritable now.

"True, but my gardener tells me it will clear up with afternoon."

"I hope so."

"Might we speak in private for a moment?" Florentia asked.

Amelia looked at her mother. "Mama, do you mind if I step out for a few moments?"

Her mother did not respond, so Amelia stood and straightened the magazine on her lap, then followed Florentia into the corridor outside. When she closed the door, Florentia pulled an envelope from her skirts.

"A letter? For me?" Amelia couldn't think who would write to her except perhaps her father's heir. Perhaps he'd finally been located in India.

Florentia glanced at it. "No. It's for Nicholas, actually. But he gave me leave some time ago to open his correspondence. He doesn't like to bother with it unless there's something that needs his attention. I believe this needs his attention." Florentia held out a hand, and Amelia took the envelope and withdrew a card.

"It's a response to an invitation," she said. She glanced back at the card. "The Duke and Duchess of Mayne accepted the invitation to the house party. What house party?"

Florentia raised her brows. "I was hoping you could tell me."

Amelia glanced at the letter again. "I don't know anything about it. I certainly am not acquainted with a duke." But there was a niggling memory of having seen that title before.

"He only became a duke recently. Before that he fought with Nicholas during the war."

"If he's a friend of Lord Nicholas, then perhaps Nicholas invited him." Florentia raised a brow, and Amelia nodded. "I know. I know. Nicholas is not the sort to organize a house party."

"Which is why I came to you."

"But I had nothing to do with it," Amelia insisted. "I've never hosted a house party in my life, and I would never invite a duke and duchess to one without consulting you."

"Even if you wanted the event to be a surprise for Lord Nicholas?"

Amelia straightened. "Are you accusing me of lying?"

"Of course not," Florentia said, taking the card back. "I'm sure you had every good intention, but knowing my brother as I do, I would advise against this sort of function. He is a solitary man. You think it will draw him out, but he will just retreat. You'll be forced to explain his absence day after day. I speak from experience." She took hold of Amelia's wrist and squeezed it in what was most likely meant to be a show of sympathy, but Amelia shook her off.

"That's all very well, but I did not organize a house party." She gestured to her mother's closed door. "I have enough on my hands at the moment."

"Then who did?"

"Ask your brother." Amelia turned away. "I'm sure you speak to him more than I."

She returned to her mother's chamber and closed the door, taking just a moment to lean against it and draw in a calming breath. Why did it feel as though everything were falling apart? First her mother had fallen ill. Then Nicholas rejected her. Now his sister thought she was a liar. She didn't see how things could get worse.

"What's wrong?" her mother asked.

Amelia blinked and stared at her. It was the first time in days her mother had spoken of her own volition. Usually, Amelia had to ask her a question and then coax an answer.

"Everything is fine." Amelia pushed away from the door. "Just a misunderstanding."

Mrs. Blackstock nodded. "Marriage is difficult the first few years."

Amelia froze midstep on her way to the bedside. She could not remember her mother ever speaking to her about the first years of her marriage to her father.

"I remember how your father and I struggled," her mother said.

Amelia could only stare. Gradually, she forced her feet forward and made herself sit on the bedside. "That's difficult to believe." She tried to think of something else to say, anything to keep her mother talking. "You two always seemed so happy together."

"Did we?" Mrs. Blackstock gave her a faint smile. Amelia might have fallen over if she hadn't quickly steadied herself. She hadn't seen her mother smile in days. Perhaps speaking about Papa was good for her mother.

"You did. Even after his injury, you were always the one who could make him laugh."

Her mother smiled again and ducked her head. Amelia imagined she was remembering the times her father had smiled. "Yes, well, it wasn't always like that. We had our share of squabbles. Some were even screaming matches."

Amelia laughed. "I don't believe that."

"Oh, believe it! It's bound to happen when two people who are different try to make a life together. That first year of marriage, we seemed to quarrel about everything. He didn't like the way I cooked potatoes. I didn't like how he left his boots in the middle of the floor."

"I was always tripping over his boots," Amelia said. "He just left them wherever he removed them."

"Bad habit of his, but I learned to love him despite it. No man or woman is perfect, and flaws can be as endearing as those perfections we fancy."

If Nicholas had a flaw, it was only that he didn't want her. And perhaps that was more her flaw than his. "I'm afraid Lord Nicholas and I have more to overcome than boots in the middle of the floor."

"I was afraid of that. You knew so little of each other before you wed. I think that makes it even harder, especially when difficulties come."

Amelia watched her mother's gaze shift to the window. She thought Marianne would go silent again. She often had that faraway look on her face when she was about to fall silent and pensive for hours, but instead she reached over and took Amelia's hand. "Do you know what we argued about?"

Amelia shook her head, but as her mother was still looking out the rain-streaked window, she spoke too, "No."

"I don't mean a small argument, either. I mean an explosion of tempers." Her mother's gaze left the window and landed on Amelia. "It was over you."

"Me?"

"Not you, specifically, but over a baby. We both wanted one so very badly, and it took several years for us to conceive. It was a trying time for both of us. We both blamed ourselves and we didn't speak about it to each other and started to turn inward. Then we blamed each other."

"Oh, Mama. I'm so sorry." Amelia had known her parents had difficulty conceiving. She had asked many times as a child why she had no siblings. Her father always said that they had the perfect child on the first try and there was no need to have another. When she'd gotten older, her mother had told her they'd tried for more and the Lord had not blessed them.

"So was I and so was your father. We apologized to each other and decided that if we weren't meant to have children, then so be it. Imagine our surprise a year or so later when I found out I would have you."

Amelia squeezed her mother's hand. "Thank you for telling me that." She leaned forward and hugged her mother. "I'm so glad you are here with me, Mama. I have missed you."

"Oh, you don't need me." Her mother patted her back. "What you need is to speak to your husband. Talk to him. Don't let those miscommunications stand. Don't let hurt feelings linger."

"I will, Mama." She lowered her cheek to her mother's shoulder and breathed in the familiar scent of lavender and moth balls.

"Amelia," her mother said softly. "What are you waiting for?"

Amelia pulled back. "You mean you want me to speak to him now?"

"Why put it off? Besides, I'm tired and want a nap."

Amelia bit her tongue to keep from pointing out that her mother had only been awake a few hours. She was taking steps in the right direction. Small steps, but steps nonetheless. "Will you tell me more stories about you and Papa when I come back later?"

"Do you like them?"

"I do." And she liked to see her mother's smile and her eyes light up.

"Then we'll speak later."

Amelia tucked the covers around her and left the room quietly. She hadn't thought to go seek out Nicholas this morning, but her mother was right. Why put it off? She had only made it halfway down the stairs, though, when a groom came running into the foyer. "My lady!"

Amelia grasped the banister hard. "What is it? What's wrong?"

"It's your pig, my lady! She's gone."

***

Nicholas heard the commotion all the way from his library. He'd been reviewing ledgers and attending to correspondence, something he did almost daily in order to keep the estate running and ensure his brother was apprised of what was needed at Battle's Peak. But he could hardly concentrate with all the shouting. By the time he stood up, had a grip on his walking stick, and had made it around the desk, the shouting had ceased.

Nicholas swore, decided not to go into the foyer and ask questions, and had just settled back into his chair when he happened to glance through his window. The view was of the stables and barn, and a dark green dress came into view, the skirts whipping in the wind and rain.

"What the devil?"

He looked again and swore. Why was Amelia out in the rain? She hadn't even donned a coat or taken an umbrella. He doubted she'd changed her slippers for boots, and she must be sinking to her ankles in mud. He'd sink to his ankles in mud as well if he went out there. He wouldn't really be any use, but he stood again and made his slow trek out of the library and into the elements. Of course, he'd paused long enough to grab a coat and umbrella. He already wore boots as he'd been in the stables earlier that morning.

He made his way toward the barns, making sure to stay away from the mud puddles. He was almost there when Bowen noticed him and rushed over. "My lord, I am glad to see you," the stablemaster said. "Would you please talk some sense into Lady Nicholas? No disrespect to her, but we have everything in hand."

"What seems to be the problem? Why is she out in this weather?"

"One of the grooms, my lord. He's new and young, and I think he has a slight infatuation for Lady Nicholas. He ran in to tell her that her pig was missing."

Nicholas swore.

"Exactly, my lord. You know how much she loves that pig."

"I suppose she wants to help look for her."

"She does, but I told her I already sent a few men out. They'll find her and bring her back. If nothing else, she's a pig. She'll be fine on her own for a few hours and will come back when she's hungry."

"Where is Lady Nicholas now?" Nicholas asked.

"In the stable trying to convince the grooms to saddle a horse."

Nicholas nodded and started that way. "My lord, it's a bit muddy," Bowen said, stating the obvious.

"I'll make it." He had to. With determination, he fought his way to the stable, almost losing his balance several times. He was glad to step inside, even if it was only to hear his wife barking orders at his grooms.

"—saddle a horse immediately, I shall do it myself. Then when I fall and break my neck, my death will be on you."

"No, it won't," Nicholas said.

She spun around, and the sight of her was worse than he'd feared. She was pale and her lips tinged blue. She was soaked through and shivering in her thin dress. "Lord Nicholas, Sweetie—"

"I heard," he said. "Bowen tells me we have men out looking for her."

"But they don't know where she likes to roam. I do. I must go and look for her."

"Not in this weather, you won't."

He saw her jaw tighten and though he didn't know her well, any man or woman would recognize the look of determination that came over her face then. He knew exactly what she would do next. She'd forego the horse and go on foot. Unless he could stop her.

And there was only one way he could think of to stop her.

Damn it.

Nicholas released the walking stick and made a show of falling. He fell on his good side, of course, so he could control it, but the jolt still hurt when he landed on the wooden slats of the stable.

"My lord!" As predicted, she ran to him, kneeling at his side and grabbing hold of his arm. "Are you hurt?"

Pretending to be annoyed, Nicholas pushed her arm away. Damn and bloody damn. She was even colder than he'd anticipated. The bare skin of her forearm was like ice. "I'm fine." He didn't have to pretend to struggle to rise, but for once he did want her assistance.

"Should I fetch the doctor, my lord?" the groom asked.

"No. Get back to your work. I'm perfectly fine."

"May I help you to your feet?" Amelia asked.

He grunted and grudgingly accepted her help to stand. He could do it on his own, just needed something stable to help him regain his balance. Amelia had her arm about his waist and felt remarkably stable at his side. She tried to move away, to reach for his walking stick, but he held her tightly to his side. She was definitely shivering, and he needed to get her inside and in front of a fire as soon as possible. "My stick," he said, pointing to the groom. The lad swept it up.

Amelia didn't try to disengage from him, but she looked up and said, "If you are steadier now, I will go look for Sweetie."

He'd thought she would at least see him into the house before he had to play his next card. No such luck. "Do you—would you—" He did not have to pretend to stumble over his words. Even when it was a calculated move, he hated asking for assistance. "Walk inside with me." He thought he'd better soften the order. "Would you?"

"I—" She looked through the open door of the stable, probably toward the direction she thought Sweetie might have taken, but she must have also seen how muddy the ground had become and how hard the rain was still falling. "Of course," she said. "I'll see you settled then go out."

They started back toward the house, Nicholas using his walking stick, but also keeping Amelia right at his side. He wanted to warm her, but he also liked the feel of her tucked against him. "You should put on boots before you go back out," he said. "And a coat."

"You're right. I forget how these summer storms bring a blast of cold air with them. My grandmama always said they blow down from Scotland."

"The weather will warm once the sun comes back out, but my father always cautioned that we'd catch our death of cold if we traipsed about in wet clothes." The marquess had never said any such thing, but he'd heard it somewhere. Might as well throw more ammunition Amelia's way.

"A coat will have to be enough," she said. "I have to find Sweetie."

"Surely she is adapted to this sort of weather. And with all the mud puddles, she'll probably be enjoying one right now."

"It's a myth that pigs are dirty," she said as they neared the house. Nicholas had never been so glad to be close to home. "They only wallow in mud on hot days to cool off. It's chilly today, and she'd have no reason to seek out mud."

Nicholas supposed he had known this, being that he'd spent much of his life at Battle's Peak. But he'd really only ever cared about the horses. Other animals were always about, of course, but he hadn't paid much attention to them.

"The mud certainly does give them a dirty appearance," he pointed out.

"Yes, but they are actually quite clean. Did you know that pigs prefer to eliminate away from their eating and sleeping area? It was far easier to train Sweetie to go outside for her needs than any dog we ever had. Pigs are as smart as dogs, you know," she said, seeming to warm to her subject. "You can teach them tricks and commands, but their intelligence also has a downside."

"Does it?" he asked as they entered the foyer.

"Yes. Sweetie has always been very good at managing latches and gates. That's the reason we gave up keeping her in the barn at night. As soon as she was big enough, she managed to open the door to Catmint Cottage, and we'd find her curled up in my room every morning. Of course, she never learned to close the door, so if we didn't want our door standing open all night, we thought it would be easier just to bring her inside from the start."

Tiggs rushed forward. "My lord, may I take your wet coat and umbrella?"

Nicholas handed the items to the butler. Amelia spotted her maid and asked for a pair of boots.

"You can have the boots," Nicholas said, "after you put on dry clothing."

"I don't have time for that."

Bloody hell, but she was making him work for this. "At least help me up the stairs so I might change then," he said. The request was so uncharacteristic of him that his butler dropped the umbrella with a loud thwack on the marble floor. Nicholas could feel his neck turning red with embarrassment at asking for assistance, but he held his head high.

"Of course," Amelia said, as he'd known she would. She'd never refuse anyone in need. It was an admirable quality, and one he didn't like exploiting. Of course, he liked her coming down with a fever even less.

"Go stoke the fire in your mistress's chamber and lay out dry clothing," Nicholas instructed O'Malley. "And tell my valet to do the same."

Nicholas approached the dreaded stairs and put one hand on the banister. Amelia kept her arm about his other side, providing support. Negotiating the first step was awkward, but once they got the rhythm of it, they moved well together. He found it was actually easier to ascend the steps with her at his side. They turned toward the master bed chamber, and she went with him through his door. His valet took one look at the two of them and made an excuse to depart. Nicholas made a note to give the man a raise. And he'd be even more generous if he managed to see that O'Malley was scarce as well.

The fire was roaring in the hearth, and he and Amelia stepped in front of it. "That does feel much better," she said, moving away from his side to spread her heavy wet skirts.

"You're shivering," he said. "Take a moment to change out of your wet clothes before you go." He worried she would treat him like a child and ask if he would be alright without her—something he deserved after the way he'd behaved for the past quarter hour—but she left his side without any coddling. She used the door adjoining their chambers to exit and when she'd passed through, he heard her calling for O'Malley.

"Where is she?" she seemed to ask herself.

His valet definitely deserved a raise in wages. Nicholas stripped off his own wet coat—mostly wet from Amelia leaning against him in her soaked garments—then went to his boot jack to tug off his boots.

"Oh, damn." He heard Amelia curse in the neighboring chamber.

"Need help?" he asked, opening the door to peer into her chamber. She was still in her wet clothes and seemed to be struggling to unfasten the bodice of the dress herself.

"Could you pull the bell again?" she asked. "O'Malley isn't here, and my fingers are so cold I can't manage the pins myself."

"I'll do it," he said. The look she gave him mirrored the shock he'd felt when the words had come out of his mouth. But then perhaps he was only shocked he'd said the words aloud because surely undressing her again was what he'd intended all along. It was almost all he'd been able to think about since the night before.

"I'm sure O'Malley—"

"I won't have you shivering while we wait for her to return. This might be difficult to believe, looking at me now, but I have undressed a woman or two. I know how it's done. Turn around," he ordered.

She gave him her back, and he made quick work of the fastenings. She was able to slide the sleeves off and then shrug the bodice off. Her back was to him, but he could see she was wet to the skin. Her shift was transparent, showing the outline of her pale upper back.

He reached for the knot of her skirts. It was wet, and he had to work at the tight fabric.

"It's not difficult to believe," she said.

"What's that?" He was concentrating on the blasted knot. He almost had it.

"That you've undressed your share of women. That's not difficult to believe, not with your looks."

Nicholas freed the knot and tugged it loose, causing her skirts to fall to the floor. Of course, that still left the bloody petticoat. He started on that string, which was blissfully tied in an easy bow. One tug and the petticoat was out of the way. "That was before," he said. "And a long time ago."

"Before what?" She turned to look at him, and he couldn't help but drop his gaze to her chest. The stays pushed her breasts slightly upward so that the rounded tops were plump and inviting at the neckline of that sheer shift.

"Before the war," he said, unable to follow the conversation. "Your underclothing is wet," he said, reaching behind her to loosen her stays. The action caused her to step closer, meaning that she was close enough to kiss as her stays fell away. That left her in only her shift and stockings, and one pull would rid her of the shift.

"I should put on a dry chemise," she said, her voice little more than a murmur. "O'Malley put one on the bed."

"Then we'd best get you out of this one."

She nodded, and before he could reach for the ribbon at the neckline, she did. She pulled, and the garment slipped down. He followed its progress as it slid off her arms, down her pale breasts, over her belly and rounded hips, and then down those shapely legs to a puddle on the floor. For a moment, Nicholas forgot he was a cripple. He forgot his fears of rejection. He was a man, a husband, and his wife stood before him in nothing but stockings tied with pretty green garters. His hand went around her bare waist, and he noted her skin was still too cold. He pulled her close to warm her, at least that was his rationale. But as soon as he'd touched her, he'd wanted nothing more than to feel her body pressed against him. He wanted to warm her. He wanted to touch her.

He wanted.

He wasn't certain who kissed whom first, but their mouths came together in a searing kiss that sent a jolt of heat straight through him. There was no wondering if she felt as he did in that moment. Her tongue tangled with his and her arms came around his neck as she stood on tiptoe to press closer to him.

She wanted too.

He deepened the kiss, his hands moving over her warming flesh, tracing the curve of her lower back, the flare of her bottom, the swell of her hip. Then his hands were cupping her breasts, and she was moaning as she had the night before. The sound of her pleasure made him hard, made him want more. He ran his thumbs over the hard points of her nipples, circling them until she seemed to writhe against him. Her tongue stroked in and out of his mouth in an imitation of an act he missed more than he could say. How long had it been? Years now since he'd had a woman in his bed—hell, since he'd touched a naked woman.

Her skin was warmer now and heating rapidly under his touch, and he slid one hand away from her breast, down her belly, and to the soft thatch of curls between her legs. He heard her quick intake of breath and then felt her short nails dig into his shoulder. She wanted him to touch her there.

His fingers slid into the curls and the heat of her was like its own fire. "Yes?" he asked, his fingers itching to explore further.

"Yes," she said, her voice eager and low with desire.

He stroked over the lips of her sex, feeling the wetness there already, knowing he was responsible for it and that she desired him. Well, she desired his touch. He slid one finger inside her hot channel, and she let out a startled, "Oh!" Her muscles clenched around him, and her head fell back. He managed to hold onto her, but he couldn't support her and himself if she lost herself in pleasure. And he intended for her to lose herself in pleasure.

He withdrew his hand, then put both on her hips and began to walk forward, pushing her backward.

"Where are we—" she began.

"The bed."

"Sweetie—"

"You can find her as soon as you're warm."

"I'm warm," she protested.

"Not warm enough."

Her gaze met his, and her eyes darkened at whatever she saw in his face. They reached the edge of the bed, her bottom hitting the mattress. He didn't have to ask her to slide onto it. She pushed up and onto the mattress, and he parted her legs and stepped between them. He thought he might have startled her with his forwardness, but her legs went around his waist, pulling him even closer.

His cock throbbed at the proximity to her sex. He tried to ignore the insistent urge to free himself and plunge inside her. Instead, he wrapped his hand around a section of her hair that had fallen down her back and kissed her. His other hand started a slow exploration of her body again. His mouth followed, kissing her neck and her shoulder then her collarbone. She fell back, catching herself with her elbows, and that was the perfect opportunity to kiss her rounded breasts. She made unintelligible sounds of pleasure as he took a nipple in his mouth and sucked lightly, and the sounds only became more demanding as his hand moved between them and then between her legs again.

She was already open to him, and he need only take a small step back to work a finger inside her. She was hotter and wetter than before, and he used that moisture to slide upward and find that nub hidden in her folds. He slid over it with a fingertip, coating it with dew, and Amelia cried out so loudly that he worried the servants would hear.

And then she fell back, her legs open, and he didn't care about anything at all except making her cry out like that again. She was beautiful. Her curls were the same amber as the hair on her head, and her sex was pink and glistening. He glanced up at her face and found her eyes on his as he admired her.

"You're beautiful," he said. He half expected her to turn modest, and close her legs, but she bit her lip.

"Take off your clothes," she said.

In that moment, he wanted to. He wanted to lie naked with her, exploring, kissing, taking. But he was painfully aware that he was a cripple. Painfully aware that the desire in her eyes would fade when she saw his legs. Painfully aware that he couldn't make love to her as an able-bodied man might.

Instead of undressing, he teased her by sliding his finger in and out, then brushing that nub with his thumb. She bucked, her eyes closing in what appeared to be bliss. It wouldn't take much to bring her to climax, but he didn't want this to be over that soon. He wanted to make it last.

Instead of finding that nub of pleasure again, he teased her by moving closer, circling round the center of her pleasure then moving away again. Every time he inched closer, she writhed and bucked. He bent at the waist and kissed her upthrust breasts. Her hands speared into his hair, pulling his head down so he could feast on her. She seemed to relish his mouth on her, seemed to want more.

Her reaction was a revelation to him. He'd known she wouldn't be a virgin, but he also knew she had little experience. Not to mention, she'd been secluded in the countryside caring for her father since the age of sixteen. But this was no demure country miss. This was a woman who wasn't afraid to embrace pleasure and wring every last ounce of it.

He had to take control or lose his own completely. Gently, he pushed her back on the bed and when she protested, he silenced her by moving his mouth to the underside of her breast and then her abdomen below. He felt her tense, could almost hear her thinking, hear her wondering what he would do next.

He kissed a path to her navel then began to move lower. In his peripheral vision, he saw her hands lift then fall then lift again in uncertainty. "You're wondering where I'll go next," he said, his mouth on the rise of her lower belly. "You're wondering if I'll do what you've only heard whispered about."

He moved lower still, kissing and licking a slow path to those amber curls.

Her hands fisted in the bedclothes.

"You didn't know whether to believe there was a man who would touch a woman with his tongue. Who would touch *you* with his tongue." He kissed her curls, the soft springy hair tickling his cheek as he moved to one leg and kissed the juncture at her thigh and then the other. "You wondered if you would like it," he whispered. He put his mouth just above her sex and looked up at her. Her dark eyes were impossibly large, saucers of chocolate.

"Shall I satisfy your curiosity?"

"*Yes*." The single word had so much need behind it that he almost felt pity for her. *Almost*. The more she suffered now, the more she would feel in a few moments.

He lowered his mouth and laved his tongue along her seam. She would have bucked and set him off balance if he hadn't grasped her hips and held her in place. He took his time exploring her. Her skin was petal soft and smelled faintly of the soap she used for washing, and underneath, the scent of woman. The scent of her.

He used his tongue to part her folds and tasted the slightly salty evidence of her desire for him. And then slowly, very slowly, he inched upward, closer to her clitoris, closer to where he knew she wanted him. When he tapped it with his tongue, she said his name like a prayer. "Nicholas."

He touched her again, lightly, so very lightly, until what sounded like a sob escaped her lips. Her body was vibrating beneath his fingertips, her dawning pleasure like the crackle of lightning just before a storm. He flicked his tongue over her again then, just as she tensed for another wait, he circled her, surprising her so that her body jerked. "Yes," she moaned, and he circled her again. "Yes." That sounded like a plea. He circled her a third time. "Oh, *yes.*"

Her taut body was so tight he felt it might snap at any moment. He could have drawn this out. He could have moved away from that swollen nub and let her pleasure build. But he wanted to see her climax. He wanted to know what she would look like, what she would sound like.

And so he slid his tongue over her again and felt her soar off the cliff. He worked her then, pushed her up and up as his tongue raked over her. He lifted his eyes and saw her head was thrown back, the tips of her breasts dark cherries thrust upward. And then she broke and cried out. Her head snapped forward, and he saw her face. In that moment, he almost forgot what he was doing. She was beautiful, so beautiful. Her cheeks were rosy, her lips red and plump, her eyes wide and dark. She cried out again, her body giving a last jerk of pleasure. And then she was floating down, and he wanted so badly to climb onto the bed and pull her into his arms. She would be warm and soft and drowsy.

But it wasn't so easy to climb into a bed, and if he tried, she would want to help him and concern would replace pleasure on her features and the moment would be lost.

To his surprise, she pushed herself up and put her arms around him. Her head rested on his chest, her legs on his hips. He pulled her close, feeling the softness of her loosened hair against his hands and the rapid staccato of her heart.

He wanted to say something. He'd never felt the need before, but she wasn't a merry widow or an actress. This was his wife. But what to say? Some declaration of feeling seemed the thing, but he couldn't tell her he loved her. She'd know it wasn't true. They barely knew each other. She didn't love him any more than he loved her.

Yet.

The thought came unbidden, and he pushed it away almost as quickly. He didn't want to think about falling in love with her or her falling for him. Too late, he reminded himself he had wanted to keep the marriage platonic—separate bed chambers. Fat lot of good separate bed chambers did if he came into hers and performed cunnilingus on her.

Now she'd want more, want this again, and then he would want and when his guard was down, she'd be reminded of what he really was. She wouldn't want him then and it would be too late for him to put his feelings back in the hat box and stow them away. Better to never open that box and keep the hat safely on a shelf.

He stepped out of her arms. "You must be freezing," he said.

"I'm perfectly warm," she insisted. "Come lie beside me."

Already she was asking for things he couldn't give. "You'd better put on a robe before you catch a chill." There was one hanging precariously off the corner of the bed, and he stepped to the side and lifted it. "Here."

He handed it to her, and she stared at it for a long moment before finally taking it. Nicholas stepped away, turning to give her privacy as she pulled the robe on. It had been only a few seconds before he heard quick footsteps outside the door. A quick tapping sounded, and he glanced back at Amelia. She had the robe on but the color in her cheeks and the wildness of her hair made it quite clear what they had just been doing.

"What is it?" she called.

"My lady!" The voice belonged to O'Malley, and it had the high pitch of excitement which was uncharacteristic for the veteran lady's maid. "They've found your pig."

"Sweetie!" Amelia practically leapt off the bed and, hand holding the robe closed, raced to the door, and yanked it open. "Is she well? Is she hurt?"

The maid took one look at her mistress then darted a gaze to Nicholas behind her, and her cheeks colored. "I'm so sorry to interrupt."

"O'Malley, you were saying they found Sweetie," Amelia said, grasping the servant's arm before she could step away. "Where is she?"

"Oh, that." The maid seemed to try and not look at Nicholas. "It seems she had never left. She'd found a way to open the door to the tack room and had curled up in a pile of horse blankets there. Bowen said they might not have found her so soon, but she was snoring so loudly one of the grooms went to investigate."

"I should go and see her," Amelia said.

"Er—" The maid looked at him again. "Should I help you dress?"

That was his cue to go. "Yes," he said. "And make sure she wears something warm." He moved back toward his chamber. "Good day," he said, closing the door between them.

So much for that declaration of feeling.

Twelve

"Now, isn't this better than sitting in your chamber all day?" Amelia asked her mother as they sat on a bench near the fountain.

Mrs. Blackstock patted her hand. "It's lovely, but it's exhausting. I'm ready to go back inside."

Amelia bit back a sigh. They had only been in the garden a quarter hour, and it had taken her at least an hour to cajole her mother out of bed and then another half hour to help O'Malley dress her. She had to remind herself that though the progress might be slow, this was progress.

Amelia patted her mother's hand. "Let's sit five more minutes, then I promise I will accompany you inside. We can both have a nap."

Amelia did want a nap, though it was only eleven in the morning. Even though Sweetie had been found and was hale and healthy, Amelia hadn't slept well the night before. No wonder, considering what had happened between Nicholas and herself yesterday morning. That interlude alone might have kept her awake and thinking, but the fact that she hadn't seen her husband the rest of the day had not helped.

She'd been so happy after he'd brought her in from the rain. Amelia had thought it might take weeks or months to break down his barriers and convince him they could be more than polite strangers. And then he'd stripped her naked and pleasured her on her bed and—

She dug her fingers into the wood of the bench and stared, unseeing, at the greenery around her.

She hadn't realized how much she'd wanted him to touch her until he was touching her. And then once his mouth was on her neck, her breasts, her belly, she couldn't get enough of him. She'd heard some of her friends who were young wives hint at what Nicholas had done to her, and she'd thought if a man ever put his mouth between her legs, she would be mortified.

But she hadn't been mortified at all. He'd made it seem like the most natural thing in the world and that her reaction was exactly what he'd wanted. It wasn't until later that she'd thought back to her reaction and second guessed it. In the moment, she had just reacted. She'd liked the way he made her feel, and she embraced the pleasure. But perhaps he wanted a wife who was more modest and less…er, enthusiastic.

He knew he hadn't married a virgin, but perhaps he wanted her to behave as one?

These were the thoughts that kept her tossing and turning until the wee hours of the night. Those thoughts and the desire to sneak into his chamber and beg him to do it all again.

More than five minutes had passed as she and her mother sat in companionable silence on the bench, and Amelia finally took her mother's arm. "Shall we?" she asked.

They rose and started back toward the house. Out of the corner of her eye, Amelia thought she saw a glint of a golden head, but when she turned, no one was there. Where was Nicholas? In the stables? Should she go to him or let him come to her? *Would* he come to her?

She had to believe he would. She didn't think he would have pleasured her as he had if he didn't feel anything for her, if he didn't want her. And she suspected he wanted her quite a lot to have taken the time and care that he did because he hadn't just brought her to climax. He'd teased and tortured her until she was practically begging for it. The end result had far surpassed her quite limited experience. Her body had thrummed for hours afterward. It was still humming, reminding her that she wanted him to do it all, and more, again.

Her mother was far more compliant returning to her chamber than she had been leaving it, and it took very little to coax her back into bed. She fell almost immediately into a light sleep, and Amelia sat and watched her with worry. Though she had improved the last few days and the doctor had been pleased with her recovery, Amelia still didn't understand why she should be so weak and lethargic. She was still a young woman, just over fifty, and yet she acted as though she were thirty years older. Amelia was beginning to wonder if she would ever again glimpse the person her mother had been before her father's death.

She yawned and decided she would take the nap she'd promised herself. But as she approached her bed chamber, she saw that Florentia was waiting for her outside. And she was holding a letter.

"There you are," Florentia said. "I was hoping you might come this way. Look what arrived."

Amelia took the card reluctantly. It was another acceptance to the house party and this one was from Lieutenant-Colonel Draven and Mrs. Draven. Amelia realized where she had seen Draven's name most recently. One of the letters the vicar had given her had been addressed to him. She remembered the name because she'd seen it in the local papers before. Colonel Draven was a hero from the war, and he'd been Nicholas's commanding officer. Being that Lord Nicholas was considered one of their own, all of Hungerford had known Draven's name and often gathered to discuss the exploits of Draven's troop and speculate on the role their own Lord Nicholas of Battle's Peak might be playing.

Amelia now knew where she had seen the Duke of Mayne's name as well. It had also been in that stack of letters.

"I suppose you know nothing of this," Florentia said, her tone accusing.

Amelia looked up. "I have an idea. I think I know who might have invited these guests to a house party."

Florentia frowned. "Who?"

"I want to confirm it first, and then I promise we will deal with it together." Amelia started away. She'd ask the housekeeper which chamber was the vicar's and start by confronting him.

"Amelia," Florentia called after her. "It really wasn't you?"

"No," Amelia called over her shoulder. "It really wasn't."

She found the housekeeper in her office belowstairs. She told Amelia which chamber the vicar inhabited, but before Amelia could head that way, a footman pulled her aside.

"My lady, forgive me for detaining you, but I couldn't help but hear that you are looking for the Vicar Osgood."

"Yes, that's right, James."

He straightened. "You know my name?"

"I should hope I know everyone's name by now," she said. "I've been here almost a fortnight." Had it really been that long? It seemed like only yesterday that she'd married. Of course, in some respects it also felt like ten years before. "But you were saying something about the vicar."

"Oh, yes, my lady. He is not in his chamber. My sister is the chambermaid for that room, and she was complaining about the state it's in. She's in there now, still straightening up."

"I see. Where is he? Do you know?"

"I believe someone mentioned seeing him slip into the library."

"Thank you, James." Amelia lifted her skirts and hurried toward the library. The door was closed when she reached it, but she knocked lightly and then pushed it open. For a moment, she hoped she might see her husband at his desk, but the desk was empty. The couch was not. The vicar was sprawled on the dark velvet furnishing, looking much more like a debauched rake than a vicar. His dark hair spilled over his forehead, his violet eyes were sleepy, and his clothing was slightly rumpled—just enough to make a woman want to reach over and straighten it.

Amelia kept her hands at her side. "Vicar."

"Lady Nicholas." He rose to his feet, but in a leisurely manner. He moved far more languidly than any vicar she had ever known moved.

"You're not really a vicar, are you?" she blurted out.

He lifted a brow, making him look very rakish indeed. "No, I'm not. I'm a rector."

"Rubbish. Who are you really? More importantly, why are you inviting people to a house party neither Lady Florentia nor I know anything about?"

He clasped his hands behind his back, looking bored rather than worried at her questions. "I have no idea what you mean, my lady. House party?"

He was not a good liar. If she'd had to guess, that was likely because he'd had little experience with lying. He was so handsome and charming, he probably never needed to dissemble to get his way.

"Mr. Osgood—if that is your name—a few days ago you handed me a stack of correspondence to mail. I did so. In the process I happened to note the names of several of those to whom you addressed your correspondence. Two of those people have now accepted in response to an invitation. I can only assume you sent the invitation."

"That wasn't an invitation I sent," he lied.

She put her hands on her hips. "Then what was it?"

"It was...hell's teeth. I'm no good at this."

"No, you're not. You might as well tell me the truth."

"Well, I can't do that, now can I?" He seemed to be speaking to himself more than her. "Might we sit? It's too early for all of this standing at attention."

"It's noon," Amelia said, but she gestured for him to return to the couch, and she took the chair opposite. "Now, who are you really?"

"I'm not a clergyman."

"I've worked that out for myself. You're not from Yorkshire either. Your accent, when you remember it, is all wrong."

He drew back. "Now I take offense at that. I practiced that accent. It's perfect. Listen. *How do*? I dare you to do better."

Amelia stared at him. He appeared serious, but she was not about to enter into a competition for who had the best accent. Besides, she had already heard him speak enough to discern other information about him. "You're a gentleman."

"I never said that."

"You don't have to. Your actions and your words speak for you. Are you really a friend of my husband's?"

Now he looked offended. "Of course. Nickers and I have known each other for years. And years."

Amelia tried to remember the other names on the correspondence he'd given her. She thought she remembered a Lord Jasper Grantham and a Mr. Duncan Murray. She knew she had seen Colonel Draven. Were the others members of Draven's troop? Could the man before her be part of that troop? It was difficult to imagine him a soldier.

"Don't tell me you fought with my husband in the war," she said.

"Hell's teeth, but you are good. I can't take it anymore. You've tortured it out of me."

Amelia shook her head. "I didn't touch you, sir."

He waved a hand. "My story is torture, and as much as I dislike contradicting a lady, I will stick to it."

"Who are you?"

"Oh, no. I can't reveal that. Not even under pain of death."

She gave him a long stare, and he grimaced.

"I will stand strong," he said, voice strained.

"Sir, did you or did you not invite your fellow soldiers here for a house party?"

"I did, and I'm not sorry."

Amelia spread her arms. "But why would you do that? If you do know my husband as well as you claim, you must know that he prefers solitude and surely does not want an influx of people here."

"Yes, well, it's for his own good."

"You did this for his own good?"

"Mostly, yes. Well, partly."

Amelia closed her eyes and tried to hold on to a semblance of patience. "Does Lord Nicholas know what you have done?" she asked.

"Not yet," he said.

"And when did you plan to tell him?"

"Er—when the guests arrived? Now, hear me out, my lady." Amelia had risen and was of half a mind to throttle the false clergyman. He spoke quickly. "If I told him before the guests arrived, he would have told me to call it off."

"Then you should call it off."

"No, I should not. The men I've invited are our closest friends. We've lived through experiences no one else can understand. We've saved each other's lives many times over. They are who he needs right now."

"Needs for what?"

"To let go of the past. He hasn't done that yet. He was sent home from the war before the rest of us because of his injury. He never had the chance to celebrate the victory with us. He never had the chance to mourn our dead and celebrate our lives."

"Surely he has seen you since the end of the war."

"He's seen a few of us at the Draven Club but not all of us together. We haven't all been together since…I don't know when. Unfortunately, this may be our last chance."

Amelia slid back into her seat. "Why is that?"

He looked at the door to the room and said, "Go ahead and tell her, Florrie."

To Amelia's amazement, the door opened, revealing Lady Florentia standing just outside. She'd been eavesdropping!

"Don't call me *Florrie*," she said, her tone icy. "You know I've always hated that."

Amelia looked from the false vicar to her sister-in-law. "Do you two know each other?"

"We do," Lady Florentia said. "Lady Nicholas, allow me to introduce Mr. Rafe Beaumont, youngest son of the Earl of Haddington and a traitor to his king and country."

"Now wait a moment," Rafe said, standing. "I never betrayed my king."

"And your country?"

He shrugged. "Depends who you ask." He made a brushing away gesture. "The horsehair heads wanted a spy so they could parade her about and make long, tedious speeches. In the end, they would have discovered what I had—she hadn't given the French anything they didn't already know."

"But they weren't able to ascertain that since you helped her escape the country." Lady Florentia closed the door behind her and spoke harshly but quietly so the servants would not hear.

Beaumont spread his hands. "What was I supposed to do? I love her."

That admission seemed to take Florentia by surprise. "I never thought I'd hear you say that about any woman."

"She's not any woman, she's my wife and the mother of my son."

"Oh, Lord. I can't imagine *you* a father."

"Just keep it in mind when you think about turning me in."

"I'm not turning you in. At this rate, I won't need to."

"Pardon me," Amelia broke in. "I'm quite confused."

Florentia crossed to her and took her hand. "I can imagine. Let me begin by apologizing to you. I accused you of planning this house party and did not trust you when you said you knew nothing of it. I am sorry for doubting you. That was uncharitable of me. I do hope you will forgive me."

"Of course. There is nothing to forgive."

Florentia squeezed her hand. "You are very generous, and I don't deserve it. But let me explain further. As I am sure you have worked out, Mr. Beaumont is a friend of my brother's. They knew each other before the war and fought in it together. But Mr. Beaumont fled England a couple of years ago before he could be taken into custody for treason."

"Treason?"

Beaumont snorted. "It sounds worse than it was."

Florentia gave him a narrow look. "Regardless, he is obviously supposed to be hiding here at Battle's Peak under the quite flimsy persona of Vicar Osgood."

"There's nothing flimsy about my persona."

"In any case," Florentia said, ignoring him, "you can see why it is a very bad idea to invite a group of people here. Not only will my brother dislike a party, it risks Mr. Beaumont's life." She straightened her shoulders. "I will send letters immediately, calling off the event."

"No!" Amelia and Beaumont cried in unison.

Florentia started. "I know why *he* does not want it called off, but why do you wish to continue with it?"

"Because I think Mr. Beaumont made a good point. Lord Nicholas never did have a chance to, in essence, finish the war. He was sent home before our victory and then when we celebrated at home, he was in recovery from his injuries. I think Mr. Beaumont is right that this will be good for him."

"Thank you," Beaumont said, looking smug.

"Forgive me if I disagree," Florentia said, "but I know him better than either of you. A house party is *not* good for him."

"He's a grown man," Amelia said, "why don't we simply ask him?"

"No!" Florentia and Beaumont said together.

Amelia gave them both annoyed looks. "Why not?" She looked at Florentia. "Because it will upset him?" she said, then looked at Beaumont. "Because he might say no?"

"Precisely," Beaumont said. "And this is the part where I make another confession."

"Save me," Florentia muttered, sinking into a chair.

"Go on, Mr. Beaumont," Amelia said.

"This may be my last chance to see all of my friends. When I left for—er, parts unknown—I thought it would be temporary. I thought I would be home in a year or so. But coming home now I realize this misunderstanding may not blow over as quickly as I'd hoped."

"Treason never does," Florentia muttered.

"This may be my last chance to see the Survivors—that's the name we gave ourselves," he explained. "Since we came home while others were lost."

Amelia glanced at Florentia and was surprised to see that she looked moved.

"I want the opportunity to see my friends one last time," he said. "All of us together. I want to tell them goodbye and thank you. I never had the chance to tell them thank you."

"If you go on with this rubbish, I will cast up my accounts," Florentia said. Amelia gasped, and Florentia rolled her eyes. "He just wants to have a party. Beaumont is about as sentimental as that vase." She pointed across the room to a pedestal with a large vase atop it.

"I can see nothing I say will sway you," Beaumont said, his tone laden with the frost of one deeply offended. "In response, I throw my support behind Lady Nicholas's suggestion. Let's ask Nickers."

"He will say no," Florentia predicted.

"We won't know until we ask," Amelia said. "But we can't exactly ask him tonight at dinner. We must continue to keep Mr. Beaumont's true identity hidden from the servants."

"We'll make a secret rendezvous!" Beaumont said. "Do you have an old crofter's cottage about?"

"No," Florentia said.

"An abandoned dower house?"

"No."

"What about Catmint Cottage?" Amelia suggested.

"That doesn't sound very mysterious," Beaumont said.

"That's actually a good suggestion," Florentia said. "There's only your one servant there at night."

"Yes, and tomorrow is Sunday. She usually goes to visit her great aunt and doesn't return until Monday midday."

"Then we meet there tonight," Florentia said. "I'll tell Nicholas I've seen the vicar and want to have a private word with him about the man. He'll know I recognized Beaumont right away."

"Not necessarily. I had a very good disguise."

Florentia sighed. "Mr. Beaumont, I won't flatter you by saying what you already know. Your face is unmistakable."

"I think that's a compliment," he muttered.

"So we are in agreement then?" Amelia said. "We meet tonight after dinner at Catmint Cottage?"

"You two go over after dinner," Florentia said, "and I will bring Nicholas shortly thereafter."

"Let's hope this works," Beaumont said.

"Let's hope it doesn't," Florentia said. "If it does, we have to figure out where to put eleven men and their families and servants."

***

Nicholas did not feel like sparring with Florentia this evening. He'd known she would most likely see Rafe at some point and confront him about their guest. He just wished it hadn't been today. He had enough on his mind without having Florentia try and worry him about Rafe being discovered before he could return to the United States.

For one, he had to come up with a plan for how to keep from breaking down the door between his chamber and Amelia's and doing what he wanted with her. He'd only barely restrained himself the night before. How would he resist tonight? The problem, he told himself, was that he didn't even need to break down the door. She would have left it unlocked. And she would welcome him into her bed. She wanted him, and that made everything that much more difficult.

They'd taken the coach the short drive to Catmint Cottage and since the coachman and outriders were nearby, neither Nicholas nor Florentia discussed Rafe on the ride over. But as soon as they arrived at the cottage and sent the coach away, Nicholas prepared for a tongue lashing. They stepped into the vestibule of Catmint Cottage, and Nicholas immediately said, "I can explain."

"I've already done that, Nickers," said Rafe, stepping out of the dining room.

"It's no wonder she found you out," Nicholas groused, following his sister toward the candlelight spilling out of the dining room. "You refuse to stay in your chambers."

He stepped into the dining room and then halted. The room had been lit by candles, and at the other end of it was Amelia, dressed in blush pink with an anxious expression on her face.

Rafe closed the door behind Nicholas.

"What is this about?" Nicholas asked, looking from Amelia to his sister to Rafe. "Does my wife know who you are as well?"

"She does," Amelia answered.

"You're even worse at this than I thought," he told Rafe.

"We've brought you here for a reason," Florentia told him. "Mr. Beaumont has a confession to make."

"Do I need a drink before I hear this?" Nicholas asked.

"That might be best," Amelia said, bringing him a glass of port.

"Do you want to sit?" Rafe asked.

"No." He preferred to stand, one hand on the back of a chair to keep his balance and the other holding the port.

"Then I hope you don't mind if I do." Rafe sat as did Florentia. Amelia stood beside Nicholas. He appreciated the gesture even if her presence distracted him. Already he'd begun to plan how he might return home with her alone in the coach.

"I've done something you might not like," Rafe said.

"That's nothing new."

"This is even more egregious," Florentia added.

He'd already surmised that being that the four of them were gathered clandestinely to discuss whatever it was Rafe had done now.

"Just spit it out," Nicholas said.

"I've invited Draven's Dozen for a house party."

"All of them? Where?"

"Battle's Peak," Florentia supplied.

Amelia took the port from his hand as it had begun to slip.

"All of them?"

Rafe nodded. "All ten of them and Draven himself. Plus wives and children, where applicable."

"I don't understand. You've invited the entire troop to my home for a house party. Without my consent?" He looked at Florentia. "Did you know about this?"

"Not until the acceptances began to arrive. Initially I blamed Lady Nicholas, but she was as innocent as I in this."

Nicholas felt the anger rising up, and he took his port back and sipped it. He wasn't sure if he was angry because Amelia had been blamed for Rafe's idiocy or because he had known Rafe was an idiot and had allowed him to stay at Battle's Peak regardless. He should have known something like this would happen.

"Just hear me out before you begin yelling," Rafe said.

"I don't yell."

"Right. Well, before you say no."

"I don't think there is anything you could say that would convince me, but you are welcome to try."

Rafe opened his mouth to speak, but Amelia's voice was the one Nicholas heard. "It's his last chance," she said.

Nicholas turned to her. "Pardon?"

"He'll be leaving the country again soon, and this is his last chance to see all of his friends. Perhaps for the rest of his life."

Nicholas didn't believe that. Rafe would be back. He was as British as they came. He would find a way to return to his home. But there was no guarantee it would be anytime soon. No guarantee when he did return everyone would be hale and hearty and able to gather.

"That's right," Rafe said belatedly. "I might never have another chance."

How was Nicholas supposed to oppose that argument? How could he sentence Rafe to never seeing his friends again? He was already facing the very real possibility that he would never see his parents alive again. And Rafe was no traitor. He'd done nothing but save the woman he loved from capture—a woman who was only suspected of wrongdoing.

"There's another reason," Rafe said. "With the war several years behind us now, we are all moving on with our lives. We'll never forget the bond we have, but perhaps now is the time to bid farewell to the past and embrace the future."

Nicholas narrowed his eyes. "You have definitely been spending too much time alone."

Rafe laughed. "I know. Another week and I'll be writing philosophy."

"I wouldn't go that far," Florentia muttered.

Amelia put her hand on Nicholas's arm, and he glanced at her in surprise. It was such a comforting, supportive gesture. He wasn't used to having anyone standing at his side and supporting him. "You don't have to agree," she said quietly. "We've only received three acceptances. We can still call it off." She looked up at him, her chocolate brown eyes large and full of understanding. A man could melt in those eyes.

"You could call it off," Rafe said. "Or you could put on your dancing shoes and prepare to dance with the devil."

Nicholas slanted his gaze toward Rafe. The phrase was one they'd always used before going into battle or embarking on a dangerous mission. The fact that Rafe was using it now proved he understood how difficult this situation was for Nicholas. Even before his injury, he hadn't enjoyed large groups of people. Several hours at a ball or a dinner party was enough to tide him over for days. He liked quiet and solitude.

In the army, he had cherished the friends he made and grown quite close to several of the men from Draven's troop. Not all of those men had returned from battle. But those who had—Ewan Mostyn, Neil Wraxall, Phineas the Duke of Mayne, Colin FitzRoy, Jasper Grantham, Nash Pope, Duncan Murray, Stratford Fortescue, Rowden Payne, Aidan Sterling, Rafe Beaumont, and Draven himself—were like brothers to him. Though he might prefer them one-on-one, as opposed to in a large gathering, Rafe was right—damn him. Perhaps they all did need the opportunity to say farewell to the era of the Survivors and begin anew.

"If I agree to this—"

"Huzzah!" Rafe shouted.

Nicholas held up a hand. "*If* I agree to this, I want no part in the planning. I don't want to be consulted on who will sleep where and what activities everyone will partake in."

"Florrie and I will handle everything," Rafe said. Florentia looked less than pleased at that declaration. "In fact, we will walk back now and discuss."

"It's the middle of the night," Florentia argued.

"I'll keep you safe." Rafe rose. "We'll have them send the coach back to collect you two." He gestured to Nicholas and Amelia.

"I can wait here for the coach," Florentia said.

Rafe shot her a glare. "Sometimes couples newly married like time alone," he said out of the corner of his mouth. "So let's leave them alone."

Florentia rolled her eyes. "Fine. If I'm attacked by wild beasts, I'm throwing you to the wolves." She took Rafe's proffered arm.

"Are there wolves in this part of England?" Rafe asked as he led her out of the dining chamber.

"He sounds a bit worried," Amelia said when they were gone.

"He's not as brave as he pretends to be."

"I don't know," she said, moving toward the decanter of port. "He's risked his life to return to England. That takes daring."

"Or idiocy." He shook his head when she lifted the decanter. "No more for me."

She set the decanter back on the sideboard and an uncomfortable silence descended. Nicholas searched for a topic. "How was your mother today?"

"She seemed a bit better," Amelia said, brightening. "We sat in the garden." She looked down at the sleeve of her dress and toyed with the lace. "She did not want to stay outside for long, but I think the fresh air is good for her."

"That seems promising."

"Yes, but the real progress has come when she talks about my father. I don't think her melancholy will lift until she's able to let him go."

"You don't think she has already?" he asked.

She shook her head. "She cared for him every day, almost every hour for the last ten years. And then he was simply gone. She feels as though there is a void in her life. I understand because I felt it too at first. It's a strange, rudderless feeling when all of a sudden the tasks you spent every waking moment attending to are suddenly gone. But for her, it's even worse. They loved each other, you see." She looked at him, and for just a moment Nicholas couldn't catch his breath. "They didn't start their marriage in love, but they grew to love each other. He was the other part of her, and now she mourns not only his death but the death of that part of herself."

Nicholas couldn't help but wonder what it would be like to have a love like that. To feel as though the other person was another piece of you. For so long, he'd felt completely alone. It seemed no one could understand the pain of losing his mobility and losing his greatest passion—riding—in one fell swoop. But he wasn't alone in his loss. Amelia had suffered loss as well. It was not the same loss, but it helped explain why he felt a connection with her.

That and he wanted to tear her clothes off every time he was in the same room with her.

"You are a good daughter," he said. "You seem to understand what she needs and have the patience to help guide her through it."

She smiled. "Thank you. I feel as though I am fumbling in the dark most of the time, but I keep trying." She lifted her gaze to him. "In addition to being a good daughter, I would like the opportunity to be a good wife."

She took a step closer, and Nicholas felt his throat go dry.

"Should we discuss what happened yesterday?" she asked. "Or should we forget the words and just do it all again?"

Thirteen

Amelia could hardly believe she had been so bold as to suggest Nicholas ravish her again. But then he didn't seem inclined to do so on his own. Perhaps he needed a slight nudge. He was staring at her, and she wasn't certain if that was a good sign or a bad one. She counted to five in her mind, and when he still didn't speak or make any move toward her, she decided she'd miscalculated. He probably detested forward women. Or perhaps he regretted what had happened between them and did not want to be reminded. "I'm sorry," she began. "I shouldn't have—"

He reached out and pulled her to him. She hadn't been expecting the gesture, but her body was drawn to his, and she went easily into his arms. He'd been standing behind a chair, and now he positioned her between the chair and himself, placing his hands on the chairback, effectively enveloping her.

"You are a good wife," he said, his voice gruff.

Amelia looked up at him. That was the encouragement she'd needed. "I'd like to be a better one. I'd like to be your wife in truth."

"That's not possible," he said, but he didn't move back. This close she could feel the evidence of his arousal.

"It feels possible," she said, nudging her hips forward slightly so that her pelvis brushed against his hard length. He inhaled sharply but lowered a hand to hold onto her hip before she could repeat the gesture.

"Amelia, you don't understand."

She wrapped her arms around his neck, determined not to let him keep her at arm's length as usual. "Then help me understand," she said, kissing him gently. "I want you." The words were so forward that her cheeks burned. But she had learned that life could be short and unpredictable. She had to seize the moment. "And I think you want me." She pulled back and looked into his sky-blue eyes. "Do you?"

"Never doubt it," he said. His hand tightened on her hip, and he kissed her. Though she could feel the strength of his desire, he held it back and kissed her gently. It was a coaxing kiss, a sensual kiss. It was a kiss that left her breathless. He pulled back slowly. "But I can't give you what you want."

He stepped back, leaving her wanting. Leaving her feeling cold and lonely without his closeness.

She'd lain awake considering what the problem might be the night before, and now she tried to work out how to broach the subject. "Will you tell me why?"

"How can you not know?" he asked, obviously frustrated by her.

"Is it a disease?" she asked, as that was the reason she had settled on after tossing and turning.

"A disease?"

"I thought you might have visited a brothel and caught one of those unmentionable diseases."

He blinked and then his lips quirked so that he was almost smiling. "No. I haven't visited a brothel, and I don't have the pox. Or any other of those conditions. Do I really have to spell it out for you?" His expression turned to anguish, and Amelia wished she knew what it was so she did not have to make him tell her.

"I'm sorry."

He sighed loudly and raked a hand through his hair. "My legs," he said finally, avoiding her eyes. "I'm a cripple."

Amelia waited for the rest of the explanation. Perhaps there was an injury she didn't know about. But when he didn't continue, she said, tentatively, "Is it only your legs that were injured?"

His brows rose. "Isn't that enough?"

"Yes, but..." She wasn't sure how to continue. No one had ever taught her how to have these conversations. Then she remembered what her mother had told her about the early years of her parents' marriage. They had argued and not spoken and turned inward. If nothing else, she did not want to bottle up her thoughts and feelings. She would say them, and she could die of mortification later. "You don't need your legs to bed me," she said quickly. "You only need, er—your manhood." At his look of incredulity, she hastily continued. "But I have very little experience. Perhaps there is something I don't understand."

Nicholas turned his head and looked at her directly. "You're right," he said. "You don't have as much experience, and I shouldn't have assumed you would understand. I shouldn't have been so humiliated that I wouldn't be honest with you. I've hurt you." He reached out and stroked her cheek lightly. "I'm sorry for that."

She grasped his hand. This was why she was so attracted to him. He was so kind and understanding. She just had to push past the thorny exterior to reach the soft interior she adored. "Please don't ever feel humiliated around me," she said. "We should always be honest with each other."

The way he looked at her was like an explorer might gaze at a new species. "It's not so easy for me to be vulnerable," he said.

Amelia took his hand and held it, holding her breath so as not to spoil the moment with too many words. He would tell her the problem, as he saw it, or he would not. She couldn't force it out of him.

"I do need my legs to bed you," he said. "Most positions require a man to use his legs for balance and control."

She only knew of one position, and she could see how Wickersham had used his legs for that purpose. But she had also grown up in the country, surrounded by domesticated animals. They didn't copulate with the male and female lying down and face to face.

"Aren't there other positions?" she asked. "Like farm animals?"

He swallowed hard. She saw his throat working. Was he angry? Embarrassed at her frankness? Aroused? She hoped he was aroused. His hand on hers tightened. "There are other positions." His voice was rough and low. It sent a shiver of need through her, but she resisted pulling him close and kissing him. "That's not the only concern."

She raised her brows, waiting for him to go on.

"My injury is..." He swallowed again as though he were trying to clear a lump from his throat. "It's ugly. Disgusting. If you saw the state of my legs, it would turn your stomach."

"Oh, I doubt that," she said matter-of-factly. "I cared for my dying grandmother and my paralyzed father for years. I'm not one of your Society misses who never so much as emptied a chamber pot. I've emptied hundreds and tended infections, bed sores—"

"I'm your husband, not your patient," he interrupted.

She saw her mistake then. He didn't want to be seen as an invalid. He wanted her to see him as a man and a desirable one.

"I hear the coach approaching. We should douse these candles and go out and meet it." He released her hand and lifted the snuffer, putting out several candles in quick succession. The room was thrown into shadow, the only light left was that flickering from the vestibule. Amelia grasped his arm before he could walk away. She had to say something, do something, to show him she desired him, no matter his injury or she would lose him again, and this time he might retreat out of reach.

He paused, allowing her to hold him, but he didn't turn to look at her.

"My mother told me that our flaws and imperfections can be as endearing as the parts of each other we fancy. There's so much that is perfect about you," she said, hoping he was listening. Hoping her words were penetrating his wall. He had such a stoic look on his face, his expression hard and unyielding. "Your eyes," she said. "Your eyes are like the summer sky, and every time you look at me with them, I want to melt into you. I feel warm all through."

Slowly, he slid his gaze to hers, and she was thankful that it was dark, and she couldn't see how blue his eyes were.

"Your hair too. It's such a beautiful shade of gold. I've imagined running my fingers through it."

She saw a flicker of interest in her words.

"That's not all I've imagined," she said. "Your lips. I've imagined kissing them so many times. I love the way you kiss. I love the line of your jaw and the glint of stubble on it in the sunlight. I'd like to kiss your cheekbones. A man shouldn't have cheekbones like you do. It's not fair." She paused to breathe. "Do you want to know what else I've imagined?"

"Yes." His voice was low and velvet.

"Undressing you," she said, moving closer to him. "Taking your coat off slowly, then your waistcoat, and pulling your shirt over your head until your chest was bare, and I could run my hands over those broad shoulders and down to that narrow waist. Then I'd unfasten your trousers and slip my hands over your buttocks."

With a jolt, he pulled her hard against him, her breasts pressed against his chest. "And what would you do when my trousers fell to the floor, and you saw the state of my legs? You'd pull away in disgust."

This was at the heart of his resistance then. The fear of rejection. How could he really think that she cared what his legs looked like? But fear wasn't always rational. She knew that from experience. She'd always had a fear of spiders. Every time she saw one, she panicked and couldn't seem to stop herself from screaming. She was a thousand times bigger than a spider, and most were harmless. Yet she had an irrational fear of them. She wasn't afraid of beetles or ants or flies. Only spiders. If she spotted one in a room and wasn't able to see it removed, she wouldn't enter that room for days.

Amelia put her arms around Nicholas's neck and tugged his head down. "Let me tell you what I would do when your trousers were around your ankles. Come closer so I can whisper it."

He lowered his head until his ear was next to her mouth, and she allowed her lips to graze his ear, felt him shiver as she breathed lightly against him. "I would start at your ankles and kiss every scar, every imperfection, every bit of your legs."

"No," he said.

"Yes." She didn't allow him to pull away—not that he tried very hard. "I'd work my way up to your thighs, and I'd kiss them too. You'd be hard by then, wouldn't you?"

"Yes." He groaned. She could feel that he was hard now.

"I'd kiss that hardness too. I'd lick you and er—"

"Take me into your mouth," he suggested.

Was that what he wanted? "Yes. That too. Anything you liked. *Everything* you like." She bit his ear lightly, and he groaned again. "Until you feel as much pleasure as you gave me yesterday."

He stood so still, like a stone statue. She could almost hear him thinking things through, trying to balance his desire with his fear. "Give me a chance," she whispered. "I want to do more than imagine."

"Fine." He pulled back, and she almost stumbled as he released her. "If this is what you want."

Amelia rather thought it was what they both wanted, but she wasn't about to quibble over details when she was getting her way.

"Come to my bed when we return. I'll make you my wife."

Before she could throw her arms about him, he walked away. He left her standing in the dark dining room and went into the vestibule. A moment later, while she was trying to still her racing heart, he doused the candles. "My lady, are you coming? The carriage awaits."

Amelia practically ran after him. She'd been waiting as well, and that wait was almost at an end.

***

Nicholas sat across from Amelia in the carriage, his body in a perpetual state of arousal. He was always aware of her when she was near, always catching the scent of crisp green apples or the low ring of her laugh or the flash of her smile. She drew him, like opium drew an addict, and tonight he had lost the battle to resist. He'd been losing it ever since he met her, losing it little by little each day he spent with her. But tonight, the things she'd said, no man could resist the words coming out of her mouth.

She didn't shock him. Widows and actresses he'd bedded had said things far more scandalous. But he expected that from women of their experience. Amelia had little experience and such a sweet, innocent face. Clearly underneath that innocence was a woman who desired more. A woman with needs and wants, and who wanted him to satisfy those desires. He'd never thought he'd have a wife willing to be open about her needs. He expected to marry a pampered young lady who was just past girlhood and who knew nothing of men and wanted to know even less. She'd suffer through the rituals of the marriage bed or be glad to be excused from them, and eventually she'd birth a son or daughter and they could both pursue other lovers.

That was his assumption before his injury. Afterward, he thought he'd never marry. And now he had married a woman, not a girl, and she was not all that shy about what she wanted. The more she told him what she imagined doing to him, the more he wanted her to do those things and do them to her in return. He could keep fighting it, but why?

He'd end it tonight. He'd strip bare and let her see his deformity, and that would be the end of it once and for all. Better to do that now than after he tasted more of her, after she'd got under his skin, and he began to want her more than he did now.

They didn't speak in the coach, and when they arrived home, he escorted her to her door and bid her goodnight. She went inside, giving him a look of promise before O'Malley closed the door. He retreated to his own chambers then and allowed his valet to help him prepare for bed. But instead of lying down, he told his valet to prop him up against the pillows and took up a book he didn't intend to read.

Once the valet was gone, he stripped off his nightshirt and waited. He was naked but the bedclothes covered him to the waist. When Amelia came to him—*if* she came to him—he'd tell her to pull them down so she could see the state of his legs. Then they'd see what happened.

He didn't have to wait long. It had been no more than two or three minutes before he heard her tap lightly on the door and then open it a crack. "My lord?"

"I'm here," he said. Her head appeared first, and her eyes went directly to his bare chest. He watched as her tongue darted out to wet her lips, and then she stepped into the room, closing the door behind her. Her hair tumbled down her back in waves the color of ripe wheat. Her face was freshly scrubbed, her cheeks a bit pink from either the cloth she'd used or her anticipation. She wore a thin robe cinched at the waist and her bare feet peeked out at the hem.

"Are you—?" She gestured to the part of him covered by the bedclothes.

"Naked? Yes."

"Then I'm overdressed." Before he could protest, she unknotted the tie of her robe and let it slip off her shoulders into a puddle on the floor. Then she wore nothing but her thin night rail. And it was quite thin, so transparent he could see the pink of her aureoles and the honey of the curls between her legs through the material.

She came to him, hoisting herself onto the other side of the bed and moving toward him on her knees. She had to tug up her skirts to manage it, and he had more than a glimpse of creamy calf. How the hell was he supposed to think when she came toward him with that smile on her face? He'd had a plan. He'd intended for her to come to his side of the bed and pull back the covers so she could see his legs. But he hadn't even had a chance to suggest that, and now he didn't want to. He didn't want to risk that she'd run away. She paused beside him, still on her knees. Without even thinking, he reached forward and nudged a lacy strap off her shoulder. It fell to her upper arm, tugging the garment down to reveal the top of one breast.

Their gazes met, and Nicholas thought he could feel the spark flare between them.

"May I kiss you?" she asked.

God, yes. But instead of speaking, he pulled her to him and kissed her with a slow, sensual patience that he didn't think he'd be able to maintain for long. "Come here," he said between kisses, and he tugged her on top of him, settling her over his straining erection.

She pulled back, her eyes wide as she felt him nudge her core. "So this is one of the positions you were talking about?" She wiggled, and he grasped her hips and held her still. "Did I hurt you?" she asked, freezing instantly.

"No, but if I'm to have any measure of control, you can't wriggle like that."

"And what if I do?" She wiggled her brows and then shimmied her hips in challenge.

"Then this will be a short night." He knew it would be a short night regardless once she saw his legs.

"I don't care." She reached out and smoothed his hair back. "As long as I'm with you." Her voice held a note of loneliness in it. He hadn't thought that she might be lonely, but he should have. She was in a new house, taken away from the home where she'd lived all her life. He should have been there to help ease the transition. Instead, he'd left her to sleep alone in a bed chamber that probably didn't even feel like her own.

"You're with me now," he said, and slid his hand up her back to cup the back of her neck. She leaned forward and kissed him, her lips sure and needy. The weight of her hair was like a silk skein over his arm, and when he slid his hand down, her back was just as soft and smooth. He should stop this. He should tell her that before they went on, she should see his legs. But he didn't want this to end. It wasn't only that it had been a very long time since he'd been with a woman. It was this woman. He wanted her, only her, *all* of her.

She pulled back and gave him a look he could only describe as saucy. "You would make a good tavern wench with a look like that," he said.

"Do you like tavern wenches?"

"Not as much as I like you." He slid the other strap from her nightrail down her arm, and she rolled her shoulders back allowing the garment to slip lower. Precariously low so that it would take only a nudge to reveal her breasts. Nicholas tried to resist, but his hands had other ideas. He crooked one finger and rested it on the material in the valley of her breasts. And then he lowered his finger and the linen slid down to her waist.

"Oops," she said.

He wanted to say something teasing and lighthearted as well, but he couldn't think. His hands slid up her sides and then cupped her breasts, his thumbs teasing the distended points. She gave a low moan and rolled her neck, letting her head fall back. It was such a sensual movement that his cock actually throbbed in response. He rolled his hips, and she moaned again as his hard cock nudged her core. He wanted the sheets between them stripped away. He wanted to be inside her.

He could still show her his legs. He should show her, but dear God, look at her. How was he supposed to resist her? How was he supposed to put a stop to what was coming next? Nicholas leaned over and blew out the candle beside the bed. The chamber wasn't completely dark, but the fire in the hearth was low and banked and gave off only the weakest glow. He could barely make out her features in the darkness. But he could feel them.

He slid his hands down to the garment at her waist, grasped it, then pulled it up and over her head. He tossed it away then clasped her bare hips. He ran his fingers over her hips, the curve of her bottom, her thighs, then slid his hands to the inside of her thighs. He felt her stiffen in anticipation of his touch. Then, to his surprise, she slid her hands from his shoulders over his chest and down his abdomen. Her own hands paused at the juncture of the bed sheets. Then she rose up on her knees and slid the bedsheets down almost to his knees.

Her hands returned to his abdomen, and he clenched his fingers on her thighs as she made a slow trek down to his groin. Now she paused as well, her hands just a fraction away from where he wanted them, wrapped around him.

He moved his fingers closer to her core, brushing over the dewy skin there, and she followed suit, brushing her hand over the root of his shaft, several fingers lightly touching him. He parted her intimate lips and slid one finger into the seam of her, feeling her heat immediately. She closed her hand around him then moved her hand up to the head of his erection and back down again. Nicholas couldn't stop a groan. She must have felt encouraged because she did it again. If she kept that up, he would spill his seed on her hand, and that wasn't where he wanted to be when he climaxed. Distracting her, he slid a finger inside her then another. Her hand on him stilled as he pushed deeper inside her and found that sensitive nub with the pad of his thumb.

She inhaled sharply, and he felt her inner muscles clench. Her hips moved out of instinct, and he knew that though she might never have experienced this position before, it was made for her. Her hand on his cock moved again, sliding up until her thumb teased a drop of arousal from his head.

"Do you want me inside you?" he asked.

"*Yes*," she said on a breath. "Please."

"Then take me," he said.

She stilled, seeming not to understand. He withdrew his hands and put them on her hips, guiding her body until she rested against his cock. He nudged upward, sliding against her warm channel, and she responded with a similar movement. He lifted her bottom slightly until the head of his cock rested at her entrance. Now it was up to her to take him inside.

"Oh, I see," she said, wonder in her voice as she moved her body down to take a half inch of him.

Now Nicholas was the one who inhaled sharply. He wanted to demand she take more, but more than that, he wanted her to discover the pleasure of their joining at her pace. She slid down another fraction, and Nicholas tried to think of something banal—pastures, corn, horseshoes.

Less tentative now, she surprised him by lowering herself quickly and sheathing him to the root. His hands on her hips tightened, and she let out a surprised gasp. "Is this right?" she asked, her voice breathless.

"God, yes," he said, his own voice low and hoarse.

"What do I do now?"

"What do you want to do?" He knew exactly what he wanted her to do. He knew what he wanted to do to her. He wanted to thrust hard and fast into the heat of her. He could hardly stop himself from doing so. The pleasure of being inside her tight body was making his head spin. "What feels good to you?" he asked. "Whatever you like. I'll like it too."

She moved her hips, pulling back and then taking him deep again. "Do you like that?"

"Yes," he said through clenched teeth.

She did it again, finding her rhythm on the third try, and Nicholas had to concentrate not to dig his fingers painfully into her hips. *Pastures. Corn. Horseshoes…riding.* No, not that image.

"Nicholas," she said, her voice like a breath.

"I'm here," he said. "You feel so good." He couldn't hold back much longer. Her movements had quickened, and he knew if he could last longer, she would find her climax. But he couldn't last much longer, and he wanted to help her to it. He slipped his hand between them, letting his thumb slide against her swollen nub. As she moved, she rocked against his thumb, and her movements became more deliberate until she had him buried deep inside her and she was grinding against him.

"Oh, yes." Her voice would probably carry as would the cries she made, but Nicholas didn't care. He could barely keep his own groans contained. "Oh, Nicholas."

He loved the way she said his name even as he felt her inner muscles tighten and grip him hard. The last of his control slipped away, and he followed her over the edge into pleasure. He was dimly aware of her crying out, of her body bowing back, but mostly he was slammed by his own hard, jolting climax. He couldn't stop a surprised shout as he spilled inside her, his hips pumping into her and lifting her up.

And then he was falling back down, and she falling with him, her body limp as she crumpled against him. Their breaths came fast but in unison, and he lifted a hand to brush it down her bare back. It had been a long time. It had been years since he'd been with a woman, but it hadn't been so long that he didn't remember how the act had felt.

And it had never felt like it had just now. He had never come so hard or been so utterly spent. He could hardly move, and all he wanted was to roll over and gather Amelia in his arms. The feel of her against him was everything—the warmth of her body, the softness of her skin, the sweet fragrance in her hair.

But he couldn't roll over and hold her—not easily at least. His legs were stiff and difficult to maneuver. And now that he was coming back to himself, he realized his left leg was beginning to ache.

"Amelia, could you—"

"I'm too heavy. I'm sorry."

He hated the way she seemed to scramble off him. He hated that she felt the need to be careful with him. He should be the one taking care with her. Instead, he'd ruined the moment by making her feel guilty and worried that she'd hurt him.

She moved away, and he quickly pulled the bedclothes over his legs and up to his waist. He should have showed her before things had gone too far. She'd hate him when she saw his scars and remembered what she'd done with him. But he was selfish and always had too much pride. He'd wanted to pretend he was whole again one last time.

"Where should I…" Amelia began, obviously not certain where she belonged in his bed. It was a large bed with plenty of room for her, but if he allowed her to stay, she might see his injuries in the morning.

If he allowed her to stay, he might want her to stay every night. And then it would be that much harder to adjust to being alone again.

"If you don't mind," he said, trying to keep his voice gentle. "I prefer to sleep alone."

Even in the darkness, he could see the way she tensed. "Of course," she said quickly. "I don't mind." She looked about, probably for her nightrail.

"Over there," he said, gesturing to the floor.

"Thank you." She slid off the bed, and he didn't watch as she retrieved the garment. She paused at the door adjoining their rooms, and he glanced at her then. In the shadows, he could make out that she held the nightgown to her chest.

"Goodnight then," she said.

"Goodnight." And he closed his eyes and didn't open them for a long time after the door clicked shut between them.

Fourteen

Amelia had never been so confused or so hurt. She'd wanted to be with her husband so badly. She'd wanted *him* so badly. For some reason she had thought that once they made love, everything between them would be different. All the distance between them would evaporate.

But now, alone in her chamber, lying in her cold bed, she felt the separation even more keenly. What bothered her even more was that she felt...*used*.

She had not felt used after she had lain with Wickersham. But perhaps that was because she'd had no expectations of him. He'd used her, and she'd used him, and her feelings had not been so much as bruised when he'd left a few days later with his regiment. Why did she feel so awful now, after lying with her husband?

Because she cared about him.

Because she loved him.

Amelia shut her eyes tightly and willed the emotion away. She did not want to be in love with him. She did not want to care for a man who didn't care for her.

He does care for you, that small voice inside her head said.

"It might have been better if he didn't," she told the voice. "Then I wouldn't have hope that he'd come to love me as well."

He's scared, the inner voice said. *He doesn't want to be hurt.*

"I don't want to be hurt either. But I am."

Because she couldn't sleep and she didn't relish another few hours of conversing with herself, Amelia rose and dressed and crept to her mother's room. To her surprise, her mother was not sleeping. She was sitting in bed with a candle lit, paging through the magazine Amelia had brought her earlier.

"Mama, you are awake," Amelia said, closing the door softly, extinguishing her candle, and setting it on the dresser.

"So are you," her mother said, and Amelia was glad to see that her eyes were clear and lucid. They were still sad, the melancholy still lingering, but her mother was present, not lost in her grief or her memories.

"I couldn't sleep and thought I would come and check on you."

"I couldn't sleep either. I probably slept too much this afternoon. But then I rather like being awake in the wee hours. It's quiet and peaceful."

Amelia crossed to the bed and sat on the edge. "You always watched over Papa through the night," she remembered. "I remember waking on nights when he'd had a difficult day and coming out to see you sleeping in the chair beside him, holding his hand." For some reason, the remembrance made her eyes sting and a tear trailed down her cheek.

"What's this now?" her mother asked, putting the magazine aside and gathering Amelia into her arms. It felt so good to have her mother hold her that Amelia burst into harder tears. She buried her head in her mother's bosom and wept. Mrs. Blackstock didn't say anything, but stroked Amelia's hair and patted her back as she had when Amelia had been a little girl.

Finally, her tears subsided, and she said, "I miss him too."

"I know. Of course, you do."

Amelia looked up at her mother. "I don't want to lose you too, Mama. We lost Grandmama and then Papa. I don't want to lose you."

Her mother cupped her face. "You won't lose me."

"Promise?"

"I promise." She patted the space on the bed beside her. "Now come get under the blanket and tell me what else is bothering you."

Amelia felt as though she were eight again, climbing into bed beside her mother after a nightmare. And just as she had all those years ago, her mother gathered her close and held her. She didn't prod any further, and Amelia knew she would wait until Amelia was ready to speak. It was tempting to close her eyes and fall asleep there. She was drowsy now that she'd been comforted and spent all her tears.

Amelia murmured, "The problem is I'm in love with Lord Nicholas."

"I see," her mother said. "And he doesn't love you?"

"He doesn't."

"Not yet," her mother added.

"Not ever. He cares about me."

"Yes, he does. I've seen the way he looks at you, how he speaks to you. He cares about you a great deal. I would not be here if he did not."

"He's a kind man," Amelia agreed. "But he's…afraid." *Afraid* didn't seem the right word, but it was the one that came to mind.

"Oh, that doesn't surprise me."

Amelia drew back. "It doesn't?"

"No. Look where he has come from. Look at what has happened to him. It won't be easy for him to love you back. It's a risk."

Amelia considered this. "His father was a marquess."

"A fact his mother won't let you forget. Your husband grew up in a family that valued appearances more than anything else. Their title, their family name, their status was everything. Those ideas are passed down from generation to generation in order to keep the family name strong and prestigious."

"But Nicholas was injured. He no longer has the perfect appearance."

"The dowager might have groused about him marrying you and pretended it was all for appearances, but she was glad not to have to push him back on the Marriage Mart. She knows others of her class also value appearance over anything else. It's why she allows Lady Florentia to stay here as well."

"What's wrong with Lady Florentia?"

"Nothing except she has no interest in marriage. That's not acceptable to her mother, so she prefers to keep her hidden away and show off her married daughter and her two so-called perfect sons."

"I hadn't considered that his past might be a reason he's afraid to trust me." She looked up at her mother. "We are having a house party."

Her mother's brows rose. "Lord Nicholas agreed to a house party?"

Amelia couldn't tell her about Mr. Beaumont. "Not exactly. But all of his friends from the army are coming. The men he served with under Colonel Draven. They call themselves the Survivors." Amelia put her head on her mother's shoulder again. "He lost so many friends during the war. When he was injured, he had to come home before the end of the war. He never said good-bye to some of the men he served with."

"You think he fears he'll lose you too?"

"He may be afraid to risk it."

"Give him time, my sweet girl. No one can resist loving you."

Amelia laughed. "That's not true."

"I think it is. You'll break down his defenses sooner or later. I know you will."

Amelia smiled and closed her eyes. Her mother blew out the bedside candle and put her arms around her. Amelia began to doze, and the one thought that drifted through her mind was that she very well might win Nicholas over. But she was only human, and she just hoped that when and if he came to love her, his rejection of her hadn't killed her love for him.

***

"Must the pig be present for this committee?" Mr. Beaumont asked, eyeing Sweetie warily.

"I haven't spent any time with her all day," Amelia said, stroking Sweetie's head. Sweetie, in the meantime, was grunting and rooting about, looking for crumbs. Mr. Beaumont, Lady Florentia, and Amelia had gathered in the library after dinner. Lady Florentia had declared it was the best insulated chamber in the house and the servants would find it impossible to eavesdrop. She had tried many times when she was a girl and her father had important men in the library.

"I was never able to hear more than the faint clink of a glass," she'd said. "Even with my ear pressed to the door."

Mr. Beaumont had immediately discarded his large hat upon entering and seemed to have discarded the role of vicar as well. He slouched in his chair with one leg thrown over the arm, a drink balanced on the other arm. Sweetie had ventured close to him, sniffing for any possible morsels in that part of the chamber, but Beaumont had shooed her away, a task he did quite well and which hinted that he had more experience with farm animals than he allowed.

Florentia was seated at the desk, and now she lowered her pen. "These are the responses we have received thus far," she said and lifted the paper. "Colonel Draven and his wife, the Duke and Duchess of Mayne, Lord and Lady Jasper, Mr. Mostyn and Lady Lorraine and their child."

Beaumont perked up at this. "He's bringing the child? Oh, this I cannot wait to see."

Florentia frowned at the interruption then cleared her throat. "Mr. FitzRoy and Lady Daphne, and the one that arrived today, Rowden Payne and his wife."

"Nothing from Duncan Murray?" Mr. Beaumont asked. "Or Nash Pope?"

Florentia frowned. "I read the list of those who have responded."

"Those are the two I worry won't come."

"I worry Mr. Wraxall and Lady Juliana *will* come," Florentia said, "and bring the entire orphanage with them."

Beaumont shuddered. "Children and rats," he said, taking a long drink. "If they bring that whole brood, *I* may not attend."

"Very amusing," Florentia said without any hint of amusement.

Amelia thought she had better intervene before the two of them began to argue. "We don't have much time before the guests begin arriving. We should plan the menus."

"You don't need my help to plan menus," Beaumont said. He was right. Amelia and Florentia would have to meet with Cook for that. Since he was to be seen as little as possible, he would conveniently be excused from that chore.

"Very well, then we can discuss sleeping arrangements. I've spoken to the innkeepers in Hungerford, and I think—"

"I'm no help there either," Beaumont interrupted.

"There appears to be a theme," Florentia observed wryly. "What are you good at, Mr. Beaumont?" She hastily lifted a hand. "Don't answer that."

Amelia glanced at him and saw the wicked glint in his eyes. "I don't mind answering that, actually," he said.

"Mr. Beaumont…" Florentia's tone held a warning.

"I excel at planning diversions. That's what we should discuss, and that's the point of a house party—the diversions."

"I thought the point of a house party was to matchmake single people and give married ones a chance to swap bedmates."

"That too," Beaumont said, "but I don't think there will be any of that at this gathering. You, Florrie, will be the only unmatched person and the Survivors are all intensely loyal and sickeningly in love with their wives. So we must think of other diversions."

"How about a scavenger hunt?" Amelia suggested. "The gardens would be perfect."

"Good idea." Florentia drew out a clean sheet of vellum and noted down Amelia's idea. "And perhaps a tour of the stables. We are known throughout the country as premier horse breeders. Bowen could discuss some of our award-winning steeds."

Beaumont stared at her. "That is your idea of a diversion?"

Florentia crossed her arms. "Some of the guests might enjoy it."

"Fine." Beaumont looked dubious. "But we plan an alternate activity for those of us who are not horsemad."

The door opened, and Amelia's heart jumped into her throat. She half feared it would be a servant. And she half feared it would not be.

"Speaking of horsemad," Beaumont said as Nicholas entered.

Amelia watched as Nicholas's confused gaze swept the room. Despite still feeling hurt at his dismissal of her from the night before, she couldn't look away from him. She was gratified to see his eyes slide over her then back again. Their gazes met before he quickly looked away.

"You have arrived just in time, Nickers," Mr. Beaumont said. "We are planning the diversions for the house party. Your sister thinks the guests will want a tour of the stables."

Nicholas nodded. "We are known throughout the country as premier—"

"Yes, yes." Beaumont waved his hand. "But what shall we do that is actually amusing?"

"Card games?" Florentia suggested.

"A night at the gaming hell," Beaumont said. "We'll have the servants furnish the drawing room like a gaming hell in Town. The footmen can dress as croupiers."

"What about a musical evening?" Amelia suggested, keeping her gaze on Sweetie and away from her husband.

"I have it," Beaumont said. "A show of talents. Each person or couple can display his or her talent. We'll call it a Night at Vauxhall, since the gardens have music, rope walkers, jugglers, and fireworks." He sat forward. "I don't suppose you could arrange fireworks."

Florentia gave him an exasperated look. "This is a house party, not a fête for the King."

"What about a ball?" Nicholas asked. The room went silent as everyone stared at him. His cheeks colored slightly. "I wouldn't dance, of course," he added.

"A ball is a splendid idea," Amelia said, hating that he seemed self-conscious.

"We can call it—"

"A ball," Amelia said before Beaumont could turn it into something else.

"Doesn't seem very creative," Beaumont muttered. "I suppose that's it then. Sprinkle in some nature walks, a picnic, and lawn games, and there you have it." He leaned toward Nicholas. "While the ladies enjoy a nature walk, we'll see if we can convince Ewan and Rowden to give us a demonstration of pugilism."

"I don't want to know anything about bare-chested men fighting bare-knuckled," Florentia said. "It's certainly not part of the official activities."

Amelia had never seen boxing before, and she was rather intrigued. Her mind flashed back to Nicholas's bare chest the night before—his broad shoulders, the toned muscles of his arms, and his flat abdomen...

"Don't you agree, Amelia?" Florentia asked.

She hadn't heard a word her sister-in-law had said. Everyone was looking at her expectantly, even her husband. "Of course," she said, glancing at Nicholas and then away.

"Good, then I shall see you in the morning," she said to Amelia, who still had no idea what she'd agreed to.

"I should crawl back to my hidey-hole," Beaumont said, rising. "I've another letter for Collette," he told Nicholas as he passed him. "Do you think you can manage to have it sent?"

"It's dangerous to send her too many letters. If someone sees them and makes the connection that you are here, we'll all be in jeopardy."

"That's why I've asked you for help," Beaumont said, patting his shoulder. "You always were the best at slipping through enemy lines." He gave Nicholas a slap on the back and opened the door, made a point of looking left and right, then made a dash for it. Lady Florentia sighed.

She had gathered her papers and rose to go, also passing her brother on the way to the door. "Of all of your friends, why must he be the one to take up residence?"

"It's not permanent," Nicholas said, his voice gentler than Amelia was used to hearing it. "And he needs—"

"Our help. Yes, I know. Would that he had asked one of the other Survivors for help. The one in Scotland, for instance." She reached up and kissed Nicholas on the cheek. "Good night," she said. "Good night, Amelia," she said then left them alone.

Alone with Nicholas was exactly the place Amelia did not want to be. "I should take Sweetie back to the barn," she said. Hearing her name, Sweetie looked up and trotted over.

"Have a footman do it," Nicholas said.

"I'd rather—"

But he had already opened the door and called for a servant. Amelia recognized the man as one whom she had seen scratching the pig's ear and slipping her sweets, so she allowed him to take Sweetie, who was eager to go once he mentioned the word *sweets* to the pig.

Nicholas closed the door, and they were alone again.

"If you wanted to speak with me, you might simply ask," she said. "I don't like being managed."

"I haven't managed you."

She raised a brow. "You've done everything but ordered me to stay."

"I object to that characterization."

"Very well. Good night, then."

His hand shot out, catching her arm. She shot him an accusatory look, and he rolled his eyes. "I've been told I can be a bit heavy-handed."

"A bit?"

"Will you stay a moment and speak with me?" he asked.

"If the expression on your face just now is any indication," she said, "that must have been painful."

"The request wasn't painful. The realization that you may refuse me, for good reason, is."

"I won't refuse you," she said, softening. She stepped back so she was in front of him, and his arm dropped away. She missed his touch already, but she would not think of that. "What did you want to discuss?" she asked.

"I…" he began. He turned and paced away for a moment then looked back at her. But instead of speaking, he seemed at a loss for words again. Now he was making her nervous, and as the silence dragged on, she hurried to fill it.

"Why does your sister dislike Mr. Beaumont?" she asked.

"Pardon?" He turned and gave her a bewildered look.

"Your sister. Why does she dislike him?"

"I suppose because when she came out, she liked him a great deal and the sentiment was not reciprocated."

Amelia had not expected this response. "She was in love with him?"

"I wouldn't go that far, but she's always had a soft spot for him, and you see how he is. I don't think he meant to encourage her."

"He's very charming. I can see why half the ladies in London fancied him."

"More than half, and not a one ever turned his head until Collette Fortier. He's left a trail of broken hearts in his wake, and my sister has one of them."

"Is that why she never married?"

He raised his brows. "Because of Rafe? No. I can't say he didn't contribute to her dim view of the institution of marriage, but he's not the reason."

"What is the reason?"

"That's for her to tell."

She nodded. "I suppose you're right." She looked down at the carpet, digging her slipper into the thick blue and gold material. "I never thought I would marry. All of my friends my age married years ago."

"I suppose you regret marrying now," he said.

Her head jerked up. "Why should you say that? I dare say I married better than any of them." She gestured about the room. "After all, you are the son of a marquess, you have a large stately home and piles of blunt."

"I don't know about piles."

"A large breeding stable, gardens, dozens of servants."

He took a step toward her, and she trailed off.

"And you don't care a whit about any of that."

She shrugged. "The money is nice."

"Which is why you haven't spent so much as a shilling of it. No shopping trips to the village, no redecorating, no summoning a modiste from Town to make you new dresses."

Amelia looked down at her dinner dress, which was perfectly lovely, if a few years out of date. "Should I summon a modiste?"

"Not on my account. I prefer you in nothing at all."

Amelia gave him a wary look. Last night she would have leapt at the chance to flirt with him. But tonight...after he had all but kicked her out of his bed the evening before, she was not so eager to be rejected again. "What is it you wanted to speak to me about?" she asked. "You were about to say something before I brought up your sister."

He took a breath, let it out, then took another. "I owe you an apology," he said. His voice was strong, but his hands were clenched at his sides. "I upset you last night."

"You all but booted me out of your bed," she said.

"I should have explained before we—er, began. I like to sleep alone."

"I see. Then I would have known I would be booted out before it happened."

He gave her a dark look. "I'm sorry for the way I behaved. I didn't mean to hurt you. I just felt…"

She waited, but he didn't seem to be able to find the words.

"Vulnerable?" she suggested. He gave a slight nod. "I'm familiar with the feeling."

"Very well. I deserved that. You have been vulnerable with me. And I—I did promise to show you my legs, and I…"

"This is the thing you do not understand, Nicholas," Amelia said in a tone so filled with exasperation that he looked at her in surprise. "I do not care about your legs. To you, your injury is a huge weight you carry on your back. You keep setting it down between us. You want me to take some of that weight and carry it too, but I don't want it. And you don't need me to carry it. We can throw it off a cliff and be free of it."

"You say that you don't care because you haven't seen the damage."

"I say I don't care because I don't. Your injury matters to you. Not to me. I'm falling in love with you, and I'd feel the same even if you had no legs at all because your legs do not make you who you are any more than your arms or your hair or your eyes do." She moved close to him, shaking now because she had just made herself vulnerable again—damn him. She hadn't meant to tell him she was half in love with him. And judging by the look of shock on his face, he hadn't expected her to say that. "Do you know why I married you?"

"You thought you were pregnant and ruined."

"There was that, but then after that dinner with your mother, I almost called it off. But I kept remembering how kind you were to me when I was just a stranger crying in your stable. Most men of your station would not have taken the time to even come to the stables."

"Well, the grooms said you were upsetting the horses—"

"I'm trying to make a point here," she interrupted. "And even if you were only motivated by the welfare of the horses that time, what about how you've brought my mother here to care for and had one of your land managers oversee Catmint Cottage?"

He waved a hand. "That's just duty."

"You brought your friend here, even though he's wanted for treason, and agreed to have a house party so he might see his friends one last time." She shook her head. "You"—she poked him—"are a good man. I'm already half in love with you. Stop trying to push me away."

"I'm not trying to push you away."

"You are. You think if you push me away now then you won't be hurt when I reject you because of your legs. But I won't reject you because of your legs, Nicholas."

"You can't know that."

"You can't know I will. Let's put an end to the argument right now. Drop your trousers."

Fifteen

Drop your trousers. That was the last straw. He couldn't resist her any longer. He'd been wanting to kiss her since the moment he'd walked into the library and now she was standing in front of him, cheeks flushed, chest heaving, eyes bright telling him to drop his trousers. A man could only take so much.

Nicholas took a step closer, and Amelia shook her head. "Oh, no," she said, skirting around him and backing toward the desk. He raised a brow. "I know that look." She pointed at him. "That wasn't what I meant when I said *drop your trousers.*"

"You can explain later," he said, moving toward her again. Obviously, she could easily outmaneuver him. She could have put the desk between them or even slipped past him and out the door. Instead, she backed up until her legs hit the back of the desk.

"We have to talk about this, Nicholas." Her voice was stern, but as he took another step toward her, she licked her lips in anticipation.

"We'll talk afterward," he said.

"We'll never come to a resolution if we don't talk."

"I think I can bring us to a resolution." He finally reached her and pulled her into his arms. She went without protest, wrapping her arms about his neck and kissing him. It always amazed him how much she wanted him. He wanted to believe that the state of his legs wouldn't change her mind, that seeing the true horror that he dragged about each day wouldn't disgust her. But every time he was with her like this, he feared it more and more. Every time he touched her, it became harder to lose her.

"We need to talk," she said, even as she nipped at his lip and pressed closer. Nicholas tightened his grip on her waist and lifted her onto the desk, pushing the inkwells and the sheets of vellum Florentia had not used out of the way. He placed his palms on either side of her, shifting some of his weight onto his arms, and kissed her again.

"We can talk after," he said as his mouth moved to her jaw and then her neck. "I promise."

"I will hold you—" She gasped as his tongue darted out to taste the hollow at the base of her neck.

"Go on," he said, pulling pins out of her bodice so it fell open, revealing her breasts encased in white stays. He pushed the garment down, freeing one and then bent to kiss it. He might have wished the desk was a bit higher as bending was difficult for him, but then it wouldn't be the right height for what he planned next.

"I was saying I will hold you to it."

"Hold me to what?" He freed her other breast, thumbing the hard nipple. She was so soft, so responsive. Her moans and gasps aroused him even before she pulled his shirt from his waistband and slid her hands underneath. He'd been an idiot to ever think their relationship could be platonic. Sparks had flown between them since their first meeting, and he only wanted her more now.

Her hand slid into his waistband gripping his hard cock, and any further thoughts fled. He was starving for her, eager to plunge back inside her and feel her clench him in pleasure. But instead of pushing her onto her back, he stepped away to make room to pull her to her feet.

"Yes, we should go upstairs," she said, trying to fix her bodice.

"I want you here," he said.

"But the servants—"

"Will stay away as long as that door is closed." He turned her so her back was to him then bent and kissed the back of her neck. Then he grasped her skirts and pulled them up to reveal her stockings, her knees, her garters, and finally the creamy skin of her thighs. "Bend over the desk," he murmured into her hair.

"You want me to…" She trailed off as he nudged her bare bottom with his erection, straining through his trousers. She bent, and he slid her skirts the rest of the way up, pooling them at her waist. She had a lovely round bottom, plump and perfect. He skated his hands over it then down between her legs to the heat of her core. She moaned and parted her legs to allow him entrance. He slid one finger inside then used the moisture to slide up to that small, sensitive nub hidden between her folds.

"Yes," she moaned, her hands clenching and releasing as he toyed with her. She looked back at him, over her shoulder, and her dark eyes were hazy with desire. Nicholas unfastened the placket of his trousers, allowing his erection to spring free.

"Open your legs wider," he commanded even as he moved between them to better position himself. She obeyed, seeming not to feel any self-consciousness. He liked that about her. She wasn't shy and overly modest. She seemed comfortable with her body and unashamed to take her pleasure. He guided his cock to her sex and slid inside.

She went completely rigid, and he paused, waiting until she adjusted to the feel of him at this angle before moving. "Did I hurt you?" he asked.

"No, I…I didn't realize."

"Do you want the rest of me?" he asked, moving his fingers over her sensitive bud again. Her breath caught.

"There's more?"

"I'll go slow," he said. "Tell me if I hurt you." He pushed deeper, knowing from this angle she felt him more fully. She let out a low moan as he sheathed himself fully, and Nicholas held still, allowing her to grow used to him filling her. But he was still stroking her clitoris lightly, and that motion was bringing her closer to climax. He felt her clench around him then she rocked back, taking him even deeper.

Nicholas's vision went almost completely black, and he couldn't stop himself from thrusting. She moaned, and he paused. "Did I hurt—"

"Don't stop," she demanded.

Thank God. He wanted to do anything but stop at that moment. He pulled back, thrust deeper, and the two of them found a rhythm. It seemed to Nicholas the two of them had been lovers for years. He was attuned to a change in her breath that let him know she liked something, and even before he could tell her to rise on tiptoes or bend over more, she was doing it. He held out as long as he could, and when the orgasm was upon him, he circled her swollen nub with his fingers until she arched back and clenched him, small cries beginning in the back of her throat.

They came together, which was a rare thing, and which meant he couldn't enjoy her climax as much as he wanted. But the way her body gripped him and the way she bucked made his own release all but blinding.

When it was over, he paused to catch his breath. Amelia was breathing heavily too. Keeping one hand on her back to steady her, he withdrew and reached for his trousers, tugging them up and over his legs. As he fastened the fall, she stood and straightened, turning to gaze into his face. "I didn't know people could do it that way as well," she said. She had lived on a farm most of her life, so he understood exactly what she was saying. He might have even been able to think of a reply if she hadn't looked so completely and utterly beautiful in that moment. Even though they should both be rearranging their clothes, he pulled her to him and kissed her again, this time slowly and sweetly, saying with his lips what he wasn't quite ready to think too much about in his mind.

She'd told him she was falling in love with him. He couldn't allow himself to feel the same.

She pulled back, her expression scolding. "You promised we would talk."

He didn't want to talk. He wanted to sit in a chair, pull her onto his lap, and make love to her all over again. But as much as he'd rather speak with hands and bodies, he had made a promise.

"Let's sit down," he said. His legs were throbbing, and he needed to take some of his weight off his left leg. He hadn't so much as removed his coat, so he tucked his shirt into his trousers and hobbled to the couch across from the desk. He sat, stretching his left leg out in front of him and watched as Amelia pinned her bodice back in place and straightened her skirts. Her hair was a complete wreck and would give her away, but given that they were married, it didn't really matter. Besides he liked her hair loose and tumbling about. She sat beside him on the couch and glanced at the desk.

"I don't think I shall ever see that desk in quite the same way again."

He smiled. "Neither shall I, and that's a good thing."

"Why? Did it hold bad memories before? Memories of late nights and endless ledgers?" she asked, speaking as someone who probably had experience with both.

"There's that, but this was always the room my father called us to when we were in trouble. We'd stand on the other side of the desk. The side we, er—"

"Knew each other?" she said, using the Biblical term.

"Yes, I'd stand there while my father lectured and doled out punishments."

"What sort of punishments did he give out?"

"It differed for each one of us, but mine were usually time away from the stables. I wouldn't be allowed a ride the next morning and had to spend my time mucking out stables instead. Little did he know, I didn't mind mucking out stables. As long as I could be with the horses, I didn't care what I was doing."

"Was he a very strict father?" she asked, moving closer to him so their bodies were touching. He liked being close to her. Liked their thighs and arms touching.

"He was a marquess," Nicholas said, and to him that seemed to sum up his father completely. She tilted her head in confusion, and he clarified. "He was raised with high expectations, and he passed them on to us. Of course, Henry received the majority of those expectations. As the heir, he wasn't allowed much room for error. Richard wasn't treated much differently being that he was the spare. But Florentia, Anne, and I were superfluous. We were expected to toe the line, but he didn't take much of an interest in us beyond that."

He felt her hand close around his and pulled his gaze back from the desk and the past to look at her. "I'm sorry," she said. "That must have been difficult. Surely your father would have been proud of you when you went into the army. Even I heard of your distinguished exploits against the French."

Nicholas shrugged. "Thank God he died before he could see what's become of me."

"What's become of you?" she demanded, her voice suddenly sharp. "You're a war hero."

"War hero," he made a derisive gesture. "There's nothing heroic about war. It's death and fear, and all the soldiers bear the scars. Mine are just more visible."

Her hand squeezed his, and Nicholas appreciated the comfort. "How did it happen?" she asked and nodded at his leg. "I heard your horse fell on you. Is that what happened? Is that why you don't ride anymore?"

"You want to know how it happened?" he asked. He hadn't really told anyone except Colonel Draven the full story. He hadn't ever wanted to tell it again, but Amelia was his wife. She deserved to know.

He must have been staring, unseeing, at the desk for several moments because she reached over and took his face in her hands, gently turning his head to face her. "You don't have to talk about it if you don't want to. I want to know you, Nicholas, but only what you're ready to reveal of yourself to me."

Her words were telling, being that he hadn't yet revealed his physical injury. Somehow talking about it seemed safer than showing her. He took her hands in his. "It happened during a battle in France. The troop had been in France for almost a year by then, skulking about, collecting information, sabotaging supply wagons, stealing munitions. The ultimate goal had been to get close enough to Napoleon to assassinate him. Ewan Mostyn—you'll meet him at the house party—was to kill him if it were to be done hand-to-hand and Nash Pope—our sharpshooter—would shoot him if we couldn't get close."

"And what was your job?"

"I did a bit of everything. Mostly I made sure we could keep moving. I procured horses and conveyances, and Aidan Sterling and I stole food provisions when we ran low. It wasn't easy keeping twelve to fifteen horses fed and watered and out of sight, and it mainly fell to me. By the time I was sent home, there were sixteen of us left. We'd started at thirty and were down to sixteen." He looked down at their joined hands. "Rafe Beaumont and Neil Wraxall had been away for a day or two, trying to gather intelligence as to where Napoleon might be lodging. The idea was we could go there and make a plan to kill him. When Neil returned, he said he had different orders. Rafe looked worried and that made the rest of us worry and for good reason. We were being sent to the front to shore up a flank of the British army. There would be a large battle in a few days, and they needed every available man."

"You must have been terrified."

"I don't remember," he said honestly. "I think by that point I'd been terrified for so long that I was used to the feeling. We broke camp and rode for the front immediately, arriving the night before the battle. The others were officers or had been trained as infantry. They were either put in charge of units or sent to join a unit. I'd been trained in the cavalry, and I was sent to join those men."

"You were separated from your troop."

He nodded. "It was supposed to be temporary. We made a plan to meet after the battle. We all assumed Bonaparte would be on the retreat, and that would make him vulnerable.

Stratford Fortescue had an elaborate plan to track him, ambush him, and kill him. It would have ended the war and we could have all gone home."

"Considering Bonaparte was exiled to St. Helena where he died, I assume your plan failed."

It had failed but not because Stratford Fortescue's plan hadn't been sound. It had failed because the British had lost that battle. Nicholas didn't even remember who the general in charge had been, not Wellington, but one of his underlings. He'd sat awake most of the night with the other members of the cavalry, waiting to hear what the plan for the next day would be. When morning dawned, a low haze of campfires lingering between the enemy camps, he still didn't know. The cavalry was usually first to attack, so the uncertainty made him and his fellow soldiers uneasy. They'd gotten into a standard formation and waited for their orders.

As the smoke had burned away and the sun had risen, glinting off the swords and buttons of the French soldiers in blue across the field, Nicholas hadn't been able to stop himself from looking about for one of the general's aides who would deliver their orders. Finally, with tension building like the sound of the drums across the field and the enemy side already in formation, a man came running and handed the major a paper.

"He seemed bewildered when he read it," Nicholas told Amelia, summarizing the confusion of the morning. "He even asked the aide if he was certain, and of course, the aide barked at him to do as he was told." Nicholas shook his head. "I knew then we would lose. I could feel it."

"What do you mean? Like a supernatural sense?"

"No. I'd been in enough battles by then to know what it feels like when we are all united. When the men around you are confident and committed. The men around me were frightened and unsure. The general had waited too long to convey their orders and the orders were unclear. And it was frustrating to those of us in my cavalry regiment because we'd been told to hold back and wait for the signal to attack. And so we were left on the side, watching as our fellow soldiers fought and died."

Amelia lifted his hands and kissed them. "I cannot imagine how awful that must have been. Your friends were fighting, and you were standing by, helpless."

"I was never so glad to ride into battle as when we finally received the signal. I don't even know if we received a signal or if the major couldn't wait any longer. I just know we charged into the fray and sent some of those Frenchies running."

Now came the part that was hardest to talk about. He hadn't mentioned Charlemagne yet, but he couldn't continue without doing so.

"I had a warhorse," he said. "I'd brought him with me from Battle's Peak."

"I thought you were a horse thief," she said, and he appreciated her smile and the way she tried to lighten the mood.

"I stole horses for most of the other men, but a few of us had our own. I cared for Charlemagne as though he were a part of myself. I remember when he was born. Everyone said he would be magnificent. We could have sold him for a thousand pounds. His dam and sire were highly credentialed. But my father had decided by that point that I was to go into the army. I didn't want to go, and he offered me Charlemagne to stop my protests." He was silent then, remembering the hours he'd spent with the horse, training him, grooming him, bonding with him.

"I imagine a cavalry officer and his horse must trust each other completely," she said.

"Yes. We fought together many times before Colonel Draven pulled me aside and asked me to join his troop. I actually thought it would be a break from the drudgery of life in the cavalry. I don't think that saying—out of the frying pan and into the fire—was ever more apt." He released her hands and struggled to push himself to the edge of the couch.

"What's wrong?"

"I have to stand." He managed to get on his feet, and his leg protested with a sharp jab of pain. Nicholas ignored it. If he sat beside Amelia, holding her hand, gazing into her sympathetic eyes, he'd break down in tears when he told the rest. He had no intention of crying over the past any longer. He'd shed enough tears when he'd been lying in bed, worrying if he'd ever walk again.

He took a few steps, then paused before the hearth. "I was riding Charlemagne that day. He was thrilled to be on the battlefield. I think he'd missed it. Our orders had been to support the infantry, and we chased off a number of soldiers." He didn't tell her about slashing the men with his sword or stabbing them through with his bayonet. Those were moments he never spoke of, moments he'd pushed far back into his mind and which had become the stuff of nightmares. He'd been pacing as he spoke, but now he paused and looked directly at Amelia. "Have you ever had a moment where everything is perfect and then like this"—he snapped his fingers—"it shifts?"

She nodded. "The day my father was shot was like that. One moment I was outside under a sky as blue as your eyes with the sun on my back, and the next moment I heard a shot. I don't think ten minutes passed before I was helping to carry my father into the house, my hands covered in blood. My world was never the same after that." Her gaze was steady on his. "I understand that life can change in an instant."

"That's how the battle felt," he said. "It changed in an instant. One moment we were pushing the French troops back, and the next their cavalry charged us. I don't even know where they came from. It felt like they came from the side, which means they flanked us. Neil would know. He always analyzed the battles afterward, but in that moment, it didn't matter that we'd been flanked. What mattered was we were fighting for our lives." He shook his head. "Do you know that I never once considered I wouldn't come out of it alive? Even with the odds as they were. Even seeing my fellow soldiers shot off their horses, I never thought it would be me. Until Charlemagne stumbled."

He clenched his fists and swallowed.

"He stumbled?" Amelia asked quietly.

"Bastards shot him," Nicholas said, forcing his voice from a throat that felt raw and tight. "Cowards shot my horse out from under me." He glared at her. "There's no honor in that."

She shook her head, tears filling her eyes.

"And there was no need. They were winning at any rate. Our men were in retreat by then. I didn't know that. I only knew that Charlemagne was falling, and I was falling with him. I knew what I had to do. I had to jump clear, but my boot caught in the stirrup. I couldn't free it and by the time I did, by the time I jumped free, it was too late. All I did was manage to trap both my legs under Charlemagne's weight. The only thing that saved me was that I hit my head when I fell and lost consciousness. The enemy must have thought I was dead and left me. I woke in the dark, in pain, the sounds of men's groans surrounding me."

"Oh, Nicholas." A tear slid down her cheek, and Nicholas watched it linger on her jaw before dropping to her dress.

"I was one of those men groaning," he said, refusing to give into his own instinct to cry. Tears wouldn't help. They wouldn't change anything. "I couldn't feel my legs. Little did I know in that moment not being able to feel them was a blessing. I tried to free myself, and that's when I felt them. The pain was so sharp and intense, I must have passed out again. I woke to the sound of my name being called. Neil had been searching the dead for me. He and Rowden Payne. They found me and Rowden stayed with me while Neil went to fetch Duncan Murray and Ewan. They were the biggest and the strongest. It took three men to free me from Charlemagne. Duncan carried me out of there over his shoulder." He didn't say that his last image of Charlemagne had been the horse's unseeing brown eyes as Duncan walked away. "The next weeks are something of a blur," he said. "I mostly remember pain. And fear I'd never walk again. They said I wouldn't."

She gave him a faint smile. "And that only made you more determined."

"Exactly." He looked into the fire again. "But that was later. After I'd come home."

He heard her rise, and a moment later, he felt her arms go about his waist. "I've only met your mother briefly," she said against his back. "But I can't imagine that she was a doting nursemaid."

He smiled. "She was not, but to her credit, she also didn't interfere with my care. When I was strong enough, Florentia suggested I come here to finish my recovery."

Amelia slid her arms around him and looked up into his face. He liked being held by her, being surrounded by her scent and her softness. "She probably hoped being around horses would help."

That had been the plan, and Amelia was clever enough to discern it.

"It was, and I believe it worked. Working with the horses gave me a reason to get up every day, and my being here has had other benefits. My father would turn over in his grave if he heard me mention money, but since I've been in residence, we've made more from the breeding operations at Battle's Peak than several other larger estates have made from farming and selling crops."

"But you never rode again?" Amelia asked, her eyes seeing too much. Of course, she would focus on that one point.

"I can't." He moved to disentangle himself from her, and she released him.

"You could if you wanted."

"I can't control the horse with my legs as a rider should, and I have too much pride to allow a groom to lead me about like a young child."

"You do have too much pride," she said. "But that's not why you don't ride any longer. Or not the whole reason. What happened to Charlemagne?"

She was too astute, by far. "Buried in that field in France, I imagine," he said, his throat tight as he thought about the horse who had been at his side for so many years. "I owed him better than that." He raked a hand through his hair. "I don't want to ride anymore. My mother thinks it's because I'm afraid I'll be injured again. But that's not it."

"There's no joy in it for you any longer," she said. "It will only remind you of your friend."

He hadn't thought of Charlemagne as a friend, but of course, the horse had been his friend.

"After my father was shot and paralyzed, there were things he no longer cared to do. Sometimes I think they were because it was too difficult for my mother and I to manage them, but I think others just made him sad to remember what he had lost."

Nicholas nodded. That was it. It seemed fitting for Charlemagne to be the last horse he had ridden. It honored the warhorse in a small way. "I didn't know your father. I met him only a handful of times, but I can't imagine he wanted you to spend your youth caring for him."

Now she was the one who looked away, her expression pained. "No, he didn't, but there was nowhere I wanted to be other than his side. I wouldn't abandon him, just as I won't abandon my mother." She glanced back at Nicholas, seeming to say she would not abandon him either. "You don't have to show me your legs," she said. "If you never show me, that's fine. I'll respect your wishes. But don't push me away. Don't assume I will turn away from you without ever giving me a chance to prove otherwise."

"I haven't been fair, have I?"

"No, but you've made amends tonight." He lifted his brows and glanced at the desk. Her cheeks colored slightly. "I meant because you told me how you were injured and about Charlemagne." She gave the desk a direct look. "The other didn't hurt either." She moved to him, stood on tiptoe, and kissed his cheek. "Good night, my lord."

He'd rather been thinking about exploring the desk further. "Good night?"

"I should check on my mother and then sleep. Now that I know something about these men coming to Battle's Peak, I want to make sure everything is perfect."

The door clicked closed, and she was gone. Nicholas couldn't help the words that ran through his mind: *She is perfect*.

So why couldn't he open up to her? Why couldn't he trust her?

Because he was far, far from perfect.

Sixteen

Amelia sat at the window in the drawing room and watched Nicholas move slowly and awkwardly across the yard toward the stable. His progress was slow and looked painful, especially since he wasn't aware anyone observed him. If he'd known she was watching, that she could see him, he would have hidden how much the effort cost him.

And yet he went every day, no matter the pain or how it must have tired him. He was a fighter, like her father had been. That only made her care for him more.

"Have you finished then?" Florentia asked from across the room. Amelia glanced her way and saw that both Florentia and her mother were looking at her. She wondered if they had spoken to her before and she'd been too engrossed in her thoughts to hear them.

"Not quite yet," she said. She'd been tasked with writing the topics for charades. She had about two dozen already, but with so many attending the house party, she needed twice that. "How are the place cards coming?"

Mrs. Blackstock and Amelia sat at a table with heavy paper and watercolors between them. Florentia had written the names of all the guests who would be dining with them tomorrow (goodness! so soon!) in lovely black calligraphy, and Mrs. Blackstock and Florentia were decorating each place card with watercolor flowers.

Florentia sorted through the small stack of cards remaining. "We have Mr. and Mrs. Murray and Mr. and Mrs. Pope left."

"Oh, Mr. Pope confirmed he would attend then?" Amelia asked. As of the night before, he'd been the only Survivor who had not replied to the invitation.

"Not exactly," Mrs. Blackstock said. "But his wife wrote and said she would—what was it she said?" She glanced at Florentia.

"She said she would do her best to drag him kicking and screaming from Wentmore."

"I think I will like her," Mrs. Blackstock said. Amelia nodded, but she was not thinking about meeting Mrs. Pope. She was thinking how much her mother had changed in the past week and a half. The changes hadn't been all that observable at first. She argued less about going out to the garden. She ate a bit more and slept a bit less. And then she would sit and listen to Florentia and Amelia plan the house party. Sometimes Beaumont and Nicholas joined them as well. The next thing Amelia knew, her mother was helping to organize things. Florentia said that having a purpose and something to look forward to had done the trick, but Amelia thought Florentia also played a role. The two women were years apart in age, but they got on so well that it seemed to Amelia they had known each other all their lives.

Amelia couldn't remember her mother ever having friends. Surely, she had when she'd been younger, but she'd spent so much of her married life caring for her mother-in-law and then her husband, no doubt she had very little time for friendships. But it had become quite clear that Florentia and her mother were good friends now. Amelia had thought she might feel jealous, but she didn't. They never excluded her or made her feel unwelcome, and she was happy to hear their chatter and laughter. She had been right to bring her mother to Battle's Peak, and it pleased her that her mother would most likely be staying on for some time to come.

Her gaze went back to the yard, and she noted that Nicholas had made it to the stables and stood just outside speaking to the stablemaster. Her husband had his hands on his hips and his head cocked as he listened, which was a stance she knew well. It meant he was listening seriously and considering what action to take.

It was a stance that always made her breath quicken slightly. She liked that he did not shy away from or avoid responsibilities. She liked that she could look to him when she needed something. It was no mystery why his authority appealed to her. For years she and her mother had to handle every crisis—small and large—that materialized. Now she knew that though she could handle a crisis, she could also count on her husband to stand at her side. He was a partner, and she wanted to be satisfied with that, but of course, she wanted more.

Since that night in the library, he hadn't avoided her bed. He'd made it clear he wanted her as much as she wanted him. But he always came to her in the dark. He liked to take her from behind or pull her onto his lap when he sat in a chair. Amelia knew she shouldn't complain. He aroused her to the point of madness and brought her to shattering climaxes. He held her, kissed her gently, told her she was beautiful and clever.

But he didn't offer any more of himself. He didn't allow her to see his legs, and though they didn't matter to her, she knew they mattered to him. There would always be a wall between them while he still didn't trust her to see all of him, to love all of him.

And she did love him. Even now her gaze roamed over his body hungrily and she had the urge to run to the stables just to tell him good day and see his blue eyes crinkle when he smiled at her. And though she had much to do today to prepare for the guests arriving tomorrow, she wished the day would hurry and pass so she could feel his arms around her, his hands on her skin, his mouth on hers.

"Don't you think so, Amelia?" her mother asked.

"Of course," Amelia said, her gaze still on her husband through the window.

"I told you she's not listening," Florentia said.

Amelia looked at the two of them. Florentia was packing up the watercolors. "I am listening," Amelia argued.

"Then why did you just agree we should make mud pies and catch frogs one afternoon?"

Amelia frowned. "Do you mean an activity for Lord Jasper's son?"

"No, dear," her mother said. "Though that's not a bad idea for him. But Lady Florentia was saying whatever came into her mind because you hadn't responded to a thing we've said for the last quarter hour."

"Too busy mooning over my brother." Florentia made a face. "I'll put these away and then we will help you finish charades." She carried the paints out of the drawing room. As soon as she was gone, Mrs. Blackstock patted the seat beside her.

"Come help me spread these out to dry."

Amelia knew her mother didn't need help spreading cards to dry, but she went and assisted. It was a good chance to review the guests for the last time. She lifted each card and studied the names.

Lieutenant-Colonel Draven would attend with his wife whose Christian name was Catarina. Draven had been the leader of the troop, the man who had organized it and given the orders. His given name was Benedict, but Amelia had never heard Nicholas or Beaumont refer to him thus.

Rafe Beaumont was next, though his card had his alias written on it. From what she'd gathered, he had been known as The Seducer and had been tasked with gathering intelligence.

She lifted another card and read *Mr. Mostyn and Lady Lorraine.* Ewan Mostyn had been the brute force of the troop, the Protector, and he'd married the daughter of a duke and they had a baby they were bringing.

The next card was Mr. Wraxall and Lady Juliana. Wraxall had been the man in charge of carrying out Draven's orders, the commander. His wife was the daughter of an earl, thus the title, and she was a leading benefactress of Society, going so far as to run an orphanage for boys, though she wouldn't be bringing the orphans with her.

Lord and Lady Jasper Grantham, she read on the next card. Lord Jasper was known as the Bounty Hunter. He could find anything and anyone. His wife was Olivia, and she had a son, Richard, who Jasper had adopted and who would attend and possibly play with frogs and mud.

Mr. Colin FitzRoy and Lady Daphne were the next card. Lady Daphne was another daughter of a duke. Colin FitzRoy had been a master of disguise and known as the Pretender during the war. Amelia questioned his talents as his efforts with Rafe Beaumont had been less than successful.

The Duke and Duchess of Mayne were the couple Amelia worried most about. She had never met a duke before. Nicholas assured her she could simply call him Mayne or even Phineas—Phin, as his friends called him—but Amelia doubted she could be so informal. His duchess was Annabel. Apparently, there had been some sort of scandal when they wed, but Nicholas said Phin had always been called the Negotiator as he was a master of tactics and compromises.

She shuffled the cards and read the next, which was Rowden Payne. He had been a pugilist and was now married to a woman named Modesty. Known as the Fighter, appropriately enough, he was one of Nicholas's closer friends.

Then there was the man Nicholas called the Thief, though Amelia couldn't think why. Aidan Sterling was one of the wealthiest men in England, so wealthy even she had heard of him. He had married very recently, and his wife was...Amelia had to think. Jenny, that was her name.

The Strategist was next. His name was Stratford Fortescue and his wife was Emmeline. Nicholas said Stratford was a master of planning, and Amelia almost wished he could be here now to help with all their party arrangements.

Finally, there were the two men coming from further away. The first was Duncan Murray and his wife, Ines. They were traveling from Scotland. Amelia was a little nervous that Duncan was called the Lunatic. The other Survivor, and the one they were the least sure would attend, was Nash Pope. His wife, Prudence, was the one who had written to say she would do her best to convince him, but apparently the man was as much a recluse as Nicholas. He had been the Sharpshooter in the troop.

Amelia set the last card down and hoped she could remember all of this. She glanced at her mother and Amelia grasped her hand. "I am so glad you are out of bed and helping, Mama."

"Yes, well, I hardly had a choice. Every day you hounded and cajoled me to get up and go outside." She squeezed Amelia's hand. "Thank you for that."

"It doesn't mean you miss him less," Amelia said. "Living life, getting out of bed. I still think of Papa all the time. I miss him."

"I know, and do you know what else I realized?" Amelia raised her brows. "He would not have wanted me to wither away, mourning him. He would have wanted me to live my life and to continue to care for the one person we both loved more than anything else. You."

Amelia threw her arms about her mother and held her tightly. "I love you more than anything else too, Mama. I am so glad you are feeling better."

Her mother pulled back and looked at Amelia with concern. "Why the tears? What's wrong?"

Amelia shook her head. "I'm just happy. For a few days, I was scared I would lose you too."

Her mother nodded. "I'm sorry. I cannot promise you I will not still have bad days, but I will keep fighting."

Amelia embraced her again, and her mother patted her back and stroked her hair as she had when Amelia was a child. It was comforting and exactly what she needed in that moment. "You said you love me more than anyone else," her mother said. "But I wonder if there isn't someone beginning to take up a portion of your heart."

Amelia groaned. "I don't want to speak about Lord Nicholas." She pulled back.

"That's fine. You are a grown woman, and I don't want to pry. Should we go over the seating charts again?"

Not the seating charts. "I am starting to care for him," Amelia said. Her mother set down the sheet with the drawing of the table on it.

"That's only natural, of course."

Amelia could appreciate that she didn't point out that Amelia had said only a moment before that she didn't wish to discuss the matter.

"I'm definitely"—she looked down at her dress, twisting the chocolate brown fabric between her fingers—"in love with him."

Her mother gasped. "Oh, but this is good news. Amelia—"

Amelia held up a hand. "He still doesn't feel the same."

Her mother frowned and tilted her head to one side. "Why do you say so? Has he been unkind?"

She shook her head. "Nothing like that, no." In fact, he was always solicitous of her, always complimenting her, telling her he wanted her. Those words were lovely, but not the three she longed to hear. "But he hasn't said he loves me."

"And you have told him?"

"I've not said it directly, but I've intimated as much."

"Why haven't you said it? If you do love him, why not tell him?"

Amelia shrugged. "Fear, I suppose? What if he doesn't say it back?"

"Oh, chances are, he won't say it back."

"Mama!"

"Not because he doesn't feel the same about you, but because he may not realize it yet. Or he may not be ready to risk his heart by saying it."

"But I should risk my heart?"

"If you love him, yes. Give him your heart. Trust him with it, and in time, he may give you his as well."

"In time." Amelia made a face.

"Patience, my dear."

"I hate being patient," Amelia said.

"You always did. Now"—she lifted the drawing of the table again—"one last look at the seating chart."

Amelia sighed and took the paper.

***

It was well after midnight by the time she retired to her bed chamber and allowed a sleepy O'Malley to undress her. As she was used to country hours, she was exhausted and equally excited and nervous about the following day. Nicholas's friends and fellow Survivors would all be arriving. Some had probably been traveling for several days already. She'd finally meet the men she'd heard about—and she'd have to entertain them and their wives for the next week. What if it rained every day and they were stuck inside? What if Nicholas disappeared as he always did when there were too many people about? What if Mr. Beaumont was discovered and the magistrate knocked on their doors?

"Good night, my lady," O'Malley said, stifling a yawn.

Amelia realized she was dressed in her nightrail and robe and her hair was plaited. She'd been so lost in her thoughts, she hadn't even spoken to her poor lady's maid.

"Good night. Thank you."

O'Malley closed the door behind her, and Amelia blew out the candle at her dressing table, leaving only the lamp beside her bed. She rose, starting for the bed, then glanced at the door separating her chamber from Nicholas's. Should she go to him? She didn't know if he had retired. She'd seen him briefly at dinner and he'd mentioned that he needed to have a word with the vicar after dinner, which meant he had escaped the endless conversation about the house party that had dominated everything else between Florentia, Amelia, and Mrs. Blackstock the past few days.

Had he gone to bed already? Usually, she waited for him to come to her. But what had her mother said about risk? She started for the door then paused. She really was tired. Perhaps she should tell him how she felt tomorrow. Yes. She would just bid him good night. She went to the door and tapped on it.

"Come in." His reply was immediate, almost as though he'd been waiting for her to knock.

She lifted the latch and peered inside. Nicholas sat in a chair near the fire, dressed in a robe over his trousers, book in hand.

"I'm sorry to interrupt," she said. "I wanted to tell you good night."

"Come here," he said. She entered, leaving her door open, and crossing to him. There weren't any other chairs beside him, so she stood awkwardly. "I should apologize," he said.

"Why?"

"I ran away. I don't usually shy from a battle, but I couldn't bear to hear one more word about the house party tonight."

"And now you feel guilty."

"A bit." He reached out and took her hand. "To ease my conscience, I thought I would ask if you need me to do anything tomorrow before the deluge of guests begin to arrive. Florentia mentioned going over the meals with Cook one last time. I could do that."

She pressed her lips together to keep from smiling at the face he made.

"Even if I agreed to that, your sister would insist on doing it herself. I think she rather enjoys this sort of thing."

"She does," he said in a tone of incredulity. "You must be tired."

She nodded, looking into his eyes. She forgot all about her exhaustion when she was near him, when she looked at him.

"Come here," he said again, and this time he tugged her into his lap. She went and was surprised when he didn't shift her to straddle him. Instead, he put his arms around her. Amelia closed her eyes and rested her head on his chest, listening to the steady thump of his heart.

"Are you nervous?" she asked. "To see all of your friends again after so long?"

"No. War makes men brothers. No matter how long has passed, whenever we see each other, there will always be a bond." He paused for a moment. "Now, their wives... Some of them make me a bit nervous."

She smiled. "All of them make me nervous."

"Don't be," he said. "You have an easy way with people. It's hard *not* to like you. I probably won't be able to find a moment alone with you once the guests arrive. You'll be far too popular."

"I'll always have time for you, my lord," she teased. Her heart was pounding, and she knew if she didn't say it now, she would give in to cowardice and not say it at all. She looked up at him. "Nicholas?"

"Hmm?"

"I love you."

He didn't stiffen. He didn't have any reaction for a very long moment. Amelia wondered if she had made a huge mistake. Now she'd made things awkward between them. She started to pull away, to get to her feet, but Nicholas pulled her closer. Then he lowered his mouth to kiss her forehead. She looked up at him again, and his mouth met hers in a slow kiss that made heat rush into every part of her, from the top of her head to the tip of her smallest toe. She wrapped her arms about his neck, and the kiss deepened. She loved kissing him, loved how everything but his mouth and the feel of his body against hers melted away in these moments. The kiss might have gone on for seconds or hours. She had no idea.

And then he shifted her so she faced him, and he took her face between his hands, taking her mouth with his and exploring her body with his hands. Her robe fell away and then her nightrail. Somehow his robe was gone as well, and her hands were on his bare shoulders, his chest, sliding down to the waistband of his trousers. He let her free him, but he didn't lift her hips. Instead, he broke the kiss and took his time tasting her neck, her breasts, touching her everywhere and making her begin to wriggle with impatience. And then his hands slid between them, stroking her in that most sensitive place until she was bucking her hips and crying out.

Only then did he lift her hips and plunge inside her. The pleasure was exquisite, and by now they moved together as one. He knew the rhythm she liked, and she knew just how to slow down to tantalize him into growling her name.

She finally couldn't restrain herself and fell over the edge of the climax. He followed, and they lay for a while, panting in each other's arms. Amelia would have stayed like that for longer, but her leg began to cramp, and she was even more sleepy than before. She pulled back, but before she could rise, he took her face in his hands again and kissed her gently. "Good night," he whispered.

"Good night." She gathered her things and returned to her chamber, trying not to dwell on the fact that they still slept separately. He needed his space and privacy. That was understandable. She'd always been a restless sleeper and would probably keep him awake if they lay together. On the other hand, she wanted more.

Her mother had told her to be patient, she reminded herself as she washed and pulled on her night clothes then climbed into bed. She'd taken the risk and told him she loved him, and now she just had to give him time to realize he loved her too. Surely, he did. The way he kissed her and made love to her. He must love her. She could feel that he loved her.

But as she lay in bed, alone, it didn't escape her notice that he hadn't said it.

***

Colonel Draven was the first to arrive, of course. He was always punctual. Nicholas and Rafe met him on the drive. They'd decided it would be better for the other Survivors to catch their first glimpse of Rafe and be informed of his false identity away from the servants and all the ears about the house. This meant Nicholas himself opened the door to Draven's conveyance and was met with the smiling face of a lovely dark-haired woman. "Mrs. Draven?" he asked.

Draven came into view, his red hair sticking up, and pushed out of the coach. "Playing footman now, my lord? I—" His gaze landed on Rafe, who was still dressed as a vicar. But anyone who knew Rafe wouldn't be fooled by that disguise for long. Draven paused for a moment, staring hard enough that his wife peered out after him, but he recovered quickly. He turned, held out his hand to his wife, and helped her out of the coach. "Lord Nicholas, might I introduce my wife, Mrs. Catarina Draven." She gave a pretty curtsy.

Nicholas kissed her hand and clapped Draven on the shoulder then gestured to Rafe. "You remember my good friend Mr. Osgood?"

The colonel raised his brows. "Of course. Osgood. A pleasure to see you again. Catarina, might I introduce you to Mr. Osgood."

"The pleasure is all mine," Rafe said with a flourish of a bow. He glanced at the colonel. "I'm a vicar now. Had you heard?"

The colonel gave him a dark look. "I hadn't, no, but we should discuss why you are here and not where I put you when we have a moment alone." He glanced pointedly at the servants standing off to the side.

"The vicar will see you inside," Nicholas said. "My wife has refreshments ready."

It was easier for Rafe to bring the guests in and out of the house so that Nicholas had to walk less, but he wished he could have done it himself. He would have liked to see the colonel's reaction to Amelia. She'd looked so incredibly lovely this morning. She wore a blue-green morning dress he had not seen before, and her hair was piled on her head in a sophisticated style that left a long curl over one shoulder. Every time he caught a glimpse of her, he wanted to wrap that curl around his fingers and pull her close for a kiss.

Of course, then he remembered what she'd said the night before.

I love you.

She'd hinted that she was falling in love with him, and she hadn't made a secret of her growing feelings for him. He liked that about her. That she was open and honest and didn't play games like many of the ladies he'd known in London.

Still, when she'd said she loved him, his reaction had been pure terror. No woman had ever said that to him before. He supposed his mother or sisters had said it, but none of the women he'd ever been involved with romantically had professed their love. He hadn't loved them either. He hadn't thought something like love mattered to him. Yes, he wanted to be desired and respected and cared for, but he hadn't known he wanted to be loved.

He hadn't known he *needed* to be loved. And that was what was truly terrifying about her declaration. He'd needed to hear those words, and now that he had he feared they'd be taken away. What if she fell out of love with him? What if she saw his legs and realized she could never love a man who had such an injury?

The worst realization was that he was beginning to care for her. Once he cared for her, if she stopped loving him, he didn't know how he'd recover from the blow. And yet, if he didn't risk his heart, if he didn't reciprocate her feelings, would he be hurting her?

As another carriage approached, this one large and so grand he knew it must be either Aidan Sterling or the Duke of Mayne, Nicholas reflected that life had been much simpler when he'd been a bachelor.

He caught sight of the ducal crest and craned his head for a glimpse of Phineas, Duke of Mayne. Phin was known as The Negotiator, and it meant he was easy to talk to and almost as charming as Rafe. Nicholas stepped forward when the coach stopped and opened the door to greet his friend. He looked as he ever had with his straight blondish hair and his light-colored eyes. His wife, who Nicholas had once heard called the Wanton Widow—before her marriage to Phin—was a beautiful, tall redhead. "Your Graces," Nicholas said as they exited the coach. But Phin didn't bow back, he pulled Nicholas into an embrace then stepped back and looked him in the eye. "It's good to see you again, Nickers," he said. "Annabel, might I introduce Lord Nicholas St. Clare. Lord Nicholas, my wife, the Duchess of Mayne."

Nicholas didn't have the chance to say more than a brief greeting before Rafe returned. "And I am Mr. Osgood, the vicar."

Phineas gave Rafe a long look. "You're an idiot is what you are," he said with a shake of his head. His wife gasped and then looked bewildered as the duke embraced the so-called vicar. "I'll explain later," the duke told his wife as Rafe escorted them inside.

Very little time passed before Nicholas spotted a third conveyance, this one with a man riding beside it. He knew the rider's stance immediately, and recognized the man as Neil Wraxall, their commander. He still had an air of command about him as he raised his hand to greet Nicholas before spurring his horse to gallop ahead. He was off his mount and clasping Nicholas in mere moments. Nicholas hadn't expected so much warmth from his former brothers-in-arms, and now he wondered why he hadn't made more effort to see them sooner. He'd thought they would pity him for his injury, but they seemed only happy to see him.

"It's been too long," Neil was saying. "And you ignored every single one of my letters. I'd have you flogged for that if we were back in the army."

"Fortunately, we're not," Nicholas said, and Neil smiled at his matter-of-fact statement.

"Colin has been suggesting we have a reunion for months now," Neil said, "but he lives in Town, and that would have only let me escape the madhouse for a few hours. You've given Juliana and me a few days, and I owe you for it. Here she is." He gestured to the carriage, then waved the footman away and opened the door himself, pulling out a petite woman with coppery hair and large brown eyes. "Lady Juliana, might I present Lord Nicholas St. Clare."

She greeted him and then her smile faded as Rafe made his appearance. He was obviously timing his arrivals for the best effect. Lady Juliana gave him a stern look. "You are not supposed to be here," she said.

He put a finger to his lips. "It will be our little secret."

Neil seemed frozen in shock, but once it faded, he embraced his friend so hard he practically lifted Rafe off the ground. Nicholas remembered they had always been good friends. Now they started for the house with their arms locked about each other. Nicholas followed, wanting to make certain Amelia and Florentia didn't need any help inside.

That was when a blood-curdling scream rent the air. Everyone halted and looked about as the sound of hoofbeats came closer. Nicholas spotted the man on the horse rushing toward them and realized it hadn't been a scream but a war cry—a Scottish war cry. There, on a large black horse racing toward them, was the Lunatic, Duncan Murray. The woman who must have been his wife, a small dark-haired woman, was right beside him on another large black horse. Neil pulled his wife out of the path of Duncan's beast, but there was no need, as he stopped the horse in plenty of time then jumped down with an ease Nicholas envied.

"Well," he bellowed. "Doona stand aboot with yer mouths agape. I'm here now. The festivities can begin."

"He hasn't changed," Rafe said. Colonel Draven's wife ran forward to greet Mrs. Murray, and Nicholas thought he remembered hearing that the two were sisters. They embraced and then there were introductions all around. Duncan told Rafe he was a numpty bampot then pulled him into a crushing embrace. Phineas was talking with Neil and the colonel was trying to make introductions. The ladies were laughing and behaving as though they had known each other for years, and Nicholas stood still and looked about at the chaos around him. Seeing his fellow soldiers brought back memories of war, but not as many as he would have thought. It helped that Neil wasn't ordering everyone about and Draven wasn't looking stern and as though the weight of the world rested on his shoulders.

Duncan, Phin, and Rafe hadn't changed at all, and Nicholas hoped they never did. He wondered what the others thought of him. Did they see a changed man or one who was very much like the Nickers they'd known in France?

Amelia slipped easily through the crowd of people, and Nicholas was glad when she came to stand at his side. She slipped her hand into his. "How many more are coming?" she asked, trying to be heard over the din of voices.

"Too many," he said, grateful for the security he felt with her at his side.

"I like all of them already, although that one"—she inclined her head toward Duncan—"is a little bit frightening."

As though he'd been summoned, Duncan looked over and tromped to them. "There ye are," he said by way of greeting to Nicholas. "It's been too long. And who is this wee lass? Doona say yer wife. Are we all married now?"

Nicholas made the introductions and sometime later Amelia and Florentia managed to corral everyone inside for tea and refreshments in the drawing room. Nicholas was tempted to escape the noise and hide in the stables, but Florentia had taken up residence near the doors and gave him dark looks whenever he moved that way.

"Is that another coach?" Lady Juliana asked, moving to peer out the window. "Oh, but it's two, and they are quite large."

Her husband joined her and after a look through the window announced, "They're Aidan Sterling's coaches."

"Ah, then that means Mr. Mostyn and Mr. Payne will be with him," the colonel announced.

"Oh, Lady Lorraine will have the baby with her!" Lady Juliana exclaimed, and the room emptied except for Nicholas and Amelia.

Amelia went to his side and smiled. "Ready for more?" she asked.

"Not just yet," he said, and pulled her into his arms

Seventeen

Amelia hadn't expected the kiss, but she rather liked that it took her off-guard. Her breath hitched and her belly tightened as Nicholas pulled her close and teased her mouth open before licking inside.

Amelia pulled back. "My lord! We should go down and greet the guests."

"In a moment," he said. He gave her an instant to decide, and she knew he wouldn't stop her if she stepped away. But she didn't want to step away. Servants and guests and the million tasks she had to attend to be damned. She wrapped her arms about Nicholas's neck and kissed him back. She'd been afraid her declaration the night before would unnerve him and cause distance between them. She wasn't sure if she should be worried or happy that telling him she loved him hadn't seemed to change things.

The kiss was long and slow and sweet, and finally Nicholas broke away and rested his forehead on hers. He was breathing hard, and Amelia had to struggle to catch her own breath as well as refrain from grasping his coat and pulling him back for another kiss.

"We should go meet Aidan Sterling and the others," he said.

"Yes, we'll be considered extremely rude if we don't," she agreed.

"I definitely can't escape with you to the bed chamber," he said.

Amelia felt a knife of heat slice through her. "I fear we will have to postpone that pleasure until later."

He lifted her hand and kissed the back of it. "Until later then."

She went out with him, the two of them arriving just as the large conveyances slowed to a stop. They were probably the most sleek, luxurious conveyances Amelia had ever seen. "Goodness," she said under her breath as Aidan Sterling's coaches drew closer.

The Duchess of Mayne was nearby, and she nodded in agreement. "I hear they are equally lavish on the inside," she added. "We should have a peek later. I heard one of them even has a bed." She raised her brows and gave a mock look of shock. Amelia smiled and then watched as Nicholas greeted the dark-haired man who exited the first coach. He was as tall as Nicholas, and she glanced up as Nicholas gestured for her to move forward so he could make the introductions. She gave Aidan Sterling a curtsy and then smiled as his wife, Jenny, a lovely woman with blue eyes and dark hair, stepped out. Then both were swallowed up by the group behind them, and she watched as an even taller man stepped out of the coach. He was a bit rougher looking. It appeared as though his nose had been broken at least once. He had broad shoulders and moved in a way that told her he must be the retired pugilist she had heard so much about.

He was introduced as Rowden Payne, and he gave her a huge smile. "So you do exist. I thought maybe Nickers made you up to escape back to the country again. My felicitations," he said. He assisted his wife out of the coach and introduced her as Modesty Payne. She had lovely, bright red hair but a very serious expression. Her face softened when she smiled.

She curtseyed then pressed a hand on Amelia's arm. "I have family nearby in Hungerford."

"Really? I have lived here all my life. Who is your family?"

Amelia didn't know the family well, but she had met them a time or two. "Of course, we must arrange for you to visit tomorrow or the next day."

"If it's no trouble, I'd like that," Mrs. Payne said. "And I want to echo my husband's well wishes on your marriage.

I can already tell you are good for Lord Nicholas." Her hazel eyes shifted until she spotted Nicholas and nodded in approval.

Amelia wanted to ask why she would say so, but the second coach, which seemed even larger than the first, moved forward. To her surprise, Mr. Beaumont pushed everyone aside and opened the coach door himself. "Let me see him! Little Rafe."

A sort of growl came from the coach and then everyone stepped back as a blond man stepped out. He straightened and Amelia raised her brows. He was probably the tallest man she had ever seen. He had icy blue eyes, and he looked out over the others as though he had come to conquer them. He made a motion, and everyone stepped back.

Nicholas had moved to Amelia's side, and she glanced at him in alarm. He smiled. "That's Ewan Mostyn. He doesn't talk much."

"Oh, the one with the baby?"

He nodded. "No doubt that's why he wants everyone to give his wife a wide berth."

From inside the coach a woman leaned forward and handed Mr. Mostyn a bundle. It looked tiny in his large arms, but he took it, and then Beaumont was allowed to step forward and extend his hand. Lady Lorraine was a beautiful woman with striking green eyes. She took the hand and allowed Beaumont to assist her down. In contrast to her husband, she was all smiles. She glanced about and Nicholas nudged Amelia forward. Before introductions could even be made, Lady Lorraine grasped Amelia's hand. "You must be Lady Nicholas. I have been so eager to meet you. And you must be Lord Nicholas," she said. "I've heard a great deal about you. Forgive me for my bad manners."

"Not at all, my lady," Amelia said, instantly charmed by her. Beaumont made the introductions and then held out his arms.

"Let me see little Rafe."

Lady Lorraine gave him a playful swat. "His name is Charles, after my father."

Beaumont rubbed his arm. "That hurts. I always thought you'd name your firstborn after me." He nudged Mr. Mostyn, which Amelia thought seemed to be a little like poking a lion. But Lady Lorraine nodded, and her husband placed the baby in Beaumont's arms. Beaumont, for his part, appeared to have held babies before because he took the infant confidently and pulled the blanket back from his face.

"Thank God he looks like you," he said to Lady Lorraine, who laughed. And then everyone surged forward to see the baby, and Mrs. Payne and Lady Lorraine embraced and finally Ewan Mostyn took the child back and Florentia came out and led them all inside.

Amelia held back for a few moments, though. She had known she might feel a bit like a misfit as she didn't know any of the men or women. Living her whole life in the country meant she'd never gone to balls and soirees with the nobility. She'd known Lady Lorraine, the Duchess of Mayne, and Lady Juliana would already be acquainted. And, of course, Mrs. Draven and Mrs. Murray were sisters. She had hoped she might be able to make friends with Mrs. Payne, but it appeared she was already acquainted with Lady Lorraine. Of course, everyone was still arriving. She would have to take time to get to know everyone. Strange that she should feel so nervous. She'd always loved being in company before and made friends easily.

But she'd never been married to the son of a marquess before and expected to host a house party for his friends who hailed from the highest circles. It was all a bit overwhelming.

"I 'ope I'm not disturbing ye," said a female voice. Amelia turned and smiled at Jenny Sterling. She remembered Lady Florentia saying that Aidan Sterling had married a woman who had grown up in the rookeries. Judging by the accent, this must be she.

"Of course not, Mrs. Sterling."

"Call me Jenny. Do ye mind if I join ye for some fresh air?"

"Not at all," Amelia said as she watched the lads from the stables direct the Sterling coaches away. "You should call me Amelia."

Jenny held out her hand. "Lovely to meet ye."

Amelia shook it. "Do you like the countryside?"

"Love it. Aidan's coach is enormous, but I just need a moment to stretch my legs and breathe." She took a deep breath.

"Lady Florentia told me you are renowned for your expertise in appraising antique artifacts," Amelia said.

Jenny raised a brow. "Is that all she told ye?"

"I—"

Jenny smiled. "I thought so. But I don't mind not being one of ye nobs. I could pass, but why keep pretending?"

"You shouldn't pretend at all," Amelia said. "I was actually just feeling out of my element."

"Stick with me then," Jenny said, linking arms. "I'm always out of my element."

Somehow Amelia doubted that. The two finally went inside and Amelia spent the next few hours helping everyone get settled. The Mostyns were staying at Battle's Peak and had two rooms, one for Lady Lorraine and Ewan Mostyn, and another for the baby and his nurse. They'd put the Dravens and Murrays at Catmint Cottage and Lady Juliana and Neil Wraxall at the inn just a half mile away. Mrs. Blackstock had remarked that since Lady Juliana ran an orphanage, she might appreciate not being wakened by an infant's cries in the middle of the night.

Beaumont was still in his room, of course, and the Duke and Duchess of Mayne took the room next to his. Amelia worried they might require something grander, but Beaumont had said they wouldn't care. Rowden and Modesty Payne and the Sterlings were also at the inn, which left a room for Lord Jasper and his family, who hadn't arrived yet, as well as Nash and Prudence Pope, who no one was certain would actually attend. Mr. Pope was almost blind, and Lady Florentia had thought it would be easier for him to stay at the house and not have to learn the layout of multiple places.

By the time everyone was settled, it was almost dinner, and Amelia had just finished changing when O'Malley returned to tell her another coach had arrived.

She hurried downstairs and was met by Nicholas. She almost stumbled when she saw him. He looked so handsome in his formal attire—a black coat, embroidered silver waistcoat, and an expertly tied cravat. He wore trousers in lieu of breeches, probably because of his injuries, but she liked him in trousers. They made him look tall and lean, and she wanted to run her hands all over him.

He gave her a warning look. "I know that look," he said. "It will have to wait."

She tried to pretend she had no idea what he meant, but when they stepped outside to watch the coach pull up the drive she reached back and lightly pinched his bottom.

"Saucy wench," he teased.

Beaumont had been right about this gathering. She could sense the change in Nicholas already. He was lighter and happier. He seemed to have shed some of the metaphorical weight he carried on his shoulders. She hoped that seeing his old friends, being accepted by them regardless of his injuries, would give him the closure he needed to move beyond the past and the war.

As Beaumont was inside, they allowed a footman to open the coach door and a man wearing a black mask over the upper part of his face stepped out. She knew it must be Lord Jasper, who had been burned in a fire during the war. Following him was Olivia, a woman with dark hair holding the hand of a small boy of perhaps seven with bright red hair. Nicholas moved forward, hand outstretched, but Lord Jasper pulled him in for an embrace. "It's good to see you, Nickers."

Nicholas started to make introductions, but Lord Jasper said they might as well wait for Colin and Daphne FitzRoy, and a moment later a man with dark curly hair emerged followed by a lovely blond wearing a profusion of pink with more bows that Amelia could count.

Amelia made herself commit all the faces to memory as the masked man was introduced as Lord Jasper and his wife Lady Jasper, though her Christian name was Olivia. She appeared to be in the early stages of pregnancy, only a bit of rounding of her belly evident. The boy was her son, Richard, and he almost immediately started asking questions about horses. Amelia promised him he could have a tour of the stables tomorrow—take that, Rafe Beaumont!—and then she was introduced to Colin FitzRoy and his wife Lady Daphne.

The Dravens and Murrays arrived from Catmint Cottage then and everyone started talking at once. Amelia was drawn into several conversations, but after a few minutes she felt a tug on her skirts and looked down to see Richard Grantham looking up at her with his big blue eyes. "Do you have any food here? I haven't eaten all day."

"Richard!" his mother chided. "That's not true. You had a meat pie in the coach."

"But that was ages ago!"

"Actually," Amelia said, "we are about to sit down to dinner."

Richard's face turned suspicious. "At a long table?"

"Yes."

He shook his head. "Mama, I don't like dinner at long tables."

"He knows long tables mean a formal dinner," Lady Jasper explained to Amelia. "I don't suppose you have a nursery, but—"

"Actually, we do," Amelia said. "Master Mostyn is there with his nurse."

"Oh, of course! Lady Lorraine brought the baby." She looked down at her son. "Shall we go see the baby?"

Richard nodded eagerly. "Yes. I can practice being a big brother."

"That's right."

Amelia led them to the nursery and left them with the nurse and Lady Lorraine and then went down to the dining room to make sure all was ready. Her mother was there already and assured her dinner would be ready momentarily. "You look a bit flushed, my dear. Are you well?"

"Just trying to keep up with everything," Amelia said. "Everyone but Stratford Fortescue and Nash Pope have arrived. Colonel Draven said he sent Stratford Fortescue to find a way to make Mr. Pope come since Mr. Fortescue is apparently an expert at strategy."

"I'll have Cook keep something warm for them in case they show up later. Should we call everyone else to dinner? Have the guests from the inn returned yet?"

"I think just a few more minutes."

"Then you have time to sit down." Her mother led her to a chair and sat beside her.

"I am supposed to be caring for you," Amelia said.

"Oh, I'm fine." Her mother waved a hand. "But you seem…out of sorts."

"It's the baby, I think," Amelia said.

"Oh, yes," her mother said. "I heard him crying. He must have his father's lungs."

"I don't mind the crying," Amelia said. "I don't mind the baby at all. In fact—" Her voice hitched, and she was shocked to find she was almost in tears.

"My sweet girl, what is it?" Her mother sank down in the chair beside her and took her hands. "What has upset you?"

"I'm not upset," she said, tears streaming down her cheeks. "I'm happy."

"I see. What are you so…happy about?"

"Lady Lorraine and the baby. I went to bring Lady Jasper to the nursery with her little boy, and Lady Lorraine was there holding her baby and rocking him in the rocking chair. Mr. Mostyn stood behind her, his hand on her shoulder, smiling down at her and the child. Well, maybe not *smiling* exactly, but looking tenderish."

"Oh, I see."

"I'm envious. Mama, I could *feel* the love between them. I could feel their love for the child. I wanted that so badly in that moment. I still want it."

"Of course, you do." Her mother took her face in her hands. "You will have it. Patience is all you need. Lord Nicholas will come to love you, if he doesn't already. How could he not?"

Amelia laughed because her parents had always behaved as though she were perfect and anyone who wasn't immediately smitten with her must be dicked in the nob.

"There. That's better. I don't like to see you cry."

"I should stop behaving like a watering pot or everyone will ask what the matter is. Are my eyes dreadfully red?"

Before her mother could answer, the door opened and Florentia peeked in. "I think we should call the—what is the matter?" she asked as soon as she saw Amelia. "What did my oaf of a brother do now?"

"Nothing." Amelia took the handkerchief her mother offered and dabbed at her eyes. "I just saw Lady Lorraine and Mr. Mostyn with the baby, and the picture was so sweet, I started watering."

Florentia gave her an incredulous look. "We'll all be crying tonight when the child keeps us up until dawn. But I suppose they had to bring him. Do you need another moment or shall I sound the gong?"

"Oh, do sound the gong," Amelia said, having not heard it since she had dined there with her mother the night before her wedding. As Florentia went to do just that, Amelia straightened her dress and hair and went out into the foyer so she and Nicholas could escort everyone to dinner.

***

Nicholas had always hated long, drawn out dinners, but though the dinner that evening must have gone on for more than three hours, it seemed as though it was over with a snap of his fingers. The ladies had left the men to their port and war reminiscences after perhaps two hours, and Nicholas found himself enjoying the stories everyone told. Of course, Phin and Rowden had the most amusing stories, and Colin and Jasper's stories were the most hair-raising. Duncan argued with everyone's account and insisted on giving his own, which always cast him in a more heroic light. Ewan said almost nothing, but he laughed a great deal, which was something Nicholas didn't remember him ever doing. Aidan seemed to remember details everyone else had forgotten and settled most of the disputes, and Neil and Colonel Draven insisted upon telling every embarrassing anecdote centering around Rafe that they could think of.

Finally, Rafe suggested a toast to their fallen brethren, and Draven gave a speech to honor them. Colin was three sheets to the wind by then and Neil offered to take him back to the inn. As soon as they rose to leave, the others did as well, and Nicholas bid them all good night.

He would have waited until the house was dark and quiet before making the painstaking trek up the stairs, but Ewan told him to put an arm about his shoulders and all but hauled him up in just a few minutes. Nicholas would have never allowed him to do it if he'd been completely sober, but it was nice not to struggle for once. He slapped Ewan on the back, and Ewan apologized in advance for the baby who he promised would wake at three in the morning and cry for at least an hour.

"He quiets if I take him outside," Ewan said. "Tell the staff not to be alarmed if I'm in the garden later."

Nicholas couldn't quite imagine Ewan walking about the garden with a small infant, but then he would not have imagined himself inviting a dozen men and their wives and servants for a house party and enjoying himself.

His valet helped him to undress, and though it was late, Nicholas couldn't stop himself from putting his ear to the door adjoining his chamber with Amelia's and listening. It was quiet, and he cracked the door open and peered inside. He could just make out the figure under the covers on the bed. She didn't move when he entered, and though he wanted her, he didn't want to wake her. Funny how he had not even known her a month before, and now he'd spent most of the day imagining when they could be alone together.

Did that mean he was in love with her? How was he supposed to know? He'd grown up among people who had married for position and wealth. No one had ever spoken of love. Even his brothers and sister hadn't married for love. They married because their partner had been deemed a good match. Most couples he had known had no interest in sharing a bed or much else after the first few months of marriage.

Clearly, that was not the case with the Survivors. All ten who were present seemed completely in love with their wives. Rafe certainly hadn't married the daughter of a French assassin because it was a good match. His love for her had forced him to flee to America. Phineas had made a poor match in the eyes of the *ton* as well. His wife was several years older than he and had a scandalous reputation. He didn't seem to care a whit. Duncan had all but kidnapped his wife, who was Draven's sister-in-law, and Draven had pursued him with every intent to punish him. Even Colin, who had been one of the few Survivors married during the war, had fallen in love with his wife after returning. And then of course, there were the unlikely pairings of Rowden, who was a pugilist, and his wife, who protested blood sports. Not to mention the large, silent Ewan who had married Lady Lorraine, who could probably hold a conversation with a plant.

Nicholas moved toward the bed and leaned down to kiss Amelia's cheek. She didn't stir, and he returned to his chamber, closing the door between them. He climbed into bed and lay awake. When the baby began to wail, he glanced at the clock and saw it was quarter after three. Rafe had told Nicholas he'd wanted this party to say good-bye to his friends, since he wouldn't be able to return for several years, if ever. Nicholas had known that was not the whole reason. Rafe and Florentia, and probably even Amelia, had thought it would be good for Nicholas as well.

Nicholas had to admit that they were right. Why had he avoided seeing these men? Why hadn't he gone to the Draven Club more? He'd avoided London because he didn't want his former friends and acquaintances to see him and pity him. Here at Battle's Peak, he was far away from any who might pity him, but he was also isolated and lonely—less lonely now that Amelia was here, but even with her, he had made attempts to distance himself.

A change was needed. He'd lease a town house in London to use for a few weeks throughout the year. Though travel was painful and difficult for him, he'd plan a trip to Scotland to see Duncan and the wild land he'd heard so much about but never laid eyes on. He'd take Amelia, once her mother recovered. Amelia hadn't been outside of Hungerford more than a handful of times. They could see the world together.

And one day he would trust her enough to show her his scars. One day he might be able to believe that she cared enough not to leave him when she saw them.

***

The next morning, Nicholas, Rowden, and Neil had just finished breakfast when they heard the wheels of an approaching coach. Rowden went to the window and said what they all suspected: "Nash and Stratford are here."

Nicholas took longer to make it outside, and by the time he did, Rafe and Ewan had joined them. Stratford Fortescue climbed out of the coach first, gave everyone a wide grin, then helped his wife Emmeline, a curvaceous brunette, out as well. They were greeted warmly, with Stratford asking where Duncan was and his wife asking after Mrs. Murray, and then Nash Pope climbed out.

"What the devil?" Rowden said as soon as he saw him. "Look at you!" He embraced Nash, who seemed to tolerate it, and then practically pulled Mrs. Pope out of the coach. Prudence Pope was tall and freckled and said something right away that made Rowden laugh. Nicholas moved forward to shake Nash's hand and saw what Rowden had been exclaiming about. Everyone had said how gaunt and ill Nash had looked when they'd last seen him. But he was the picture of health now. His black hair had been carefully styled to hide the injury to his left eye, but if Nicholas hadn't known he had very little sight, he would not have guessed. Nash had a healthy color and he greeted Nicholas warmly, which was rather unusual for the sharpshooter as he'd always been somewhat detached and aloof.

But Nicholas realized he had always been more of a loner as well. Until recently.

It wasn't long before Jasper appeared, and then all of the wives came out, and Nash and Stratford were shepherded inside to break their fast. Nicholas tried to catch Amelia's eye, but she was playing the good hostess and seeing to everyone's needs. Finally, the guests from the inn and Catmint Cottage arrived, and the crowd moved to the garden with the promise of a picnic luncheon in a few hours. Nicholas stayed in the foyer and caught Amelia as she tied on a bonnet and started for the door.

"Good morning, my lord," she said with a smile.

"Where are you off to?" he demanded.

"I promised Master Richard I would give him a tour of the stable and let him pet Sweetie. Lady Jasper is waiting for me with him just outside."

Nicholas glanced where she pointed and saw Jasper, his wife, and adopted son out on the front lawn.

"I won't keep you then," he said, his voice gruffer than he'd intended. But he'd wanted a moment alone with her.

"Is anything amiss?" she asked.

"No." And he walked away to join the others in the garden. It didn't take him long to realize he and Rafe were the only ones who were without their wives. Florentia had set up easels about the garden as well as paints and some of the ladies were attempting to play artist. Nicholas couldn't quite stop himself from glancing toward the stables.

"She will come back, you know," Rafe said after Nicholas had to ask him to repeat himself for the third time.

"Who?"

Rafe gave him a knowing look. "I really had no idea you were so smitten with her."

Nicholas made a dismissive sound. "We just married. I hardly know her."

Rafe shrugged. "Sometimes it doesn't take long."

"Keep your sentimentality to yourself." And he refused to look toward the stable for the rest of the morning.

The picnic had been a success, and then they'd all returned to the lawn for games. Nicholas watched as Amelia floated from group to group, checking on each guest and making sure he or she was doing well. She seemed intimidated to approach Duncan Murray, but once his wife, Ines, joined the conversation, Amelia relaxed. Soon Emmeline Fortescue and her husband, Stratford, were telling Amelia a story, which had her laughing so hard she bent over. Later he caught her speaking with Prudence Pope, Nash's wife, and Modesty Payne. Amelia seemed to convince Mrs. Pope to tell stories about her life traveling with her missionary parents, while Mrs. Payne, who had been raised by strict Methodists, listened intently. Amelia left the two of them laughing before stopping to speak with Nash and Jasper.

That was when Nicholas took note. The day was warm and breezy, a perfect summer day really. The breeze had pushed Nash's hair off his face, and his damaged eye was visible. Nicholas had heard the scar was quite horrific, but seeing it now, he thought the gossip overblown. It was just a scar, and Nash didn't seem quite so self-conscious of it. But what really took Nicholas by surprise was that Jasper had removed his mask. Nicholas remembered when Jasper had been burned in that fire, trying to save his fellow soldiers. Jasper had almost died in that fire and one of their fellow soldiers, Peter, had died. Nicholas could still remember Ewan carrying Jasper out of the burning structure, still remember the awful smell of burnt flesh and the raw skin of Jasper's face.

Nicholas hadn't seen the wound since that day. When he'd seen Jasper afterward, the man always wore his mask. But apparently now he felt confident enough to remove it. And Nash felt confident enough to let his hair fly off his face.

And there was Amelia speaking with both men, looking directly at them and not at all seeming repulsed or even discomfited. Lady Daphne joined them, wearing another of her dresses that looked more like a sugar confection, and Nash—Nash!—said something that made the women laugh. It shocked him that Lady Daphne, who was perhaps the most typical example of the ladies of the *ton* Nicholas always avoided, seemed to accept Jasper and Nash without hesitation.

But then she hadn't married either one of them. She'd married the darkly handsome Colin FitzRoy. But the whole afternoon made Nicholas think that perhaps he had built his injury up to be more than it was. Perhaps no one would find it as hideous as he'd feared.

And he continued to believe that until he changed for dinner. He deliberately moved to where he could see his reflection in a mirror. Reflected back at him were two legs, one thinner than the other and obviously misshapen. The knee protruded at an odd angle, and scar tissue from the surgeries he'd endured crisscrossed the skin.

Nicholas turned away. He couldn't bear to look, and he would never believe anyone else could stand to not look away either.

Eighteen

"*Caramba*, but this is difficult!"

Amelia stood in the foyer and looked up from the menu she'd been perusing to see Ines Murray and her sister, Catarina Draven, puzzling over the paper with the scavenger hunt clues. They'd just come in from the garden, arriving quite late as all of the other guests had already found the inside clues and were outside looking for the rest.

"Can I help?" Amelia asked.

"*Por favor*," Ines said. "This clue I do not understand at all." Ines and her sister spoke Portuguese as their first language.

"I think we are not as good with English as the others," Catarina added. "And since we are playing against the men, our husbands will not help."

"Let me see it." Amelia held out her hand. She wasn't helping them cheat. Florentia had written the clues, and Amelia didn't know most of them, though she had helped to hide a few outside.

Ines passed over the sheet of paper and pointed to the third clue. Oh dear, they really did need help if they were only on the third clue.

Amelia read, "These objects can be sharp. They aren't for beginners. If you need to snip a thread, just look for some—" Amelia glanced at the women, brows raised expectantly. They were lacemakers. Surely, they would have guessed scissors.

"What is *snip*?" Catarina asked. "I don't know this word."

"It means to cut."

The women looked at each other, their faces lighting up. "Into the parlor," Ines said. "I saw a sewing basket there."

Amelia watched them go and smiled. She was about to look back at the menu when she felt a prickle along her back. She turned slowly and spotted Nicholas leaning against the stairs, watching her. He must have been in the library, a room she tended to avoid now as every time she even thought of it, her cheeks heated.

"My lord," she said, feeling a bit flustered that he'd just been in the library.

"My lady." His tone seemed mocking. He moved forward, and she realized she was crumpling the menu with her tight grip. "I haven't seen you in days. I almost began to believe you were ignoring me."

"You saw me last night," she said, and then glanced about, worried someone might have heard. His brows rose, and she knew he was remembering how he'd come to her room, dismissed O'Malley, and bent Amelia over the bed.

Amelia had liked how in command he'd been and was reassured by how much he'd obviously missed their lovemaking and wanted her. And though he'd given her pleasure, he hadn't given her what she really wanted.

He hadn't shared any part of himself. She was aware that even as he shared his body with her, he didn't trust her to share all of it.

"I remember." He gave her a look that made her breath catch in her throat. "Might we speak a moment?" He held out his hand, and she took it, her breath growing a little short when she saw his destination was the library. They stepped inside, and her gaze went to the desk. Was she a complete wanton for hoping he would toss up her skirts and bend her over it? It was a bit hard not to think about bedsport when she was constantly surrounded by couples so obviously in love.

Yesterday she'd interrupted a rather passionate kiss in the corridor between Neil Wraxall and Lady Juliana. At the start of the scavenger hunt, she'd spotted the duke and duchess sneaking toward one of Aidan Sterling's carriages. It wasn't hard to guess why.

But Nicholas closed the door of the library and backed Amelia against it. His body pressed against hers, and she looked up at him, her heart thudding hard in her chest.

"I've missed you," he said, his hand trailing down a stray curl and then continuing downward to brush over her breast. She shivered.

"I'm right here." She reached up and kissed him, and he flattened his hands on the door on either side of her and kissed her back as though he hadn't seen her for weeks. Amelia couldn't stop a small moan from escaping her lips.

"You like that," Nicholas murmured, moving his lips to her jaw and then her neck. "Why are you avoiding me if you like how I make you feel?"

Amelia stiffened.

Nicholas pulled back. "You didn't think I'd notice?"

"It's not that. It's just...I thought..."

He looked down at her, his usually sunny blue eyes dark with a storm coming. "Have I done something?" he asked.

"No." She shook her head. "Of course not."

"You haven't come to my bed chamber in three days."

"Last night you came to mine."

"I half wondered if you would turn me away," he said. Amelia tried not to show her surprise at the admission. She wasn't used to him being vulnerable.

"I'd never turn you away."

"But you don't want to come to me anymore either."

"I do. I just…" She swallowed. "I thought maybe a bit of distance would give you time to think."

"About?"

"Your feelings."

He frowned, looking confused. "What feelings?"

She bit her lip and told herself he didn't mean that as it had sounded. "Your feelings for me."

"I should think that would be obvious." He looked directly into her eyes, and she saw desire in his blue depths—desire and need. She wanted to reach for him then. She wanted to give him what he wanted, satisfy both of their needs. But the problem was, as it had been, no matter how satisfied her body was, her heart would still be yearning.

"There's a difference between the physical and emotional," she said. "I know you desire me, but you haven't told me how you feel toward me." She was trembling slightly. The words had been difficult to say. Now she was the vulnerable one.

He took a step back. Never a good sign. "You want me to be more emotional?"

She might have found the look of panic that crossed his features amusing if she didn't want some admission of his feelings for her so badly. Even the idea of giving her that seemed to terrify him.

"You're my wife," he said. "I care about you."

"As in you care for my welfare?" she said, her tone a bit more confrontational than she'd wanted.

"Of course." His face froze for a moment as he seemed to realize his error. "I care for you."

"Like one of your horses?"

He gave her a searing glare. "Like my wife."

Amelia knew she wouldn't get what she wanted at this point, but for some reason she seemed to invite heartache. "And what is that feeling?"

"I told you. I care for you."

She closed her eyes and reminded herself to be patient. Patience had always been one of her strengths, but perhaps she'd used all of it up over the years caring for others. Or perhaps spending the last few days with twelve men and women who loved each other so fiercely she could all but taste it, left her wanting the same more than ever before. She needed him to say the words. Or, if he did not love her, she wanted to know that as well. She wanted to quit hoping and waiting and being unsure.

"I told you I love you," she said, raising her gaze to his. "I love you, Nicholas."

His shoulders eased down. "I know. Then why haven't you come to me?"

She closed her eyes and shook her head. "Because I was hoping I might hear those words from you," she said finally. "I was hoping a bit of distance might make you consider whether you love me. I suppose, like a fool, I was hoping you would come to me—which you did—but it was only for physical release."

He reeled back as though she'd slapped him. "You felt used?"

"No." She hadn't felt like that at all. He'd never made her feel that way. "No," she said again. "The way you touch me, kiss me, look at me. I don't feel used, but I also don't feel…" She bit her lip then forced herself to speak. "I don't feel loved. I want that, Nicholas. I wanted to be patient and to wait for you, but all of your friends and their wives are so in love that it's made me long for that too."

She'd thought he might retreat further at her words. Instead, he moved closer and took her in his arms. He held her tenderly then kissed her head. "I care for you, Amelia. Very much."

Amelia waited for more, but there was none. After a little while, the sounds of voices rose, and Amelia knew the guests were returning from the scavenger hunt. Nicholas released her, kissed her cheek, and said they had better see to their guests. She let him go and stood in the library alone. She'd asked for what she wanted, and he hadn't been able to give it. Just as he couldn't reveal his injury to her, he couldn't reveal his heart.

Or maybe he had revealed it, and *care* was all he did feel for her.

***

Nicholas was drunk. It had been some time since he'd been this drunk, and if he were smart, he would keep on drinking. He was just drunk enough to be dangerous, as Rafe would say. Rafe had drunk enough to be sloppy. His words slurred as he made a sentimental toast to the other men. "I love all of you," he said, spilling some of his brandy as he raised the glass. "I love you so much."

Love. It seemed to be the word of the day. First Amelia had asked him for it, and now Rafe was throwing it about as though it meant nothing. As though saying that word didn't crack one's chest open and invite someone to rip out one's heart. But then Rafe had said he loved the Survivors. They had risked life and limb—his limbs—for each other. Nicholas loved them as well.

"Where are the ladies?" Colin asked. He too was drunk. He stood up after he asked and had to grab hold of the chair to keep from toppling over. "I want to make a toast to my beautiful wife."

Rowden, who seemed relatively sober, rose to grab Colin before he could fall over. "Maybe you could make that toast later. When you're alone."

"I want to toast my wife too," Phin said. He might not be as drunk as Nicholas or Colin, but he'd had his fair share. Despite Rowden's suggestion they leave the ladies to their tea in the drawing room, the other men agreed with Colin and Phineas, and the entire troop was soon streaming out of the dining room and stumbling toward the drawing room. They burst in upon the ladies, who were talking and laughing, but who gave each other knowing looks as soon as the men stumbled in.

Ewan and Rowden made the apologies. Ewan had barely imbibed, and like Rowden he was a big man who would need a great quantity of drink to intoxicate him. Of course, Duncan seemed to have no trouble downing a great deal of whisky. At one point, he'd had a glass in each hand. They'd started making toasts to the fallen members of their troop, and after raising a glass eighteen times—and several times in-between—most of the men had succumbed to inebriation.

"I have a few things to say," Colonel Draven began when all the men were in the drawing room and seated beside their wives. Most of the women looked bemused at the state of their husbands. Amelia leaned over and whispered, "Are you well?"

He waved her concern away as Benedict Draven continued his speech. "When I was given the order to form a troop of expendables"—he held up his hands as the men made sounds of protest—"men who had skills and talents but whose loss wouldn't be a burden to their family or country. Men who weren't the heir or the spare." He looked at Phineas. "At least not likely to be. Men who weren't married." He looked at Colin. "Or at least not happily."

Colin cursed and lifted his wife's hand, kissing it.

"When I was given that task," Draven continued with a smile, "I knew I would be asking thirty men to make the ultimate sacrifice. I was given a preview of some of the missions the troop would be sent on, and I knew few men would survive. So I chose carefully. I chose men I thought could defy those odds. And, if you recall, I approached each one of you with a question."

Neil Wraxall piped up. "Are you afraid to die?" he asked in a low, gravelly tone that sounded menacing.

"That's right," Draven said. "And all of you except Nicholas were fool enough to give me the same answer—no."

Aidan Sterling cleared his throat, and Draven laughed. "That's right, Mr. Sterling. You gave me a look as though I were an idiot and said *of course*."

Aidan took a mock bow.

"Do you remember what you said next?"

Aidan smiled. "I said, *But I want in anyway*."

"He's nae afraid tae dance with the devil," Duncan Murray said, his Scottish brogue so thick from the drink Nicholas could barely understand him.

"None of you were," Draven said. "And twelve of you put on your dancing shoes and came back home. I want to tell you something I've never said before." His voice hitched slightly, and his wife stood and put her arm around him. He gave her a look before taking a steadying breath. "I didn't think any of you would come back, and the fact that twelve of you did is a testament to not only your skills but the strength of your bond. You truly had each other's backs."

"And we still do!" Stratford Fortescue said.

"We always will," Jasper added.

"I'll drink to that," Neil said. "And I'll drink to my beautiful wife." He tipped his glass toward her. "I love you more than words, Juliana."

Lady Juliana's face colored, but she smiled and everyone drank.

Rafe, not one to surrender center stage for long, stood. "My wife isn't here, but I want to raise a toast she'll hear all the way in the Americas. To Collette, the love of my life!"

"To Collette!" the men echoed with a roar.

"Scotland isnae so far, but we'll raise a glass tae my wife and make a toast they'll hear in the Highlands. I love ye, Ines."

"To Ines!" the men echoed.

Phineas stumbled to his feet, and the duchess gave him a concerned look and muttered, "Oh, dear."

"I want to say something," the duke said, sloshing brandy over the rim of the glass a footman had just refilled. "Fighting the French was bloody hard, but winning over this one"—he gestured toward his wife—"was even harder. To the fight," he said raising a glass. "And the sweet spoils of victory."

"To the spoils!" the men echoed then drank. The duchess pulled Phin down beside her for a kiss.

"I'm not one for speeches," Nash said, and the room actually quieted. "But when I lost my sight, I thought I'd lost my life."

Nicholas stared at him. He knew exactly what Nash meant, but he didn't think the man would have ever said it out loud if he wasn't deep in his cups.

"Pru showed me I still have my whole life ahead of me. I love you, Pru."

"And I love you!" She jumped up and hugged him while the rest of the company smiled and drank.

"I think you all know that my life was relatively devoid of meaning," Aidan said as Nash and Prudence sat down.

"But not devoid of blunt," Rafe added.

"I never thought I'd say this," Aidan remarked. "But money isn't everything. So I want to raise a glass to the woman who was at my side when I had nothing. Now that I have her, I have everything."

"Oh, 'ell," Jenny Sterling said, swiping away a tear. "Look wot ye did."

"As long as we're giving speeches," Rowden said, rising. His wife turned bright red and hid her face in her hands. "I want to say thank you to all of you. You lot saved my life more times than I can count."

"I'll drink to that," Colin said.

"And this woman made that life worth living. To Modesty!"

"To Modesty!" the men said and raised their glasses. Nicholas observed the footmen were busy filling glasses again as Jasper stood. He wasn't wearing his mask, obviously comfortable enough without it among them.

"I know we'll never forget the eighteen who didn't come home with us," Jasper said. "And I know we're all living with the scars of the war." He gestured to his face. "Some more obvious than others. But we have each other, and I've relied on every one of you to see me through my darkest days."

"Giving someone else credit?" Rafe teased. "Now I know he's foxed."

"I am foxed," Jasper agreed. "But not so foxed that I don't know who deserves the most thanks. She loves me no matter what I look like. To Olivia!"

The men echoed his sentiment and Nicholas, who was near Jasper, heard Lady Jasper murmur, "You're beautiful."

Amelia leaned toward Nicholas. "Should we suggest everyone retire to bed? Mr. Fortescue can barely keep from falling over."

As though on cue, Stratford lurched to his feet. "I love you, Emmeline. Toast to my Emme."

Everyone toasted, and then Colin FitzRoy stood. "I was one of the few Survivors married when we went to war. Sorry to say, Daphne probably wouldn't have cared if I'd come home or not."

"That's not true," Lady Daphne protested.

"But thanks to all of you"—he raised his glass to the men—"I did come home. Thank you for giving me another chance," he said, turning to Daphne. "I love you, bows and all."

"To bows!" Rafe said and everyone echoed the ridiculous salute.

Ewan Mostyn cleared his throat, and everyone quieted. "I don't have much to say."

Everyone chuckled as he was stating the obvious. And he obviously wasn't foxed, but then Nicholas wouldn't expect that from him. After all, he had a three a.m. appointment with Master Charles.

Ewan pointed to Lady Lorraine, who looked speechless, for once. "But I love this woman."

Nicholas felt himself rising. He hadn't planned to speak, but if Ewan could do it, he could. "I came home before the end of the war," he said, wincing a little at the sound of his slurred words. "I was wounded just after Nash and Aidan."

"All three of you made it longer than me," Jasper said.

"Some men will do anything to get out of obeying orders," Neil joked.

Jasper made a rude gesture, and Nicholas continued, "I never thought I'd walk again. And I know I'll never ride again." His chest felt tight as so many of the emotions he'd kept locked inside started to well up. "But there was one thing I knew, even when I was lying in the dark on that muddy battlefield, my legs trapped under the best horse a man could ever want." He raised his glass. "I knew you lads would come for me. And you did."

"I wouldn't leave a man behind," Neil said. "I'm only sorry we had to leave Charlemagne."

"He was the best horse," Nicholas said, his eyes stinging. "He was a hero. To Charlemagne." Nicholas raised his glass and the other men echoed him. A few of them looked teary-eyed as well. He sat back down heavily, and Colonel Draven rose.

"Well, this is a lot more sentimentality than I ever thought you lads capable of. You're going soft in your old age."

"Speak for yourself, old man," Rafe joked.

Draven gave him a look, and Rafe held up his hands. "I mean, sir. I apologize—"

Draven pointed at him. "Got you." And he smiled. He lifted his glass. "One last toast. No, two. Raise a glass to my beautiful wife, Catarina. The love of my life."

"To Catarina!"

"And then finally, one last drink to all of you. The best troop of soldiers—the best group of men—I've ever had the privilege to serve with and call friends."

"Hear, hear!" The men drank and then the colonel ordered the footmen to collect the glasses and his men to take their wives to bed. That sounded like an excellent idea to Nicholas, but when he looked about, Amelia was gone.

He felt a tap on his shoulder and turned to see Draven standing there. "Looking for your wife?"

"I thought she was beside me."

"She left after your toast," the colonel said. "Can I give you a word of advice?"

"Do I need advice?" Nicholas asked, still looking about for Amelia. Why had she left?

"Twelve men toasted their wives, Nickers. You toasted your horse. I think you might need a wee bit of advice."

Nicholas sank down. He had toasted his horse, hadn't he? Amelia had been right there, and he'd not even looked at her.

"I know you're newly married," Draven said, "and the marriage was, as they say, one of necessity. You might not be in love with her yet, but anyone who looks at her can see she loves you. Take that power she's given you and use it wisely."

Nicholas stared at him. Power? He hadn't thought of himself as having any power since the accident. He was a cripple. He was lame and powerless.

But Amelia didn't care about his injury. She'd told him she loved him. She'd made herself vulnerable to him. He had more power than he realized, and he'd been careless with it.

He'd been a fool.

"Yes, sir," Nicholas said. "I'll go speak to her."

Draven put a hand on his shoulder. "My advice is wait until you're sober. Anything you say now she's likely to attribute to drink."

"Benedict?" Mrs. Draven said from the doorway. "The coach is here to take us to the cottage."

Draven slapped Nicholas on the shoulder. "You'll find your way, Nickers. We all do."

But Nicholas wasn't so sure.

Nineteen

Amelia had wanted to stay in her chamber with her head under the covers and the door bolted shut. She hadn't ever wanted to show her face again. How could Nicholas have humiliated her so? He might not love her, but did he need to announce it to their guests?

She'd lain awake that night, hoping, for the first time, he would not come to her. He'd either be drunkenly apologetic or completely unaware of what he'd done. Either way, she did not want to see him. If she saw him, she didn't think she could stop herself from bursting into tears and then he'd just think her pathetic.

But Amelia didn't have the luxury of wallowing in bed. Though her mother had been doing well for the last week or so, Amelia had seen her improve only to decline again rapidly. Most recently, it had happened right after Amelia's wedding, and she still hadn't forgiven herself for not checking on her mother sooner. And so, when the chambermaid came to her room in the hour before the dawn to stoke the fire and leave fresh water and linens for washing, Amelia rose, washed, and dressed. She was already brushing her hair when O'Malley tiptoed in with a tray of tea. Amelia pretended as though she was always awake and dressed this early.

"Are any of the guests awake yet?" she asked as O'Malley took over brushing her hair and began to pin it up in a simple style.

"Lady Lorraine and Mr. Mostyn and the baby are awake. They've asked for one of Mr. Sterling's coaches to be readied for the journey to London."

Amelia nodded. "I'm sure they want to be in their own home. It can't have been easy to come to Battle's Peak with the baby. Have you seen Mrs. Blackstock?"

"Not yet, my lady."

"Then I will seek her out. If you could just help me button my boots…"

A half an hour later, Amelia had greeted Lady Lorraine, who looked tired but still beautiful, and Lady Juliana, who was bright and cheery. "I saw Mrs. Blackstock walking in the garden," Lady Juliana said in answer to Amelia's inquiry. "I flung open the curtains to allow the sunlight in and spotted her from my window."

"I'm sure your husband appreciated that," Lady Lorraine said with a smile. Neil Wraxall had been quite inebriated the night before. "Are you certain you won't mind being trapped in the coach with the baby? He was quite fussy on the way here."

"Of course, I won't mind. I love babies."

Amelia excused herself and went out into the gardens where she found her mother, just as Lady Juliana had said. Her mother looked up from where she knelt, pruning some roses. The gardener would have done it, but Amelia knew her mother liked to work with plants. She had been the one who did much of the pruning and tending of the catmint around their cottage.

"What's happened?" her mother asked as soon as she saw Amelia's face.

"Why do you ask?"

"You've been crying."

Amelia sighed, hoping it was only her mother who would notice the pink of her nose and the slight redness about her eyes. Mrs. Blackstock stood and brushed off her dress then took Amelia's hands. "Is something amiss?"

Amelia wanted to tell her mother. She wanted to spill the entire story of how all the Survivors had toasted to their wives and expressed their love, while her husband had raised a glass to his warhorse and completely forgotten her. But this was between Nicholas and herself. Her mother could not solve the problem. Even she could not solve the problem.

She couldn't make Nicholas love her.

"I'm just tired," Amelia said. "I can only stay a moment. The guests will be leaving this morning, but I wanted to see you before the leave-taking begins. How are you feeling?"

"Much better, thank you." Her mother squeezed her hands. "In fact, I have been missing home and thinking of taking my own leave as well."

"Oh, Mama. I don't know. Everything there reminds you of Papa and—"

"That's why I miss it. I think I won't mind being reminded a bit now."

Amelia frowned. She didn't like the thought of her mother being alone at the cottage again, even if it was only a short walk away.

"I miss my bed and my things," her mother said. "And of course, I miss Rose."

"When do you want to leave?"

"Tomorrow, I think. I won't add to the commotion today."

Amelia nodded. "Why don't I go with you?" Amelia suggested, the idea taking shape even as she said it. "I'll help you settle back in."

Mrs. Blackstock gave her a sharp look. "But your husband is here."

"I'm sure he can spare me for a few days. Besides it's a short walk, and he can send a servant to fetch me if I'm needed."

"Has something happened?" her mother asked. Amelia should have known her mother would see right through her. "Has Lord Nicholas done something?"

Amelia shook her head. He hadn't done anything. He just didn't love her, and that was no one's fault. But she needed some time away to tend her hurt feelings. Time to let her wounded heart heal before resigning herself to patiently waiting for Nicholas to fall in love with her.

Or perhaps resigning herself to the fact that he might never love her.

"Not exactly," Amelia said. "Do I need a reason to spend time with my mother?"

"Of course not, but I have to caution you. You cannot run away from your problems."

"That is good advice," Amelia said. But she didn't intend to take it. She had come to Battle's Peak expecting a platonic marriage. Instead, she'd fallen in love with her husband and offered him her heart. Now she needed to take that heart back and fortify it before returning and trying again to be Lady Nicholas.

"I see one of Mr. Sterling's coaches is being brought around. I should go inside." Amelia gathered her skirts.

"I'll follow in a few moments, my love."

By the time Amelia was inside again, it seemed the whole house was awake. Servants bustled about, barely avoiding smashing into each other as they carried valises and portmanteaus down the stairs and then went back up again. Neil Wraxall and Ewan Mostyn were standing outside, Wraxall leaning on Mostyn a bit. Nash Pope was speaking with them. The carriage that had been used to take the Dravens and Murrays back and forth from Catmint Cottage was coming up the drive, and Amelia supposed the guests staying at the inn would arrive any moment as well.

Amelia was saying her farewells and directing servants as the drive became more crowded. Rafe Beaumont, looking disheveled and rakish, approached her with his satchel.

"You aren't planning to leave as well, Mr. Osgood?" she said.

"I am, Lady Nicholas. I had a long talk with Colonel Draven, and he thinks he can get me on the next ship to

Boston. If there's a chance of setting off for home, I want to take it." He missed his wife. Of course, he did.

"I do hope I will see you again one day," she said, feeling suddenly terribly sad that he was leaving. He'd been in the house as long as she, and he felt like a brother to her.

"You will," he said with a wink. "I'm not that easy to be rid of." He gestured to the group. "None of us are."

A hand landed hard on her shoulder, and she jumped then turned to see Nicholas beside her. For a man who had been three sheets to the wind last night, he looked remarkably well. Damn him. It would have been easier to hate him if he weren't so handsome. But she knew she could never hate him. She loved him too much, and perhaps that was why she needed time away.

"Amelia," he said. "I was looking for you this morning."

She moved away so the hand on her shoulder fell off. "I have been helping arrange the leave-taking," she said, avoiding his eyes. "And not doing a very good job, as you can see." She gestured to the chaos and smiled at Rafe Beaumont, who was watching them.

"We'll talk later," Nicholas said.

She nodded and then turned as she heard her name called by Emmeline Fortescue, who had brought her a parting gift of lovely hair combs as well as fresh apples and a large wide red ribbon for Sweetie. Both Emmeline Fortescue and Ines Murray had enjoyed spending time with the pig. They'd taken Olivia and Jasper's son, Richard, to visit Sweetie every day.

For the next two hours, Amelia was able to forget Nicholas. Almost.

He was at her side, but they were both busy with bidding their guests farewell and making sure everyone got off without incident. The first to leave were Lady Lorraine and Ewan Mostyn with Lady Juliana and Neil Wraxall. Next was Duncan Murray and his wife, Ines, as well as Nash and Prudence Pope, who would travel with them as far as the Pope's estate Wentmore. Then the Murrays would continue on to Scotland.

Emmeline and Stratford Fortescue were next followed by the Duke and Duchess of Mayne, who were traveling to Berkshire where the duchess's daughter resided.

Finally, the second of Aidan Sterling's luxurious coaches pulled forward, and he and Jenny Sterling took their leave along with Lord and Lady Jasper, much to the obvious excitement of Richard, who had loved playing in the large conveyance the past week almost as much as playing with Sweetie. They waved farewell and then Lady Daphne was hugging Amelia. She was so beautiful that Amelia was almost always intimidated by her, but she'd been nothing but kind even though her husband, Colin, was a bit aloof.

That left the Dravens and Rafe Beaumont and Rowden Payne and his wife, Modesty. Mrs. Draven had kissed both of Amelia's cheeks as she said good-bye. "Save me from all the talk of pugilism," she whispered and nodded at her husband and Rowden Payne. "Come visit us in Town," she said, echoing the invitation every one of Nicholas's friends had issued. "Oh, please do," Modesty Payne chimed in. "I'd love to repay your kindness in hosting us."

"And you are welcome here whenever you come to visit your father," Amelia said.

Modesty gave her a quick hug, and the ladies were helped into the coach.

Come visit us.

The gentlemen and ladies had arrived as strangers to her but were leaving as friends. Amelia hadn't expected that nor had she expected to feel as though she now belonged to a larger family than just her mother and herself.

Nicholas had finished his good-byes to Colonel Draven and Rowden Payne, and she shook their hands as well. Then she held out a hand to Rafe Beaumont, but he pulled her in for a quick kiss on the cheek, lingering just long enough to whisper, "Give him one more chance."

Amelia began to ask what he was talking about, but Nicholas cleared his throat. "Beaumont—I mean, Osgood—that's my wife you are handling."

"I daresay that's not the first time he's heard those words," the colonel said.

Beaumont raised his hands in a gesture of innocence. "I only handle my own wife these days!"

The men climbed into the coach and Amelia and Nicholas stood side by side and waved until the conveyance was out of sight. And then Amelia did the one thing she hadn't before—she ran quickly inside and left Nicholas behind.

***

Nicholas hadn't bothered to call after Amelia. He knew she wouldn't stop. She'd been avoiding looking at him all morning. She was hurt, and she wanted to escape him. The realization cut him to the bone. He'd never wanted to hurt her. In fact, he'd tried to put limits on their relationship to avoid this sort of pain—except he thought *he* was the one who would be hurt. He'd worried he would be the one rejected. But that wasn't what had happened at all. She'd been nothing but accepting and open with him, and he'd been the one to break her heart.

This was why he hadn't wanted to marry. Relationships could be so complicated, and he had been happy alone.

Hadn't he?

He wandered into the house, which now seemed too big and too quiet. He half expected Duncan's laugh to boom from the drawing room or Jasper to slide around a corner. Strange how he'd dreaded having them all here, and now he wished they were back again.

He looked up to see Florentia coming down the stairs, her face pinched. "Are they all away?" she asked.

He nodded. "Even Rafe has gone."

She paused on the second to last step. "You seem despondent. Don't tell me you will miss them." She studied him. "You *will* miss them. Rafe Beaumont was actually right about having them here. I worried it would bring up too many bad memories from the war."

"I worried about that as well, and they did bring up painful remembrances. But there were good times as well, and there's a...kinship, I suppose. We have been through something no one else can understand. I've felt isolated, as though I was the only one in the world feeling a sense of loss from all I have been through." He gestured to his legs, but he meant the years of his youth spent fighting and the men he'd killed or seen killed as well. "But being with the other Survivors has helped me to see, I needn't be alone."

And he could stop feeling sorry for himself. He wasn't the only one who'd left the Continent with injuries, but Nash and Jasper weren't hiding away. Jasper hadn't even worn his mask for much of the week, and no one had retreated in disgust at the scars from his burn. No one had cared.

"About that," his sister said.

Nicholas narrowed his eyes.

"I believe your wife is packing to depart. O'Malley is gathering her things to take back to Catmint Cottage."

"What?"

"Her mother wants to go home, and it appears Amelia will go with her. You didn't know?"

"The hell she's going," Nicholas said, forgetting for a moment that his legs were not what they once were and that he could not run up the stairs to stop her. He started the slow, painful climb. Why were there always stairs?

"Have you quarreled?" Florentia asked.

"No. Not exactly. I…made a mistake." He wished he could move faster not only to reach Amelia but to avoid Florentia's questions.

"It must have been rather serious if she is leaving. She isn't a petty sort of person."

No, she wasn't. She was patient and kind and open-hearted.

"What will you say to her?" Florentia asked when he paused halfway to the top.

"I'll tell her…" But what would he tell her? That his heart was racing? That he felt a ball of fear settle in the pit of his belly? That he didn't want to lose her? Couldn't lose her? Because…

Why? Why was he so afraid of losing her? She would be less than a mile away in distance, but if she went, she'd be a million miles away emotionally. He might never get her back. And he needed her here. He needed her with him because…

Damn it. He paused to catch his breath and assess his progress. Just a few steps left.

Because he loved her.

Nicholas clenched the banister hard and held on. The feeling he had now was like the one he had when he was searching for a favorite book and couldn't remember where he'd placed it. And then out of nowhere he would recall, and the book would be exactly in the place he'd left it. Realizing he loved Amelia was like finding that book in the place it had been all along. He'd known it was there, but it had just taken his mind a little longer to realize it.

Nicholas climbed the last of the stairs and looked down at Florentia who was watching him with curiosity.

"I'll tell her I love her," he said and arrowed for Amelia's chamber.

He slammed the door open with more force than he might have wished, and Amelia and her lady's maid looked up in surprise. Nicholas pointed to the maid. "Out."

"Yes, my lord." O'Malley lifted her skirts and was gone. Nicholas closed the door with a thud.

"What is the matter?" Amelia asked. "I wish you would ask before sending her away. I need her help."

"To leave."

She opened her mouth then closed it again, her gaze lowering to a pile of clothing that needed careful straightening. "Not leave," she said. "My mother wants to go home, and I want to help her settle in."

Nicholas gestured to the valise on the bed. "You don't need to pack to help her settle in. You're leaving."

"I'll be back. It's only for a few days." She still hadn't met his eyes, and he almost believed that she meant what she said. But a few days would turn into a week or two and the longer they were apart, the harder it would be to come together again.

"Is it because of last night?" he asked, moving toward the bed. Now her gaze darted to his.

"It's because my mother—"

"Because I raised a glass to my horse and not to you?"

"Of course not."

"Because I am sorry about that," he said, pausing on the other side of the bed. The furnishing suddenly felt enormous and impenetrable. "I was foxed, but that's no excuse. Everyone else toasted their wife, and I didn't mention you."

She glanced up at him, tears shimmering in her large brown eyes.

"Amelia," he said, his heart clenching at the pain he saw in her face.

She swiped at her tears. "I'm fine. I know you don't love me, but in that moment, I just wanted to be acknowledged."

"You're wrong," he said. He started around the bed, and she watched him with a wary look.

"Wrong to want to be acknowledged?"

"Wrong to think I don't love you."

Her head jerked back as though she'd been slapped.

And then he was beside her, taking her hands. "I do love you, Amelia."

She stared up at him, but her expression was not what he'd hoped. Instead of seeing the joy and pleasure he wanted, her brows came together. "I don't understand."

"Neither did I. Not until this morning. I love you." He pressed her hands, but she slowly pulled them out of his.

"You realized you loved me this morning," she said carefully. "After you found out I was leaving?"

"What does it matter?" he asked. "I love you."

Slowly, she shook her head. "I don't think so."

Now Nicholas was the one who reacted as though he'd been slapped.

"You are a man and a warrior. You're telling me what you think I want to hear because you're afraid of losing me."

"I'm telling you what I feel because yes, damn it—I am afraid of losing you." The words had wanted to stick in his throat, but he'd forced them out. She was right. He was a warrior, and this was a battle. One he couldn't lose because if he did, he would lose Amelia. "Because I love you," he said.

"And I love you." But she didn't look happy about it. Tears streamed down her face now, and her mouth was turned down in a painful expression. "But I just don't know if that's enough any longer. You say you love me, but does that change anything? I saw more emotion and vulnerability from you this past week with your friends than I ever have when we were alone. I want more than just words of love, Nicholas. I want *you*."

He spread his hands, bewildered. "I'm here."

But she pressed her lips together as though disappointed. "I'll be gone for a few days," she said, going back to her pile of dresses. "We can talk more when I return."

"Amelia—"

"I think a few days apart might do us both good."

But he didn't want a few days apart. He wanted to pull her in his arms and kiss her and never let her go. Clearly, that was not what she wanted. And devil take him if he understood what she wanted. He'd told her he loved her. He'd gone to her and apologized. If that wasn't enough, then maybe she should leave.

"Fine." He turned and went to the door between their chambers, pulling it open, and slamming it closed.

***

Amelia was very good at managing tears. She'd had years to practice the art of putting on a smile for her ailing grandmother or her dying father while wailing on the inside. Dinner that night was no different. Nicholas didn't come down to dinner, which didn't surprise her. He was hurt and angry. She was sorry for that, but what more could she do?

She'd opened her heart to him, and he'd thrown some words at her. He hadn't meant to hurt her, but he had. She needed to fortify herself, erect some walls before she returned so she could protect her heart.

Then they would both have walls.

After dinner, she kissed her mother on the cheek, and claiming a headache, retired to her room. She readied herself for bed and had just finished brushing her hair when the door leading to Nicholas's chamber opened. Amelia almost dropped her brush when she saw him standing there. He wore his trousers, but his feet were bare and so was his chest. His hair was brushed back from his forehead in a golden wave, and his sky-blue eyes looked almost stormy.

"Y-you startled me," she said.

"That wasn't my intention."

She knew that look in his eyes. He wanted her, and as much as she might want to resist him, she wasn't certain she could. Already her body felt the pull of his, and she wanted to go to him, even though she knew that making love with him would only hurt her later. She would give him all of herself, and he would give her only a little, hiding from her and making sure he only showed her what he wanted her to see.

"I have a headache," she said, trying to erect some defense before her legs betrayed her and raced to him without her permission.

"I won't trouble you then," he said and turned to leave, but not before she saw the flash of hurt and rejection in his eyes. Immediately, she regretted the words. They were hurting each other now, and she didn't know how to reverse course. He would close the door and that would be the first brick of her wall.

***

Nicholas reached for the door latch, but he paused when he took hold of it. Yes, she'd rejected him. He'd rather thought she would. And he didn't really blame her. How could he expect her to be vulnerable and open with him, to be naked not only physically but with her desires, if he could not do the same?

She'd said she wanted him. She wanted emotion and vulnerability. He hadn't known what she meant. Until now.

He knew what he had to do. His hands were shaking, and perspiration beaded on his lower back. He was terrified, and that's how he knew he was doing the right thing. He reached for his trousers.

"There's just one thing I want to show you first," he said and loosed the fall of his trousers.

Her eyes widened, and Nicholas decided that if he was to do this, he would do it right. He closed his door and moved into the light shed from the lamp on her dressing table. "I promised to show you my legs and the wounds I received from the war," he said. "I want to do that now."

"Nicholas, you don't have to."

"I want to. I should have shown you before. I should have trusted you."

His hands were shaking so badly that he could hardly grasp the wool waistband of the trousers to tug it over his hips. Though he wanted to watch her face as the material slid down, he focused on a point above her head as the trousers slid down his thighs and he knew the first of his scars became visible.

He darted a quick glance at her expression, but she wasn't looking at his legs. She was looking at his face. "You don't want to see?" he asked.

"Only if you want me to," she said so quietly it was almost a whisper. "Your hands are shaking. You don't have to do this."

"I'm terrified," he admitted. "But that's how I know this is right because the only thing I'm more frightened of is losing you." And he released his hold on the trousers and let them fall to the floor. The material pooled about his ankles, and he stepped carefully out of it. He was naked now, completely exposed. And yet Amelia didn't look away from his eyes.

"Are you certain?" she asked.

"Yes," he said. "I want you to see."

"One thing first." And to his astonishment, she stood, loosed her robe, and slid it off her shoulders.

"What are you doing?" he asked when she reached for the ribbon at the bodice of her nightgown.

"I don't want you to be the only one standing naked in this room." And she slipped the nightgown down her body, revealing her lovely curves and soft skin.

Unlike him, she had no flaws, no imperfections. He could have looked at her all day, and he didn't stop his gaze from sliding over her. When he'd finished his perusal, she said, "Are you ready for me to look at you?"

Nicholas squared his shoulders. "Yes."

Her gaze lowered slowly from his eyes to his lips and down to his chest. Her bold gaze would have aroused him if he hadn't been so nervous about what would happen when she saw his legs. He clenched his hands as her eyes dropped to his waist and then to his stiffening cock, which was reacting to her nakedness despite his anxiety.

Her lips curved into a smile at his body's reaction, and she glanced back up to his face, her expression reassuring. Then her gaze dropped again, and he knew she was seeing the scars on his leg. His right leg was perfect until below the knee, but his left leg was misshapen beginning above the knee all the way to the ankle. The skin was pale, the leg smaller than it should have been, and angry red slashes marked it where bones had protruded or the surgeon had cut in an attempt to reset what he could. The knee itself looked like a grotesque blob and his calf bowed strangely inward. His right leg was not as bad. It too bore the red scars of the surgeon's blade and the calf was smaller than it should have been, but the knee was recognizable and the calf was straight.

Amelia's gaze rose back to Nicholas's face, and her expression held not pity or disgust but understanding. Nicholas felt his shoulders lower slightly as some of the tension fled.

"I can't imagine the pain you must have felt," she said. "The fact that you walk as well as you do is a miracle."

"I don't walk well," he said without thinking.

"You walk extraordinarily well," she countered, moving toward him. "Any other man would be an invalid."

"The doctors said that was the most likely scenario."

She took his hands. "But they didn't know you are a warrior. You fought your way back on your feet, and most days I imagine that fight costs you."

She seemed to see inside him with her piercing gaze. Had she known how he'd felt all along or had seeing his legs revealed it to her? And why hadn't he trusted her sooner? Why had he been so afraid?

"The pain is manageable."

"I hate that you have pain," she said. "But I love your strength and your determination. You're beautiful, Nicholas."

He frowned at her. Women were beautiful, or paintings or vistas, not crippled men. He told her this, and she arched a brow. "May I show you?"

"How?"

"Come lie on the bed." She tugged his hand, but he hesitated. It was awkward for him to climb into bed, and he didn't want her to see him struggle. He glanced at her face, though, and all he saw was desire and love. He hadn't trusted her before. It was time to trust her now.

She hopped on the bed and moved over to make room for him. He sat then swung his legs over and worked to adjust them and then sit back against the pillows she arranged for him. "Comfortable?" she asked, kneeling beside him. He reached out and ran a hand down her bare arm, forgetting about his legs now.

"Come here," he said.

She seemed to have been waiting for his invitation. Throwing one leg over his, she braced herself on her knees as she straddled him then leaned down to kiss him. Nicholas's desire went from simmering to boiling. His hands went to her waist and slid over the curve of her hips and up to the peaks of her breasts. She moaned with pleasure then lowered her mouth to kiss his neck, his collarbone, his chest.

"Come back here," he protested as she moved lower.

"Patience," she teased, and he watched as she moved down his chest toward his stiff cock. Her mouth skated over his body with sensual slowness, her tongue darting out here and there to taste his skin. As she neared his cock, he gripped the bedclothes, uncertain if she would dare put her mouth on him. That was something they hadn't done before, though he'd wanted it. But he'd been too damned afraid she'd catch a glimpse of his legs. Even now he wanted to lower the lamps and hide. But then he wouldn't see the way her lovely body moved or her hair fell over her shoulders or her mouth inched closer to his throbbing member.

And then moved right past it.

Nicholas blew out a breath and Amelia looked up at him, a mischievous glint in her eyes. "Did I miss something?" she asked, voice low and seductive.

"No," he said through clenched teeth.

She smiled. "Don't worry. I'll work my way back up."

Which meant... "No," he said as he divined her intentions. She didn't listen. Of course, she didn't. She moved lower kissing his left thigh and scooting down the bed so she might better reach his legs. "Amelia."

"I want to show you how beautiful you are to me," she said, glancing up at him, her look pleading. "How much I love all of you, Nicholas."

He pressed his lips together and tightened his grip on the bedclothes until his hands were white with the effort. Finally, he nodded, and she lowered her lips to the first of his scars. She kissed it gently, almost reverently, then moved lower to kiss knotted skin, deformed flesh, and all of the ugliest, weakest parts of him. And then she moved to the other leg and repeated it all, moving back up as she did and ending with her lips inches from his cock.

She met his gaze, and he held his breath as her mouth parted and her tongue emerged to lick from the root to the tip. "Amelia," he gasped as her tongue teased the head of his member then closed over it briefly with a light suck.

"Don't you dare tell me you love me right now," she warned, glancing up at him.

"Is there a word stronger than love?" he asked, and she gave him a warning look then closed her mouth over him again. He was all but delirious when she finally inched her way back up his body and positioned him at the entrance to her sex. He could feel the heat of her, and his hips bucked reflexively, wanting to be inside her.

"You're beautiful to me, Nicholas," she whispered as she lowered herself, taking him in inch by inch by inch. He groaned.

"You are the one who's beautiful." He met her gaze as she moved, thrusting slightly to nudge the place that would give her pleasure.

"You always make me feel so," she said, taking him deeper. They moved together in a dance they both knew well. And when she found her pleasure and arched back, he came as well, holding nothing back.

***

Sometime in the night, Amelia woke and turned her head to find Nicholas still in bed beside her. The lamplight was weak, but she could see his gaze was on her, his blue eyes dark. She smiled. "You're still here."

"I don't know why I didn't sleep with you before," he said.

"You were an idiot before." She rubbed her eyes and propped herself on her elbow. "Comfortable?"

He hesitated as though he hated to ask for anything and then he said, "Could you adjust the pillows behind me?"

She rose, did as he asked, and when she climbed back in bed, he pulled her close so that her head was on his chest. Two hours ago, Amelia would not have thought anything he said or did could make her decide to stay or heal the pain that lanced her heart. But he'd found a way to bandage her wound—by showing her the scars from his past. She'd understood the risk he'd taken when he'd done that, though she'd always known it would be no risk at all. She'd asked for more of him, and he'd given it. She'd asked for his trust and vulnerability, and he'd given that as well.

She loved him more than she'd ever believed possible. As though he read her mind, his arm tightened about her. "I love you, Amelia."

She looked up at him. "It took you long enough to realize it."

"I can be a bit thick sometimes, but I promise to tell you every hour upon the hour when you return from Catmint Cottage."

"Now you want to be rid of me?"

"Your mother—"

"I'll help her settle in, but I've spent my last night in bed alone. I shouldn't have decided to leave. I was running away when I should always stand and fight for what I love."

"I didn't exactly make it easy for you. And"—she looked up at his sheepish tone—"your threatening to leave made me realize how much I wanted you to stay and that my fear was pushing you away."

"I love you, Nicholas, scars and all. Nothing will ever change that."

"Come here," he said.

"Why?"

"I'll show you."

And he did, showing her with his hands and his body and his words how much he loved her.

Epilogue

Five years later

"Papa! Papa! A letter came for you."

Rafe Beaumont looked up from his face in the mirror and set down his razor, half his jaw still lathered with shaving soap. His son was practically bouncing up and down, holding the letter out like a holy offering. "Thank you, Henri. Put it on the breakfast table."

"But Papa, Mama says you will want to see it right away. It comes from across the ocean."

"Really?" He glanced at the bedchamber door as Collette entered, wiping her hands on her apron. She smiled at him, but he saw the trace of worry in her eyes as well.

"All the way from England," she said, her words accented with the lilt of her native French.

"Not my—"

She shook her head. "Not from your family, no."

"Then who—"

"Papa!" Henri waved the letter impatiently. "Open it!"

"Yes, yes!" He took the letter and moved to the bed, taking Henri on one knee. Collette came to sit beside them and watched as he broke the seal. He unfolded the paper and smiled as he read it. His gaze met Collette's, a question in his eyes.

"Monsieur Draven will not be happy," she said.

"He worries too much. Surely everyone has forgotten all of that hubbub."

"What's hubbub?" Henri asked.

"It is about to be the state of the house," Rafe answered, "because we are packing everything for a long trip."

"Really?" Henri's eyes widened. "Where? Philadelphia?"

"Even better."

"New York?"

"Better!"

"Paris?"

"Even b—"

Collette cleared her throat. "Almost as good. London."

"Where is London?"

"Across the ocean," Rafe said. "It will take weeks to sail there on a big ship, but when we arrive, we'll go to a big party in the countryside with lots of horses and pigs and sheep for you to play with and other children as well."

"When do we leave?" Henri asked.

"Go pack now," Rafe said. As soon as he had jumped down and scurried away, Rafe pulled Collette close. "Ready for another adventure?"

"With you? Always."

And the paper fluttered to the floor.

Lord and Lady Nicholas request the pleasure of Mr. and Mrs. Rafe Beaumont's company for a week of entertainment with Draven's Dozen at Battle's Peak. The festivities will commence in six months' time. Please join the other Survivors on the 7th of June 1823.

An answer is requested.

It was signed *Nickers*.

About Shana Galen

Shana Galen is three-time Rita award nominee and the bestselling author of passionate Regency romps. Kirkus said of her books: "The road to happily-ever-after is intense, conflicted, suspenseful and fun." *RT Bookreviews* described her writing as "lighthearted yet poignant, humorous yet touching." She taught English at the middle and high school level for eleven years. Most of those years were spent working in Houston's inner city. Now she writes full time, surrounded by three cats and one spoiled dog. She's married and has a daughter who is most definitely a romance heroine in the making.

Would you like exclusive content, book news, and a chance to win early copies of Shana's books? Sign up at her website for monthly emails with exclusive news and giveaways.

Coming in summer 2022—a new series from Shana Galen!
The Royal Saboteurs—Protecting the Crown at Any Cost!

A disparate group of men and women board a train in the middle of the night. They aren't told where they're going or why, but they have one thing in common: they are the best at what they do. These strangers—the best pick-pockets, forgers, ciphers, and spies in England—might not know each other, but each will come to trust the others with his or her life. When the group arrives at the rustic farmhouse in the wilds of northeast England, they're met by a leader who's more legend in their circles than man. He offers them the opportunity of a lifetime: to become elite operatives for the Crown, to live a life of adventure protecting their country. For some this is compensation enough. Others require further inducement. So begins their training at a camp for saboteurs, where the skills they learn and the missions they're assigned will test their mettle and their loyalty. From glittering ballrooms to the grandeur of the royal palace to the most dangerous slum, the bonds they forge may save their lives, but it's their hearts that are irrevocably transformed.

From RITA-nominated, national bestselling author, Shana Galen, the queen of "fast-paced, action-packed, cat-and-mouse spy thriller that will leave you breathless," (*RT Book Reviews*) comes a series that perfectly mixes intrigue with sizzling passion.

Pre-order the first book in the series, *Beauty and the Thief,* now and enjoy chapter one.

One

Bridget Murray consulted the small gold watch she held in her gloved hand and frowned. Nearby, the last train of the night blew out a burst of steam, sounding very much like an enormous, and rather impatient, horse. She looked about the deserted train station, her eyes roving over the same figures she'd observed the past forty-seven minutes. One lone porter sat on a bench, his eyelids half closed as he snoozed. Through the window of the small lounge, she noted the ticket seller beginning to gather his coat and hat. Bridget, in her dark traveling dress and old but still serviceable winter coat, stood between two columns, watch in hand and umbrella hooked on one arm.

Another minute ticked by. *Where was he?* The train would depart in twelve minutes. The rest of her charges were aboard, and she felt a twinge of unease at not being safely aboard, though she'd reminded herself several times that she still had plenty of time.

Baron wanted Kelly on that train, and Baron had asked her, specifically, to wait for the man. But she couldn't *make* this Kelly come to the train station. He knew the train schedule, didn't he? Surely, he did. Baron informed her Kelly had been given his ticket days ago. Whereas, she had held the tickets for her other passengers.

She looked at her watch again just as a gust of steam from the train ruffled her black skirts and momentarily deafened her. When she looked up again a man sprinted toward her.

He dashed down the platform, his greatcoat flying behind him, revealing dark, fitted evening clothes beneath. He'd lost his hat at some point and his chin-length hair flew back from his clean-shaven face. She might have retreated if not for the grin he wore. He looked like a man having the best night of his life.

She'd been struck momentarily immobile by his sheer masculine beauty. The way he moved, the way his eyes glittered, the way the wind whipped his hair back…

He was coming straight for her.

Bridget glanced at the train then the lounge, trying to decide which was closer should she need to flee. But even as she turned toward the lounge, the man, who was now only a few yards away, called out to her. "Are you Miss Bridget

Murray?" His voice had a lilt she couldn't place at the moment, but she understood him well enough.

"I am." She shoved her watch into the reticule hanging from her wrist.

"Sure and I'm Callahan Kelly." He skidded to a stop before her and reached up to doff his hat. Finding it missing, he shrugged and gave her a sweeping bow. Oh, yes, he was handsome. That was undeniable.

Even more undeniable was the fact that he was trouble. One look into his gray-blue eyes told her that.

A commotion at the other end of the platform caused him to straighten and cast a look over his shoulder. Just then four other men tumbled down the far stairwell. A remarkably tall men led three burly men. They paused and looked about as though searching for someone. She sighed. "They're after you, of course."

Kelly hissed in a breath and stepped behind the nearest column, pulling her with him. "How long until the train leaves?"

"Eleven minutes." She peered around the column. The men had slowed, seeming to search, and moving in the direction of the lounge behind her.

"Too long." Kelly took her wrist and yanked her out from the columns and into the shadows at the back of the platform.

"Let go!" she objected as he pulled her into an archway built into the stone.

But instead of releasing her, he shoved her against the white tiled wall and pressed himself beside her. "Be quiet."

Bridget brought her foot down hard on his shoe, and he jumped back, a look of incredulity in his eyes. She straightened. "I don't know who you think you are, but I have not given you leave to touch me."

"Bridget—"

"*Miss Murray*, if you please."

"You'll be *Miss Murdered* if you don't shut up and step back."

She might be angry, but she wasn't an idiot. She could see the men who'd come for him were not the sort to listen to reason or, more importantly, to respect train schedules. She stepped back, pressing herself uncomfortably close to Mr. Kelly and dug out her watch. "Nine minutes until the train departs."

"We'll catch the next one."

She turned to face him. "You think trains to the Farm leave every day? I have strict instructions to be on that train no m—"

He cupped a hand at the back of her neck pulled her face hard against his chest. Two seemingly contradictory thoughts entered her head at that moment.

One, she wanted to hit him.

Two, he smelled remarkably good. She had the ridiculous urge to bury her nose in his coat and press her cheek against his warm torso. Instead, she shoved back. His grip on her neck held, and they stared at each other, nose to nose.

"Unhand me!" she hissed.

"My friends are just there." His gray-blue eyes darted to the side. "Once they pass us, we make a run for it."

She wanted to argue. She wanted to stomp on his foot again. She wanted a closer look at those eyes. Instead, she pressed her lips together and allowed herself to be gathered against his chest again.

Even she would be pressed to admit her current situation was a hardship. Besides the fact that his touch was doing strange things to her belly and making her chest feel tight, his plan was reasonable. Provided the men passed them in the next seven minutes, they'd have enough time to board the train and be away.

But seven minutes with her body flush against his, her breath quickening as her breasts were flattened against his chest, the hair at the nape of her neck rustling with each of his warm breaths. She clenched her fists, determined to bear the friction as he slid against her in an effort to peer around the wall shielding them.

"Miss Murray," he whispered in her ear, making her shiver. "We have a problem."

Truer words were never spoken. "What problem?" she whispered back.

"One of the men is standing guard just outside the station lounge."

Clearly, Kelly's plan must be discarded. The thug was unlikely to move in the next six minutes and she must be on that train. She could go without Mr. Kelly, but that would mean ignoring Baron's order to wait for the man. Baron wanted Kelly at the Farm.

She looked up, avoiding Kelly's unusual eyes. Her gaze rested on his lips, but those also proved too dangerous, and she settled on one of his dark eyebrows. "Do these men need to take you alive?"

"Sure and I don't know what you're hinting at, Miss Murray."

Irish. That was his accent. "Will they kill you now or do they need to bring you to their leader alive?"

"Alive, I expect, though they wouldn't mind damaging me, if you understand my meaning."

"Now who would want to hurt you, Mr. Kelly?"

He lifted a brow, which made her chest tighten a fraction more.

"I might owe their employer a pound or two."

They'd want him alive then. Dead men couldn't pay debts. In any case, there was no more time to waste. She held up her watch and palmed it so only a glint of medal showed. "Turn around and let me put my arm about your neck."

"Are you daft?"

"Don't try me, Mr. Kelly. Turn around."

He gave her a look of incredulity then turned and hunched down, so she could hook her arm about his neck. She pressed the watch to his temple as though it were a pistol.

"You can't think this will work," he muttered.

"Hello there!" she called, pushing Kelly out of the alcove.

The wide, muscular man standing by the column spun around, his small eyes widening. "Oy!" he called to his comrades.

"Is this the person you are searching for?" Bridget pushed Kelly forward. If she could move near enough to the train, they could make a run for it.

"Hand 'im over, missus."

"No, don't come any nearer. I have a pistol to his head, and if you come any closer, I will shoot."

"Oy!" The thug called again.

"They're coming back, lass," Kelly said under his breath.

"You won't shoot 'im, missus" The burly man moved forward. He had a vicious scar across one cheek, and his nose looked to be little more than a flat blob in the center of his face.

"I will. I've shot men before. Now, I want to board this train, and I am taking him with me."

The tall man approached, slowing to a walk as he assessed the situation. "You can't do that, madam." He was obviously the leader. His speech was slightly more refined. "We work for a very important man, and he needs to speak with Mr. Kelly. Immediately."

The train hissed out another blast of steam. Now she had two men between the train and herself. She couldn't look at her watch, but she knew she was almost out of time. "That's most interesting because I also work for an important man, and he would like to speak with Mr. Kelly as well. Perhaps my employer could speak to Mr. Kelly and then you could have him back. Now, if you would move aside and allow us to pass." She started confidently forward, pushing Kelly in front of her.

"I can't do that, madam." The tall man glanced to the side as the third large man joined them. "Hand him over, and I give you my word, you will not be touched."

"Get out of my way, or I give you my word that I will shoot him right now."

The tall man's eyes narrowed. "I think you're bluffing."

She kept her gaze locked on his. Bridget was a very good card player.

The train whistle shattered the tension, and Bridget jumped at the unexpected screech. Her hand opened, and she fumbled to catch the watch before it fell to the ground.

"Get him!" the tall man yelled.

Everything happened very quickly. Kelly pushed her out of the way as the three men rushed him. She stumbled over her skirts and went to her knees. She pushed up again just as someone called, "All aboard!"

"No!" She started for the train, but she couldn't leave Kelly behind. He had his hands full with the three men circling him. As she watched, he threw a punch at the flat-nosed thug, but it glanced off the man's cheek, doing little harm. The tall man grasped his arms from behind, but Kelly slammed his elbow back, and the tall thug bent double.

Bridget was used to seeing men who could fight, and she knew skill when she saw it. The enormous wheels of the train began to move, and she started for it. She could still jump aboard, but how to free Kelly to join her?

And if that wasn't problem enough, the fourth thug was racing toward them. He had his full attention on Kelly, and Bridget unhooked her umbrella from her arm and stuck it into his path at just the right moment. He went down hard and she closed in, bashing him in the back of the head with the umbrella's solid wood handle.

One down.

The train was moving in earnest now. She had less than a minute to jump aboard. "Mr. Kelly, we must go!" she called.

"I'm coming—" He threw a punch and missed. "—as fast—" The tall man hit him in the shoulder, and Kelly reeled back. "—as I can, lass."

"Must I do everything?" she muttered to herself. She dug in her reticule and pulled out all the coins she possessed. In one motion, she flung them onto the platform. As she'd expected, the men glanced at the dropping coins, and realizing what they were, dove for them.

Well, two of the thugs dove for them. The tall man turned back to Kelly, ducking his right hook.

The train was moving quickly now. She could see the last cars approaching. She began to jog to keep up. "Mr. Kelly, now would be an excellent time to board."

He feinted left then punched the tall man in the throat. Bridget turned away and, running now, grasped the stair railing, pulling herself onto the steps of the car just as the rearmost car passed the struggling men.

"Mr. Kelly! Now or never!" she yelled as the train whistle sounded for the last time.

Kelly grabbed the tall man by the coat, pulled his head down, and slammed his forehead against the tall man's. Bridget winced, but the desperate maneuver worked. The tall man stumbled away, and Kelly began to run toward the train.

He shook his head as though dizzy, and Bridget realized he wasn't running fast enough. He'd never catch the last car.

"Hurry!" she called.

Kelly looked up at her and increased his speed then stumbled at the last moment. "No!" Bridget called as Kelly went down and the train sped away.

Pre-order it now!

Printed in Great Britain
by Amazon

46314432R00264